Praise for Jeff Rovin and *Tempest Down*

"High drama and nail-biting suspense . . . [The cast is] compelling, composed of believable, understandable characters to worry about. Rovin gets the people right and produces his best yet."

—*Kirkus Reviews*

"A story so intricate and intense, readers will find themselves clutching the edge of their seats . . . takes the reader on a bone-chilling ride [full of] nail-biting suspense."

—*Publishers Weekly*

"An exhilarating high-tech adventure. The reader is in for a whiplash ride. Watch out, Tom Clancy."

—Gayle Lynds, *New York Times* bestselling author of *The Coil*

Conversations
with the
Devil

JEFF ROVIN

TOR®

A TOM DOHERTY ASSOCIATES BOOK

NEW YORK

This is a work of fiction. All of the characters, organizations, and events portrayed in this novel are either products of the author's imagination or are used fictitiously.

CONVERSATIONS WITH THE DEVIL

Copyright © 2007 by Jeff Rovin

All rights reserved, including the right to reproduce this book, or portions thereof, in any form.

Book design by Mary A. Wirth

A Tor Book
Published by Tom Doherty Associates, LLC
175 Fifth Avenue
New York, NY 10010

www.tor.com

Tor® is a registered trademark of Tom Doherty Associates, LLC.

ISBN-13: 978-0-7653-4631-5
ISBN-10: 0-7653-4631-1

First Edition: March 2007
First Mass Market Edition: March 2008

Printed in the United States of America

0 9 8 7 6 5 4 3 2 1

For V.
And M.
And S.

I wept not, so to stone within I grew.

—DANTE ALIGHIERI, *THE DIVINE COMEDY*

Conversations with the Devil

One

1

New Englanders have always had a close relationship with death.

When the Plymouth colonists landed on hostile, unfamiliar shores in 1620, they were faced with starvation, disease, and unforgiving winter. They were saved by the Wampanoag natives, who showed them how to plant and harvest and store food. The natives were rewarded with devastating European diseases like smallpox, typhus, and "bad blood"—syphilis. But the colonists survived and prospered.

So did death, in many forms.

Free to own land, the New Englanders fought the Native Americans and each other to possess it. Free to worship, they killed those who chose heretical paths. Free to create militias, they fought proxy wars for European powers and started new ones. Weathered gravestones commemorating these sacrifices are far more plentiful than the covered bridges, taverns, and forests for which New England is popularly known.

Yet death is manifest in more than just the ancient cemeteries, those odd-shaped geometries that occupy an acre or two behind rusting iron fences, defying the lopsided roads that grew around them. Death pervades daily life. Modern families celebrate their ancestors' sacrifices in countless wars and skirmishes, honoring them in portraits and busts, on memorial streets and buildings, and with weathered ivory tombs. Dead leaders of government and industry are celebrated with post offices, official buildings, and schools.

Martyrdom is pictured and revered in houses of worship.

Along the coast of New England, death rides every breath. The salty sea air is rich with the odor of dead fish and flora. Inland, in places like Delwood, Connecticut, predators of all sizes and species move through the low hills and forests. Schoolchildren learn that the word "fall" signifies falling leaves but adults know better. Like the vespers church bell tolling day's end, it is the echo of our fall from grace. Yet those with the will to persevere and a bright slant of mind wait for hope to be renewed, stronger and more precious, on the other side of winter.

Only briefly, of course, for fall returns. Death always has the last word.

Outsiders embrace New England's autumnal beauty but the locals resent it. The creeping chill closes windows that remained cheerfully open during the summer. It wraps people in jackets and cardigans, in defiantly colorful and branded sweatshirts. It turns them inward. Grasses wither to brown, leaves burn red, and skies go pale. Spirits fade and die too, locked inside walls and garments.

There was nothing anyone could do about that. But Sara Jacqueline Lynch did everything she could to keep the skulls of Delwood from growing too dark and dreary.

The psychotherapist always saw more faces in September and October than at any other time of year. Some of those faces were familiar, like Delwood Deli owner Billy Roche. The middle-aged butcher seemed to fall for a new summer transplant every year, a New York sophisticate he fancied more than his wife. The emaciated urbanites talked to him and listened to what he had to say. It didn't matter that the only thing he had to say was about meat and barbecues. He got to look into their eyes. Roche's attractions usually died in mid-October, along with the rest of Delwood. Then there was Barri Neville who could not stand having her children come back inside and wanted to know if it was wrong to wish that she had never had kids.

"No. It's good you did," the psychotherapist told her.

Sara said it was natural to feel frustrated and that Mrs. Neville should find private time away from the house and family. She suggested the woman join a reading club at the library or do yoga at the gym of the nearby community college.

Instead, Mrs. Neville opted for two therapy sessions a week. That changed to none after a month or so, when the bills started backing up and Mrs. Neville had to increase her hours at the supermarket checkout counter.

For some patients fall marked a chilly end to cautious optimism. Computer repairman Chun Park grew drearier about the prospects of gaining his parents' approval to marry a non-Korean. Claudia Cole felt that it would be a mistake to come out of the closet. Like the trees, people shed their leaves, deprived themselves of sunlight to conserve water.

The fall invariably brought new faces at Sara's family practice as well, mostly disconnected kids who had matriculated from area junior high schools to Litchfield County High School. Sara treated adults to pay the bills, but her main interest was in adolescent problems. She felt a special connection with teenagers who felt like they didn't belong—with their families, in their communities, among their peers.

Sara listened closely and made suggestions designed to involve the parents, but only when the kids were somewhat surefooted about themselves. That tended to happen naturally when parents backed off a little. With some kids, the process was ongoing. She had written about this in her doctoral thesis at Yale. Although the larger subject was the relationship of gifted children with one or more narcissistically deprived parents—resulting in jealousy and criticism—she wrote about what she called the Fall Phenomenon. People crawled into their heads the way they withdrew to their homes in autumn. Threatened by strangers—in this case children, who bring not only their own personalities but also the ideas of other families into the home—adults often hold more tightly to their own values. They overenforce their own ideals on children in order to maintain control in a suddenly hostile environment. Many children break under the dual stresses of external and familial pressure.

Preserving families was important to Sara and getting parents to respect their children was the heart of that. She had enjoyed great success in that area, rebuilding families from the smallest members outward.

With one sad exception.

Her own.

2

There was no Mr. Del.

It was generally assumed that Delwood got its name from "dell" since the town of 2,499 people was located in a small, secluded section of the Housatonic Valley in middle-western Connecticut. Some old-timers suggested that it was actually short for "Devil's Wood." That idea was rooted in rituals that refugees from the Massachusetts witch trials were said to have performed on the far side of the river.

A number of Sara's younger patients suggested it was just the Yankee pronunciation of "dull."

The valley was on the very edge of western New England just a few miles from the New York State border. Because it was an average two-hour drive to New York, Hartford, or New Haven, without convenient highway access, Delwood was not a bedroom community. Everyone who lived there full-time was either retired or worked in the county, some of them on the local dairy farms that spotted the region, most in shops that catered to regulars, weekenders, hunters, and day-trippers. In addition to the nearby high school, "Delac," the Delwood Academy, was located off Route 6, the county's main road. The coeducational Delac was an elite private school that had been the breeding ground for two presidents, three New England governors, and nearly a dozen ambassadors. It was a pipeline to Yale, which was where Sara Lynch had met many Delacians. She herself was not one of them. She went to Nathaniel Lyon Free School, named for the first Union general killed in the war. Lyon was not from Delwood but from Eastwood. A winter storm had pinned him at the local Graham Inn for several days on his way to West Point and he became a borrowed hero.

The Housatonic River slashed through the valley from Massachusetts on its 130-mile journey to the Long Island Sound. The river had powered the early metalworking mills that caused the growth of the region, which included the manufacture of bullets and artillery shells. The munitions were shipped down the river to the navy yards in New York and Groton. It was the only time Delwood exported rather than hosted death.

The Lynch family were latecomers to Delwood. They had arrived in the late 1940s, when Sara's father Robert was mustered out of the navy. He had spent three years in the Pacific Theater and unlike his fellow sailors who settled in postwar communities across western Long Island, Robert took his new Savannah-raised bride, Martha, to Connecticut where he had it in mind to build and sell his own handmade furniture. Using funds from the G.I. Bill they bought a large fixer-upper on the river, which Robert restored while thinking about, then talking about, then taking a few steps toward setting up his business. Martha opened a small shop in town to sell antiques, which she thought would be a perfect adjunct to her husband's trade. Robert could restore the furniture they sold. He did a little of that, and it ended up being the family's sole source of income as Robert Lynch spent more time drinking, smoking, and fishing with his young son Darrell than he did working.

The way Martha later described his symptoms, Robert was suffering from what would now be described as posttraumatic stress disorder, with a list of medical and psychological ways of treating it. He would have had more at his disposal than just the self-prescribed booze and cigarettes. Because of it, Robert's business, like his life, never went much farther than ambition.

3

Throughout the postwar years, Delwood struggled with another form of death. Its own. Industries were lost to the South, its farms were marginalized by conglomerates, and its growth was limited by harsh winters and humid summers. Suburbs grew with new families but exurbs like Delwood did not.

Luckily, those families helped Delwood grow in other ways. They were ways Robert Lynch had anticipated decades before. Lately, the river had made the region popular with rafters and kayakers, fathers and sons bonding the way Robert and Darrell once did. Fishermen came for the trout and pike. During the spring and summer they brought sons and buddies and cousins. They filled the region with life. Their laughter, loud engines, and cell phone chatter were enthusiastic but transient. The quiet, uninvolved mood of the locals remained unchanged.

In one way, the teenagers of Delwood were lucky today. They had the Internet. They did not have to remain emotionally caged in the fall and winter. They did not have to leave Delwood to find people with varied interests. They could custom-create unblemished online personalities, open electronic windows, and present themselves online to kindred souls. When their identities or relationships became unsatisfying or dangerous they could be quickly and ruthlessly discarded. But that indulgence came at a price. For one thing, it was a way of suppressing rather than improving the parts of young people that were faulty. For another, it was something of an oxymoron: a support group for antisocial behavior. Delwood may have been guilty of giving people boundaries, defined by their profession or birthplace, affluence or education, but it also provided communal goals. Whether it was serving on the volunteer fire department or working at the recycling trailer at the local landfill, people contributed to the upkeep of the community. They acquired new skills and, over time, a little social evolution occurred as some managed to pick up new perspectives. Most teenagers today were isolated from those duties, lost in virtual spaces of their own choosing.

Fredric Marash was one of those teenagers.

The mid-October afternoon was cool and damp from a late-morning rain. The low clouds colored everything in the heart of town with a different shade of gray, from the drained-of-rust bricks of the Delwood Bank and Trust to the ashen color of the uneven sidewalks. Even the centuries-old oaks had a charcoal darkness across their wrinkled bark.

Sara did not usually leave her home office during the day but her mother had run out of Ambien. The seventy-four-year-old woman did not often take the prescription sleep aid. But she liked to know it was there for those times when, as Martha put it—showing her formal but dramatic Southern roots—"Consciousness is a responsibility I no longer wish to bear."

It was only a short walk up the steep hill from her office to the center of town. It was a scenic trip along a narrow street crowded with old homes fighting for river views. Though walking was something Sara enjoyed, she had driven to the pharmacy. Fredric Marash was due at three and it was nearly half past two when the doctor had phoned in the prescription. She did not want to be late for any patient, but especially for Fredric. The sixteen-year-old had been under her care for nearly ten years, ever since she had received her doctorate.

He was a special case, an extremely sensitive young man. He would take her tardiness as a personal wound.

Sara passed Fredric as she headed home. He was riding his prized bike, oblivious to the world beyond it. The distinctive bike was a familiar sight around town. The lanky high school sophomore had not yet taken his driver's test and his parents worked six days a week at their dry-cleaning store. It was one of those things the family had let slide. Fredric did not seem to mind.

Predictably, Fredric was one of the few things in town today that had no gray. He was dressed entirely in black: a black T-shirt, black jeans tucked inside black boots, coasting on the black Time Trial Machine with his black windbreaker fluttering behind him. The TTM had an extremely high seat and very low, forward-facing handlebars. Fredric's torso rode so low that his head was actually dipped toward the ground. But the young man knew the streets well and he looked up when he had to, navigating like a great echo-locating bat. In their last session he had confessed to the psychotherapist that riding the bike this way made him feel invisible.

"But I've seen you riding your bike," Sara had told him in their last session. Part of her job was to try to gently integrate the young man into a world he had stubbornly pushed away since early childhood.

"You've seen me but you haven't seen me," he said as he held his spindly arms before him, upright, in a wide, embracing triangle. "I've been in here. But you will, one day. When you are here with me." Then he opened his arms to indicate the rest of the world. "Most of them will not be."

"Where exactly will we be?" she asked.

"Here," he replied, once again making a long, reclining pyramid with his arms. This time in his lap, like he was holding an angular Buddha belly.

"The first shape you made was up, the second one was down," she noted. "Does that make a difference?"

"None," the young man assured her. "What matters is that we will be rewarded for the trials."

"You'll have to walk me through that, Fredric," Sara said. "Are you telling me we have a bond because we're friends who look out for one another? Because that's how I feel."

"No," Fredric answered. "We're just headed for the same place. I saw it and soon you will too."

"I guess I'm not too smart today," Sara said. "The part I'm missing is where 'there' is."

"Safe," he said, "in a place I made, a place where the trusted and trusting will be rewarded."

His eager confidence sounded vaguely religious. It was an interesting perspective, this sense that they were inhabiting a secure area created or accessible by some vision they shared. Perhaps it was his way of denying danger by simply rejecting it with her as a partner, a crutch. Sara hoped to learn more about that during this week's first session. But she never knew with Fredric. His mood and unpredictable levels of accessibility determined the course of their conversation. There were some young patients who Sara felt comfortable "nudging" as she called it, and she had considerable success with them. Most of them wanted to talk, and were willing to open up over time to a compassionate mother-figure.

Fredric was different. That was why she liked to see him on successive days, twice each week. Occasionally, after Fredric had a chance to sleep on the questions of their first session, he came to the second meeting with more information to share.

Sara pulled into the long curving driveway of the Lynch home at 64 River Road. Dead, brittle leaves crunched under the tires as she parked by the detached garage. She left the Grand Cherokee outside. Built by her father, the garage had never been used for cars. It was stuffed with the expensive tools, warped wood, and faded sketches he had intended to use for his business. It had been nearly ten years since his death. Her younger brother Darrell was supposed to have taken what he wanted and sold the rest. If it was up to Sara she would have the local carting service come and just take everything away. But her mother wanted the stillborn business interred with respect. So the dusty corpse sat within those walls, waiting for Darrell to deal with it. It wasn't difficult for him to come from the outskirts of town. It was just the investment of time. That and the fact that a bar or an open tailgate at the state park usually got in the way.

Sara hurried along a slate walk to the back of the house. Fresh pyramids of firewood were stacked beside the garage and covered with a tarp. Darrell had managed to bring those over the night before last. Darrell used to enjoy outdoor activities. As a young boy he would "help" Sara rake the leaves by playing in them. Keeping her company *was* a help, especially when she was old enough to know that their father was off drinking. Swinging an ax was one of the few outdoor activities Darrell still enjoyed. Sara tried not to make too much of the fact that their father once dreamed of creating things with wood, not destroying it.

The home was a seven-bedroom Victorian with two cupola-topped turrets overlooking the riverside. They were connected by a long, straight corridor. The nearer of the domed towers was where Martha and Sara had their rooms. One of the three tall, slender chimneys rose beyond the turret.

It vented smoke from the two tower fireplaces as well as the small den, which was located just beyond her office.

A cracked, wood-burned sign above the back door of the house announced that the homestead was called "the Sticks." The name had come from a small inlet that had cut its way into their backyard. The Housatonic dumped all manner of flotsam here, mostly denuded tree branches, planks from broken canoes or rafts, and the occasional two-liter soda container or used condom. It was a much different world from when her father had made that sign.

Sara walked through the tiny waiting area to her office. There were two windows, two chairs, and a table with magazines. The antechamber was literally a six-foot-wide corner of the tower that had been walled off with Sheetrock. If patients became distraught, or were ashamed to be seen here, Sara allowed them to leave by the front door. Fredric typically came and went that way. He had once said it felt sneaky, and he liked that. Sara indulged him.

Sara paused to crack one of the windows. She switched on the ceiling fan as she entered the office. Since no one was coming immediately after Fredric it would be all right to leave the door to the waiting room open.

She took off her lightweight amber-colored cotton overcoat and put it in the closet. She paused in front of the mirror that hung on the inside of the door. Sara wore very little makeup. Ever since she had looked into her grandmother's coffin when she was a child, bright makeup had been something she associated with dead bodies. She did not need makeup really. Sara had a very pretty round face with pale blue eyes. Her blond hair was cut in a bob that extended to just below the ears. It narrowed a face that was always thought of as too young-looking. It also helped to hide the wrinkles that were beginning to pinch the outside of her eyes. She applied muted red lipstick to her thin lips and pulled a brush through her hair several times. She slipped a powder-blue Pashmina shawl from a hanger and threw it over the top of her white blouse. The open-neck look was too casual, unprofessional.

Sara had completed the transformation to Dr. Lynch as Fredric rang the buzzer. She closed the closet door and crossed the large Persian rug that covered the original hardwood floors. She admitted her patient.

Fredric's gaunt, pale face was framed by the upturned collar of his windbreaker and his long, peroxide-white hair. He was looking down and muttered a solemn "Hey" as he shuffled past her. The hopeful good humor of their last session was gone. Sara was not surprised. Fredric did not seem to hold on to joy for very long. He walked past a brown leather couch and went to the paisley-patterned armchair in the corner. He didn't so much sit as drop into it, his long legs surrendering the rest of his body to the seat. He arched up briefly to pull a pillow from the small of his back. He tossed it onto the couch and sat back down.

Sara took a steno pad from a locked drawer in her old mahogany desk. She sat in the armchair across from him. The room was small enough so that they were still quite close. It was intentionally spartan, with little to look at but the doctor. The fireplace was behind her. The door to the rest of the house was between them. Sara's degrees hung on the wall behind Fredric.

They were black and white too.

The young man raised a bony finger, shut his right eye, and traced a design in the rug. Sara watched him for a moment.

"Do you want to talk a little more about what we were discussing last week?" she asked.

He didn't answer.

"The place you were telling me about," she gently coaxed him. "The one you and I share."

"No."

"Is there any reason in particular?"

"I finished it. I'm tired," he said.

"Are you finished *with* it?" she asked.

"No," he said. "I did what I needed to. Now I have to wait. I don't want to talk about it."

"All right." Sara watched him as he turned curlicue paths along the rug. He had never seemed to notice it before. "What do you see?" she asked. With Fredric she had found it was best to work her way into his reality, his area of interest.

"I bet those old dudes hid maps there."

"In rugs?"

He nodded. "Maps are from people who were *there*. They're like eyes we get to borrow."

"That's a very interesting thought," she said.

"Sometimes it's good. Sometimes it's bad."

"What makes you say that?"

"I was reading," he said softly. He was staring at something that wasn't in the room. "I think there were things hidden there too."

"Where?"

"In the Bible," he replied. "It's such bullshit."

"In what way?"

"Probably most ways. I don't think the earth was made in five or six days, and that Adam came from dust and Eve came from a rib or that a snake told her to eat an apple. I mean, that's like *Stargate* stuff. Then I was thinking even though that's what it says I bet that isn't what it means."

"What do you think it means?"

He rolled a shoulder.

"May I ask what prompted you to read the Bible?" Sara asked.

"I was cold," he said.

"Physically?"

He nodded. "I was on the computer in my room. I went out to turn on the heat and I saw the Bible in the bookcase."

"When was this?"

"Coupla weeks ago," he said. "I remembered the first time I went to church was in the summer and it was real hot. So I was thinking that if I used it to focus, maybe I could remember the heat."

"That's a pretty sophisticated idea," Sara said. "We call that a radical memory exercise, when you try to obtain results in the present by using an object to re-create experiences from another time. Why did you want to try that?"

Fredric grew a little antsy. He usually did that when he didn't want to answer. This was one of those times when Sara felt she had to nudge.

"Did someone else try it? Did someone online recommend it?" Sara asked.

"Because my father was bitchin' over dinner about the price of oil and said we should wait till winter to use the heat."

"You were going out to adjust the thermostat and thought you'd try this instead," Sara said. "To keep the peace."

He shrugged. That meant "yes."

Sara made notes as she said, "You tried to accommodate him. That's very admirable."

"It has teeth marks on it."

"What did? The Bible?"

"No," he said. "The dining-room table."

"When did you notice that?"

"Years ago. They're little ones, in the bar that holds up the leaf. I rubbed them while he was talking. It was like a message from little me to me now."

"What was 'little you' saying?"

"He said, 'Bite the table,' and I wanted to. The way my dad was talking, all 'Thou shalt not.' It made me mad."

This was a first. Fredric's recollections of early childhood rages were deeply suppressed. She had worked hard to keep him from reliving the feeling of exile he'd felt as a six-year-old.

"But you didn't bite the table."

"No."

"Or anything else, like your pillow or your hand?" Sara asked. Those were subjects of his aggressive behavior in the past. The side of his left hand and his right thumb still bore slight scars.

"No. No biting," Fredric told her.

"And you didn't turn up the heat."

"I wanted to."

"But you didn't. You found another way."

"Yeah," he said. "Reading the Bible made me mad. That made me warm."

"I'm very proud you respected your father's wishes," Sara told him.

The young man winced and his shoulders rose and fell, body language for "Whatever." But it was a big step.

When Fredric was first brought to her he was suffering regular, increasingly feral outbursts, biting everything he could fit his mouth around. Contacted by the elementary school's guidance counselor Miss McMahon—an old-school psychologist who believed in severe parental punishment as a means of behavior modification—county social services could detect no signs of physical or mental abuse. The young boy's attacks seemed to be triggered whenever someone told him "no," even in the playground. His first-grade teacher, a fool of an old-school marm, suggested to his face and his parents that he was just "born bad." Sara had him pulled from the class and, temporarily, from the school. Rather than try to get people around him to stop saying no, Sara convinced the boy that the word was only a suggestion, not a command. It was up to him to decide whether to stop what he was doing.

It was not a sophisticated concept, a variation of what one of her professors, Dr. Martin Cayne, had called the "roll-over-for-a-dog-biscuit" technique. She hadn't approved of that analogy but the idea itself was sound. With Sara's guidance, plus a semester of home-schooling from a patient, soft-spoken tutor and the buffering presence of a gentle maternal grandfather who came to live with them, Fredric quickly learned that a cessation of disagreeable acts led to approval. The biting stopped, even after he returned to public school. Sara concluded that Fredric's aggression was actually rooted in pro-social behavior. It was a means of preemptively preventing exclusion from domestic activities and peer groups.

But there was still the matter of his outstretched arms from the session before. They indicated that Fredric had gone in the opposite direction. He had created a partnership that was designed to exclude the rest of the world. He had lately contacted other teenagers on the Internet. Perhaps he was trying to translate that sense of exclusivity to the real world.

"Did something specific in the Bible make you mad?" Sara asked.

Fredric squirmed slightly in the chair. He seemed to withdraw, to shrink inside his windbreaker.

"Was there a story?" Sara nudged. "A phrase? An illustration?"

"Eve," he said.

"In *Genesis*?"

"Yeah. She really pisses me off. God too." He looked squarely at the psychotherapist as he spoke. "Eve did something wrong and God blamed the snake, made him crawl on his belly. I don't like the way people believe that shit and I hate all those fuckin' old dudes like Abraham and Moses talking about 'Thou shalt not' and don't have idols and all that crap. If that's so important why are there all these motherfuckin' churches with idols on the walls and on the outsides?"

Fredric did not usually go off like this. She was glad. It was better to have the anger on the outside than stored on the inside.

"Those are not idols, they're icons," Sara said. "They're images of respect."

"That's just a different word for the same thing," he said. "They're grave images and God himself said they shouldn't be there."

He meant "graven" but she let it pass. He was not only huffing discomfort but expressing himself with full sentences. Their sessions tended to be spotted with short answers: "chicken pecks," as she called them, most of which had to be coaxed out. His open dialogue suggested that the Bible—and his father's command—had tapped an important keg of resentment. He had gone from fearing he would be excluded from activities to experiencing subordination. In his mind, the onetime fantasy was becoming a reality. That was unhealthy.

"It sounds like you learned an awful lot reading the Bible," Sara said.

"I did. And I remembered stuff from church."

"Do you think Abraham and Moses were bad people?" Sara asked.

"Yeah," Fredric said.

"Why?"

"They were sick."

"They were very *strict*," Sara suggested. "They lived in a different time, often in the wilderness where a command structure was necessary."

"Abraham—that fool was gonna knife his son," Fredric said. "What kind of 'structure' is killing your own kid? God sent his own son here to have him crucified and his mother just let him go get nailed up."

"People do things that seem right at the moment," she explained. "Parents are human too. Sometimes they misunderstand situations."

"Abraham was gonna *knife* his *kid*," Fredric repeated angrily. "And God *told* him to! Jesus had a way out, he could have taken the deal to be a king, but God didn't want him to."

"That deal was with the Devil," Sara said.

"Big friggin' whoop," Fredric said. "The deal would have kept him from being hammered to a cross. I read online how that feels. What parent could possibly want that for their kid?"

"Okay. We can agree that was a bad way to die," Sara said. "A deal with the Devil might not have been a good way to live."

Fredric said nothing.

"Let's talk about another aspect of the Bible," Sara said. "What about 'Thou shalt not kill'? Is that bad?"

"It's another lie. Abraham was gonna kill, Moses killed that builder and drowned all of Pharaoh's men. Jesus' peeps were fed to lions and crucified and all kinds of shit. God kills with floods and disease and war. My granddad got Alzheimer's and his brain got erased. God could have stopped that. Who is He to talk about 'Thou shalt not kill'?"

"God."

"Yeah?" Fredric leaned forward. "Well, what I'm saying is that don't mean shit. You know what God is, what the Bible is? It's people telling us we can't make up our own minds and then doing it anyway while they sell us a lot of stupid shit that doesn't make sense."

"Why do you think they do that?" Sara asked.

"Mind control," he said. "They don't want us to think. They don't want us to make our own maps. That's how the churches stay rich and powerful." He sat back in the chair, his foot tapping quickly, his eyes on the fireplace. "Just because a billion people say something, that doesn't make it right. In China and India no one gives a shit what God has to say."

Fredric's extremism wasn't surprising. Teenagers had passion. That was export of their body politic. She was more impressed by how little of the Old Testament Fredric had apparently gone through to draw the conclusions he did.

"I have a question for ya," she said. She elided the word to try to reconnect in an informal, peer-level way. It felt unnatural, but only to her she hoped. "If you had to draw your own map where would it take you?"

The youth's dark eyes held her. "To the truth," he said without hesitation. "It's there."

"Where?"

The young man looked at her. He raised his arms slowly. He formed the triangle again.

"The place where you and I will meet again," she said.

He nodded. Then he lowered his arms. The moment of tranquility passed and he started tapping his foot again.

Sara was accustomed to Fredric being laconic or vague. But this overt reticence was something new. He did not seem confused. To the contrary, he seemed unusually sure of himself. Almost enlightened.

The psychotherapist tucked her notebook at her side. She folded her hands and leaned forward.

"I like the way you're questioning things," Sara said. "We read, we process information, we make informed decisions. You're doing that. But I think you're doing something we call 'transference.' You're angry at your father, or maybe a teacher, and so you're raging at Abraham and Moses, at God. I'm not qualified to say whether they deserve it or not. My friend Sister Grace could talk to you about that if you're interested. I'm more interested in what is behind this anger."

"Stupid decisions," he said.

"Like not being allowed to use the heat."

"Yeah."

Sara sat back again. "I'm curious, Fredric. What would happen if you talked to your dad?"

The young man's shoulders slumped into his chest. He seemed very young just then. "He would give me a lecture and make me feel like an idiot. Also, you shouldn't do that."

"Do what?"

"Be curious. It kills cats."

Sara smiled. "You know, that happens not to be true. Hundreds of years ago the saying was 'Caution kills the cat.' Cats take time to explore things. Whack it around a little. Sit and look at it, watch it. What the expression really meant was that you can wait too long without satisfying your curiosity. That's what killed the cat. People changed the word and the meaning got lost. That's why I like how you're questioning things. Better that than have caution kill you."

Suspicion touched his innocence. "Did you just make that up?"

"No. I read it in a book, actually, one I pulled from the shelf in my library the other night. It belonged to my brother."

"Darrell."

"That's right," she said. "I gave it to him on his birthday years ago."

"Who's younger?"

"He is, by four years," Sara said.

"Did you boss him around?"

"I tried not to. I had to babysit for him after school, so I had to make sure he did his homework and chores around the house."

"But you fought."

"He fought. I just scowled." She smiled after making a face.

The boy said nothing. He was closing up again. He turned and put his face against his shoulder. Tightly, as though he were trying to hide. Sara didn't want him to.

"I'm over here, Fredric," she said.

"Do you tell Ms. Blair things?" Fredric asked, as if he hadn't heard.

That was a surprise. Chrissie Blair was twenty-six years old, a University of Connecticut graduate who was brought in at the end of the last school year to replace the part-time counselor who served the entire school district. Fredric did not have regular sessions with Chrissie, though Sara did give the guidance counselor general updates on Fredric and other students. She wondered when he might have seen them together. Sara made a point of going when class was in session.

"I talk to Ms. Blair, but I don't tell her what you or anyone else says," she told him. "That's against the law. I give her my interpretation."

"Your maps of people."

"If you like," she said. "But I give you my word, nothing you tell me leaves this office. Getting back to the Bible, you've formed some pretty sophisticated opinions about the Bible. We should talk about those, not about—"

"That isn't true," he said, his eyes shifting toward her.

"I disagree. You've started to interpret some pretty complex metaphors—"

"I mean that nothing leaves this office."

That caught Sara with her guard down again. "Nothing leaves," she assured him. "That's a rule, the *basic* rule. When I'm away the doors and windows are locked and the key to my desk is always with me. There is no way for anyone to hear us or to read my notes."

"You say that, but things leave," he insisted. "People know."

"They leave *how?*"

Fredric Marash raised his arms and formed the triangle and once again seemed very much at peace with the world.

TWO

1

Sara left her office after making extensive notes about the session.

Another one down, she thought when she finished. It was frustrating work. Sometimes she had to be content just holding ground. Psychotherapy was a lot like dieting. Sometimes the biggest, most satisfying results happened early on, at what was called the "crisis juncture." After that, the improvement—like pounds—came along grudgingly.

She would return to finish after delivering the pills to her mother. Martha didn't need them now but she liked to know they were there. Sara was holding the long pharmacy bag in one hand and her notebook in the other. If she had a flash of insight about Fredric she wanted to be able to jot it down. Her ideas tended to evolve quickly, sometimes in the wrong direction. If she needed to backtrack it was important to have intellectual station stops.

Whenever the psychotherapist worked with young people she liked to ask progressive questions. Children and teenagers did not typically think or converse in linear fashion. It was best to lead them gently using information they provided. At some point during this session Fredric had uncharacteristically taken charge. In effect, he had dared her to defend the Bible, to explain inconsistencies, and to justify acts by revered holy men that could not be easily explained. She had to be careful in that arena. Defending violence against a family member could be interpreted as giving leave to do so. Given Fredric's past, that was a bad idea.

She was especially puzzled by Fredric's willingness to read the Bible instead of use it in a more totemistic fashion. If he had wanted to get warm, he was more likely to have recreated the setting of the church by sitting on a chair with the book in his lap. He was not a reader. Fredric was primarily an image processor who responded to visual stimuli better than words and ideas. He played computer games, downloaded movies and videos, spent time in chat rooms—she had checked one of them, CTGOTHTEENS—which were filled with variegated typefaces and graphics to dramatize communication. He also enjoyed creating "photomanips" of famous faces, structures, or art. Sara found out about these just a few months before when he used the term and she asked what it meant. He didn't want to tell her so she looked it up online. Armed with the *jargon de jour* she kept after Fredric—coaxing, encouraging, until he agreed to send her three of his favorites. The young man had put a saber in the upraised arm of the Statue of Liberty, added Moses-like horns to all of Michelangelo's sculptures—they made David seem even more attractive somehow, she had to admit—and restyled Abraham Lincoln's beard as though the president were one of those magic wand toys full of metal filings. The photo-manips were powerful, aggressive works. To provide control data, she had asked three of her other young patients what they would put in the statue's hand in place of the torch. They said a flashlight, a remote control, and a banana. Those answers were benign and unsurprising.

Because Fredric was so visually aware, there was a second haunting curiosity about the session: the triangular shape he had made with his arms, not once but three times. The form contradicted what he was saying. An embracing shape would have been a circle. The sharp lines of his arms and the tense, rigid placement of his fingers suggested a prison, not an exclusive, caring club.

One thing Sara did know was that Fredric was too angry with the Old Testament patriarchs to be angry *at* the patriarchs. Some deeper, unarticulated injustice seemed to be gnawing at him. She spoke with Franz and Goldwyn Marash regularly and they did not seem to be pushing him. A request to keep the heat down would not have been sufficient to draw this kind of reaction. Someone at school, perhaps? What was frustrating was that Fredric could also be picking up fuel in chat rooms. Hearing about restrictions other parents laid on their kids might cause him to see demons in his own life.

The psychotherapist walked through the pentagonal den to the narrow "north wing" corridor beyond. Except for the two- and three-girl dorms at the University of Bridgeport and then at Yale, the Sticks was the only home Sara had ever known. She had moved home to take over the mortgage when the store finally closed. But supporting her mother was not the only reason that Sara came back. There was comfort here, good memories tucked among the bad. And she had enjoyed being with her mother. The two of them had been profoundly disappointed by men in their lives. "The Sticks" was an isle of sanity, like the all-women Paradise Island in the *Wonder Woman* comic books Sara had read when she was younger.

The hall was lined with fading, floral design wallpaper. There was a staircase to the left with a small closet for storage space. It was stuffed mostly with Christmas decorations, seasonal items like deck chairs, and suitcases they never used except when Martha went to visit her older brother Bob in Georgia. He was a pilot and came to visit more often than Martha went south. There were family photos on the wall to her right. Doors between the photos led to a coat closet and to the basement. Cellars were one of the few things that came alive during the New England autumn as oil burners growled heat from their old iron bellies. The dark wood floor of the hallway was covered with a Kashan rug. The wine-red fabric was spotted with golden hooplike shapes, unlike the Kerman curlicues that had fascinated Fredric in her office.

That was new too, Sara thought, making a note in her pad as she started up the staircase. *It was as though Fredric had noticed the rug for the first time.*

It was a visual presentation, true. But it might be related to his sudden fascination with maps. And that interest might have some bearing on the triangle he kept showing her.

Martha was in her room, in her big rattan chair, watching TV. The slender, white-haired woman watched a lot of cable TV during the "inside months," as she called them. She liked home fix-up shows and lately she had been watching shows about science on the Discovery Channel and PBS. Martha Lynch was not a college-educated woman and she seemed to enjoy learning about the world. Not history but science. She said she liked finding out more about natural things, not the mess that people made of them.

It wasn't just the learning she liked, Sara suspected, but the escape. During the summers Martha spent most of her days on the Delwood green, bathing in sunlight as she fed ducks, chatted with friends, or read—paperbacks with happy endings or simple crossword puzzles, never newspapers or anything that would trip up her mood. The breezy humidity that crawled through the Housatonic Valley never bothered her. Compared to Southern mugginess, she said, the muggy wind was like air conditioning. She would walk to the green and back and she would always come home contented, tired, and looking forward to the next day.

But fall and winter were ugly to her, and she got cranky right back; always ladylike, but with an edge. As a girl, Martha had thought the changing of the leaves and snowy December nights would be romantic. That was why she had agreed to go north with Robert. She learned otherwise. The fall brought eye-swelling molds, depressing skies, and roads made slick by dead leaves. In the winter there were joint-stiffening temperatures and skin-blasting cold. In New England, the early darkness of the seasons was not like a silky Southern scarf bright with moonlight and stars. It was like a quilt, heavy and thick.

At the first loud whispers of fall Martha's mood changed with the leaves, going from soft green to pique yellow. She went inside and stayed there, spending most of her time in the second-floor bedroom that abutted but did not connect with her daughter's room. Martha became more critical of everything, Sara included. Sara had learned not to take it to heart, though sometimes it got under her skin.

Even though Martha Lynch had not been outside all day she was wearing a cashmere sweater and matching lime-green slacks. Martha did not believe in jeans or sweat clothes on ladies. That was not how she was raised. Her one concession to household comfort were her slippers.

"Here are your pills," Sara said as she walked in.

Martha took the bag and looked at it low through her progressive lenses. "Thank you, dear." It came out "deah." Martha's accent was traditional "Georgia gracious," as Robert used to describe it.

Sara glanced at the TV. Someone was holding a fistful of Spanish moss toward the camera. "Anything interesting?" she asked.

"It's a program about window boxes in cities," she said. The remote was on her lap, pointing toward the TV. She pressed the mute button. "They're telling folks how to grow on sills what we grow on actual trees back home."

"They give the windows a very New Orleans look," Sara said as a brownstone facade filled the screen.

"I prefer flowers in parks and gardens," Martha said.

"They don't have to be mutually exclusive," Sara said. "It adds color to a rock face."

"It's like putting ice cream sprinkles on mashed potatoes, dear. They are out of place."

Point Martha. Just shut up, Sara.

Sara had tried, but there was no reason to discuss anything when her mother decided to be contrary. Sara felt a thin, chill wind against the back of her hand. She went to the window and made sure it was entirely shut. It was time to get the foam-filled "draft dodger" rolls from the storage closet.

"Before this there was a program about the universe," Martha went on. "They worry too much about figuring out how it will end. There doesn't seem to be much we can do about that."

"People like to understand things," Sara said, ignoring her own counsel.

"Well, I don't understand *that*. We live on a river. We enjoy the middle of it. Do we really need to know where it starts or ends?"

"We do if we're nineteenth-century lumberjacks or fishermen or trappers who need to sell our goods in another town," Sara said.

"We aren't, dear," Martha grumped. "Besides, we know what's there. God is waiting for us. And if we ever get there by other than honest means—by spaceship or this 'astral projection' they talked about on another program—he's going to flick us out with his finger, like a ladybug off a screen."

Sara shook her head. Martha Lynch was not a traditionally religious woman. She was Episcopalian and her husband had been Catholic. Sara had been raised Catholic at her father's Irish-stubborn insistence. Whereas Sara had left it all behind after her confirmation, Martha still held to the parts of her faith that gave her comfort.

"We're having a little party for Alexander tonight," Martha said.

"I noticed that on the calendar this morning," Sara told her.

"When you were six we went bowling. Do you know how I remember?"

"No, Mother."

"Because we had lane six," she said. The woman frowned. "There's a word that describes why we remember certain things. Do you happen to remember what that is, dear?"

"A mnemonic."

"That's it. Spell it?"

"M-n-e-m-o-n-i-c."

"The 'm' is silent. That's a little pain, isn't it? You need a mnemonic just to remember it's there."

And sometimes the crossness was endearing. Sara smiled and gave her a kiss on the forehead before leaving.

2

It was four-thirty when Sara returned to her office. Her mother liked to have dinner at six. She wondered if Alexander would always remember *his* sixth birthday because of that.

Alexander was the son of their housekeeper, Tonia Tsvardin. Tonia's husband Piotr had been a senior lieutenant in the Russian army. He dismantled mines and bombs and was killed by an explosion in Chechnya before his son was born. Unable to care for Alexander and survive on Piotr's inadequate "death pension"—which arrived sporadically—Tonia emigrated to the United States. She settled with relatives in New Haven five years ago. A dear friend at the Yale Divinity School, Sister Grace Rollins, knew Tonia's family and put her in touch with the Lynches. When Robert was alive, Martha had been motivated to try to make their house a home. That stopped when he died. Sara hired Tonia to work for them, hoping Alexander would bring her mother back from depression. The Russian woman and her boy moved into the tower in the south end of the house, which used to be Darrell's bedroom and the guest room. Martha loved having her "little Russian daughter and grandson" around. Though Tonia did the cleaning now, Martha was no longer in retreat.

Tonia was a devoted and grateful woman, and Alexander was an exceptionally sharp young man. He spoke two languages and his command of English was better and more precise than most of the American youths Sara saw. His poise gave her hope when some of the local children got her down.

The psychotherapist went to her office and shut the door. There was something reassuring about the solid *click* the door made when it closed. She sat behind the desk and dropped the notepad beside her laptop. She liked sitting here, in her high-backed swivel chair. Out there, on the rug, in the stationary armchair, she was as vulnerable as her patients. That's the way it had to be. She got into their problems with them and often there was emotional backwash. Here at her desk she felt more like a coach than a player. The game was over. It was time to evaluate the playbook. She liked both aspects of the job, but this was more intellectual than emotional.

A job, she thought. *That is my life.*

Since she "got so smart," as her father used to put it when she got into Yale—with admiration and perhaps a little envy—Sara had forgotten what it was like simply to watch anything from the grandstand. Just attending one of the few conferences she did, or visiting a friend, or even stopping at the pharmacy, she felt the way an artist must feel at a museum. She needed to deconstruct everything.

So what do you end up with here? the psychotherapist asked herself, thinking about the last two sessions with Fredric. *A design that doesn't make sense.*

She sketched the young man's triangle on a page of her notepad.

"Talk to me," she said aloud. "What are you really saying here, Fredric?"

The woman had been treating Fredric for so long she had

gotten used to both his obtuseness and the glacial pace of his treatment. It would have been wonderful if she could find a unified theory of Fredric that suddenly made him "happy." But that wasn't the way he was built. He was bored by the *abba* rhyme scheme of reality. His only real joys seemed to come from short, regular swims in disorder. Even his bike was a manifestation of that, heightening his personal speed and creating a little wind and generating an adrenaline rush. As long as it stayed mild and nonviolent, his localized chaos-making didn't concern her. It was expected.

That's why the simplicity and order of the triangles intrigued and frustrated her. *That* didn't fit.

Fredric had been reading the Bible. Could he have meant the Holy Trinity?

No, she decided. Being a part of that would not make him feel secure. She also dismissed another symbolic aspect of the shape, the ontological image of man as an integration of body, mind, and spirit. Fredric was visual, he could be surreal, but he was not abstract. Even his most "out there" photo-manips were still playful or ironic extensions of reality.

That wasn't the only reason Sara felt the triangle was about the shape itself and not just the three points. There was a strong suggestion of intimacy in the way Fredric had displayed it. The triangle came from his body, like a hug. If he merely wanted to illustrate a shape he probably would have done so with his thumbs as the base and his index fingers as the sides. Fredric tended to be a minimalist.

Sara refused to accept that she was making too much of the shape. Not yet. She got a *ping* and made a note to check with Fredric's teachers. Perhaps one of them had discussed Nazi oppression during the Second World War when different-colored triangular patches were used to identify undesirables, from communists to alcoholics to gays. If Fredric was feeling oppressed he probably would have traced the design on his shirt, but it was worth finding out.

Sara opened her laptop and looked back at his saved file of photo-manips. She looked for triangular design components and found just one—the jaunty goatee he had given Lincoln in place of his regular beard. It was probably a coincidence. The proportions were not the same as the shape he had made with his arms.

The image of Lincoln made her smile. It was irreverent and funny. She liked seeing Fredric confident enough to take on an icon.

Sara went through a decade of notes about Fredric Marash to see if there were some reference she may have forgotten. She looked back at the results of the psychometric testing from when he was six and seven. For the first test she had given him shapes that were all black, since color itself generates an emotional response. Fredric's reactions were classic. He preferred shapes that suggested adult human physicality, ovals and circles, and laid them out in a tiered way to indicate size. He put the smallest circle, himself, in the middle. The results suggested a normal kid intimidated by larger individuals. It also explained his biting. Fredric was not very talkative and had trouble expressing his fears. His confidence handling the cutouts showed a strong nativistic sense, meaning that he was born with well-developed spatial perceptions. Sara's analysis accurately foreshadowed his subsequent visual growth and also his inevitable boredom in school, where the emphasis was on reading, writing, and numeric education. She had encouraged his parents and grandfather to give him an Etch-A-Sketch, Colorforms, and other media that would provide an outlet for self-expression.

Fredric's second test, administered exactly one year later, showed a dramatic growth in his empirical skills on top of a greatly strengthened nativism. He demonstrated complete command of the black shapes, constructing more recognizable human forms. When Sara added colored shapes he was drawn to red regardless of the configuration. Red stimulates human metabolism. It is the color of hunger, of aggression, of sexual desire. Even though the biting had stopped, Fredric still felt as though he were outside the mainstream of social activity.

There was one use of a triangle, she noted, and it had been dramatic. In one set of designs, Frederic had used a triangle like an arrowhead to cut down a large human figure he had constructed. He drove the wedge into the neck. Their subsequent discussion about the decapitation revealed it wasn't the size of the adult that troubled Fredric but what he imagined was coming from the mouth.

"Red," he said.

She had not yet put the colored shapes on the table.

Innately, Fredric saw adults as a restrictive force. His visualizations and comments suggested impotent rage. That was not uncommon in children, but it was very strong in this boy. It took years of hard work to socialize him to the point where he could be with other children and not feel cowed, cornered, and inevitably violent because of adults. She wondered, though, about that triangle.

Sara closed the file and sat back. She had not given Fredric further psychometric tests because he was charting along a classical pattern of development. His spatial skills were evolving, his ability to organize small shapes into larger ones, narrative ones. Additional shape-shifting exercises would have frustrated him because the cutouts would not be enough to express his growing visual sense.

The triangle he made today is not the same as the triangle he made then, she thought. Thinking about his remarks during the session, Sara wondered if Fredric might have been introduced to the design online. She logged on and found several small, independent religious orders that used the triangle to represent faith, hope, and charity. The sites were graphic-intensive and she wondered if Fredric had visited them. Many such sects—which were based in places like Abadiânia, Brazil, and Blue Sulphur Springs, West Virginia—were considered "Christian-aberrational." Their selective use and outright distortion of dogma could account for Fredric's attack against the Old Testament patriarchs.

Sara looked over the notes she had made after the session, key words that reflected her initial impressions. "Guarded, smug, teasing, resentful," she had written on her way to see her mother. The shifts in Fredric's mood and manner were greater than she usually saw. She wondered whether the young man would feel empowered by the way he had successfully taken charge at certain moments. That could be the first sign of a new phase of growth, of confidence. Or it could be the first stirrings of resentment against Sara and other authority figures. That could be dangerous, especially if Fredric started to feel like he wasn't being heard, the way he did when he was six years old. That was one way aggressive children became violent adults.

Sara called the Marash store. His father answered and Sara said that she would like to see Fredric again the following day.

"Is something wrong?" he asked.

"I don't think so," she said. "We ran out of time today and there were some important ideas I didn't want to leave hanging for a week."

"But he's okay?"

"He's still Fredric," Sara said reassuringly. But there was something in Mr. Marash's usually flat, even voice that suggested an elevated concern. "Has he been all right at home?"

"Tell the truth, he's been really distant the past few days," Franz admitted. " 'Distracted' might be a better word, like he's trying to figure something out."

"Such as?"

"I don't know. It's not like he's trying to decide what kind of decal to add to his bike. It's almost like he's in a trance."

"Why didn't you call me?" she asked, trying not to sound annoyed.

"We were hoping we could get him to talk to *us*," Franz replied. "You've had him all these years and we were thinking it's time we—I don't know. *Pushed* him a little, encouraged him to trust us."

"Did he respond?"

"If you call grunts and shrugs responding," the man told her.

"Has he been doing anything else out of the ordinary?"

"He's been spending a lot of time outdoors, but we figured that was a good thing as long as it's not too cold yet. At night he stays in his room."

"Does he stay around the house when he's outside?" Sara asked.

"No. I've seen him head off to the park, but I don't know why or where," Franz said. "Maybe he's got a girl. That's what we were hoping."

"That would be nice," Sara agreed. "Is there anything else? Thoughts or impressions—you know the drill," she said with a reassuring laugh.

"Nothing," he said. "But I promise, I *will* let you know if anything occurs to us."

"I'd appreciate that," Sara said.

Franz thanked her and said he would tell his son to come at the usual time.

Sara sat back. Sometimes it was tougher dealing with the parents than with the kids. Therapist-patient privilege existed between her and the young people who came to see her. She was obligated to involve the parents only when she needed their cooperation in a program of off-premises treatment, or when the child or other members of the household might be at risk. But there was usually such longing when she spoke to the parents, a desire to know, to be reassured.

This was about as far as she could go with Fredric tonight. Sara spent another hour going over notes from other patients she had seen. Then happily, even defiantly, she called it a day. There was another little boy who required her attention.

Sara took the gift she had bought from her desk drawer and, locking the back door, went to a party.

3

The dining room was just large enough to accommodate eight people plus a credenza—where several wrapped presents were stacked—and a narrow hutch for the fine china. The eight-light chandelier was Bohemian glass, made in the 1930s and a wedding present from Robert's parents. One of the last things Sara's father had done was put in a dimmer. Martha liked to eat in low light. She said it made her feel elegant.

Martha was already at the table when Sara arrived. Alexander was seated to her left. Sara sat on her right. Tonia and her son usually dined with them. Martha referred to Alexander as the man of the house and he was proud to tell guests that his name meant "defending men."

Tonia Tsvardin was a petite woman with a round, open, angelic face. She had long brown hair worn in a ponytail and blue eyes that came from her Lithuanian grandfather "Bundy." She was always smiling, sunniness that carried into her disposition. She was grateful to be living in Delwood, grateful that her son could grow up in America. She spoke English well enough after just a few years and listened carefully to others so she could speak it better.

Alexander was his mother writ small, though he had black hair that came from his father and the restless curiosity that came from being a six-year-old boy. He was not a large child—his father was around five-foot-seven, as far as Sara could tell from photographs—but his curiosity and spirit filled a room.

They were all there when Sara arrived. She had gone upstairs to change into slacks and a sweater and tried to join the group mentally. Her mind was still on Fredric.

Darrell was also coming, Martha said, though only for cake.

"He said he might be bringing a lady friend," the woman added.

"One we've met?" Sara asked.

"He didn't share that information."

Not that it mattered. They all seemed the same to Sara. Lonely, single mothers who did not have the money for a night out. A little overweight, a little too made-up, just wanting someone to drink with and hold her. There was nothing wrong with any of that. But it was all very superficial. She didn't know about the women, but she knew her brother had more to give than a quick laugh and an anonymous tumble.

Alexander had selected the menu items, which is why they were having franks drowned in chili with sides of potato chips and corn on the cob. He had printed up a colorful menu and program in art class that included the price for the meal: "presents." Martha remarked over and over how handsome the menu was. The first few times were for Alexander. The remaining times were for a lost time of young motherhood, or perhaps unrealized grandmotherhood.

Sara eased into the relaxed mood, riding in on her mother's surprising gaiety. It was encouraging to see Martha so relaxed, especially after a dreary fall day. Martha Tappert Lynch was from a time and place when dinner had strict rules and stricter manners and matriarchs were reserved, when men courted women and kisses were modest and polite. From what little Sara had heard from her father and mother, Robert brought a soldier's "new manners" with his dashing figure to the patio of the Tappert row house adjacent to Forsyth Park. He had just returned from the South Pacific and was looking to rent a room for a few weeks while he figured out what to do next. He was frank but kind, jovial but not rude, deferential but not fawning. Martha enjoyed being around him and respected, deeply, the sense of duty that had compelled him to enlist and fight overseas. When the young seaman returned to his native Boston, Robert told his mother two things. He didn't want to take over the family fish shop and he thought he met the woman he wanted to marry. Mrs. Lynch told her son she didn't blame him, and to go back and get her. He did.

The post-traumatic stress didn't show until a year or so later, when Robert had a place to fall apart and someone to land on. Maybe that was why Sara had never wanted to bring her problems to her mother, even the biggest one. Martha's lap always seemed so full.

Alexander passed out party hats and horns. They were

left over from the little celebration they had at school. As per the program, the boy played a slow, soft march on his horn in honor of his father. It sounded like a dirge as he struggled to sell the melody on a one-note instrument. Tonia smiled softly. She was not one to mourn loss but to keep memory active, and she did that with Alexander. Once a week they looked through an album of curled and faded pictures of his father.

"Piotr was a man of strength and honor," Tonia once said. "He fought death, to not die, even after the doctors thought he would not survive. If my son is in a troubled situation ever, I want him to think what his father would do."

Tonia probably didn't realize what a great service she had done for her son. A dead father became the equivalent of a cartoon superhero to a young boy. He knew everything, could vanquish any foe, was a constant companion in difficult times. That kind of role model was vital for children.

After dinner—and as per the program—Alexander was a whirlwind of fingers and big eyes as he tore into his gifts. Everything was "just what I wanted!" even the sweater Martha had knit for him. When he was finished, Alexander secured his booty in his bedroom and returned for dessert. Tonia was a wonderful cook and had made her son a giant cupcake cake, piled deep with pale blue icing and a rich green "Happy Birthday Alexander" on top.

Darrell arrived just as Sara dimmed the chandelier and the lighted cake made its brilliant "Happy Birthday to You" entrance. Darrell was announced by his big, off-key baritone coming from the front hallway. Whatever Sara thought of her brother's lifestyle, whatever Martha's disappointments were with her son, they were careful not to show any of that in front of Alexander. Darrell and the boy got along like best buddies. Her brother had inherited that best pal bonhomie from their father, who used any excuse to take Darrell here or there to fish or have a catch or sail a radio-controlled boat on the river. The soldiers they had used as "Japs on Okinawa" still sat on the shelf of Darrell's—now Alexander's—room.

When the song was finished and everyone had offered a little cheer, Darrell gave Alexander a hug. The big man's arms enfolded the boy tightly. Then he handed him a plastic bag that had been looped around his arm. Even though she was halfway across the room Sara could smell the Jack Daniel's under his heavy aftershave.

Alexander needed two hands to hold the present that had been in the bag. While Tonia cut the cake her son opened the gift. It was a rug with the boy's color photograph on it.

"Thank you, Darrell! That is *so* cool!" the boy cried. This expression was sincere. "How did it get my face?"

"Your mom gave me the picture," Darrell said. "I scanned it and sent it to these guys I know who do computer graphics. Pretty neat, huh?"

"Yes!" the boy said enthusiastically.

"It's very nice," Sara said.

"Thanks, sis."

"Mommy got me a book about religion," Alexander said. "My favorite is—what was his name again? The god with four heads?"

"Brahma," Tonia said. "He is Hindu." The woman said, half apologetically, "I felt my son should know about the world."

"Absolutely." Sara smiled reassuringly.

"Sara got me a book of stories that has a CD of somebody reading them," Alexander said.

"Did she?" Darrell asked.

"*Bulfinch's Mythology* read by Anthony Hopkins," she said. "Alexander can follow along and learn new words and ideas."

"That would seem like a good Muppets project," Darrell said. "Kermit as Mercury, Oscar as Pluto."

"Oscar is a grouch. Pluto is a dog," Alexander said.

"Pluto is also the god of the underworld in Roman mythology," Sara informed him with a little wink. "That was a long time before Disney."

"Oh," the boy said.

"I just don't know which Muppet would be Zeus, though," Darrell said, wrestling with the problem as he stood beside Alexander. "Miss Piggy is the natural, but that doesn't quite work."

"What you call him? Gonzo?" Tonia suggested.

"That could fly," Darrell said.

This was great, Sara thought. Now everyone was populating Olympus with Muppets. Martha left to make decaf. Sara passed out slices of big cupcake.

"No date tonight?" Sara asked.

"Erin's in the car," Darrell said, his blue eyes and big smile flashing. He pushed a strand of long, dirty blond hair from his forehead. "She's shy."

"Ah."

Sara gave Darrell dessert. He forked his way through while standing there. He was clearly content to be here with Alexander. He was happy with his cake, hurrying just a little so he could move to the next pleasure. He seemed such a boy, still, that while it was easy to be disappointed in him it was difficult to be angry. Sara even envied him just a little. There was something to be said for Darrell's quick, absolute attachment to the moment.

He scooped the crumbs with the edge of his fork, then

put the plate on the table. He used a finger to score extra icing from the cupcake itself, winking wickedly at his sister as he did so.

"Hey, tiger, I gotta go!" Darrell told Alexander, holding out his arms and scooping the boy into them. "Hope you have a happy seventh."

"I'm not seven, I'm six!"

"Really?" Darrell said, winking at Tonia. "Coulda fooled me, lieutenant. You're so darn big!"

"Why did you call him that?" Sara asked.

Darrell put the boy down and pointed to his shirt. "He's carrying my old Lieutenant Stone figure in his pocket. He's the only one with a bayonet."

Sara smiled warmly. She didn't have to ask why it was there. It was Alexander's way of having his father at his birthday.

Alexander thanked Darrell again for the gift and he left with a wave at the table. He had hardly spoken to their mother.

Sara excused herself and trotted after him. She caught up to him as he was opening the door and grabbed his elbow. "Darrell, are you okay to drive?"

He looked back at her. "Yeah. I had a shot before I left the auto shop."

"Just one?"

"Just one."

Sara released his arm and stepped back. He slumped a little. He seemed hurt rather than offended.

"I'm fine," he assured her.

"Are you sure?" she asked.

"Yeah. How's Mom doin'?" he asked.

"You know how she gets in the fall."

"Isn't there anything you can do about that?"

"Such as?"

"I dunno. Talk to her, give her shrink advice, something."

"It's not a good idea to provide therapy for your own family," Sara said.

"Since when?" Darrell asked, mimicking her own tone slightly.

Sara frowned. There was a difference between analysis and sisterly concern and he knew it. "Have a good night," she said.

"You too."

"And drive carefully."

"Haven't woken up in the ER yet," he said.

The click of the door sounded hollow as Darrell left, and the hall seemed unusually unhappy as Sara turned and walked slowly to the dining room.

Alexander was just finishing a second piece of cake when Sara arrived. He asked to be excused, then went to his room to check out his gifts. Tonia did not yell after him for running down the hall. She knew what Sara did: that there were times when you had to let things go.

"It was very nice of Darrell to stop by," Tonia said as she cleared the table.

"Yes," Sara said.

Tonia went to the kitchen and Sara sat beside her mother. The woman was sitting at the small butcher-block table. She was holding her decaf and staring at nothing in particular. Sara slid into a chair across from her.

"Are you all right?" Sara asked.

"Oh, fine."

"What are you thinking about?"

The woman smiled slightly. "He called you 'sis.' I like when he does that."

"Me too," Sara admitted.

"I was trying to remember the last time he called me 'mom.'"

"When was the last time you called him 'son'?" Sara asked.

Martha's expression became cross. "Do I call you 'daughter'?"

"No, but at least you speak to me," Sara said. "The two of you are like big cats who circle each other with menacing looks."

"I don't think I like being called a big cat," Martha said.

"I'm sorry."

"I'm a civilized woman who expects to be treated civilly, and with the respect a wife deserves."

"A mother," Sara said. "You're his mother."

"That's what I meant," Martha complained. She took a long sip of coffee.

It hurt Sara to see her like this, asea in bitterness and unfocused memories. Unable to rouse herself from disappointment and find new goals. Sara had learned from her own experience that little victories were the only way to claw from big disasters.

"All I'm trying to say is that sometimes an older and wiser individual has to overlook things in a younger one."

"I overlooked your father for almost fifty years," Martha said. "I can't pretend to like how your brother is spending his life. He's thirty-three. It's time to grow up."

"I'm thirty-seven and I'm still living at home," Sara said with a grin.

"It's not the same thing."

"I know. I was trying to lighten things up a little."

Martha drank more decaf. "Thank you, dear."

"Mom, Darrell is living the life he wants," Sara said. "I don't like it either, but it's not my life and it's not yours. I realized tonight that what we need to do is follow his example."

"Your brother's?"

"*Yes!*" Sara insisted. "We should grab the good times, even if they're measured in minutes like tonight. We can use those to connect with him, maybe help him to change over time."

"I can't," Martha said. "I love him too much to pretend I like how he's wasting his life."

"He fixes cars, he apparently pays his bills, and he seems happy," Sara said. "It's not overly ambitious but it's not a waste. I think what you're really saying is you don't like seeing so much of Dad in him."

"It's funny, isn't it?" Martha said. "Your father and Alexander's father both fought for their country. How can the memories of them be so different?"

"War is black and white, good versus evil," Sara said. "Piotr never got to be anything but a hero."

"I guess," Martha said. "Life should be like that too. It was, once." The woman excused herself, kissed her daughter on the cheek, then went upstairs.

Sara didn't feel like going to the office or the den. She sat there for a moment, then got a shawl from the hallway and went to the backyard. She headed toward a small vine-covered gazebo where the backyard sloped toward the river. That was another of her father's early contributions to the estate. He had painted it just before she was born. The white coat was dirty and peeling. It had not been touched since then.

The sky and grounds were a dark blue, the nights coming earlier and falling faster. The soggy leaves from the surrounding oaks sighed underfoot as she walked over. The gnats and mosquitoes, so prevalent in the summer, were gone now. There was a cool but gentle wind and some of the drier branches creaked overhead. The fallen twigs that had massed in the inlet sounded like little wet bones as the current knocked them one against the other. The rush of the river grew louder as she approached the slope. The sound was enhanced by the nearly thousand-foot-high line of hills on the other side. There was still the faintest ruddy hint of sun where the treed hilltops met the overcast sky.

Sara entered the gazebo and walked to the far side. She looked up at the tumbling gray clouds. "How about it, Dad?" she asked. "Was the world sharply defined when you met Mom? Were you upset that it changed so much after the war, is that what pushed you into your own safe place?"

Sara didn't often talk to her father—"address" him, really, since he never answered. Once in a while, though, she had to put a thought or question out there like a message in a bottle. It was called "extrinsic argumentation," a fancy term for devil's advocacy. Just expressing the question and taking a walk around it helped her to examine it from a point of view other than her own.

"We could have been your world," Sara said, tearing up a little. "Or did we disappoint you too?"

Sara didn't know. She doubted she ever would. All she knew was that the Lynch household was a lot like the Lynch garage, full of unfinished projects and unrealized aspirations. She wished she knew how to change that. But a big part of their life was gone, the part that had both galvanized and polarized them. He was a part that could not be replaced.

The wind picked up and Sara turned back to the house. Behind her, the branches of the inlet clacked angrily beneath the threatening skies.

Three

1

"Is there anything *you* want to talk about?" Sara asked.

Fredric raised a bony shoulder and let it drop. He had been in Sara's office a few minutes and showed no signs of leaving behind the characteristic warm-up period. That felt like a setback. He was less animated and far less engaged than the previous afternoon. He had said fewer than a half-dozen words, and most of those were "no." The young man had been unenthusiastic about discussing his school day, his parents, his feelings, what he was doing outdoors or in his room, and—again—most adamantly the triangle. He was not just reticent about that subject, he had positively shut down on Sara. When the psychotherapist tried to pick up the conversation from the previous session, asking how the triangle "knew" what went on in the office, Fredric just sat there staring intently at the carpet. She was going to have to try some back doors and second-floor windows to get into that topic.

"Can I ask you something a little personal?" she said.

He looked at her.

"I had lunch at the Yankee Doodle Inn the other day," she said. "A pizza burger. Ever have one?"

"That's personal?"

"No." Sara smiled. "That's what we call a 'lead-in question.'"

"A trick."

"More like an appetizer. What I really wanted to ask you about—tell you about—was a waitress who was working there."

"Waitstaff," he said. "Ms. Blair told us to call them 'waitstaff,' because it's not gender specific."

"Do you agree with what the guidance counselor suggested?"

He nodded.

"Why?"

"Because a person shouldn't be defined by whether they have a cock or a cunt," Fredric said. He was still looking at her, hard. For a young man who had trouble discussing members of the opposite sex, let alone sex itself, this was atypical.

"That's good advice," Sara agreed. "Out of curiosity, why did you say it that way?"

"Say what what way?"

"'Cock' and 'cunt' instead of 'male and female'?"

"Does it bother you?"

"A little," she confessed.

He snickered.

"Why does that make you laugh?" she asked.

"They're just words. We talked about kill and murder the other day but that didn't bother you."

"'Waitress' and 'waiter' are just words too and you said they're inappropriate," Sara said.

"That's a stereotype, and stereotypes are wrong."

"Terms like you just used could also be considered wrong in this context," she suggested. "They are a demeaning way to describe the essence of what it is to be a man or a woman."

"I was talking about reproductive parts. Would it have been better if I'd said 'penis' and 'vagina'?"

"It would have been better to describe the entire person as a man or a woman," she said.

"Better for you, not for me."

"If you were drawing them, how would you draw a penis and how would you draw a cock?" she asked.

Fredric thought about that for a moment. He seemed intrigued by the idea. "A penis would just lie there. A cock would be hard. A vagina would just be a vagina. A cunt would have a cock in it."

"So they're not *just* terms that describe men and women," Sara pointed out. "They are nouns that describe a specific, active purpose."

"I guess so," he said. "I guess that's what men and women should be doing. Being active with them."

Aggressive opinions were another form of biting. Typically, it was used to dominate a group to which one had already been admitted. Fredric was using it to put Sara on the defensive. When patients were ashamed or afraid they tended to be silent. When a normally taciturn person became confrontational like this it was invariably because he had something to conceal.

"Okay," Sara said. "We managed to get a little bit off-topic there. What I was going to say about the waitstaff was that the woman I met had a tattoo on the small of her back.

I could see it peeking over her apron string. It was a butterfly. Would you ever get a tattoo?"

"Do you have one?"

"No, and we were talking about you," Sara reminded him. She did not like to push but sometimes it was necessary to push back.

"I do not have one," he said. "If I did, it wouldn't be a butterfly."

"What, then?"

"A snake," he answered without hesitation.

"Why?"

"'Cause that dude got fucked and needs a home."

Fredric did not routinely use the word "fuck" either. Only when he was agitated. Something was definitely up, something that had happened between this session and the last.

"Where would you put the snake?" she asked. Fredric wanted to be invisible. Sara was curious to find out whether the young man would want the snake to join him or to speak for him.

"I'd have him crawling up my nose with his tail here." He touched his middle finger to his philtrum, just above the upper lip. "Then I'd have his head looking out from between my eyes."

"Did you ever read about Medusa in Greek mythology?" Sara asked.

"Snakes for hair. Very cool."

"She turned people to stone with those snakes," Sara said. "Is that what you'd want to do?"

He shook his head. "I don't care."

"About?"

"What people do or what they think," Fredric said. "The snake and me would do our own shit."

"Do you care what I think?" Sara asked.

"You're like my mom. You're gonna like me whatever I do."

"Is there anyone whose opinion matters to you?" Sara asked. "Someone in the triangle, maybe?"

Fredric looked away. He was silent for a long moment.

"Fredric?" Sara said. "What about a teacher? What about Ms. Blair?"

"She's fine," Fredric said.

"Fine as in 'okay' or fine as in 'sexy'?"

Fredric smiled. "She's fine. We were talking in the hall. She doesn't judge. She's interested in shit and doesn't get all over you about how you look or talk. She's not like McMahon or Hardass."

"I want you to answer without thinking about this, Fredric. What kind of tattoo would Ms. Blair have?"

"A red apple," he replied.

"And Mr. Harkness?"

"A cross on his whole fucking body," he said. "I'd like to see a cross tattooed with him."

John Harkness was the very conservative principal of Litchfield County High. He had fought hard for a dress code against baggy jeans and thug attire but the Board of Education felt that adopting one would discriminate against the lower-income "agrarian children" who were bused to the school from the northwest corner of the state. Many of them wore loose-fitting overalls because they worked before coming to school. Harkness did succeed in blocking students from going to certain blogs on school computers, however, when he saw that one of them encouraged violence against teachers. Harkness didn't care that it was a satiric site by "Mahandgun Gandhi" promoting "impassive resistance." It was his way of exerting authority.

"Fredric, has Mr. Harkness said anything to you recently, something that made you angry?" Sara asked. The young man had suggested the cross as though he wanted Harkness on it, not behind it.

Fredric nodded.

"What did he say?"

"He said I looked like the walking dead."

Sara jotted the remark in her notebook. "When did he say that?"

"Today, when I was talking to Ms. Blair," Fredric said. "He's a fool. People who judge are assholes."

"He had no right to say that and I'm sorry he did." Sara intended to call the principal after the session and tell him to keep his big mouth away from her patients. He wasn't a quarterback shouting signals anymore. He wasn't hanging with his jock friends in a locker room. He was a principal responsible for all his students. "Has anyone else said anything that upset you?"

"Just God."

"What you read or did He say something to you?" Sara asked. It never hurt to check.

"What was written in that stupid book."

"Fredric, I need you to tell me why the Bible is suddenly bothering you so much," Sara said.

"It always bothered me," he said.

"You've never mentioned it before," Sara told him. "You've been unhappy with bullies, you've been upset by adults who didn't understand you, and you didn't like being forbidden to do things. All of that is valid, I understand it. This is the first time I've heard you angry at injustices done to others—"

"You said you wouldn't judge me—"

"Fredric, please. I'm *not*."

"It's about the snake, isn't it? People rescue dogs and cats and fix broken wings on birds, but because it's a snake—"

"You're seeing things that aren't there," she said. "We should applaud anyone who takes up the cause of a creature that can't speak for itself." Sara was getting unusually agitated. She took a moment to pull back and then smiled. "I'm not criticizing you at all, Fredric. You have to believe that. You're upset about snakes, you're upset about what Abraham did to Isaac, you're angry about Moses and Jesus. What I'm wondering is why now?"

Fredric leaned forward in the chair. "Why *not* now?"

It was a fair question, if elusive.

"Forget the Bible," Sara said. "Talk to me about snakes as snakes. I've seen garter snakes in my backyard, and there are some pretty big water snakes in the river. Have you ever seen any?"

"Only online."

"Are you upset by something other than what God did to him?"

"Man, I hate God," the teenager said through his teeth.

Sara leaned forward. "Go on," she said softly.

"He's like the principal. He has all this power and He does nothing to help unless He likes you."

"What do you want Him to do?"

"Die."

"How would that help us?"

"Someone else would be everyone's God."

"Do you have someone in mind?"

Fredric did not answer.

"You told me yesterday that you read the Bible because you were cold," Sara said. "Was that the only reason?"

He turned his face toward the back door. He was not just avoiding her, he seemed to be looking for something. Help. Encouragement.

"Did someone recommend it to you? An acquaintance online? Did one of your teachers say something that intrigued you?"

Fredric continued to look away. Now he was making a point of it. Sara tilted her head to the side to try to catch his eye. She extended her neck slightly. She smiled.

"We've known each other a very long time, too long to play games with each other," Sara said.

"I'm not playing a game," he insisted.

"You're keeping a secret. As far as I know, that's something you've never done before."

He faced her. "Would you answer any question I asked you, just because I asked it?"

"I might," she said. "But *I* am the doctor and I'm trying to help *you*."

Fredric looked at her a moment longer and then his long face suddenly crumbled into tears. Sara was surprised but didn't show it. She watched as his shoulders, lethargic until now, heaved like pistons. He put his open hands on his face, becoming invisible again. He said nothing as he sobbed. Sometimes people spoke when they cried and Sara always listened very closely. It was the truth trying to break through.

It was Sara's practice to give hysterical patients physical and emotional room and a box of tissues, no more. Her job was not to slow their fall or to catch them but to help them get up again. She believed that this kind of blind free fall, when it occurred, was a necessary part of shedding emotional inhibitions.

The psychotherapist took the box of tissues from her desk, leaned forward, and lay it on the floor beside Fredric's boot. She went to the dimmer switch and lowered the over-head light. His eyes would be sensitive when he stopped crying. Sara's slender fingers drew a static "ping" from the faceplate. She backed into her chair, watching for a break in his outburst. There was a clock on the wall behind him. Time had run out on the session several minutes before and, once again, there was no one scheduled for the rest of the day. Sara did not want Fredric to leave until they were done.

The young man's hysteria ebbed. Sara looked at the clock again. He lowered his left hand, noticed the box, and pulled out several tissues. He wiped his eyes and then his forehead, then took several more and blew his nose.

"I don't like these scented kind," he said, holding up the tissue.

"I'm sorry. I'll get others."

"I have to go," Fredric said. He stood unsteadily.

"Would you sit down a moment?" Sara asked. "Please?"

The young man hesitated, then sank deep into the cush-ion, into himself. He stretched his hand across his forehead. He was hiding again, making himself invisible.

"Are you okay?" she asked gently.

He nodded behind his hand.

"Is there anything I can do, anything you want to tell me?" she asked.

He shook his head.

"You know I'm on your side, that I care about you."

He nodded.

"Good. Then I want you to do *me* a favor."

"What?"

"Come back tomorrow before school."

"Jeez," he said, adding a sigh that asked, *Haven't we done enough?*

"I'm going to be truthful with you, as always," Sara told him. "County regulations require that Social Services be informed about changes in the behavioral patterns of young men and women under their care. If you're better tomorrow, even just a little, I won't have to do that."

In fact, what CSS required was a report of potentially dangerous, aggressive behavior in troubled youths. Fredric was not that but Sara wanted to make sure he had stabilized.

"More stupid rules," Fredric complained. "Thou shalt. Thou shalt not."

"I don't like them either," Sara admitted. "So let's fix this. Say, at seven tomorrow?"

"Yeah. Sure."

Sara rose and dropped her pad on the chair behind her. She hoped that a touch of informality might give her a last chance to get something from him. "Before you go can you tell me—*will* you share with me—what it was that upset you just now? Were you thinking about what Principal Harkness said?"

"I wasn't upset," he said, getting up from the chair.

"What were you, then?"

"I was remembering," he said. "I thought about being alone. I didn't like it."

"When were you alone?"

"Always," he said.

"Do you feel that way now?" Sara asked.

He shook his head.

"What makes you feel like you belong?" Sara asked.

Fredric stood as still as she'd ever seen him. He didn't answer.

"Is it this shape," she asked, forming the triangle with her arms.

His eyes were unusually cold and his mouth was down-turned as though it were made of clay. "That looks like a church steeple," he said.

"Help me. Was the one you made different?"

"Yeah," he said. "It was."

So saying, he grabbed his backpack and left.

2

It wasn't what Sara wanted but it was an acceptable place to stop. At least Fredric had agreed to take her to the "beginning" of whatever that triangular shape was—or was not.

She made a few quick notes about the session. She noted the duration and intensity of the young man's outburst. It had lasted over half a minute. Fredric had never gotten this upset during a session. Sara did not want to prescribe anti-depressants for any child, and for Fredric in particular. Drugs anesthetized whatever was wrong and gave a false sense of well-being. Not only was that a temporary solution but there would be physical side effects—nausea, anxiety, and aggression—and they would have to severely curtail his bike-riding. The endorphins released by activity would either neutralize or magnify the drugs, depending on which ones she might prescribe.

Sara did not think it would be necessary, however. She suspected the tears had come partly from memory, but also from uncertainty about dancing around his big secret. It was not unusual for Fredric to keep his deepest thoughts and expressions to himself and panic a little when they were exposed. That made him less invisible. A lot of what Sara learned about his attitudes toward art, music, comic books, clothing, and bicycles—and asked him about in sessions—did not come from him directly but from his online postings.

Today's emotional spike aside, what surprised Sara about today's session was how fully formed this mysterious shape was to him. He was very confident about its meaning and symmetry. She re-formed the shape with her own arms. Her build *had* made the shape narrower than the one he had made.

Sara called Goldwyn Marash and left a message on her cell phone about the early session, assuring her it was nothing to worry about. Sara decided not to simply call John Harkness. She wanted to see him. She phoned to make sure he would still be there, then got in her car to make the nearly half-hour drive.

Main Street was the only way in or out of Delwood. River Road dead-ended in the center of town; two blocks in either direction and you were out. Sara turned left, heading north. Posters in storefronts announced Litchfield County's "Fall Afire" promotion, with a map of the region showing the best spots to see the foliage. One of them happened to be on the small green and duck pond in the center of Delwood, right in front of the town hall—and the center of the shopping district.

Driving beneath a canopy of flaming maples, amber oaks, and sagging black power lines, Sara passed the deli, the pharmacy, and the Marashes' dry-cleaning store on the west. On the east side were a comic book and videogame store, a bakery, two antiques shops—one of which used to belong to Martha Lynch—and a mom-and-pop candy store. They were all housed in wood-framed buildings, including Victorian houses and converted barns built in the late nineteenth century. A sixty-year-old town ordinance mandated that all frontage signs be rendered in black and white, which made even the contemporary stores seem vintage. The Burger

King at the northern end of town—across from town hall—
was also obliged to comply. A McDonald's near the Delwood
Academy, just yards beyond the town limits, was the first
blast of color that was not a tree.

Main Street became Route 6. It was still a two-lane road
but it was bounded now by hills and fields and, farther out, by
landfill. She drove past the cabin of State Trooper Maggie
Brown before reaching the high school. The winding drive
took her past the front of the sleek, modern white building to
the teachers' parking lot. The students' parking lot was beyond. Three late buses were still parked there. To the left,
along the shores of the river, were the athletic fields. The
football team was just finishing their workout and several
teachers were lapping the track. A few kids were scattered
through the grandstands, waiting for athletes or rides. A slow,
cool wind moved through the expanse, tugging dying leaves
from the trees and stirring the state and national flags that
flew from separate poles. The head custodian was just coming out to the lot to take the banners in for the night.

Sara parked her Jeep and went inside. The skies were a
little clearer here and the sun was just dropping behind the
Taconic Mountains, a string of low peaks that are part of the
Appalachian Trail. The flat, dark olive color of the evergreens
somehow seemed deader than the autumnal colors of the
bulk of the trees.

The administration office was directly inside the main
entrance. Only one assistant was still on duty—a student volunteer. She took Sara to see John Harkness. The principal's
office overlooked the river and the football field.

Ms. Blair's office was next to his. The door was closed,
which meant she was gone for the day.

Harkness was a big, powerfully built man with a beefy face, a military-short buzz cut, and nearly matching pants and a sports jacket that looked like they came from Wal-Mart. A former high school quarterback and college wrestler he had served in the Persian Gulf after getting his teaching degree. He spoke with a heavy Boston accent, which gave gravitas to his unashamedly Puritan beliefs. On his traditional gunmetal desk were a computer monitor, photographs of his wife and two daughters, and stacks of manila folders.

The principal offered Sara a bottle of water that she declined. He opened one for himself, shut the door, and sat behind his desk. Sara sat on a small, worn sofa across from the desk.

"How can I help you?" the principal asked with a forced but courteous smile.

"Fredric Marash is going through an unusually difficult period," the psychotherapist said. "It would help very much if he did not receive negative reinforcement from the school staff."

The principal plucked a pen from a holder and took a pad from a drawer. He tossed the pad on the blotter in front of him and leaned toward it. "I assume you've got an instance of that? Name?"

"You," Sara told him. "Fredric told me that you referred to him as 'the walking dead.'"

Harkness put the pen down. He folded his hands on the pad and stared at the woman. The fake smile was gone. "Dr. Lynch, I'm afraid you made the trip here for nothing."

"Why? Did you *not* say that?"

"I did, but I was trying to *talk* to the boy."

"Your idea of trying to talk to someone is telling them how dead they look?" she asked.

"I smiled when I said it. I thought I was giving him exactly the response he was looking for." The principal shook his head. "Jeez Louise. I was standing outside the office after school, talking to Chrissie Blair, when Mr. Marash walked by. He was wearing white pancake makeup and he had on a necktie. Only he wasn't wearing it like a normal necktie, it was knotted like a noose and hanging over a black T-shirt that had 'zombie' in bloodred letters. He stopped and said good morning to Chrissie and just looked at me. I didn't want to ignore him so I acknowledged that he looked like what he clearly *wanted* to look like. And for the record, I believe I phrased it as a question—I said, 'Who are you supposed to be, the walking dead?' "

"You didn't think that was at all judgmental?"

"I did not," he said.

"And it wasn't *really* a question, was it? You'd already decided that's what he looked like."

"Well he did!" Harkness snapped. "If he'd walked by in a smock and beret I'd've asked if he were trying to be Picasso."

"You don't see the condescension in that?"

"Frankly, no."

"If a young lady walked by in fishnet stockings and a short skirt would you have called her a hooker?"

"Now you're being ridiculous—"

"Answer me."

"—and confrontational. What you just described would be in violation of our dress code and I would have sent her home. But making the comment you suggest would have been sexual harassment."

"You're missing the point. If a young man from the Scatacook Reservation came in wearing a headdress and moccasins, would you have asked him if he were supposed to be an Indian chief?"

"I would have said, 'That's a fine expression of your heritage,'" Harkness told her. "Mr. Marash was not doing that. He was calling attention to himself."

"That's your psychotherapeutic evaluation?"

"It's my parental, principal's evaluation," Harkness replied angrily. "It's what my gut tells me. You've had the boy—"

"The young man."

"—for what, ten years? What kind of dent have you made in that big firecracker on his shoulder? The kid still looks like he's ready to blow."

"My job is to help Fredric understand his own skin and make sure he doesn't harm himself or others," Sara replied. "That was the mandate and that's what I've done. What happened here today undermines that work. Fredric was hiding behind a disguise. He's adopted a look that makes him part of a Goth fraternity—"

"A group, I understand—from one of the Social Services bulletins sent to this office that I do read and do take seriously—a group that celebrates the dead."

"So do we in our own way," Sara said. "If he were wearing a cross instead of a tie that looked like a noose would you have said anything at all?"

"'Nice cross.'"

"Why not just 'Good morning, Fredric?' or 'How are you classes, Fredric?'" Sara said. "Why provoke him?"

"Y'know what?" Harkness admitted, "You win. I thought I was giving him what he wanted. But I also think you're overreacting. At least I caught my initial response which was, 'I thought Halloween is next week.'"

Sara was even angrier now than when she had arrived.

"But I guess that's why you have letters after your name and I don't," Harkness said. "A student who was born a Native American and comes to school wearing skins and beads like his grandparents did—that I understand. A student comes to school like something out of the *Rocky Horror Picture Show*, in pasty makeup and a noose, maybe a little red lipstick—that I *don't* understand. One's about pride. The other's about rebellion."

"You say that as if it's a bad thing."

"Are you going to trot out the 'this country was built by rebels' defense?" Harkness asked. "This is a high school, not the Continental Congress."

"This is America. Fredric has the right to express himself."

"No one stopped him!" Harkness declared. "Look, if you'd like to speak with Mr. Edwards, the school attorney, for an opinion on whether I overstepped my authority, I'll give you his number. The Board of Ed has a very full and specific list of regulations on race, religion, and sexual orientation. I have memorized them and I follow them from One-A to Seventeen-C, subsets inclusive. I believe my comments were correct and appropriate and I am sorry if the sensitive Mr. Marash was put out. Tell me, do you have any children in our school system?"

"I do not."

"I have two in Delwood public school and they are *my* little laboratory. I get to see what works and what doesn't work as a parent, and within B of E regulations I try to extend that hands-on, twenty-four/seven experience to the greater family of this institution. For six years here, my number one goal, *numero uno*"—he held up a thick finger in emphasis—"has been to set a very strong center so that our five percent or so of fringe individuals like Mr. Marash—whom I think we would agree is *not* a centrist, not a mixer—do not stray too far without being noticed. It also gives them something to hold on to if they decide to join the mainstream."

"That's a sound policy," Sara agreed.

"Sound and proven, not just here but in the world. The mainstream is where most of the kids will be spending their adult lives. Those who are looking for a life outside the norm require the kind of attention this school is not equipped to provide. I do the best I can in the moments presented with the wits that are available to me. Which brings me to something I'm itching to ask, Dr. Lynch. Frankly, I'm puzzled by why this young man's costume doesn't seem to concern you."

"He's an artist. He uses his body as a means of expression."

"He's expressing *death*," Harkness repeated.

"That's today," she said. "Yesterday it was something else and tomorrow it will be something new."

"All of it freakish. That's what worries me."

"In what way?"

Harkness looked at his watch. He was getting impatient. Sara didn't care.

"After you called I pulled his file." Harkness tapped the pile of folders on his desk. "This kid was brought to you because of—and I quote—'extremely violent tendencies toward other children.' I've got 1,011 other students to consider. I need to worry about their safety."

"Fredric has not had a violent episode in nine years," she said. "I don't believe you need to be concerned about anything extraordinary."

Harkness whistled. "Dr. Lynch, there are a lot of qualifiers in that statement."

"Nothing is guaranteed. But the long period of tranquility speaks for itself."

"Fair enough," Harkness said. "Look. In the interest of getting home before dark, I agree not to comment on his attire again. It'll just be, 'Hello, Mr. Marash' and 'How are you today, Mr. Marash?'"

"Thank you," Sara replied. "By the way, do you happen to know if there's anything being taught about Nazi persecution in any of his classes?"

"That is not on any of our syllabi," the principal replied, showing real concern. "Why?"

"There's a particular design he seems fascinated by," Sara said. "I'm sorry, I can't say more—I was just curious."

"You're saying no one's at risk?" he asked.

"I have no evidence that would suggest so," Sara replied.

The big man rose. "I'll pass the word to Mr. Marash's teachers to watch what they say. I don't agree that coddling is the best thing for him, but the county says we have to do things your way."

"Their way, actually. Thank you," she said.

Sara felt better when she left the office. She had covered one flank for her patient and had gained some information about his condition. As she climbed into the Jeep, the psychiatrist wondered about the noose. He hadn't been wearing the tie or makeup when she saw him. Sara did not see it as a death threat against the school or as a form of acting out. A noose was a guaranteed shock, like using the word *cock* in her office.

Still, Fredric was a moody young man with a former history of violence, some of it directed at himself. She was glad he was coming to see her in the morning. She wanted to make certain that the necktie was a statement and not a warning.

She decided that she would stop at the Marash store on the way home, just to have a chat with Franz or Goldwyn.

Sometimes idle conversation turned up information that seemed unimportant or normal to those close to a situation.

Checking her cell phone messages before she set out, she headed from the parking lot and back along Route 6.

Darkness was nearly upon the valley, the sharp-edged hues of the road becoming the muddy rust of Delwood as she made her way home.

Four

1

The Marashes' dry-cleaning store closed at six during the week. It was five minutes before when Sara arrived. She had phoned Tonia to tell her she would be late for dinner. Martha Lynch could decide whether to eat without her daughter or wait. Sara bet that her mother would wait and then complain a little about having to do so. It was autumn, after all.

Sara parked in front of the shop. Goldwyn Marash had already left but Franz was still there. Sara knew a little about the family history, which came from conversation at the shop and not from Fredric. It was her way of talking to them about something other than their son. Franz's grandparents had come to the United States from Hungary during the anti-Soviet uprising of 1956 when Franz was just a baby. The family had been tailors in Eastern Europe and Franz was expected to learn the trade. Goldwyn's mother, Judy, was a former Hollywood extra who had struggled to achieve semi-stardom during the early 1950s. After a few minor successes on some independent films she finally gave it up, returned to her native Delwood, and married her childhood sweetheart. Judy directed amateur plays in a converted barn and was one of the more notoriously flamboyant figures in Delwood's past. She was said to have had a number of lovers, one of them a New York theatrical producer who summered in town. The relationship got her to Broadway. In a limousine, not onstage. Though Franz was an artful tailor, Sara had always suspected that whatever dramatic flair Fredric possessed came through her side from her mother.

Tall and bony like his son, Franz Marash had short-cut salt-and-pepper hair and an ever-present smile. He did the mending, Goldwyn ran the business, and a Filipino couple from nearby Angton, New York, did the actual cleaning. Fredric did not help out. He had tried, several years before, but Delac kids saw him working on the motorized racks and said they brought their clothes here to get them clean, not dirty. Franz did not want to subject his son to that, but he could not afford to lose the business of Academy kids. It was fine with Fredric who didn't want to work there anyway. Franz was smart, though. He paid his son to create the window signs and also to design the boxes that clean shirts were packaged in. Fredric came up with a comic book–style superhero who had a cape, boots, and mask with a plain white shirt. Franz gave those to families with young kids. He called it a "coloring box." Fredric drew several others over the years—a pirate, a circus aerialist, mermaids, and more. Franz stopped a year ago when Fredric's vision turned to the victims of witch trials and graphic Civil War battle scenes, both of which they were studying in school.

That had also been the first time in years that Franz had expressed concern about his son's mental condition. The boy's parents had stopped by Sara's office after Franz had delivered the artwork.

"It's a positive sign that your son is expressing violence in art instead of in reality," Sara had told the Marashes at the time.

"Why is he suddenly feeling violent, though?" Goldwyn had asked.

"This is a natural evolution of Fredric's socialization," Sara had told them. "He feels anger toward Delacians, and possibly to students and teachers at his school who don't 'get' him. He experiences what we call 'impotent rage' and he expresses it through art. That's actually a healthy thing."

"Wouldn't it be better if these things didn't bother our son so much?" Goldwyn asked.

"That's the goal," Sara said. "But it's a process, and it takes many years."

"I don't understand what we did to make him this way," Goldwyn said.

"You probably didn't 'do' anything," Sara assured her. "People are born with genetic baggage—racial memory, some call it—and some children pick up quirks as they go along. A mobile in a crib may have glinted in the sun 'just so' and a child may develop a lifelong fear of, or love for, birds or butterflies or rainbows. The fact that he doesn't cram these feelings inside is a good thing."

The Marashes accepted her judgment then, as they always did, even if she sensed that they didn't always agree. They were concerned, they were involved, but they did not meddle.

The night air was cooler than it had been the day before. There was winter on the wind. She crossed the broken, lumpy sidewalk that had been so much smoother when she was small. The roots of the street's largest oak were visible through the cracks.

Everything in the world is a process, an evolution, she thought as she opened the glass door of the shop.

Franz was finishing with a customer when she walked in. Rudy "Rowdy" Brown was leaning on the counter, his torso too large for his flannel shirt and waist taxing the limits of his belt. He was the body-shop owner and husband of Trooper Brown. He was also Darrell's boss and the head of the region's volunteer fire department, which was located in the southern end of town. The Marashes cleaned the Delwood VFD uniforms for free.

"Evening, Dr. Lynch," Franz said as she approached.

She returned the greeting.

"Y'know, you got it easy," Rowdy said, looking back without getting off his elbows. That qualified as a greeting from the man.

"How's that?" she asked politely.

"In your business people talk to you. They let you know what's wrong," he said. "I was just tellin' Franz I've got this Bentley I picked up at a police sale—"

"A silky beige beauty," Franz told her. "I saw it in the trooper lot with the other crime repos."

"Yeah, but there's this rattle and I'll be damned if I can figure out what's causing it," Rowdy said.

"Well, the good news is you can dismantle it and spread the parts over the garage floor," Sara said. "I don't have that luxury."

"Hah!" Franz chuckled.

"I guess," Rowdy grumped. "Thing is, I did that and I still don't know what the problem is."

"Maybe it's haunted," Franz suggested, still grinning over Sara's comment.

"I considered that too," Rowdy told him. "This vehicle used to belong to a Russian mobster and I'm guessin' the SOB had more in the trunk than a spare tire and coolers of beer."

"'Dead gangsters haunt a dismantled Bentley,'" Sara remarked with a grin. "That's one for the *Weekly World News*."

"Hey. You sayin' you don't believe in that stuff?" Rowdy asked.

"I'm a therapist, and therapists are scientists," she said. "We fill our open minds with fact."

"Well, here's a fact for ya," he said quietly as Sara reached the counter. His red hair smelled of cigarette smoke from the shop. "Remember five, six years ago when they had that late-night fire at the Goldsmith Nursing Home? The one when two of the residents died?"

Sara and Franz both nodded.

"When we went in to make sure nothin' was still smoulderin', I was alone in the basement and I coulda swore I saw one of the dead people. He was still wearin' his white pajamas and everything."

"Did you tell anyone?" Franz asked.

"What're you, nuts?"

Franz looked at Sara. "Am I?"

She smiled.

Rowdy scowled. "If I said anything I woulda been benched. You're the first people I ever told."

"Maybe it was smoke," Sara suggested. "Hot air meeting cold air—it could form unusual shapes."

"Or it might have been burned clothes or drapes blowing in the wind," Franz said. "I've seen garments move in strange ways sometimes."

"Smoke doesn't *talk*," Rowdy said. "This guy walked from behind me, glided across the wet floor, no reflection, said 'Can I leave now?' and just floated up the stairs. I followed him but he was gone."

"No one else saw him?" Sara asked.

Rowdy shook his big head portentously. "Guy vanished by the time I reached the first floor."

"That is weird," Franz agreed. Nonjudgmental Franz, a man who was so dependent on his community that he noticed cars in the police lot, was pleasant to everyone who walked into his shop, and talked easily to people whatever the color of their collar. "Maybe your problem with the car is a critter of some kind," he suggested. "It's that time of year when a lot of them go to ground."

"I checked the air intake, which is where field mice usually go."

"Why do they do that?" Sara asked.

"Warm air from the engine."

"What about squirrels?" Sara asked.

"If I didn't see a mouse I didn't see a squirrel either," Rowdy said. "I didn't see fur at all."

"I don't mean that," Sara said. "When you asked if we thought you were nuts, I started thinking. There are trees around the lot at your wife's outpost. They might store nuts somewhere. Maybe the tailpipe?"

"I checked it for rot. Clean."

Franz snapped his fingers. "What about one of the hubcaps? Doesn't that car have a star shape built into the tire rim?"

Rowdy nodded. "It does."

"A squirrel on its hind legs could reach it," Franz said.

"Damn. When the cap spins something inside could definitely make a noise."

Franz held up his hand to Sara. It took her a moment to realize he wanted a high-five. She gave it to him.

"Damn!" Rowdy said again then left, forgetting his clean fire uniform on the counter. He came back from the door to collect it, thanked them again, and left.

"If only all problems could be solved so simply," Franz said.

Sara nodded.

"So, Dr. Lynch? What do we have of yours?" he asked.

"I'm not here for a pickup," she said. "I wanted to ask you about something."

"Oh. Do I need to be sitting?" he asked with an anxious chuckle.

"Not at all," she assured him. "I was just up at the school. Principal Harkness happened to mention that Fredric was wearing a tie that looked like a noose today. It concerned him."

"I saw that but I didn't say anything. Should I have?"

"I don't think so," Sara said. "It was probably like those drawings he once did for your shirt boxes, an expression of unease."

"Unease," Franz murmured. "Restlessness. You know, that could be it."

"What do you mean?" Sara asked.

"As I said, Fredric's been spending most of his nights in his room," Franz replied. "But last night he was out on his bike."

"In the dark?"

Franz nodded. "He's got a headlight and reflectors. And he said he doesn't go where there are cars." He moved a little closer, spoke more quietly. "After we talked yesterday, I decided to try and see where Fredric went."

"Did you?"

Franz nodded again. "He went out back and walked his bike to the hiking trail in the park. I could see the headlight."

"The park" was the 2,300-acre Huston State Park. The home of iron furnaces and saw mills in the nineteenth century, it was turned into a nature sanctuary in the early twentieth. The park embraced portions of the mountain range, the river, and the Appalachian Trail and was a popular stop for hikers and campers. The cul-de-sac where Fredric lived bordered on the southeastern tip of the park.

"You have no idea how far he went?" Sara asked.

Franz shook his head. "I can't even tell you when he came back, but it was late. I went to sleep around ten-thirty. His mother turned out the light a half hour later and he still wasn't home. We asked him about it this morning but he said he didn't pay attention to the time."

Sara thought for a moment. "But he got to school on time?"

"He woke when I knocked on the door. He has more energy than his mother and I combined."

This next question would be difficult to ask without betraying confidence. "Did you happen to make a comment about the cost of heating oil recently?" she asked.

"Heating oil?" Franz said. He thought for a moment. "Yes. I asked Fredric and Goldy to watch the thermostat because the last bill we got was a killer. Are you saying I can't make *any* requests of my family?"

"Not at all," Sara said. "It's a question of tone. Would you describe what you said as authoritative or angry?"

"Maybe a little annoyed, but not at him," Franz answered. He looked at her, his eyes imploring. "Dr. Lynch, I don't ask much of Fredric. But I did ask him to watch that. When I go by his room in the morning I can feel the heat rolling out under the door. I can't turn my back on everything he does. Even you've said that."

"I'm not asking you to," Sara assured him. "I just want to make sure that your son isn't distorting events in his memory."

"Is that how he described it?"

"Pretty much," she replied.

"So I really upset him?"

Sara didn't answer.

Franz sighed. "I'm sorry. You think that's what was responsible for this noose thing?"

"I believe a string of events brought him there. I'm trying to figure out what they were and where they're headed."

"Do you think he was telling us he'll harm himself if we push him?"

"I don't think that was the message," Sara said. "I believe he was saying he felt choked, stifled."

"I mean, I've told Goldy to leave that side of things to you, to let Fredric be Fredric. She's wanted to have a lot more to do with his treatment—you can understand." Franz shook his head. "We make these important decisions but we don't know if they're the right ones. It's frustrating. It's frightening, really."

"That's a natural concern to every parent and to every therapist. When children get older and their interests and values diverge from our own, we have to step back and let them run with it."

"As long as it's not self-destructive," Franz said. "If Fredric took up smoking I'd tell him how tough it was for me to stop. If he drank . . ."

Franz's voice trailed off. He had known Robert Lynch. He knew he had gone three words too far.

"I understand," Sara told him.

She was silent for a second. He thanked her with his eyes.

"As far as the noose is concerned," she went on, "what I watch out for in patients who may be pro-active rather than simply expressive—"

"Who may commit suicide, you mean."

She nodded once. "—are comments about feeling hopeless, worthless. Fredric has not done any of that with me. I'll bet he hasn't with you."

Franz shook his head.

"People who are terminally depressed tend to say goodbye to those closest to them. They give away their belongings and exhibit self-destructive behavior such as increased smoking, drinking, and drug use. They take risks, like driving with the headlights off or walking on the railing of an overpass. That is not your son. You said you even saw him with his bike headlight on."

"That's true."

"I would say that his biking is also a very positive statement, a way he looks after himself. So is his frustration about the heat. He is interested in comfort, not oblivious to it. The people I watch for treat death as a companion, not an accoutrement."

"You don't think Fredric is that, all dressed in black and wearing a noose?" he asked. "And those drawings he did last year—?"

"Black is a statement, it's mysterious," Sara told him. "It blends with the shadows, absorbs light, makes the wearer invisible. As for the drawings, they were anti-death. Obviously, he was affected deeply by what he heard in school. He had to find a way to purge those feelings."

Franz exhaled slowly. The big smile returned. "Doctor, I'm glad you're on the case. Sometimes Goldy and I sit in front of the TV and talk about him. We turn up the volume so he can't hear and we wonder if we're doing everything we can."

"You are, and you should be very proud of him," Sara said. "Fredric is a young person with conviction. He believes in ideas when everyone else challenges them—that's a son or daughter with some steel in the back of his neck."

Franz nodded and extended a big, knobby hand across the table. "Doctor, I can't thank you enough for this talk. And for everything you've done for our son."

"He's very special to me. We'll get him through this."

"Thank you," Franz said. "We just want to see him happy."

The psychotherapist did not tell Franz that for young men like Fredric, happiness was ephemeral. During her graduate studies, the head of the Yale School of Drama had addressed the psych students. His was one of a series of guest lectures given by individuals in the arts. Professor John Sax told them that actors spent most of their lives pacing emotionally, waiting for a script to read and an actor to play off. They were only fulfilled when they were digging through the muck of a complex character and throwing that at other actors, or getting the mud thrown at them. And they were truly "happy" on those rare occasions when a performance or scene meshed—and then the connection and the joy was gone.

Speakers from the university's art and creative writing departments said essentially the same thing, that the creative life was a taxing, uncharted journey. Landfall was never a destination. It was simply a place to rest your eyes and mind, a chance to savor a new place before becoming restless and moving on.

Sara couldn't tell Franz Marash that her job was not to "cure" his son but to help him manage his self-expression, to find ways that he could integrate his unique and vital temperament into the fabric of society.

It's easier to be a jock, she thought as she got back in her car.

As she pulled from the curb, Sara happened to glance at the spotlit Sacred Heart Church across the street. She thought of Sister Grace then and wondered if it was also easier to be a nun. Probably not. Like Sara, she could not put the day's challenges in a drawer or computer file when she went home. She carried them in her head, in her heart, and—in Grace's case—in the small of her back as a knot of tension. At least Sara never had physical manifestations of her problems.

She decided that when she saw Fredric in the morning she would push to get him to talk about the woods, about the noose. Since he was obviously fond of the woods, perhaps she would take the session outside. It would be cool in the morning, but invigorating. They could sit in the gazebo. Sara had always been reluctant to put her sessions in an objectifiable setting. The simple, almost bland office made it about the patient. In a nature environment Fredric might see her as a strong earth-mother figure. For the sake of getting much needed information, she might take that risk.

Tonight, though, Sara needed to make landfall. She would have dinner, chat with her mother for a while, then shut the door to the den and pull something from the shelf. There was a mahogany bucket chair in the room. She used to sleep in it as a child, curled on the smooth gold silk and feeling protected by the high, straight back. It was still her safe place, and with apologies to Hans Christian Andersen or Upton Sinclair or Mr. Dickens, if the hour was right and the matching footstool was "just so," Sara could still fall asleep there.

It was also one of the few places in the house where the outside world did not encroach, where the only terrors and fears and disappointments were from the minds and experiences of authors. Years before, when Sara's office was still a playroom filled with dolls and puzzles and the den was a TV room and library, it was a wing where her stumbling-drunk father and her sobbing mother did not come, where she and sometimes Darrell could lock the door and banish sadness.

Everyone needed a nighttime bike path into the woods.

2

Sara never made landfall.

She had dinner, which was handmade spaghetti with anchovy sauce and veggie balls. If Tonia ever left, Sara would have to hire a chef. The woman had exceptional skills acquired from her peasant grandmother, she said proudly.

Sara took a decaf double espresso and went to her office to pay a few bills, including one of the dwindling number of student loans she had taken. Then she went to the library feeling tired and ready for her chair. She turned up the heat a few degrees—feeling a little guilty as she did so—but before she could select a volume and shut the door, her mother wandered in. Martha wanted to take a walk and asked Sara to go with her.

It was dark and it was very cool but the woman said she wanted to get out of the house.

"Any reason in particular?" Sara asked.

"You recommended it."

"That was last year."

"Well, I'm sure there's a reason but I can't think of it," Martha said.

There was no arguing with that. The women put on sweaters and baseball caps. Martha had a favorite cap for the fall, orange with a yellow sun on front. Sara had brought it back from a convention she'd attended in Georgia several years before. It still carried the fresh smell of cedar from the closet. Sara grabbed a flashlight from her office and together they walked slowly up River Road.

Her arm hooked in that of her daughter, Martha breathed hard as they made their way up the slope.

"Actually, that's not quite true, what I said before," Martha told her.

"About what?"

"Getting out," Martha said. "I was sitting with my coffee and *House Beautiful* today, thinking that maybe I shouldn't hibernate this fall like I usually do."

Martha had subscribed to *House Beautiful* for as long as Sara could remember. The woman wasn't so much looking for ideas, Sara suspected, because she never did any gardening or reupholstering or wallpapering. Sara guessed that Martha was looking for images that reminded her of a sunny and hopeful past.

"That's a very positive idea," Sara replied.

"But I do hate the cold," she said.

"Sometimes it's best to confront what we hate," Sara said. "In reality, fears don't seem as big and bad as we imagine them to be."

Martha thought for a moment. "No, the cold is as unfriendly as I remember."

"Compared to the summer you love, yes. In and of itself you may find it's not so bad."

"I see," Martha said. "What if I were afraid of being hit by a car? Should I try that too? Or be struck by lightning?"

"You're just being contrary. There are junctures in life when we face things we don't want to do and things we shouldn't. A rational, reasonable mind should be able to tell them apart."

"Uh-huh," Martha said. Her mother often said that when she was processing information. "You're probably right, dear. I wonder. Would you intuitively know things like that if you didn't have your education?"

"I don't know." Sara smiled. "I think I would have known that it's a bad idea to hide for six months of the year."

"It's my Southern constitution," Martha panted. "We are not meant for harsh winters or walks that are not level and bordered by azaleas."

Sara smiled. Some of her best memories growing up were of her mother absolutely refusing to go outside during the winter. When it snowed Sara and Darrell would actually go outside with a cookie tray, load it with snow, and bring it inside so they could build "snow freezes" with their mother on the kitchen table. It wasn't until seventh or eighth grade that Sara found out they were really called "friezes." They'd use animals from their Christmas nativity and buildings from Darrell's train set to populate the dioramas, which were usually gardens or forests. If they needed more trees or boulders one of the kids went and got more snow. When they were done, they would put the work in the freezer. By morning they were chunky and deformed, which was part of the fun. They looked like something from a Smurf cartoon. Sara also remembered the smell of chocolate cookies her mother would bake—partly to heat the house—and the times they would pull chairs up to the bay window in the living room and play tic-tac-toe on the frosty glass. When they ran out of panes Martha would move in close and exhale on them, creating a fresh playing surface. Darrell thought she was a snow queen like the one he had seen in a storybook.

Maybe Sara wasn't so smart after all. Seasons spent inside

were a little like Fredric's views of life: different, not necessarily bad.

They turned right at the top of the street and walked to the flagpole that stood in a small green near the fire station. The hoist line snapped hard against the old, peeling pole.

"Are you doing okay?" Sara asked.

Her mother was breathing hard. "I'm delicate, not frail," she said.

"Do you want to sit?"

Martha waved her hand from side to side. "Too cold. Time to go back."

Martha held her daughter tighter as they turned around. At least going down the hill would be easier than going up.

As they headed back down the deserted Main Street they passed Hobble Court, the cul-de-sac where the Marashes lived. The streetlights cast dull white cones on the curbs, leaving the rest of the street in darkness. At the end, Sara saw what she thought was a sharp silvery light bobbing from side to side. She wondered if that might be Fredric, off for a ride in the woods.

"Heeeeere, Fluffy!" she heard in the distance.

No. It was Albert Jay looking for his golden retriever. The dog had a secret way out of the picket fence that old Albert was never able to find. The dog was smart enough never to use it when anyone was looking.

"He could be a pookah," the middle-aged clerk at the post office told Albert one day.

Sara happened to be standing behind the eighty-two-year-old at the time. It was a Saturday morning and Albert's jeans were still splashed with mud from a chase the night before. The clerk, Heather Rich, was the town bookworm. She had listened to Albert complain about the dog while she wrote him mail-order checks.

"A what?" the gaunt, white-bearded man had asked as he slowly counted out the exact change from a purse.

"A spirit animal that can come and go wherever it wants," the clerk told him.

"Eyewash," Albert said.

"No, sir," Heather said. "We live on Native American grounds that are rich with such lore."

"It's all applesauce. I'd be rich with such lore too if I smoked as much loco weed as those fellas," Albert said with a chuckle. He set aside the third and final stack of bills and coins. He chucked a thumb behind him. "And if her dad had put in the new fence I'd wanted we wouldn't be having this conversation." He glanced back at Sara and winked. "No disrespect. I liked your dad. We hoisted a few in our time. He just never got around to doing what he said."

"He meant well," Sara said. "And he may still get around to it."

"What?" Albert's face scrunched into something confused and gargoylish and he looked away. "*That's* downright disrespectful, girl. To me, I mean. I'm not stupid. I know he's passed on."

"Well, we do live in a very spiritual region," Sara said. "He may yet finish it."

Heather nodded in agreement. Albert didn't know what to make of any of it. And Sara was just feeling pissy hearing this man talk about her father.

That was four or five months ago. She hadn't seen the man since. He spent summers digging and selling bait to fishermen—and looking for Fluffy who, like her mother, really enjoyed a warm night out.

It was nearly nine o'clock when Sara and her mother got back to the house. Martha went upstairs and Sara went to her office to check her messages. She had not taken her cell phone with her and checked that first. No one had called. There was one message on her office voice mail and she punched in the code to hear it.

It was Goldy Marash sobbing that there had been a fight.

Five

1

"Fredric was just—so *angry*," Goldwyn said. "He ran out."

Sara called at once. Goldwyn Marash was still very upset, still talking through tears.

"What happened?" Sara asked as she took her handbag from under the desk. She wanted to have her car keys in her hand.

"Franz and I were watching TV in the den," Goldwyn said, choking out the words. "We—we were talking when Fredric came in. He wanted to know where his new scarf was. I told him it smelled a little musty so I took it to the store to clean. Well, I forgot to bring it home and he just started *yelling*!" She cried openly. "I've never seen Fredric so angry! He ran out of the den screaming the most awful things!"

"What happened then?"

Goldwyn continued to cry.

"Mrs. Marash, what else happened?"

The woman took a long breath. "My husband went after him. He told him to calm down, said they could drive over and get it," Goldwyn said. "But Freddy just screamed that it was ruined, that he felt *raped*, and ran from the house. Franz went after him but he was on his bike."

"Is Franz still gone?"

"Yes," Goldwyn replied. "How is that a rape? I don't understand! And—he has other scarves. He wears them all the time."

"Black?"

"I—I don't know. Dark."

"Did your husband go into the woods?"

"Yes, but he came back for a flashlight—who knows where Fredric might have gone?"

Sara slung her bag over her shoulder. "I'll be over in a minute. If Fredric comes back, tell him you're sorry."

"That's all?"

"That's it," Sara said. "Don't explain, don't give Fredric words to throw back at you."

"All right," Goldwyn said. "I am sorry. I'm *so* sorry."

"One more question. Did you take the scarf from Fredric's room?"

"Yes," she said.

"The door was closed?"

"Yes. It was just hanging on the hook behind his door. I happened to smell it when I passed by, that's how dirty it was. But I didn't look at anything, I just reached in and took it."

"Where does he usually put his dirty clothes?"

"In a hamper in his bathroom," Goldwyn said.

"We're going to fix this," Sara said. "I'll see you in a bit."

Goldwyn thanked her again as Sara hung up. She grabbed the cell phone, dropped it in her bag, then hurried out the back door. As she hurried to her car she could not help but feel that the night was much colder and darker than it had been just a few minutes before.

Driving up River Road, Sara tried to figure out what in particular had set Fredric off. It was probably a dual hit of the scarf being taken and his room entered. Sara could remember Fredric having worn scarves, so this one might have special significance—for his nighttime trips into the woods, most likely. It would be very much in character for the young man to put a unique visual signature on his personal trips of discovery or introspection. The feel, the smells of the woods, were something that would instantly evoke that place and state-of-soul when he was away from it. Cleaning the scarf would have erased that security. And his room, of course, was his atelier—a private spot where he exposed his inner thoughts and feelings. That was definitely not a space he would want anyone to enter uninvited.

Sara crossed the old covered bridge that spanned the Housatonic and pulled up in front of the house. It was just to the right of the Jay place, which occupied the bottom of the cul-de-sac. Albert was no longer looking for his dog. He was peeking from behind the blinds to see who had just pulled up. Sara did not want to waste time enlisting his help. She took a flashlight from the glove compartment and hurried up the cement walk. The outside spotlights were all on, a few stubborn moths fluttering around them. Goldwyn rushed out to meet her.

"They're not back, Doctor," the woman said anxiously. "I was thinking, should I call Trooper Brown?"

Sara had been wondering that herself. She had been

weighing the advantage of having extra eyes on the search with the negative effect of the added attention, something that would certainly bother her "invisible" patient.

"Yes," Sara decided. "Tell her that Fredric was upset when he left, that he's in the woods on his bike, probably on the hiking trail, and we're afraid he might get hurt in the dark."

"I'll do that," Goldwyn said. "Thank you again."

Leaving her with a smile and a reassuring squeeze on the arm, Sara jogged off. She went around the house to where the woods intersected the Marash backyard. She snapped on the flashlight and moved quickly onto the trail. Sara had never taken a walk like this as a young woman. Their journeys were always about the river. At once, Sara felt as if she'd been cut off from civilization. There were no lights but the one she carried, no sounds but those coming from the trees above and the darkness to the sides. There were no shapes, other than what nature had provided.

She suddenly felt that the world Heather Rich had described at the post office was strangely and disturbingly real. The shuffle of the fallen leaves limited her ability to hear much of what was happening beyond the immediate area, beyond her own breathing and heartbeat. She did not hear Franz or Fredric. She did not see their lights because the terrain was so uneven. It sloped up and down, turned west and then east with sudden regularity. She saw what looked like the dark line of bicycle tires in the muck below but that could have been days old. The good news was that if Fredric had entered the park there was no other way he could have gone. The ancient rock ledges were high and in many places unpassable. There were no trunk routes to the lake or picnic grounds until much deeper into the woods.

Sara was startled by a big, hollow sigh that came from the leaves to her left. The burst melted away quickly. She imagined it was a stag standing watch or a red fox stirred from its den. There were infrequent but unmistakable full-throated *hooos* from long-eared owls in the higher branches of the trees. When Sara was a girl she thought they were angels talking to one another in the backyard. Isolated groups of crickets sounded here and there, unwilling to go quietly into the long, unwelcome season ahead. Sara once again thought of Heather because the postal clerk had been right about this much: there was a time, not so long ago, when these sounds and this darkness were the world at night. When the mysteries and wonder of the flora and fauna were as wondrous a puzzle as the moon and stars.

Sara had knowledge but she could only imagine the sense of wonder the ancients possessed. Theirs were millennia of limitless options, when every thought, every discovery, was new and filled with infinite potential. It was a time and a journey when the internal and the external were equally unknown.

How liberating that must have been . . .

Sara's breath quickened, joining the rapid slush of her feet through the damp leaves. Her head pounded slightly as she ran, driven by the urgency of the moment. She kept the flashlight constantly in motion, poking here and there and showing nothing but tree trunks, darkness, rock walls, and the occasional mirror-glint of animal eyes in the distance.

And then, somewhere ahead, she heard the voice of Franz Marash calling after his son. She slowed to listen.

"Fredric?" he cried. "Freddy, where *are* you? Please come back, son!"

Sara had never heard either parent call the boy "Freddy." It sounded lonely, desperate. She slowed. She did not want to be breathing heavily when she reached the distraught father. As in the office, she needed to be calm and composed for him and for Fredric.

Sara moved the flashlight in slow, wide, horizontal sweeps to make sure she didn't miss Franz. Unlike a young man on his bicycle, the elder Marash might have climbed one of the ledges on either side for a better view of the woods. Obviously, he hadn't spotted his son.

Franz called again and this time Sara spotted him. He was jogging slowly ahead of her, shining the flashlight from side to side. Sara hurried to catch up to him. The owls were silent now and there was no movement in the foliage atop the ledges. The man's shouts must have silenced them.

"Franz?"

The man turned the light around. "Dr. Lynch?"

"Yes," Sara said. She lowered her light from his eyes. "Your wife called—"

"It was so sudden!" he said.

"We'll talk about it later," Sara said as she approached. "Trooper Brown will be arriving shortly to help find your son."

"Are you sure that's a good idea? An authority figure—"

"It sounds like Fredric was angrier than usual," Sara said. "He might not be paying attention to the road, to the river—"

"But what you said before about him. Won't that kind of attention freak him out even more? He isn't disguised."

"He won't be happy, but the important thing is to find him," Sara said. "Then we can talk to him."

Franz nodded, then turned and continued walking. Sara walked alongside him.

"All my wife did was clean an article of his clothing," Franz muttered. "Goldy cleans *all* his clothing. The way he screamed you would have thought she had stabbed him."

"I think it was the intrusion in his space—"

"All right, she made a mistake," Franz said. "She said as much, she apologized, but it didn't do any good. It was like he was possessed—"

They were just rounding another turn when Franz fell silent. The flashlight, which had been probing at a long angle alongside the road, locked on the bicycle. It was leaning against a low rock ledge to the right. Sara's own light rose and probed beyond the bike. It spilled over the top of the ledge against a tree. She stopped. It took a moment for her to process what she was seeing.

There was a large sycamore set back from the edge of the rock wall. The clusters of pointed, drab-green leaves were thin at the bottom and much thicker at the top. There were large, nearly naked branches low in the tree. They stretched proudly from the peeling bark of the thick trunk.

Fredric was hanging by the neck from one of those fat low branches.

Sara couldn't think. She stood as still as the sycamore. The only movement was perspiration from the hike trickling down her side. It was several moments before she breathed, blinked, closed her mouth. Her brain struggled to get away. It wanted to reach back in time, to rip away the last hour, play it all differently. But she forced it to stay. She needed to work through the moments, not collect those that had gone by.

Her eyes had devoured the scene even if her brain had not. The security chain from his bicycle was fastened to Fredric's neck with the padlock. The other end of the chain was wrapped around the powerful branch. The young man's head was bent at an awkward angle and he was still swinging slightly. He had apparently climbed to a lower branch and jumped.

"Christ Jesus . . ." Franz murmured.

Franz's familiar voice gave Sara back her limbs. She walked, then ran forward. When she reached the bike she put the light on the seat and shined it ahead. Her brain was still somewhere else but her body was functioning in a survival mode. Mechanically, she fished her cell phone from her bag and punched 911. She reported their position on the trail. When asked, she informed the dispatcher that the section of road was wide enough to accommodate an ambulance.

"Please hurry," Sara said. That was not just for Fredric but for herself. She needed normal systems to engage, organization restored. Once the event was absorbed into a larger order it would become an aberration instead of her universe.

She forced herself to inhabit the moment. *Walk. Get to Fredric. Try to help.* She could not permit this shock to merge with others in her shocked and momentarily undefended brain, to form a kinship with them.

Franz had passed her and was scrambling up the rock. If it were possible for a man to tumble upward he did so, clawing and falling up the stone face but somehow managing to swing a leg over the wedge-shaped lip. He raced toward the tree with ungainly purpose. When he arrived he began pulling himself up through the branches, his big hands desperate and using any handhold.

"Lower him to me, quickly, then come down!" Sara shouted as she reached the tree.

Fredric's feet were pointed at a lazy angle just two feet above her head. He was turning slightly, slowly, back and forth. She was not thinking about reasons now, only about getting him on the ground and trying to fan whatever life still smoldered inside that slender shell.

Franz had reached the branch that held his son. The man

was curled around it like a koala, fighting with the knot Fredric had tied in the chain. The boy's dead weight was making it impossible to disentangle the links. Screaming in frustration Franz pounded the branch to try to break it. He did not succeed.

"Get *down*!" Franz cried as he dropped his flashlight and shook the branch. When that didn't work he reached around it and pulled down on the chain. He came at it from every way he could think of.

There was nothing Sara could do. Even if they had the key to the padlock, getting to it would be impossible. The metal latch was digging into the soft tissue under Fredric's jaw, glinting in the glow of her flashlight as the body moved.

The body bobbed and swung hideously. Sara just now noticed a bulge in the back of his neck, sharp lumps of flesh protruding above the knot. Flesh with broken bone beneath it.

This was a new world now. It was neither civilization nor the mystic night of Native Americans. It was a slow-motion, starkly lit nightmare. It didn't daunt her knowledge, it humbled it, made it useless.

Colored lights lit the trail. They were coming from the direction of the house. That would be the black-and-white of Trooper Brown. Sara ran back several dozen yards to get the police woman's attention. As she raced toward the red and blue lights, Sara knew there was virtually no hope that Fredric was still alive. The young man had not choked himself, he had jumped. His neck had apparently snapped. She thought of how un-Fredric-like his body had looked in the tree. The angle of his head was tortured, his neck pinched impossibly thin, his eyes shut and bulging, his mouth twisted deep to the left like a Greek mask of tragedy. The noose had even trapped blood in the flesh of his face making it ruddier than usual. Her father hadn't looked like himself in his coffin, either. He looked like painted dough. It was frightening how little of our bodies "we" really were.

The patrol car moved nearer and Sara motioned for it to hurry to the sycamore. The tires spit leaves and pebbles in all directions as Trooper Brown saw the body and sped up. She braked hard beneath the tree. Sara ran to the front bumper, dropped her handbag, and climbed onto the hood. She believed that she could reach the boy from there.

"Dr. Lynch, wait!" the trooper shouted as she got out. "You're going to need help."

"There's a padlock. I'm looking for the key," she said as she patted the boy's sides. The small key, like the key to a diary, was in the front left pocket of his jeans. She took it out. Such a small thing had enabled him to die.

The trooper climbed beside her. "Mr. Marash, please come down!" she yelled.

"My boy. What did you do?" Franz said hopelessly. He backed across the limb so that he was away from his son, then jumped the six feet to the ledge.

Trooper Brown was a large woman, a head taller than Sara with wide shoulders and a thick waist. She felt for a pulse, found none, then wrapped her long arms around Fredric's legs while Sara reached up. The lights of the patrol car threw her shadow across Fredric's chest and turned his throat an alternating red and blue. Sara took the padlock in her left hand and popped it with her right.

"I'm going to lift him slightly so you can remove it," the trooper said.

"All right," Sara said.

Fredric's musky smell touched her nostrils. It was familiar because he came to her office on his bike. But the odor was different now, tinged by a hint of smoke from his clothes, by the metallic edge of blood.

Fredric's body rose just a little. The flesh of his chin peeled away from the lock and the chain slackened slightly. The bolt had made a large dent in Fredric's neck. The mark stayed even when the padlock was removed, as though it had been punched in clay. The flesh around it was torn and bloody. Sara slipped the U-shaped bolt from the links and pulled the padlock away. She stuffed it in Fredric's pocket; it was his.

Trooper Brown's grip prevented Fredric's body from falling. Sara tossed the chain to the ground as the officer lowered the boy to the hood of the car. Sara helped her by taking his head as they laid him down, his head near the driver's side. It had been years since she had touched the hair of the very young Fredric Marash. She remembered how "boy" it felt, rough and solid. It still did.

Sara climbed down as Brown hopped off and went to the driver's side. The trooper called her dispatcher to make sure an ambulance was on the way. She also asked for a forensics specialist and a helicopter from the Western District Headquarters. Sara, meanwhile, hurried to the side of the car. She licked a finger and held it under Fredric's nose. The young man was not breathing. She pressed two fingers against Fredric's raw and oddly bent neck to feel for a carotid pulse. There was none and she reached over to begin cardiopulmonary resuscitation.

Franz Marash stood stiff and disbelieving. "You told me there was nothing to worry about," he said.

Sara ignored him. She placed two fingers of her right hand where the sternum met the bottom of his rib cage and the heel of her left hand beside them, on the breastbone itself.

She pressed firmly, rhythmically, counting out fifteen seconds. Then she breathed into his cold mouth twice to aerate his lungs and repeated. After ventilating him a second time Sara felt again for a pulse.

The teenager was dead. She performed the process one more time before stepping away from the car.

"I'm sorry," she said to Franz.

He shook his head slowly. "If only I'd run a little faster."

"This wasn't anyone's fault," Sara said softly but firmly. The psychotherapist was not just talking to Franz but reminding herself. In situations where loss is so personal it is important to keep the survivors in the "now" and out of the "what ifs."

Marash continued to stare.

"Franz, did you hear me?" Sara continued in a strong, level tone. "No one could have foreseen this."

"You should have," he said flatly. "I asked you—"

"It isn't that easy. There are no formulas—"

"You said he was in *no danger*!"

"And something happened tonight to change that," she said.

"You're a scientist," he said, his voice rising. "You told me and Rowdy you are a goddamn scientist. You're supposed to *know* these things!"

Trooper Brown walked to the front of the car. "I suggest you both move apart." She opened the back door on the passenger's side. "Why don't you sit down, Mr. Marash?" Coming from her it was a command.

Franz nodded and walked to the seat. He sat heavily, facing outward, away from the car and from his son's body. As he did that, the trooper took a notepad from her leather jacket and placed the garment over Fredric's chest and head. A distant siren cut through the sigh of the evening breeze. The leaves stirred overhead. Sara felt a chill as she recalled the stories she had read in one of her father's own childhood collections of Gaelic folktales, tales of the banshees who came to announce the death of someone close. The spirits wailed forlornly as they moved through the night skies, irrevocable and hailing the approach of the costa bower, the death coach.

"I assume there was no physiological response when you found him," the trooper asked as she approached the psychotherapist. She spoke low so her voice didn't carry far.

"None," Sara said. She noticed her handbag on the ground and picked it up. The handle dug into her neck as she slung it over her shoulder. How many times had that happened without her noticing it?

The trooper plucked a pen from her shirt pocket and began making notes. "Did either of you see it happen?"

"No."

"Did you hear or see anyone else around?"

"I wasn't aware of anyone. Just animals."

"Are you sure they were animals?" Trooper Brown asked.

"Sure? No," Sara admitted. That would explain the trooper's request for a helicopter.

"Do you know what the boy was doing out here? Was he supposed to meet someone?"

"I don't know." *You're talking about Fredric, your patient, your future artist. Dead.* Sara took a steadying breath.

"Doc, off the record—is there anything I should know about this?"

"Fredric had a fight with his mother about a scarf," Sara said.

"Was it an argument or a fight? Do you know if there was pushing, if blows were exchanged—"

"As far as I know it was just an argument," Sara said. "He ran from the house, got on his bike, and came here. His father ran after him and his mother called me. I caught up with Mr. Marash. We found Fredric the way you saw him."

"Seems like an overreaction to an argument, wouldn't you say?"

"I—I don't want to speculate until I know more."

"Fair enough. Why didn't you drive out here?" the trooper asked.

"I didn't know where we'd end up, on trail or off," Sara told her. It suddenly occurred to her that if she had driven she might have gotten here in time. The thought made her want to scream.

"Rowdy told me he saw you at the Marash shop today," the trooper said. "Were you just picking up laundry?"

"I went to talk to Mr. Marash about his son," Sara said.

"Were you concerned about this?" the trooper asked. "Do you think the deceased came here with the intention of harming himself?"

"He was not violent. As I told Principal Harkness today, he expressed his anger through art."

"Then it doesn't make sense that he would have done this to himself," the trooper said.

Sara looked at the sycamore. The branches seemed strong and defiant. "No. It doesn't," she answered truthfully.

"Why were you speaking to Mr. Harkness about Fredric?" the trooper asked.

"The principal made a careless remark about his appearance," Sara told her. "I wanted to make sure it didn't happen again."

"Was the remark 'careless' enough to make the young man want to do this?" the trooper asked.

"I don't think so," Sara answered.

The oncoming siren had disappeared behind the houses on the cul-de-sac. It reemerged now, louder than before. The sharp white lights cut through the trees adding brilliance to the scene but no clarity. Sara saw the anxious face of Goldwyn Marash squeezed between those of the paramedics. Franz got out of the police car. This was going to be a terrible moment for Goldwyn and her husband but it had to be their moment alone.

The trooper left to join the paramedics. Sara turned and walked toward the tree. Her shoes moved quietly along the mulch. The wind moaned around either side, strangely different on the left and the right.

Two banshees, not one, she thought. Maybe there were even more. Parts of several people had died here tonight. Sara stood beneath the tree. The headlights made the bark seem like the hide of some great mythical creature. The tree seemed powerful and impassive, even imperious. Its life would go on, unchanged.

Not yours, Sara knew.

She was still convinced that the noose necktie was not a warning but a statement, a way to get attention, an artistic bite against the exclusive mainstream. She couldn't have anticipated this because there was more to it than she had known. The scarf, for one thing. Why a scarf? Fredric had never seemed very particular about any other article of clothing, as long as it was black. Was it the smell that mattered to him for some reason and not the garment itself? His life had seemed to be about one sense, the visual. Had she missed something by not pursuing the others?

Sara looked down. She felt as though her chest had been scooped out and filled with cold mud. Her body was heavy, thick, sluggish. In retrospect, events often seemed ordained or foredoomed, depending on how they worked out. Her father's death by cirrhosis. Darrell's drinking.

Her relationship with Martin Cayne.

Fredric's death was not like that. The cold shock of it left her body numb but her brain sharp with analytical clarity.

Fredric Marash was not suicidal. She believed that. She *knew* that.

Goldwyn Marash wailed suddenly and loudly behind her. Sara turned, not to watch nor to make herself available for the woman's anger. She did not want to present a disinterested back to the mother's anguish. Franz was holding his wife tightly. He shielded her from the front of the police car as the paramedics worked over Fredric's body. The two men attempted to reventilate his lungs and start his heart as Sara had done. The result was the same. After two minutes they put his body on a portable gurney and wheeled it to the ambulance. Trooper Brown stopped them to take the padlock from Fredric's pocket. She handled it gingerly, with her fingertips, putting it and the chain in an evidence duffel bag and placed them in the trunk. Then she took a roll of yellow crime scene tape from the trunk. She walked ahead and strung it between roots poking through the rock ledges along the far side of the road, just past the sycamore.

Sara looked back at the Marashes. They were holding each other, sobbing into one another's shoulders. Sara wished she could go to them. She had never felt so completely useless.

"Excuse me," Trooper Brown said as she went to sling the tape across the near side of the road. The bicycle was obviously going to remain where it was. Sara recovered her flashlight and stuck it in her handbag, then moved away.

Sara stood there, still trying to imagine what had driven

Fredric to take his life. She did not believe it was an argument over a scarf. And why did he come here? There were other trees along the route, trees that would have been easier to climb. If he did this from rage, in defiance, for effect, he could have selected a strong bough nearer to home. The more Sara thought about it, the more she wondered if the scarf was just a part of what upset him. He used the word "raped." Did he mean that figuratively or literally? Was his anger about invaded privacy or about the room itself? Perhaps there was something inside that was only for his eyes.

Something too personal for anyone to have seen, even his mother.

2

The Marashes elected to drive to the morgue with their son. Trooper Brown said she would follow the ambulance to the Litchfield County Coroner's Office in nearby Sharon and then give the couple a ride back. There was no room to turn around. The ambulance backed from the trail very slowly.

"Want a lift?" Trooper Brown asked Sara as she went to the patrol car.

Sara nodded absently.

The trooper backed out as well. Sara watched the tree as darkness consumed it.

"How long were you caring for Fredric?" the trooper asked as she looked over her shoulder.

"Almost ten years."

"Off the record, what do you make of this?"

Sara barely heard. The hum of the ventilator filled her ears. The smell of dead leaves filled her nose.

"Confidentiality restrictions don't apply in a suicide investigation," the trooper coaxed.

"I know." Sara just couldn't think right now about that, about anything."

"Then let's see if I can point you in a direction," the trooper said. "Fredric was never on my radar. But that doesn't mean he wasn't a member of some kind of gang or cult. Is there anyone else we should be looking for or at?"

"If he had friends he never mentioned them. I never saw him with anyone."

"Didn't you ever ask about other kids?"

"Of course. But I didn't push. That was not the best way to relate to Fredric."

"Short fuse?"

"Not in the way you mean," Sara said. "If I pushed he closed up."

"So there may be kids out there he met with."

"Perhaps."

"Online friends or school friends?"

"I don't know about who he might have hung with at the school," Sara said. She realized what she had just said and it made her sick. The trooper appeared not to have noticed. "Chrissie Blair was his guidance counselor. She kept an eye on him there."

"I'll have a talk with her tomorrow," the trooper said.

"As for chat rooms, I wouldn't describe the people he met there as 'friends.' They talked about Goth things."

"Did you ever go there when he was online?"

"I lurked," she said. "I didn't post."

"Did he ever meet these people for real?"

"I don't know," Sara said.

"What about drugs?"

"I didn't prescribe any, and I don't believe he took any."

"What do you make of the scarf?"

"Nothing, yet."

"That's a weird trigger, don't you think?"

"I don't know if the scarf alone set him off," Sara said. "Fredric's mother went into his room. They fought about that."

"Would he have hanged himself because his mother went in his room?"

"I said they *fought* about that," Sara reminded her. "I didn't say that's why he took his life."

"But it's possible he felt violated."

Sara nodded. Fredric *had* agreed to see her the next day. There was nothing insincere or I've-got-a-secret in his manner. She believed he intended to be there.

"Did you ever see him wear that scarf?" the trooper asked.

"Not that I recall."

"Did either of the Marashes say anything about it?"

"Goldwyn said it smelled musty," Sara told her.

"It's early in the season," the trooper said. "I wonder how it got funky enough to need cleaning?"

"A couple of hard afternoon bike rides would have done it," Sara said.

The trooper was silent for a moment. "I've seen him around on that bike."

"He loved it," Sara said.

"Why do you think he used the bicycle chain?"

"I assume it was handy," Sara asked.

"It was, in one sense."

"I don't follow."

"We don't get many suicides here, and most of those are gunshot wounds," the trooper said. "But I do get county and statewide reports every day and I've read about what they call 'self-afflicting instruments' used for hanging, such as neckties, belts, and bedsheets. Do you have any idea how hard he had to work to get that around his neck?"

"No."

"I had a good look before you popped the lock," the trooper said. "He made a figure-eight around the branch and another around his neck, with the padlock pinching it in the middle. The chain wasn't very long, which means Fredric had to be leaning close to or lying on the branch in order to put the lock in. He would have had to do that blind since he didn't have a light, and he also would have been gasping pretty hard since he had already put the twist in the center of the chain."

"You're taking this somewhere," Sara said.

"If Fredric Marash were *planning* to kill himself he would have brought along a much less cumbersome SAI, something he could have knotted around the tree, knotted around himself, and jumped."

Sara felt a chill. "A scarf."

Trooper Brown nodded. "I'm no shrink, but my gut tells me he may have been planning to do this anyway. Maybe he was aging that scarf, making it smell like a grave. I don't know. Momma may have thrown him off and he tried to get back on-plan. The boy wasn't wearing a belt and sweaters have seams that tear so he used the first thing he could think of."

It was possible, Sara had to admit. She was still too shaken to think objectively. Though the trooper's previous remark did stick in her head: *"If Fredric Marash were planning to kill himself."* That was not necessarily the same as being suicidal. This could be a macabre form of self-expression. It might even be related to his fascination with the triangle. *Pyramids,* she thought suddenly. The Aztecs and Mayans both committed ritual sacrifices on and within those shapes. Unlike suicide there was no checklist for that, no fire bells. But that didn't mean there wasn't evidence, a trail of some kind.

The patrol car neared the beginning of the trail. Trooper Brown waited while the ambulance negotiated up the small incline to the Marash driveway. Then she backed the black-and-white from the woods. The ambulance left, silent running, and Trooper Brown pulled up beside Sara's car. Sara cracked the door. The officer looked at her with a sour expression.

"Are you sure there's nothing you can tell me, or will tell me, or want to tell me? I'm thinking about you too here, about our town. A boy in your care takes his life—that's going to play really bad in the papers."

"I've told you all I know. I don't want to speculate about anything else."

"Fair enough. I don't like to speculate either, but judging from Mr. Marash's reaction I also wouldn't rule out legal action."

Sara had just been thinking about both, the press and the legal ramifications, but briefly. They skipped across her mind like flat stones on a lake.

"I know that I worked hard to help Fredric Marash, and I believe that something beyond our sessions was responsible for this tragedy," Sara said. "That's my path away from ground zero. Those other possibilities you mentioned—they're completely beyond my control."

The trooper nodded. "If it helps, and I'm not sure it will, there were always angry parents ripping into the parking lot, demanding to know what their little Johnny or Mary had done. It was always something or their little tulips wouldn't be there. Fighting, drinking, drag-racing, vandalism. Always something. The parents are always a whole lot calmer in court, Doctor. By then they realize there was a problem, and part of the blame was themselves."

"Thanks," Sara said. "I appreciate the thought."

Brown sighed. "Well, we're going to give the woods and that vicinity in particular a good eyeballing, though I'll be surprised if we find anything. This looks like it was a one-hander. Sad, though. Real sad."

Sara got out of the patrol car and the trooper drove away. She stood beside her car. Albert had been peeking through the blinds. They snapped shut when Trooper Brown left. Fluffy was barking and continued to bark, more and more sporadically like a retreating thunderstorm. Except for those distant, tenacious crickets the psychotherapist was very much alone.

If Fredric Marash were planning to kill himself.

The words bothered her. Fredric had been reading the Bible. He had talked with passion about Abraham preparing to sacrifice Isaac and he was angry over the death of Jesus. Fredric's sharp reaction seemed to be the antithesis of a young man who wanted death for himself.

But maybe that wasn't entirely true, Sara realized with horror as she walked through the session. Perhaps Fredric was not just damning the authority figures but praising the heroic sons.

The thought pushed tears against the back of her eyes. Fredric was not a young man who had heroes, at least none that he ever shared with her. Yet until yesterday she didn't know that he was reading the Bible. Obviously he kept things from her.

Sara opened her eyes wide to drive away the tears. She looked over at the Marash house. She needed to know what secrets Fredric had been keeping and this might be the only opportunity to find out. Striding boldly along the driveway, Sara went to the front door of the house. She opened the screen door and entered.

3

It had been years since Sara was here.

She had been invited for a Christmas Eve caroling party six years before, along with most of the Marashes' longtime customers. Fredric had stayed in his room the entire time with the door closed, so she knew where it was. Sara had gone to the party as a dry-cleaning customer and not as a psychotherapist so she had not tried to draw Fredric out. But she remembered how bad she felt that he needed to stay inside. When she asked him about it during their next session, the ten-year-old had said that he did not want to share his Christmas tree. He had made decorations and hung them in his room. He brought one in to show her. It was Santa Claus made of clay, painted entirely red except for his beard, which was black. Sara speculated that it was a young Santa, which Fredric neither confirmed nor denied.

Staying in his room with his ornaments was one of Fredric's earliest expressions of being invisible.

Sara moved through the house, which was eerily silent. The oil burner kicked on a few moments after Sara entered, growling like the guardian hellhound Cerberus when a stranger trespassed near the gates of Hades. She was actually glad for the company. It kept the banshees away. She just now noticed how cold the house was.

The small foyer led to the living room. She crossed it quickly, making her way to a hallway that ran along the right side of the house. Fredric's room was directly past the bathroom. The door was shut. She was uneasy as she reached for the knob, not because she didn't belong here but because she could not believe that Fredric was gone. It was easier to accept that the last hour had been a terrible reverie and that the young man would be sitting in his room, invisible as he wished.

She turned the knob. It was very cold. She felt bad for Fredric having to live in such a chilly place. Maybe that was why he wore a scarf. She released the knob and pushed the door open slowly with her fingertips. She didn't walk in right away but waited. Goldwyn had left the lights on in the house but Fredric's room was dark. She felt for a light switch. She found one and pushed it up. Nothing happened. Apparently, Fredric didn't want to make it easy for intruders to see the room or him. Remembering the flashlight, Sara drew it from her handbag and switched it on. There was a fluorescent lamp on the desk to the right. She entered and pressed the button in the base. The light flickered to life. Sara jumped when she saw a giant snake beneath it, then relaxed. It was only a shadow. Fredric had used a marker to color the silhouette of a cobra on one of the two bulbs. The tongue curled menacingly onto the second bulb.

Sara clicked off her flashlight and looked into the room. She had expected it to be somewhat utilitarian, with furniture his parents had selected and a few customized elements such as posters, stacks of DVDs and CDs, clothes tossed here and there, and maybe a few toys or action figures with a science fiction or fantasy theme. That was not the decor Fredric had chosen. There *were* a few utilitarian pieces of furniture, an unmade bed, an open closet with mostly black clothing inside and a chin-up bar fixed between the jambs. Between his biking and the bar Fredric was obviously proving to himself that he could be as much a jock as the jocks. Maybe more so. None of that was a surprise. The artwork, however, was.

The bulk of the wall was covered with Fredric's photo-manips, which were push-pinned to the wall. These included at least a dozen images of what looked like Chrissie Blair, her head replaced by those of very delicate animals such as does and ewes, and her head on the bodies of snakes.

Sara noticed that all the pictures of Chrissie Blair were placed very high on the wall. She looked at the bar.

Shit.

Sara felt validated and sickened at the same time. The necktie had not been a statement about death but about hyper-experienced life.

She pulled over his desk chair and stood beneath the chin-up bar. She could see all the pictures of Chrissie from here and wondered if they had been a part of an autoerotic asphyxiation fantasy. Cutting the flow of blood to the brain heightens the intensity of orgasms during masturbation. Per-haps that was something Fredric did in his room. That would explain the turtlenecks he wore to conceal any bruises. The necktie might have been his own private joke about sex, something he could flaunt at a conservative school without anyone knowing what it was really about. That would have appealed to his sense of empowerment and art.

The scarf might have been too private for his mother to touch. The fact that she had done so, had smelled the musk of his throat, his ardor, may have caused repressed Oedipal tendencies to break through. Instead of destroying his eyes Fredric destroyed himself.

Maybe.

She needed to think about that. She needed more infor-mation, something Fredric may have left behind.

She put the chair back and looked at the art that was tacked lower on the wall. There were pages of what appeared to be downloads from the Internet. These were pictures of remarkable variety, among them etchings by Gustav Doré, copies of paintings by Renaissance masters, illustrations by line artists she didn't recognize. They all had one thing in common: a youth was being dominated, attacked, or slain by an adult. Unlike the images of Chrissie there was very little curling in the paper. She did not think the collection had been up there for very long. His fascination with tortured biblical and mythological youths had apparently come after his interest in sex.

There was one window and the drapes were shut, overlapping and as defiantly closed as Fredric himself. Her eyes moved to the dresser. Leather wristbands, sunglasses, audio CDs, and small hooped jewelry were splayed across the top. Perhaps Fredric had piercings she did not know about. That might be part of his sex life as well, the eroticism of pain. She noticed that the hoops were not plain circlets but had ridges cut into them. Looking closer, Sara saw that they were small snakes eating their own tails. The circle of life or the inevitable tragedy of being a snake?

Sara turned to the desk that had Fredric's laptop and printer. There were also stacks of books and notebooks, as well as a wooden case with pastels, a plastic container with watercolors, and several spiral-bound books of art paper. She looked down the spines of the books. The Bible was here, both Testaments, along with a *Strong's Concordance* from the school library. She looked inside. It was part of the permanent collection. The thick alphabetical guide to finding words of the Bible had not been checked out, it had been taken. Recently, since the last check-out was just two weeks before by Principal Harkness, not surprisingly. He had probably been looking for biblical validation of his repressive regime. Beside it was a paperback copy of Milton's *Paradise Lost* and behind that was a tattered leather-bound copy of something called the *Devil's Bible*. The publisher had cut a serpent in the cover. It formed the "s" of "Devil's." She touched the reverse embossing with the tip of her middle finger. The old leather was soft, smooth, even seductive.

Given her last conversations with Fredric she had expected to see the Bible. The concordance was a surprise because she did not expect such scholarship from a young man who did not—*had* not, she corrected herself—enjoyed reading or churchgoing. She looked inside the Strong's and saw that certain pages had been bent down and words had been circled: "fallen," "serpent," "sacrifice," "son," "father," "patriarch," and others. Some of them were cross-referenced by Fredric, such as "sacrifice" and "father."

Sara set the book aside. Milton's *Paradise Lost* and the *Devil's Bible* were revelations. She wondered if these had come to Fredric's attention before the Bible. She could see him looking in books like these to explain or refute things he had read in the Old or New Testaments. Then again, an outcast would certainly have been drawn to the stories of the fall of Satan. The Milton had a bookmark stuck in the front and the pages were clean. Fredric had not yet gotten to this one. She sat in the chair and drew the *Devil's Bible* under the light. According to the title page it was a reprint of an edition collected by the Dark Pope in the nineteenth century. There was no information about this individual. A name and date were written in faded fountain-pen ink: John Hamstead, 1938. Perhaps this was a recent eBay purchase. The edges of the paper were yellow-brown and quite brittle. She imagined Fredric turning them with respect and not impatience. He was not in a hurry like so many of his peers. At least, not externally. This volume suggested a far more aggressive internal life than she had imagined. She felt betrayed. She thought she had won his trust. She really wished Fredric had opened up to her. Perhaps he thought that this material went a little too far for their relationship.

Sara was alert as a car went by. She rose, listened. It stopped somewhere down the street. She sat and went back to the book.

The tome was a biography of the Devil in verse, the lines and sections numbered like the Bible, but backward. Interspersed with the narrative were quotes from Satan detailing the Eleven Earthly Commandments, the Unholy Trinity, and Delights of the Satanic Afterlife, and others. There was an appendix of Satanic symbols. She was willing to bet the triangle was there.

There was something else in the book. A section on spells for invoking the Devil and other demons.

Like the concordance, the *Devil's Bible* was dog-eared with writing in the margins. The notations were written in the same dark ink as the Strong's collection. Fredric had gone through this book making observations about words and meaning, context and logic vis-à-vis the Bible.

"Do not abstain from constructive delight," observed the first Earthly Commandment. In the margin beside it Fredric had written his own syllogism: *"Experience gives us knowledge. That means abstinence must perpetuate ignorance. Ignorance is what makes us fearful."* Then he wrote, *"God uses fear to gain followers"* but crossed out *"uses"* and wrote *"exploits."*

Sara moved the snake-decorated light closer as she turned the pages. The dark shape fell across the pages, no doubt as Fredric had intended. She read the young man's insights and questions, each of which were youthful but honest. She could hear Fredric saying many of them:

"Why is gratification a sin?"

"Can there be light without fire?"

And the one that intrigued her the most: *"The Sign is the original Internet."* The phrase was underlined in a big, thick block. Again, she suspected it was a reference to the triangle.

Sara was also intrigued by his handwriting, which she had rarely had a chance to examine. The script was tight and small, with none of the fascinating flourishes and designs he admired in the Persian rug in her office. Sara had taken a course in handwriting analysis at Yale. Fredric was accurately profiled in his penmanship: the loops instead of lines that connected many letters suggested confusion and indecisiveness; the low-crossed "t" signified a lack of self-esteem; and a loop in the stems of lower-case letters indicated paranoia: the bigger the loop the greater the desire for a buffer from watchful eyes. It struck Sara as sad and ironic that so much insecurity was hidden in such artful longhand, such beauty.

As Sara paged through the demonic volume something shone behind the laptop. She twisted the shade to shine light on it. The object was about the size of a lunchbox. It was made of dark wood with a little latch. The small aluminum plate must have been what caught her attention. The latch was secured by a small padlock, like the kind that secures a diary.

Sara slid the box forward. She felt uneasy as she looked it over. It was one thing to talk to a young man and elicit information. It was another to take it. This was something he didn't intend for anyone else to handle. It would bother him.

If he were here.

Sara turned it over slowly, respectfully. There were carvings of birds in flight on all sides. Underneath was a stick-on label from the local gift store. The box did not bear an imprint from the maker and there were metal screws instead of pegs, so it probably wasn't an antique. This might have been something Fredric purchased for himself, a place to keep valuables.

Sara shook it. There were a few smaller objects that rattled. They did not sound like coins.

Sara sat back. It would have been easy enough to pry the latch open but she didn't want to ruin the box. She believed she had a moral right to be in the room but not to destroy Fredric's property. There had to be a key somewhere nearby. Like the key to the padlock, Fredric liked to keep things private and close.

The desk was a lacquered wooden surface with no drawers. Sara did not see the key anywhere on top. She moved the books, the laptop, felt underneath the seat of the chair. She tried to imagine where Fredric would hide it. She looked in the stack of jewel cases where he stored his computer CDs.

Hidden, invisible, she thought. *Where?*

Away from the light.

Sara lifted the lamp. The golden key was sitting beneath the weighted base. She picked it up and slid it into the opening. It fit. She moved the box toward her.

No. Sara stopped.

"What are you doing?" Sara asked herself. "You could lose your license by doing this."

Going through the belongings of a minor patient, even a deceased one, without the permission of the parents was illegal. Trooper Brown was right. The Marashes might be inclined to press a malpractice suit for Fredric's suicide. If they did, unethical conduct would weigh strongly against her. So would a possible arrest for trespassing. There were other ways to get the information. Longer ways, but legal. If the Marashes wouldn't give her access to Fredric's belongings, state Social Services could make the request officially. In the event of a lawsuit the material could be subpoenaed. By comparing her notes with the young man's marginal notations they would see he had apparently been holding back a great deal.

But that was not her only concern. If he had belonged to some kind of cult, even online, there might be other young men and women involved. There might be a death pact. She owed it to them to find out.

Just the box and the book about the Devil, she thought. *That's all you need.*

Sara was already here. She might not have another chance. The Marashes never went in this room. If the material revealed anything important Sara could always say that Fredric had brought them to her to discuss in a future session.

She put the two items under her arm, removed the key, and put it in a zippered pouch in her handbag. She hesitated as she looked at the boxes containing the computer CDs.

Screw it.

She flipped through Fredric's storage media. Most of them were labeled "art." A few were labeled "blogs" and there was one that said "indexes." She put everything but the "art" in her bag, shut the light, and left the room.

The psychotherapist did not know much about the Devil. But as she hurried to her car she knew that if there was a hell for professional misconduct, she was well along that path.

Six

1

The night was very still and the air unreasonably—and unseasonably—cold as Sara returned to her car. Her footsteps sounded hollow on the asphalt of the driveway. Albert had not returned to the window. She was alone.

Except for Fredric.

Her patient, her friend, her neighbor, a dramatic fixture on the roads—Fredric was in every aspect of her thoughts as she drove home. Sara felt tight in the chest as her memories jockeyed between Fredric Marash as a young boy, as an adolescent, as a teenager, as a young man.

As a corpse.

Death had a way of redistributing time. The most recent Fredric was no more accessible than the earliest one, making her memories of him equal. The young man was also physically present in the things Sara had taken from his room. Unlike the intangible and timeless images that flipped through her mind, there was nothing unsettling about Fredric's belongings. That surprised her. It was probably because Sara did not feel as though she were robbing a tomb. To the contrary, she felt proactive. She hoped that by understanding the book and finding out what was in the box she would better understand what had happened tonight.

And that is my job, she reminded herself as an overactive conscience pricked her again. To understand, and then to use that knowledge to help others.

Sara turned onto River Road thinking how different her world was the last time she passed this way, just ninety or so minutes before. Death in the air of New England was rarely personal. Most of the time it touched the skin, scraping it without affecting the soul. As familiar reality returned, and her soul with it, Sara became more and more distressed.

I failed him, she thought.

Sara remembered Fredric riding down this street, darker than the night itself. More mysterious and unknown, at times. Her mission had been to understand his relationship with family and his interaction with peers. That was the job she had been hired to do by the State of Connecticut. Sex was something they had discussed very little. When she had flirted with the subject over the past few years he had seemed very embarrassed. He indicated that his father had talked to him about it and so had Mansfield Carr, the sixty-three-year-old general practitioner who treated virtually everyone in town. Like everyone else Sara talked to in Delwood, sex was regarded as a bestial act, the wilder practitioners best kept in a cage. Understanding Fredric's sexuality had not been part of her direct mandate from Social Services so she stayed away from it.

Besides, Fredric was not forthcoming about why he had a Bible. Getting him to open up about sex would have been far more difficult.

Unless I had brought in Chrissie Blair, she told herself as she pulled into her driveway. The school district would have screamed about Chrissie getting involved in Fredric's psychiatric care, especially involving sex. But what if that was what the young man had needed? To confront the guidance counselor with his feelings and work through them? That kind of crush was natural. It shouldn't have been kept in the dark, growing like mold beyond the boy's ability to control it.

So much of our own lives are out of our control.

Sara had realized that when her father was on his drunken rips and she was helpless to stop them. She didn't truly understand how little control of her life she had until she went to Yale. There, her own sexuality took command from her brain when she became romantically involved with Professor Martin Cayne. Her father taught her that it was possible to love hopelessly and steadfastly, regardless of the damage it did. Martin taught her it was possible to hate the same way. Sara learned something else from both of them, though for entirely different reasons: that blood holds people together in very permanent ways.

Sara parked and walked past the garage. The external world seemed strangely still and quiet here, but that had more to do with her own condition. Her heart was beating faster and her ears were throbbing with the rush of blood. Her chest was still heavier than usual, her stomach lighter. A little of it was an anxious reaction to what she had done in Fredric's room; and most of it was a classic reaction to grief. Sara didn't panic. She simply had to work through it.

She had neglected to turn the back light on before leaving. It was black by her office and she had to feel for the key to the door. It was between the front door key and the garage door key. As she ran the metal between her thumb and index finger she brushed the key ring. It felt striated, like one of Fredric's snakes. She touched it again, more purposefully, and it was smooth. It must have been a key she felt.

Her legs were weak from the hurried walk along the sloping dirt path. They trembled slightly, uncontrollably. So did her hands, a belated reaction to what she had done in the woods and then going through Fredric's belongings. She couldn't wait to sit down. In her own chair, in her own office, in a place where she had always enjoyed some measure of control.

Sara put the key in the lock. She could not hear the river but she could feel the woods off to the south of it. They were a sick, dreary hole. Like smoke from a bonfire the residue clung to her, influencing her thoughts and senses. She understood what was happening, a classic psychodramatic reaction. She was externalizing her internal psyche. Sara felt empty so the park became a personification of that feeling. This was a way people dealt with trauma and loss.

She stood there and let her arm drop. Her entire body began to shake and tears ran from the sides of her eyes. Sara put her left sleeve to her mouth to cover her sobs. She didn't want anyone to hear.

I'm sorry, she thought. *I'm so, so sorry.*

Fredric did not enter her mind until a moment after she said that. The realization caused her to start. What was she sorry about? Her father? What had happened back at Yale—?

Yes, that, she realized. Again.

She howled into her sleeve. The convulsions rocked her

hard as she stood on the old concrete step. If she didn't get inside she was going to fall. She turned the key and opened the door. She stumbled into the dark waiting room and dropped into one of the wing chairs. It was a chair where people waited for help, either with doubt or hope but knowing that there was a compassionate ear on the other side. Where was her analyst, her confessor? Sara had never sought comfort from anyone but Sister Grace. She had seen a psychotherapist for several months, back when her world had come unraveled. But Sara knew the dance. She saw the steps coming. Besides, she did not have a problem reaching detached, intellectual understanding. It was the animal side, the raging nonlogical desire to rebuild by destroying, that she could not overcome. Since she refused to give in, the best she could do was turn away from it.

And talk to Grace. Her friend was good at finding the acorns that had survived a forest fire.

She leaned on the armrest, put her face down, and cried into her sleeve. Like the faces of Fredric over the years, her own trials merged. They were all equally clear, equally painful, equally beyond reach.

After several minutes Sara managed to crawl from memories past and recent. She raised her head slowly, took a long, slow breath, and blinked out the last of her tears. She could not afford to let any of this become about her own failings. The task at hand was to gain understanding about what had happened to her patient.

The psychotherapist sat up and looked around the small room. The outside door was half open, the keys hanging low and still. She removed the ring and looked out at the bleak sky.

"If you're up there, Fredric, I'm sorry. And if God's within earshot, tell Him to go screw Himself for everything."

She shut the door and wiped her cheeks with her finger-tips. Then she went into the office itself and closed that door behind her.

2

Sara sat at her desk. She pulled the *Devil's Bible*, the box, and the CDs from her handbag and placed them before her. She retrieved the small key from the zippered pouch. She opened the lock and removed it.

Her handbag was still on her lap and she jumped when her cell phone chirped out Chopin's *Minute Waltz*. Sara fished out the phone and checked the number. It was Darrell.

"Hi," she said.

"Hey, sis. Is everything okay?"

"Why?"

"The volunteer FD picked up the dispatcher's call from the hospital—someone said you were on the scene of a hanging out at Huston."

"One of my patients," Sara told him.

"Damn. I'm sorry."

"How did you hear about it?"

"I'm at Sloppy Joe's. Simses is here."

Sloppy Joe's was one of the two taverns right off Route 6. Housepainter Mike Simses was one of Darrell's close drinking buddies. They often ended the night—and started the next day—sitting on the stoop of the Delwood FD.

"You need me to do anything, say anything?" Darrell asked.

"No thanks," she said. The last offer was sweet. By morning, everyone in town would know what had happened. This was the only chance they would have to spin the story.

"Well, if you change your mind, call," Darrell said. His

voice lowered conspiratorially. "Rowdy says you came by to see Franz Marash this evening. He's saying you didn't look stressed or anything, like you weren't worried. Should you have been?"

"Rowdy should stick to dismantling cars, not reading expressions," Sara said.

"I know. But he's shootin' shit anyway," Darrell told her.

"Was I right about his Bentley?" Sara asked.

"Huh?"

"Is it running?"

"Yeah, why?"

"Never mind," Sara said. His manhood was hurt, and he was taking it out on her. "Look, I appreciate the call. If I need anything I'll let you know."

"Okay. Take care."

"You too," she said and clicked off. As she put the phone down it beeped again. She answered it. "Yes, Darrell?"

The voice on the other end crackled and sputtered.

"You're breaking up," Sara said. She waited. She waited some more. "I still can't hear anything," she said.

"Hel . . ."

"I can't hear you," she said impatiently. "Try again outside the bar."

She was about to hang up when the voice came through again.

"Hel . . ."

The word was clearer this time but Sara still couldn't make out the voice. She looked at the display. It said Unknown Caller. She pressed it back to her ear.

"Who is this?" she asked.

The speaker was silent.

"*Hello?*" she yelled.

Sara looked at the display again. The call had ended. She pressed the directory. Not surprisingly, the number wasn't listed. Angrily, she highlighted her brother's number and phoned him.

"'Sup, sis?"

"Darrell, did one of the clowns at the bar call me?"

"*Huh?* No."

"Someone just did, the second I hung up with you. No caller ID. Are you sure it wasn't Rowdy or Mike?"

"They're standing here with me," Darrell said. "Did it sound like them? What did he say?"

"I think he said 'help,'" Sara told him.

"Not us," Darrell said. "It could've been a wrong number or maybe you didn't get the whole message."

"Possibly," she said. "All right, thanks. Sorry. Good night again."

"G'night," Darrell said.

Sara hung up. She checked to see if anyone had called while she was on the phone with Darrell. There were no calls, no saved messages. Her brother was probably right about it being a wrong number. A persecution complex was the natural evolution of a collapse in one's professional or social circle. Sara mustn't allow herself to succumb to that.

The psychotherapist sat for several moments before returning to the box. She took a breath and raised the hinged lid.

There were just two things inside. A large folded paper and a piece of thick red chalk. She removed the paper. She lifted one corner. It was onionskin, about four feet by four feet, and a design of some kind was drawn in black India ink. Pinholes had been punched along the design, four or five each inch. She took it over to the floor and opened the paper on the rug.

Sara shouldn't have been surprised to see the top of a large triangle in the first corner. She was curious to see where it led. She unfolded the paper and saw that it wasn't a triangle at all. It was one point of a star; a pentagram, a five-pointed star.

A symbol of the Devil, she seemed to recall.

She examined the five corners of the star. There was a faint outline of feet in one corner of the star.

That was what Fredric had been talking about, she thought. This must have been his corner, his sanctuary. *But from what?*

Sara was pleased with the discovery. Opening the box had already given her information she would never have figured out on her own. She got down on the rug and looked at the pinholes. She saw traces of chalk around the edges of each puncture except for the feet. Those were obviously drawn just for position. This was apparently a template, something from which to draw a pentagram elsewhere.

She went back to the desk and looked at the chalk. It was quite large. That suggested that he had not done very many transfers.

To where? The floor of his bedroom, she suspected, or perhaps a spot in the woods. That could be why he went there so often. But there was no dirt on the underside of the paper. Unless he used a boulder . . . ?

"What were you doing, Fredric?" she wondered aloud.

She went back to the desk and turned to the appendix of symbols in the *Devil's Bible*. There was a nearly two-page-long entry under the pentagram with two startling illustrations. There was a line drawing of a sexless human figure inside the star. Its arms were spread along the uppermost vertical line of the star putting the hands in the left and right points. Its legs were spread so that the feet were in the bottom two points.

The head was placed in the topmost triangle. The groin was dead-center. The caption read, "Celebrating the center of Existence."

Fredric had added an arrow that pointed down from the throat. It was drawn confidently, perhaps after he had experienced sexual excitement from his near-death hangings.

The second illustration showed the central pentagon formed by the bases of the triangles that formed the five points of the stars. A second pentagram fit neatly inside, and another inside of that one. The caption read, "The Infinite Miracle is revealed to all who enter."

Sara read the entry itself:

"The word 'pentagram' derives from the Greek *pente*, meaning five; and *gramma*, which is something written. Its origin is deeply and most profoundly rooted in the ancient astronomical observance of the pattern created by the planet Venus and its conjunctions with the Sun. Early astrological scientists ascribed to that design great powers over our lives in its magical operations. This was a truth divined from the close kinship of Venus and her glorious predecessor, Ishtar of Sumeria, the all-powerful goddess of love, fertility, and warfare.

"Early Hebrew mystics determined that the design possessed great significance because its points symbolized the truth and purity of the five books of the Pentateuch. The oldest Hebrew texts refer to the sacred geometry as 'Solomon's Seal,' a sign of inviolable truth.

"The Greeks honored the pentagram as the perfect expression of the ideal human being. With one point atop it signified the wisdom of man. With two points raised it signified the exposed womb of woman.

"The origins became secondary to the universal regard

of this symbol as a talisman of health and success. It was printed on coins in Roman Gaul, worn on sandals by holy Druids, and engraved in cornerstones of cathedrals to signify the ultimate expression of the Golden Ratio, the perfection that exists when a master shape is constructed in the same ratio as a smaller shape within, and again through each smaller rendition, linking one generation to another, in proportion and balance, through time.

"Yet the true nature of the pentagram is only partly expressed in these excerpts. The pentagram is the symbol of the choice that faces Man. When one point is ascendant, the pentagram is a symbol for the principle of docile submission to the will of the One. When two points are proudly ascendant, it represents the dual rays of the enlightened, the presence of the great Baphomet, the horned god."

Sara sat back. The author used historical and mathematical fact to establish a simple and somewhat simple-minded premise: two horns are better than one. The worship of the Devil was preferable to the worship of God. She could see a visually oriented young outsider like Fredric being caught up in the wonders of the pentagramic design and its interpretive nature.

She glanced at the paper on the floor. Yet it was also apparent that Fredric did more than read. He also wrote.

And he drew.

3

It was well past eleven P.M. when Sara put the book aside.

She had spent over an hour looking over Fredric's notes. That seemed like the place to start to seek an understanding of what role the Devil may have played in his recent life. Some of the most current notes, which bore a *September*

heading and were written on the blank rear flyleaf, were in-
spired after Fredric had encountered a Latin headline in the
text, *facilis descensus Averno*, which he had translated as *"the descent to hell is easy."* Beneath it was a list of indulgences that,
according to Fredric's notes, made a lot more sense than
turning the other cheek and the forms of self-denial it took
to get into heaven. Sexuality was one of them. He underlined
that as well. It obviously supported what he had discovered
on his own.

Yet there was also sweetness among the carnality and
aggression. At one point the young man had also written,
*"Avernus—a lake in southern Italy thought by Romans to be the
entrance to hell.* <u>*Need to visit.*</u>*"* At some later time he added,
*" 'Avernus' means 'Without a bird' because of the poisonous vapors.
Probably not an entrance. Must be some other way in. Also, a way
out for the birds."*

Sara wondered what birds he meant. That would have to
wait for another time.

Her eyes were growing tired. Before she went to bed,
however, Sara wanted to look at the computer disks. If Fredric
was one point of the pentagram there might be other young
people who were part of this.

Sara did not have all the software necessary to display the
data, though she was able to bring up several of the blogs and
chat rooms he had saved. Obviously, he visited more than just
the Goth sites. These were mostly conversations and postings
about which poster was a bigger jerk, interspersed with spells
and ingredients for spells, with an occasional digression into
philosophy. Though everyone had a screen name, she thought
she recognized Fredric's careful, somber manner in the few
postings of GOA2HEL. It took her a while to read the name as
he obviously intended: not only "go to hell" but "goat to hell,"

apparently a reference to Baphomet whom she discovered was the goat god. Most of his postings appeared in the room. There was one exchange in particular that Sara found revealing. It came from the HELOH! room the previous week:

HECATE21: U cant think he wuz together.
WALPURGUS: Goa2 iz nutz. DEM, u doin Gothfest n
     Philly?
DEMONELLA13: YePpeRz.
GOA2HEL: I think Jesus was heightened.
HECATE21: Yea up a cliff.
WALPURGUS: Jesus wuz hi.
GOA2HEL: Jesus was dehydrated. Deprivation causes focus.
DEMONELLA13: Toodles all.
WALPURGUS: Well fqq us :-P
GOTH2LUV: LMAO, WAL. SYL, DEM.
HECATE21: Wat u deprived of, GOA2?
WALPURGUS: Sex LOL.

Fredric—if it was Fredric—had signed off then. He obviously had nothing else to contribute to that particular discussion. Or rather, no one had anything to share with him. Not surprisingly, he did not participate in small talk. Sara wondered whether "WALPURGUS" knew something about Fredric's sex life or whether he or she was just "flaming" him online. Probably the latter. Sara did not imagine that Fredric would have discussed sex in a public forum.

Of the few disks Sara was able to access, none contained information about these or other individuals. Sara did not know whether they were local, though the reference to Philadelphia suggested that some of them might be in the Northeast. She did not know whether any of them were involved with Fredric beyond the chat room.

There was, however, one way to find out. Tired as she was, she slid her computer forward and created a screen name for herself. AVERNUSIAN wasn't taken and she grabbed it. She found GOTH4GOTH. The room was full and while she waited for a space to open she looked over the other names. HECATE21 was there and so was DEMONELLA13. While she waited, she checked to see whether Fredric had created a profile for his screen name. He had filled in none of the spaces. Behind an assumed name, he had succeeded in becoming virtually invisible.

As she waited, Sara was surprised to see someone slip in while she was checking the profile. Her heart slapped hard when she read the name: GOA2HEL.

That's not possible, she thought. The screen name was taken. No one else could use it unless they hacked into Fredric's account and why would they?

A space opened. She entered the chat room.

DEMONELLA13: Wb GOA2.
GOA2HEL: ty
HECATE21: Whered u go 2 GOA2? LOL
GOA2HEL: Just hanging.

No, Sara thought. She tried to instant message GOA2HEL. Her IMs were blocked. She tried someone else, HECATE21. Her IM was accepted.

AVERNUSIAN: I'm new here.
HECATE21: Create a profile fool.
AVERNUSIAN: I will. I just stopped by. A friend told me
    about the room.
HECATE21: Who?

Shit, Sara thought suddenly. People probably didn't use real names here.

AVERNUSIAN: I mean GOA2HELL.
HECATE21: brb

Sara watched as HECATE21 jumped back into the chat room conversation.

DEMONELLA13: U lofting SLASH?
SLASHAX: No. Spild hot joe.
DEMONELLA13: oWch.
HECATE21: Fred!
SLASHAX: Suin Star$$
DEMONELLA13: Whoz Fred?
GUYPIERCE: Skinny chik from ANGEL.
DEMONELLA13: LMAO. Flintstone.
HECATE21: Someone sez itz GOA2. Zat U GOA2?

Sara swore as GOA2HEL suddenly disappeared from both the chat room and from the online list.

GUYPIERCE: Blockin Aver. Must be a fed, LOL.
HECATE21: Me2, GP.

Damn, damn, damn, that was stupid! Sara thought. No one was going to talk to her, and as long as she was here no one would say anything.

Sara was angry at herself for trusting an anonymous kid— at least, she assumed it was a kid. The participants in these rooms all had porous egos, relying on each other for support. There was no way at least some members wouldn't have turned the question into a big beach ball to bounce around the arena. No wonder Fredric lurked more than he participated in these chats.

She searched for Fredric's screen name. It was listed as being offline. She had a feeling that whoever it had been was not coming back.

Sara went to the main menu and deleted her new screen name. She didn't want to receive e-mails from anyone who had been in the room, especially from whoever had assumed Fredric's screen name. And she was convinced that someone had. Like the phone call, somebody "out there" was messing with her. Maybe not someone at Sloppy Joe's bar but some other sick mind in this small town, someone with a lot of time and very little to do.

Sara walked from behind the desk, stretching. She stepped around the pentagram several times, eyeing the footprints. They were facing inward, toward infinity.

Or maybe not, she thought. *Maybe Fredric was looking from the bottom toward the upraised horns?*

Sara slipped off her shoes. She stood on the paper, which crinkled loudly. She shut her tired eyes. Exhausted and emotionally sapped, Sara wavered slightly as she stood on the pentagram. She saw in memory the old, dark tree. She saw Fredric hanging from it, pale and broken and so utterly helpless. She frowned but she did not look away. In her vision he opened his eyes.

"Why did you do it?" she asked him.

Suspended in air and time, the young man said nothing.

"Were you looking for a sexual thrill?"

No, she didn't believe that. Fredric had no way of knowing whether his father would reach him in time. Even if his neck hadn't broken, there was no way down from beneath the ten-foot-high branch of a tree. Besides, Fredric was fully dressed. The jump had not been about sex.

"What, then? What were you thinking?"

The only answer the psychotherapist received was the creaking of the branch, the howl of the banshee winds, and then the hum of her computer fan and the sound of the paper below as she adjusted her stance.

"Even in my own visions you won't talk to me," she said.

Sara opened her eyes. She jumped as, for a moment, the image of the dead young man in the woods seemed to linger in the real world.

Like the cell phone call and the chat room visitation, Fredric left quickly.

Invisible, just as he wished.

Seven

1

"You should have told me," Martha complained. "I'm your mother. I shouldn't have to find out from someone who isn't."

"Good morning, *Mother*," Sara replied.

Sara had just entered the sunlit dining room where a plate of dry toast, a sliced apple, and black coffee waited. She sat across the breakfast table from her mother as Martha Lynch fired a small but serious scowl at her. She had already eaten and was dressed in slacks and a sweater. Despite the sunshine it was a very cool morning. Tonia was getting Alexander dressed and ready for his Friday art lesson. The boy liked to draw and Tonia had arranged to have him study with a local illustrator.

"I assume you're talking about the incident in the park?" Sara said.

"I am."

"I'm sorry, but you know I don't discuss my work," Sara said. She took a swallow of coffee, then another. She was too tired and too upset to worry about how annoyed her mother was.

"This wasn't work," Martha insisted. "It was community. I shouldn't have had to hear about it from the newspaper delivery man."

"The delivery man? Is it in the paper?"

Martha nodded and pointed. The paper was on the table. Sara didn't want to look at it. She knew what had happened.

"What *can* you tell me that the rest of the town doesn't already know?" Martha asked.

"Not much, I'm sure," Sara said. She took a bite of apple. "Not the way this town gossips."

"I don't like that tone of voice," Martha said.

"Mom, one of my patients took his life last night," Sara said. "I didn't sleep very well. *That's* the tone of voice you hear."

Martha's expression remained set for a moment more, then it softened. "I'm sorry," she said. She glanced away, looking not quite ashamed of her remarks but somewhat repentant. "I truly am."

"Thank you," Sara said.

"It's just that—this is news that affects us, our family. I think I should have known about it," Martha said.

"It was late. I was upset."

"I could have helped," Martha said. "That troubles me too. Are you all right? Do you want to talk about it?"

"I'll be all right. I will need you to do something, though."

"Of course, dear."

"It's going to be a rough few days," Sara told her. "People

are going to say things, possibly do things out of grief or misunderstanding that will reflect badly on our family. I need—" Sara stopped and took a long sip of coffee. She gave help, she did not ask for it. Not even of her mother. "I need your support."

"Oh, honey, that goes without saying," Martha said sweetly. The woman frowned and asked in a half-curious, half-concerned tone, "Why? What might people say and do?"

"That I'm responsible for his death," Sara said.

"Responsible how?"

"Because I didn't prevent it."

"Neither did Goldwyn nor Franz Marash, his parents," Martha said. "Neither did his schoolteachers."

"I know."

"It's empty talk," Martha said. There was finality but concern in her voice.

Sara finished her coffee and went to the kitchen counter for more. She *had* spent a restless night, waking every hour or so in a half-conscious state, very clearly seeing either the tree and the young man or the pentagram and its infinite progression of pentagonal designs. She was not surprised by the vivid nature of the visions. She was what Dr. Arul of the Oxford-affiliated Kensington Laboratory of Anthropological Research once called "an objective self-explorer."

That was longhand for "no imagination."

It was all right, though. Sara could live with that. And when she met Arul she was definitely in a depressed state, looking for solid ground instead of another soaring Icarus-like run at the sun.

After graduating from Yale, Sara completed her studies in London. Part of that was the program offered by KLAR, part of that was the need to get away from New Haven and

Martin Cayne. One of her professors was Dr. Samir Arul, whose controversial papers she had much admired. The fifty-eight-year-old New Delhi–born psychotherapist specialized in what were popularly referred to as "past-life regressions." Arul did not believe these were necessarily views into the past but were genetically transmitted racial memories. His theory was that the "ego ideal" aspect of the self dressed general memories in specific, invented details to personalize them. It was the individual's way of rejecting the finite nature of the self and the soul and repudiating death.

The sweet and gentle Arul was considered a dangerous radical by many in the Hindu community to which he belonged. The psychotherapist regarded that as a backdoor proof of his theory: like Gandhi, he was a pacifist whom the establishment feared. People did not fear, he claimed, unless there was something legitimate *to* fear.

Sara was fascinated by the idea that very specific behavioral details of early humankind still resided in the human makeup. Many of these tendencies were revealed in detail by subjects under hypnosis. Men who identified themselves as heterosexual remembered being on lengthy hunts where there were only men for warmth and comfort. That closeness became imprinted on a cellular level. Musicians spoke about antediluvian settings where the earth spoke, such as echoing caves and lyric waterfalls. Victims of substance abuse recalled constant ice or cold, lonely peaks or shallow caves where there was no music or fellowship.

Sara herself underwent this "disconsciousing" process seven times. Within three sessions it had reached a point where she would "go under" just by hearing the soft, relaxing voice of Arul close to her ear. He had always said that it would be interesting to find out how readily Sara's children would one day succumb to the process, whether her responsiveness would be passed on genetically.

He had never said that with any of the other patients. She always wondered if he had been picking up on something about her body or soul.

What Sara discovered was that her subconscious did very little embellishing. Events from her own life came forth readily whereas memories of the communal past were extremely vague. Arul found this to be common in what he classified as "intellectual" rather than "artistic" individuals. Sara was pleased to hear that. She didn't like to think of her perceptions as being subject to whim.

Arul maintained that the only significant difference between visualizations during hypnosis and during sleep was the lack of a guide. He was not surprised that Sara's dreams tended to be relatively mundane and organized. The only time they "went off-recipe," as he described nightmares, was when death touched her life in some meaningful way. The control experiment had been a puppy he asked her to watch for two days and then lied about, telling her it had been attacked by a larger dog and killed. Her off-recipe dream that night was savage and red.

A nightmare that came from nowhere one night—no puppy, no bad news from home—was how Arul found out about New Haven.

Arul's assessment received a posthumous vindication. When he died in a car crash two years ago, Sara dreamed of him. He was a dove beset by black hawklike creatures. It was not subtle. Her nightmares never were.

Sara returned to the table. Her mother was looking at the wall, in her own thoughtful trance.

"I was thinking that we should write a letter to the

newspaper," Martha said. Concern had pushed the finality aside.

"Saying what?"

"Reminding people how you've helped this community and its children for ten years."

"We can't do that," Sara told her. "We can't identify my patients—"

"I wasn't going to name names, dear," she said.

"No," Sara said carefully, gently but firmly. "The support I want—what I *need*—is the opposite of that. We mustn't respond if people try to place blame."

"Well that doesn't seem fair, does it? To leave people free to say whatever they want while we can't speak up."

"Think of it as the high road," Sara said.

"I do. We have letters from my great-grandpa Amos saying how he used to shoot at Blues marching by on the low road. He always aimed at the leaders, knowing that the rest of the boys would probably go home—"

"But this isn't a civil war," Sara said, "and it doesn't need to become one. We have to handle this in a very private, low-key way."

Martha's lips grew tight. "I do not believe in passive resistance, dear."

"Then when you are attacked you may be as impassive as you want," Sara said. "This is my 'situation' and you need to let me handle it. Please."

Martha's face relaxed. She went from being engaged to becoming aloof. "All right," she said politely. "We will do it your way for now."

"Thank you," Sara said. She didn't like the "for now" part but—for now—she would take it. "What's on the schedule for today?"

"I'm having my teeth cleaned," Martha said. "At least I will look good when people make their indirect remarks and I simply smile back." She frowned. "No, that's not the word I want."

"Oblique?" Sara suggested.

"That's the one. Thank you, dear. You're so smart."

"Thank you."

"Just not always wise," Martha added.

Sara frowned. Her mother had set her up and bowled her over. Delwood was not the only front she'd be fighting on in this struggle.

Sara finished her breakfast and went to the office. She had a feeling what she would find there. She wasn't surprised, just disappointed. Out of five appointments for the day there were three cancellations. The three were high school students called in by Chrissie Blair. The guidance counselor's tone was unusually formal. She was obviously establishing professional distance from the psychotherapist. Her only comments about Fredric Marash were that she was sorry to hear the news and that she could be "available" if Sara wanted to talk about it. She left her home phone number. It was a thoughtful gesture.

Sara was disappointed that she wouldn't get to work with three teenagers who really needed someone to talk to. Basketball player Steve Rapp was struggling with issues of sexual aggression. He was a date-rape waiting to happen. Danny Michaels suffered from mild agoraphobia that was getting worse. And Suzi McIver was an obsessive-compulsive who couldn't leave for school each morning until she had made certain everything was perfect: all the faucets in the house shut, the burners turned off, even the ant traps facing the same way in every room.

Sara picked up the phone and called Chrissie's office number to thank her for the message. She was surprised when the guidance counselor answered. Chrissie said she couldn't talk. She was about to meet with Principal Harkness about grief counseling for students.

"Also, Dr. Lynch—" not "Sara," as usual—"after I made that offer to talk this over if you wanted, the school attorney informed me I shouldn't discuss the matter with anyone—including you. I'm sorry."

"That's all right," Sara said. At least Chrissie was being honest. "Will there be a memorial for the students?"

"Yes."

"Where and when?"

Chrissie hesitated.

"This is not about 'the matter,'" Sara said. "It's about showing respect for a patient who has died."

Chrissie hesitated a moment longer, then said, "The memorial will be at Sacred Heart Church at four."

"Today?"

"Yes," Chrissie said. "We wanted to have it quickly to help the kids with grief management."

Fredric would have hated being remembered by a priest in the house of God. But as Chrissie had said, this was for the community—not just to help them mourn but to shine a light on any potential copycats among Fredric's acquaintances.

"Thanks," Sara said. "I'll understand if you don't come over and say hello."

"I wouldn't do that," Chrissie said. "I won't let it become personal, though I can't guarantee the Marashes will feel that way."

"I don't expect them to," Sara said.

"Look, I've got to talk to the principal," Chrissie said. "I'll see you later and—good luck."

Sara thanked her.

The psychiatrist had decided not to tell Chrissie about the larger issues, including the pictures she'd found in Fredric's room. She could always say that Fredric had told her about them, but it might make the guidance counselor self-conscious and distract her from caring for students. If it turned out that other local teenagers were involved in Fredric's activities, either sexual or occult, Chrissie would need to focus on that— not on whether young men were masturbating to her likeness.

Besides, Sara did not want to get into a debate with Chrissie about whether that was normal and acceptable behavior. Sara wasn't sure herself. She was the last one to suggest that having a crush on a teacher was unusual or even avoidable. She also had to admit that such a relationship rarely, if ever, was entirely reciprocal.

With just one appointment later in the morning, Sara decided to return to the books and disks she had taken from Fredric's room.

The origins of his apparent asphyxiation activities seemed to come from a Website he found by following links from comic book artwork. He stumbled on the work of a cartoonist named Orpheus, some of whose work he had saved. She couldn't open the files but did an online search. The artist did line drawings of women in two kinds of jeopardy: gynophagia and asphyxiation. Being stripped and eaten or stripped and strangled. They were extreme examples of two kinds of fantasies, male domination and female submissiveness. Sara found it interesting that Fredric identified with the women and not the men. Perhaps asphyxiation was also his way of getting closer to the victimized sons he had read about.

The dates on Fredric's files suggested that the Orpheus

site drove him to seek out links about torture in history. From there he went to the persecution of witches, and from that point it was a short step into researching the Devil.

That was the way in. But it still didn't tell her why Fredric took his life, whether it was about sex or sacrifice or something else.

The pentagram he had drawn was still spread on the floor. She went back to it. The scarcity of chalk dust and the crispness of the folds reinforced the idea that he had not used the pin-pricked template more than once or twice. That meant the design was either permanently cut or painted somewhere, or it had been a very recent development in his life. The floor of Fredric's bedroom was carpeted so he probably didn't use the template there. Is that why he went to the woods—in the dark, when a hiker would not see what he was doing?

Sara opened the *Devil's Bible* and went through it slowly. It was clear that he had not turned to the book for information alone but for empowerment. He had made a point of referring to the pentagram as *"the original Internet."*

She stopped at a passage late in the text, one that seemed to address that aspect of the question. It was in a section called the Ritual of the Symbol:

"Extinguish the light and embrace those who share your passions. As you turn in, O Acolyte, so do you turn out."

Sara did not know what the editor/interpreter meant by "the light." Did that mean the practitioner had to divest himself of brightness, the belief in God, or life itself? But she believed she understood the rest.

Facing inward placed Fredric in a position to look out along the symbolic horns of Baphomet the goat god—which, according to the text, was simply another facet of Satan in the way that Jesus was a face of God. Perhaps Fredric did this, stood within the symbol, at the same time as others. It could be that these individuals were present at the same time and place, or they could be spiritual companions who stepped inside their own pentagrams.

The original Internet.

Stepping into the triangle of the pentagram could also have been the first step of a self-induced trance. She herself had felt that the night before when she was tired and extremely distraught, all of her guards way down. Dr. Arul had his patients lie on a small rug on the floor, what he half jokingly referred to as his "magic carpet." He did that to help condition the patient and so that he could kneel beside them, on a pillow, and be above them. If that was the case with Fredric, there were probably recitations as part of the ritual.

Sara read through more of the Ritual of the Symbol. As she suspected, it was a graduated process of detachment. Several lines were spoken aloud, then one was recited in silence. Several more lines were spoken, then two were said in silence. The process continued until the entire incantation was silent and the acolyte was entranced. But to what end?

Apparently, that would depend upon the particular ritual that was being spoken, she realized as she continued turning pages. According to the verse headings in the section called the Book of Dagon there were rituals for Sexual Desire, Wealth or Position, Youth and Potency, and Revenge. Within the verses were variants that permitted greater specificity. It was followed by a section called the Book of Baal that contained just one ritual: the Summoning of Satan, the Devil.

Sara went to the glossary and looked up both Dagon and Baal. There was a long history reaching back to the early days of the Hebrews and their contemporaries. Dagon was a half man, half fish, the chief god of the ancient Philistines of Goliath and later the Phoenicians. He was considered an equal to Baphomet who, according to the glossary, was the demonic protector of the Knights Templar, the twelfth-century Christian warriors who asked for his help defending God and pilgrims against the heathens.

"The enemy of my enemy is my ally," Sara said.

Baal was an early fertility god, later a chief god of tribal leaders who were identified with the Old Testament patriarchs. Over time, the attributes of Baal were subsumed by the being known as Satan.

The definitions cross-referenced these three as the Unholy Triumvir, with Baal-Satan on top. Sara wondered if this could have been the triangle to which Fredric had been referring. He felt he was protected by these supreme demonic deities in his section of the pentagram.

The bulk of the book was not about spells and commandments. It was a treatise, with occasional prose strains—ostensibly quotes from the Devil—called the Satanic Scripture. It was a history and philosophy of the Devil and his leading demons and a defense of those who worship him. Sara continued to skim what amounted to shrill if at times poetically written spin-doctoring on the value of pleasure versus the pointlessness of abstinence.

"Who desires to be at the side of Jehovah, where chastity and virtue are celebrated like water over wine?"

The only part that chilled her a little was a section about the Dark Pope, a figure who is elected in secret by the Coven of Magi—thirteen leading warlocks from around the world.

"The term derives from the Greek *pappas* for father and it was appropriated by early Christians as a means of seducing contented members of our flock; of drawing them from the endless pleasures of the dark to a leader clothed in the blinding gold and white of empty light."

The identity of this leader, as well as the times and places of the convocations and the issuance of papal "decrees-absolute" are known only to the Magi. Though the book was a century old, Sara suspected that the tradition continued to this day. The vote occurs whenever the Dark Pope is "called to Satan's throne" and, if the text was to be believed, has been taking place since three thousand years before the birth of Jesus. The requisites for becoming the Dark Pope included—three *again*—"S's: subscription to the dogma, submission to the will of Satan, and surrender to the eternity from which Satan will resurrect the acolyte."

Fredric had been pursuing at least two of those when he most definitely undertook the third.

The office phone beeped. Sara picked it up without looking away from the text.

"This is Dr. Lynch."

"We don't want you there," the caller said.

Sara sat up straight. "Mr. Marash?"

"We don't want you at our son's memorial," he said. "Do you understand?"

Sara said nothing. In the background she heard what she assumed was Goldwyn Marash wailing.

"You incompetent, bumbling so-called doctor," Franz went on. "You told me there was nothing to worry about. You stood in my shop and you figured out how to fix Rowdy Brown's car but you didn't know how to fix our son."

"Mr. Marash, I'm sorry for your loss. But it isn't what you think."

"You don't *know* what I think," the man barked. "I think you need to stay away from our son, from us, and from the church. We don't want people standing around pointing at the killer. This is Fredric's day, not yours."

"I did not kill your son." Sara wasn't going to take this. She just wasn't.

"You didn't do your job, which was to anticipate it and *prevent* it!" he snarled. "Go to hell, Doctor, and stay there."

Franz hung up.

Sara replaced the phone slowly. Her arm was trembling, her heart racing. She was angry but she was also sad. It was bad enough she couldn't see her patients today, young people in whose lives she was intimately involved. Now she was being labeled a town pariah. She had no intention of hiding from Delwood or her own actions. The phone beeped again and she scooped it up.

"This is Dr. Lynch."

"Doctor, this is Vic Biday with the Delwood *News-Hour*. How are you this morning?"

"Mr. Biday, I have no comment," she said and went to hang up.

"Doctor, we'd like to offer you four weeks of home delivery—"

"Excuse me?"

"Four weeks of all the local and state news, delivered by seven A.M. each morning, for just forty cents a day."

Sara laughed. Sometimes a persecution complex was just that.

"Mr. Biday, thanks for the smile."

"Pardon?"

"We already receive your paper. Martha Lynch is the subscriber."

"Then you know us. Perhaps the *News-Hour* is something you'd like to offer patients in the waiting room—"

"They prefer *Redbook* and *Sports Illustrated*, though I suspect the adults secretly read *Highlights* for 'Goofus and Gallant.' But thank you."

Sara hung up with Mr. Biday's voice fading as his pitch went on. She put away Fredric's books and the pentagram shortly before Barri Neville arrived for her ten-thirty appointment. Sara was sad to be putting the things away. It wasn't just the guilt-edged need of trying to figure out why Fredric had taken his life. There was something dangerous about the materials, something that challenged her skills and scholarship. The last line she had read stuck with her as she placed the objects in her desk:

> The Talisman of Power is the intangible Knowledge and Desire that are bred from us. Children intuitively sense His Satanic Majesty in the Dark. Adults lie and say there is nothing there. They seek the light from fear, not loyalty to the Empty Lord.

2

The thirty-two-year-old mother of two arrived looking unusually depressed. She was still dressed in her supermarket uniform. Her long brown hair, usually worn free, was tied in a tight ponytail. She was not wearing makeup. She was chewing gum. Her long doe neck was leaned forward, her big eyes sad.

"Good morning," she said as she shuffled toward the chair.

"Good morning." Sara sat across from her, half expecting to be asked about Fredric. If Barri had heard about it—and apparently everyone had—his death would have spoken to the woman's guilty feelings of anger about having her own children indoors more during the cold weather.

"I envied her," the woman said and immediately began to cry. She did not just tear up but became hysterical.

"Who?" Sara asked. The tissues were still by the chair where Fredric had left them.

"Goldwyn Marash. God forgive my sins, I wish that had been me."

Sara eased over, pulled out several tissues, and handed them to the woman. Barri crushed them in her fist.

"Tell me it's not wrong to want my life the way it was," the woman wailed. "Tell me I'm not evil."

"Evil is sometimes relative, and honesty is the key to this process," Sara replied. "This is not about your children, it's about your sense of feeling trapped—"

"I want my children *gone*!" Barri screamed. "Is that honest enough?"

"If it's what you're feeling, yes," Sara said.

"Jesus!" Barri wailed. She dug her carefully manicured nails into the tissues. "I turned on the radio and heard about the student who hanged himself and I felt *envy*. Can you believe that?"

"Do you still feel that way, at this moment?"

"I don't know," she said, sobbing. "I feel guilty now—it's so confusing."

Barri continued to cry. As she did, something occurred to Sara. She discreetly made a note in her book. Sara did not believe in the occult as such. But she wondered if it were possible for a negative ethos to invade a small, tight community. The psychotherapist had seen Delwood react to shocking national and international events, and to local tragedies like car crashes and fires. She had treated people who had trouble dealing with these things. They all had similar feelings of helplessness and rage, and in every case there was a sense of the community pulling together. She wondered whether Fredric had triggered—or possibly even succumbed to—a new, more virulent strain of the mid-October "Delwood depression."

Possible, she wrote. *If so, caused by what and affecting whom?*

Barri had begun to calm.

"Would you like some water?" Sara asked. She kept bottles in a mini-refrigerator in the corner behind her desk.

"No thank you."

"There's no reason to be ashamed about anything you feel, even something that seems extreme," Sara told her.

"Doctor, this doesn't *seem* extreme. It is extreme."

"As I said, the expression may be radical but the emotion behind it is not," Sara said. "The frustration you feel is the foundation. That's what we've been chipping at. You were pregnant very young. The father left and never came back. Jess married you and adopted Lizzie. You put off your dream of going to college and becoming a fashion designer. There are a lot of disappointments and upset in there, and you're transferring it all to the end result: Lizzie and now Petey. That's normal, Barri."

"It doesn't feel normal. I don't *hate* my children."

"You feel stifled, which is different," Sara said. She pointed to the woman's forehead. "It's a dark maze up there, Barri. For all of us. We see a light and move toward it. But we mustn't fixate on that light as if it were one big, shining truth. There are other truths, smaller ones that we can't see because of the light. Some of those truths are even more important."

The room was very still. The shades to the waiting room were drawn. The muted overhead light created a soft yellowish glow. A space heater in the corner created a comfortable, intentionally sedative effect. People who were cold tended to be more distracted and inhibited than people who were drowsily warm.

Barri stopped crying. She took a long, almost gasping breath and tried to smile but her mouth didn't quite get there. It rippled in the center. Then, suddenly, her mouth sagged sharply to the left. It dragged the right side of her face with it.

"Barri?"

There was nothing about epilepsy in the woman's file. Sara watched as her head tilted hard to the left, then jumped to the patient's side.

"Barri!"

She grabbed Barri's shoulders to turn her around. The woman's big frightened eyes looked up at her.

"Barri, what's wrong?"

The woman began to wheeze. Barri Neville wasn't asthmatic either so it had to be something else. Sara suddenly remembered that she had been chewing gum. The psychiatrist pushed hard on the sides of Barri's cheek with the fingers of her left hand to force her mouth open. Then she stuck two fingers of her right hand into the woman's mouth. If she couldn't reach it from here she would execute the Heimlich Maneuver—

The woman gagged from Sara's probing. The gum was under her tongue. She pushed the doctor back.

"*What are you doing?*" Barri screamed.

"You were choking."

"You're crazy! I was trying not to cry!" Barri shouted. "Jesus! *Jesus!*" The woman spit repeatedly into the tissues.

"I'm sorry," Sara said, backing away.

"You're sorry? You're out of control!" Barri shouted as she stood.

"You looked like you were in distress," Sara told her. "Please sit down. It was a mistake, that's all."

Barri grabbed more tissues and spit again. "I'll take that water, now."

The rest of the session was exceptional. Once the indignation and shock of the assault had passed, the fact that Barri had been treated like a choking youngster created an almost child-like submissiveness in her, almost like a waking regression. Sara was not an advocate of shock therapies but Barri listened very attentively to the likelihood that she was transferring her own disappointments to her children. The young woman left with an expressed desire to be very, very gentle with them.

Sara also realized she was going to be very gentle with her-self. Not everyone who turned away or grimaced was choking—or hanging. She also had to get over the idea, begin-ning to take shape, that maybe she had been a little hasty giv-ing up her Catholic faith in high school. It was an epiphany, in church of all places. She realized that her family kept giving without ever receiving. Money went into the plate, confessions went out to the priest, prayers went up to God, and nothing ever came back, nothing changed. Sara clearly remembered a day when she was sixteen years old and knelt in the pew, her fingers tightly knit, her eyes shut, petitioning for that which she wanted most: for her father, one of God's most loyal de-fenders, to stop drinking. It was a simple request, denied.

Sara talked to old Father Colgan at the time, asking if there was anything she had done wrong.

"Sara, it is not our place to test God by expecting a divine boon every time we request one," he told her.

She had replied boldly, "I only want this and it isn't even for me."

"Jesus himself asked for one thing, which was that the cup of suffering pass him by," the priest replied with a stern smile. "He didn't get that. Do you expect more than Jesus?"

"Jesus asked for himself. I'm asking for my father," she replied.

"As Our Lady at Lourdes said, 'I cannot promise you happiness in this life, only the next.' Child, we are in enemy territory. In the Garden of Eden we told God that we did not want His help and protection. This world is the domain of the Devil and we must struggle through it as best we can."

Sara didn't accept that. It was why she became a psychotherapist.

Robert Lynch continued to drink from his cup of suffering, the family struggled, and Sara left for college the day after she graduated from high school. Student housing wasn't opened and she moved into a Bridgeport apartment with three girls who were looking for a roommate for the summer. She didn't ask her parents for help. She worked days at Burger King and nights at a hot dog restaurant called Lums to pay her bills. When school began Sara's student loan covered most of her expenses. Lums covered the rest, plus meals. She never went to church again, not even with Grace at Yale. She never ate a hot dog again either.

Sara remembered Colgan's remarks as she opened the *Devil's Bible* again. She stopped at the frontispiece where there was an etching of the serpent that was on the cover. It showed the large, trident-tongued snake of Eden wrapped dramatically around Adam and Eve. Eve seemed to be looking down at the script below her:

"Here Your Prayers Are Answered."

Sara didn't believe that. She suspected, though, that Fredric did. Maybe it was time to look at things through his eyes, through the eyes of Eve, instead of through her own. The objectivity that Dr. Arul had noted—though not necessarily admired, she had always sensed—was getting in the way.

She turned to the Book of Baal, to the Summoning. There were, perhaps predictably, thirteen steps a worshiper had to perform in order to call the Devil. As she had read before, some were spoken aloud, some were spoken in silence. One of the steps was the uttering of the seventy-nine "Maledictive Names" which went from Adramelech to Zacharius Black. These were the demonic components to the complete being that was the Devil.

"The lesser demons can be called for specific tasks suited to their individual natures," the text indicated in a footnote. It referred readers to the Book of Dagon for these spells. Sara found it interesting that unlike the Judeo-Christian God, the Devil was made up of different identities similar to the human psyche. That made him seem more plausible to her, at least in theory. It also fit with Dr. Arul's research about humans being comprised not just of tangible matter but of intangible pass-alongs collected somehow within that matter, perhaps in what was commonly referred to as "the soul."

There was also something in the text that struck her as very familiar: that once-summoned, the Devil could be brought back with a much, much shorter invocation. That was similar to the hypnotic technique used by Dr. Arul, making the individual more immediately receptive during ensuing sessions.

Sara read through the ritual itself. The leader, known as the Officiant, was to begin the ceremony dressed entirely in black—again, not a surprise. Fredric was always wearing black. The Officiant needed to secure an altar that, according to the text, was to be made of wood or stone, representing "the source of the apple through which his Majestic

Darkness saved mankind from an existence of perverted chastity, or the lodestone of guilt which God has set upon the human backbone." The altar had to be large enough to accommodate the pentagram, which was to be rendered in "a medium of sufficient size that the Officiant and any Prime Acolytes can stand within or set their hands upon it." All other worshipers were to be gathered in rows, kneeling behind the Officiant and Prime Acolytes. The eyes of all but the Officiant were to be shut.

"Which is the perfect way for a mesmeric outer or inner voice to influence them," Sara muttered.

The ritual could only be performed after sunset and it required that three items be present. First there must be two flames that are to be the sole source of illumination for the rite. "This signifies the insignificance of the singular will of God compared to the dual radii of Satan," Sara read. *It also allows you to see what the hell you're doing*, she thought. There were instructions as to where candles were to be set in order to represent the twin horns of the True All Powerful.

The second requisite item was a drop of the Officiant's blood, which was to be spilled by pinprick. "The bleeding reminds us of the pain that must precede joy in all things, from copulation to birth," the text said.

Finally, the ritual was best performed with a specimen harvested from a sycamore tree. According to the *Devil's Bible*, "The presence of the sycamore allows the Devil to return at his own discretion to aid the needy. It is a forceful repudiation of the divinity of Jesus, for it was in the branches of a sycamore that the tax collector Zaccheus climbed to see the entry of the sanctimonious pretender into Jerusalem, and thence take him into his home where Zaccheus was turned from his honest profession to that of Jehovanic acolyte."

It was also in the branches of a sycamore that Fredric hanged himself.

Sara read through the separate steps. Her first impression held: each step was designed to disassociate the individual from his or her surroundings. The graduated steps were similar to Dr. Arul's method of detaching his patients from the familiar so that they could free-float in their subconscious. Sara could see how a true believer—or someone like Fredric, who wanted an empowering rather than restrictive authority figure—would be drawn to Satanism. Through a form of hypnosis, it gave the illusion of actually working.

It was nearly noon and the psychotherapist left her office to get lunch. Tonia had prepared her chicken Caesar salad and left it on a tray with a Diet Coke. Sara filled a glass with ice and sat at the kitchen table to eat. She could hear her mother watching television upstairs and Tonia doing the laundry downstairs.

The exurban heaven and hell, Sara thought.

Giving in to a perverse, punishing narcissism—"If I screwed up I deserve to wallow in it"—she picked up the local newspaper. She read the advertisement-packed tabloid from back to front as she ate, mostly to catch up on the local news and opinion she missed by working at home. Starting at the end gave her the option of changing her mind and tossing the paper before she got to the front page.

It was worse than she had imagined. The account of Fredric's death was the page one headline. The article was written by Juan Patiz, a hotshot transplant from New Haven whose mandate from the newspaper syndicate was to expand readership. His willingness to pay for items for the local "Overheard at the Diner" gossip column and to send young reporters into schools and bars posing as students or underage drinkers had caused a stir when he arrived six months before.

The article was relatively accurate if sensational—Juan wrote that the chain left "an ugly bruise where the neck had viciously snapped"—but only mentioned Sara in passing, saying that Fredric was under her "state-ordered care." Because this was late, stop-the-presses news the only quotes in the article were from Trooper Brown, who was interviewed by phone at the morgue.

There was a photograph of Fredric from the previous year's Halloween party at the fire station. He was dressed in black—no turtleneck, no bruises—with a white line around his entire body. Sara remembered that costume. Every now and then he would lie down on the floor in a different position.

Perhaps prophetically, but certainly innocently, he was a crime scene.

The other major articles were about a disagreement among the selectmen over how to finance an expansion of the landfill, a ribbon cutting by the first selectman at the newly restored Cowhead Bridge, and an interview with the coach of the high school football team who was tasting a state championship this year.

Small-town news seemed both trivial and reassuring as she contemplated the text she had just been reading—

"Dr. Lynch?"

The soft male voice seemed to have come from behind her. Sara turned. She looked around the tiny kitchen with its antique maple cabinets, old porcelain sink, and double window that looked out on the freestanding garage. There was only the graying daylight coming through the windows.

"Darrell?" she said.

That was stupid. He wouldn't have called her "Dr. Lynch." The swinging door that led to the dining room was still. The side door that led to the driveway was shut. No one had come in. She went to the old answering machine wired to the house phone. There were no messages. The speaker on the phone was turned off. She lifted the receiver and got a dial tone. The voice did not come from there. She glanced at the radio that still sat on the counter where she used to lean and listen for word of snow-related school closings. It was off.

"Catch me?"

The soft voice was behind her again. The psychotherapist turned.

The kitchen was empty, which meant that someone was definitely playing a game with her. Maybe some idiot who read the account in the newspaper and thought it would be funny to harass her. Or it could be someone—Juan?—had hired to wind her up before the memorial service. Then he could legitimately write tomorrow's subhead using the words "badly shaken psychotherapist." In either case, they shouldn't be here, whoever that was and wherever they were.

Sara turned on the light, moved the chairs, looked under the table, then checked the halls leading to the study, the staircase, and her office. The only sounds she heard apart from the washer and dryer were Tonia humming to herself and the muted drone of the TV in her mother's room. Sara went out the kitchen door and walked along the side of the house. No one was there. She went back into the kitchen slamming the door hard and feeling angry rather than upset. She did not like having her private space or her downtime corrupted.

"*Proserpine ad portas,*" the voice said.

Sara turned a quick, full circle. Again, there was nothing but empty air.

Damn it, she thought. She did feel herself getting rattled now. She had been starting to believe that Darrell and his

drunk friends had come in during the night and hid a microphone somewhere. But she doubted that any of his drinking
buddies knew Latin. Sara had taken two semesters in college
so she could understand medical and pharmaceutical phrases.
She recognized "*ad portas,*" which meant "at the door."

She went back to the kitchen door and checked the jamb
for wires. There weren't any. She opened the door again,
looking along the outside for a microphone, a webcam, anything. She slammed it again and stood there, looking at the
driveway.

"What *is* all the noise?"

Sara spun. Her mother was standing in the swinging
door. The woman's face was a mixture of displeasure and
concern.

"Just me," Sara said.

"Doing what?" Martha said. She noticed that the chairs
had been pulled from the table. "Is there a mouse?"

"I think so," Sara said. "It's getting cold out."

"I'll have Tonia set out traps," Martha said.

As her mother spoke, Sara went to the counter and took a
pen and Post-it from the wicker basket beside the refrigerator.
She wrote the first word of the Latin expression phonetically.

"I'm going to get the mail," Martha said.

"When did it come?"

"About five minutes ago. Didn't you hear Mr. Fleer clomp-
ing on the patio?"

"No," Sara said. The porch was well to the right of the
kitchen window, directly below Martha's room. Sara wouldn't
necessarily have heard the carrier when he came to the letter
box. Perhaps he had made a side trip to the kitchen to tell Tonia or whoever that the mail was at the door.

In Latin.

"Sara dear, are you all right?" Martha asked, concern edging displeasure. "You look a little odd."

"I'm fine, Mother," Sara said. She returned to the table, took another bite of salad, and put it in the refrigerator.

"All right, then," Martha said, turning to go. "I'll get the mail and then talk to Tonia about those mousetraps. You have a good afternoon."

"You too."

Tears forced their way through. Sara held them back long enough for her mother to leave. Then she put her wrist against her mouth and bit back the sound of her sobs and tried to get control of herself. She didn't know whether the tears were for Fredric or for herself, not that it mattered. Things were off-balance. She needed to straighten them out. Deli owner Billy Roche would be here soon to talk about his latest loves. He needed attention. Mr. Fleer or the clown playing games in the kitchen did not.

As she left the kitchen, Sara heard a voice behind her say, "I'm still here."

"Fuck you," she said, holding her ears as she went to her office.

3

Sara had a few minutes before Billy arrived. She stopped in the hall powder room to wash her eyes and consider what had just happened.

All Sara knew for sure is that it wasn't Mr. Fleer telling her he'd brought their mail.

It was rare but not uncommon for people suffering from unusual emotional stress to hear voices. These could be comforting words or sounds or they could be angry ones, created by an unsettled conscience.

Imaginary voices were also a common symptom of the onset of schizophrenia, third-person auditory illusions appearing when an individual suddenly mistrusts their own judgments; or of multiple personality disorders, when different aspects of the individual's psyche are trying to be heard, often because of suppressed emotional trauma. Tragic though it was, Sara did not believe Fredric's death—*any* death or distant loss—would move her in the direction of a major psychological meltdown.

Of course, denial is also a significant marker in behavioral and mental distress, she reminded herself.

The psychotherapist refused to allow that this was happening to her. She had always been grounded and rational, even when she was hypnotized. She had to be grounded and rational until now.

The key words were "until now." She *did* hear a voice.

Sara went to her office and spent a little time looking up the different phonetic spellings of the Latin she heard or thought she heard or imagined. The closest she could come was the name Proserpine, the daughter of the Greek earth goddess Ceres and the unwilling wife of Pluto, Lord of the Dead. Pluto had abducted her to live in the underworld and subsequently made a deal with the heartbroken Ceres to allow the young woman to return to the earth for six months every year. While she was gone, Ceres mourned and the earth above was cold and barren.

Proserpine ad portas, Sara thought. *Proserpine is at the door.* It was an appropriate comment. Winter and cold were approaching, which applied to the here-and-now of Delwood. But it was also appropriate to the reading she had done over the past day, referring to an obscure mythological figure associated with one of the oldest names for the Devil. No one knew about her research. No one except her. No one else had ever used Latin in this house.

Except for Fredric, in his footnotes.

Sara closed the book and prepared for her session with Billy by reviewing last week's notes. But her heart and thoughts were on the improbability of what had happened in the kitchen. She listened to Billy talk about his latest might-be lover, the widowed owner of Hobbs Road Bed-and-Breakfast who asked him what kind of sausage he had for her. He took that as an overt come-on. Sara did not know Thomasina Hobbs very well. For all she knew the woman *had* been coming on to the long-married Billy. Before he blundered ahead, however, Sara wanted him to be aware of what he stood to lose personally, and of the ramifications of an affair, or even the suggestion of one, in a small town.

"It could destroy your marriage, your business, and your self-respect," she said. "We need to talk about those in turn."

"Before we do, think about this: it could bring other women into the open," the burly man pointed out optimistically. "Trust me, this town is a sexual pirate's chest, buried and waiting to be discovered. People are having affairs all over, and those are only the ones I personally know about. Which are a lot."

Sara could not disagree. She did, however, advise him to think carefully about what he was contemplating while he was out of reach of temptation. She suggested that the effort he put into trolling could be better used to mark out downtime with his wife. "I realize it's an old-fashioned idea, the idea of wooing your spouse, but you may discover that novelty is best explored with someone you know. And afterward, you've got something to talk about other than escape routes and how a long blond hair got stuck in your watch band."

Sara also counseled, half in jest, that he lock up the knives he used at the meat counter. The brunette Tammy Roche was not a forgiving soul.

Billy seemed to be hearing her. And she relaxed as the session progressed. The more the minutes piled distance upon the event in the kitchen, the more she was convinced that it never happened. Sara only thought she heard the voice, and the Latin phrase must have come from something she had read or skimmed or possibly even remembered from one of her classes.

It was one-thirty when Billy left. He seemed a little less burdened than when he arrived, as though discussing the fact that he was still attractive—discussing it with a woman—made it more real. Sara did not think he would act on what was essentially an active fantasy life. She hoped he didn't. If he had misread the sausage come-on, word of his wandering eye would spread as quickly as news of an affair—and with the same result.

Sara decided not to go right back to the *Devil's Bible*. If she were imagining voices she needed to get some reality into her head. Instead, Sara went to her room, got a sweater, and sat in the gazebo. She looked out at the river on this now-overcast afternoon, and listened to the sound of the dead sticks collecting in the inlet with their wet-sounding drumbeat. Against that backdrop she thought about the memorial service to come and about loss.

The death of Fredric Marash did not feel like the death of her father. Whether intentionally or not both of them had chosen the time and means of their exit. One quick and possibly accidental, the other prolonged and unplanned but no less inevitable. She thought about those deaths and she thought of Ceres turning a mother's sadness into death for countless others. Sara had studied death in school. Grief counseling was a required course and death was the major part of that. She was taught to explain how death was a stop on the wheel of life, and that where biology ended faith began. The counseling was not about logic, it was about selling snake oil. It was about getting a person through the loss by the most convenient means possible.

Yet death was more than the loss of a person.

She looked at the dead, water-logged twigs bobbing against the shore. Death was a pain from which people recovered to varying degrees and at different speeds. But it was also a light shined on the mourner's own limited time and dwindling options. It was a powerful reminder of opportunities seized, opportunities lost, and opportunities surrendered. Death wasn't sudden for Robert Lynch, Fredric Marash, or anyone else. It was a process. Yet the process was not always all-consuming. There were intangible aspects of life that refused to die, however much you wanted them to. Maybe those were the brands that ended up on our DNA, as Dr. Arul had speculated. The pain of Sara's colossally failed relationship with Martin Cayne was one of those. She sat here as she often did and relived the moments of decision: the youthful judgments, the romantic trust, the beautiful intimacy, and the pain of the ultimate rejection—an image of him and Stephanie Reynart she couldn't crush from her brain no matter how loud she screamed or how hard she cried, then and now.

Decisions. They never changed. They were out of reach, frozen in time. They were evil and immortal.

She had made hers after finding Martin and Stephanie together. It was a decision that made the breakup not just traumatic but vile.

Did Fredric make a decision? she wondered. Did he trust Satan without question? Did he hope with his heart open and eyes closed? Did he make a leap of faith in every sense of the word?

Sara did not want to cry. She shut her eyes and focused on the cool breeze that moved across her warm cheek. Somewhere in the distance, downriver, children were laughing. She knew just where they were, at the playground in the western corner of the park. Her father had helped to build some of the log swings and monkey bars and even a little frontier cabin.

She didn't want to go back to her own rutted memory but she couldn't help it. She continued to look for a way out that wasn't there.

A life controlled by a moment in that life, she thought sadly. A seed of despair that might survive when the rest of the fruit rotted away.

She could still feel herself walking toward the car parked at the New Haven train station. She thought it would be nice to meet her lover on his return from the Sleep Deprivation Seminar in Philadelphia. The Metroliner had been scheduled to pass through on the way to Boston at nine-twenty P.M. Even if it was late, she would not mind waiting. After seven months the relationship was still gloriously new and waiting was a good anticipation, not a bad one. Besides, she had something to tell him. She wanted to do that off-campus, away from distractions.

Sara had pulled up to the station at nine-ten, shortly before the Metro North commuter train from New York arrived. It was not the Metroliner. Martin should not have been on it. But he was. She saw him step onto the platform several cars from where she was standing. That was a surprise, but not half as much as seeing him get off with Stephanie. In her left hand was a Playbill for a matinee of *Cats*. In Martin's left hand was Stephanie's right hand. They didn't see her as they walked toward his car on the bottom level of the garage. The young graduate student followed them. The couple sat in the front of the car making out.

It was crushing enough that her lover was carrying on with Stephanie, and that they had gone to see *Cats*; he hated musicals. What made it worse was the fact that he had constructed an elaborate lie to cover it. And what made it devastating was that she never got to tell him what she needed to tell him.

Sara stood in the garage for an hour, long after Martin and Stephanie had driven away. Toward his house, not the student dorms.

Sara went back to her car feeling numb. She sat heavily behind the steering wheel and remained there as light crept along the concrete floors and columns of the open-air garage. Sara's roommates were accustomed to her staying at his home off-campus so they would not be concerned about her. There seemed to be no reason to drive anywhere. The future had stopped. There was just now. She tried to tell herself that the acting major was a fling, that there was nothing in Stephanie's head that had not been shoveled in there by Shakespeare and Albee. But she was also many things Sara could never be—tall, beautiful, and charismatic. The strawberry blonde didn't think very much, or very deeply, as Sara had discovered when she assisted Martin with the Introduction to Freud course. But Stephanie laughed contagiously and was fun to be around.

Obviously more so than Sara had thought.

It was sunrise before Sara left the car and shuffled to the old terminal building. It was a minute or two past six A.M. and it had just opened for the morning commuters. She asked the ticket seller for change and went to the pay phone. There was no booth, just the phone. There also weren't a lot of options. She wouldn't phone her parents. She didn't want condemnation from her father or mother, neither of whom could get their own lives right. Sara was friendly but not close with her roommates, and in lonely desperation she called Grace Rollins. The talk was brief because she didn't want the divinity student to come and sit with her, as Grace had offered. Right now, Sara couldn't bear even the gentlest I-warned-you lecture followed by the all-life-is-sacred sermon.

That left just one number. She had to look it up in her address book. After dialing it and plugging in the required amount she huddled against the wall, her back to the room, holding the phone to her mouth as though it were an oxygen mask.

The phone rang once, twice, three times. Finally, Darrell picked up. He had just moved from the Sticks to his own attic apartment off Main Street.

"H'lo?"

"Darrell? It's Sara."

It took her brother a moment to shake off his grogginess. "Sis? How are ya?"

Sara didn't answer. She couldn't. She had to cough to cover the sobs she couldn't keep down. Just hearing a familiar, caring voice caused her to let go.

"What time is it anyway?" Darrell asked.

"A little after six," she said, clearing her throat.

"Early," he said. "For me. Is everything okay?"

No, she thought. *It isn't.*

"Sis, are you all right?"

Sara took a long, deep breath to push back her sobs. She was tired too. The young woman wanted to close her eyes.

She wasn't thinking very clearly and needed immediate peace.

"I'm at the New Haven train station. Can you come and get me?" she asked.

He was silent for a moment. "I guess so—sure," he said. "Why? Talk to me?"

Christ, this is difficult. Asking for help, not allowing herself to get hysterical. She heard the squeaking brown door open and close behind her as commuters arrived. She hugged the wall beside the phone even tighter.

"I need you to come here. Can you do that?"

"To the train station?"

"Yes."

"Okay," he said. "It'll take about two hours, I guess."

"I know."

"Are you sure you don't need a doctor or something?"

If he only knew. "I'll be fine," Sara told him. "Just get here. Please."

"On the cordless phone and dressing as we speak," he told her. "Do you have money? Have you eaten?"

"Not yet. I will."

"Make sure you have solids, not just coffee."

"Okay," she promised and even managed a little laugh. That was a sweet sentiment which was something she needed.

Then she hung up, went to the ladies' room, and started to cry. She wanted this to be over. She wanted everything to be in the past.

And now it is, Sara thought as she sat in the gazebo looking at the steel-gray water. But it wasn't over. Perhaps it never would be. She wondered if that was something Fredric had intuited, that he was at a pretty good point in life and it might be wise to lock it in.

Sara's cheeks had dampened with tears for herself and for the young man. She brushed them away and smiled at the river just because it was there, steady and clear of purpose and managing to sparkle despite the clouds.

She had to do the same. One thing she had learned when she ran from Martin Cayne was that running from problems didn't make them go away. It was certainly less satisfying than breaking his skull would have been, but there was also a middle ground. And that was where she had to be now. Leaving the gazebo, Sara went back inside to put on a properly respectful outfit.

She had a memorial service to attend.

Eight

1

Sacred Heart Church was built in 1887. The regional landmark with its narrow hundred-foot-high spire was constructed by an elderly Italian architect who was a devotee of the Christian Romanesque style of the sixth century. The church and rectory to the north and behind it were constructed of light buff-colored stone with a cream ledge, Mankato stone trim, and a tile roof of charcoal-gray. The stone was a gift from a sister church in Minnesota, which the architect had constructed thirty-three years before. The spire was covered in the same rich gray. The two buildings were connected by an enclosed arcade, which was appreciated by the clerics and their guests during the bitter New England winter. The front entrance was dominated by a carving of the holy family with St. Joseph posed to the left of the infant Jesus who was in the arms of his holy mother, who was standing slightly to his right.

Inside, there were twenty ambulatory windows that illustrated the life of Jesus. He was portrayed in solid whites amid the myriad colors of the stained-glass tableau. The arch that led to the sanctuary was carved with the Latin phrase, *"Esto Fidelis Usque Ad Mortem Et Tibi Dabo Coronam Vitae"*: *"Be Thou Faithful Unto Me and I Will Give You the Crown of Life."* On either side of the arch were two painted murals, still vivid showing the view along the Via Dolorosa in the time of Jesus. Worshipers who passed them crossed a mosaic tile floor that lined the sanctuary and vestibule. The floor ended beneath a dome with a painting of the death of St. Peter. Illumination in the sanctuary was provided by stained-glass windows illustrating the seven Sacraments.

Sara had not been inside the church since the death of her father. She did not intend to enter today. She didn't want to cower but she didn't want to become the focus of the memorial either.

Sara walked up River Road. Parking was always difficult around the church during a service and she wanted to leave the spots to people who had come from the school. She turned onto Main Street thinking about how Grace would tell her to go in, that no one was an orphan in the presence of God. That His presence would calm and heal the others. But Sara wasn't buying pep-talk philosophy. Not from God, Grace, or their imaginary proxies in her own head.

Though it might not be a bad idea to talk to Grace about Fredric, Sara thought. She didn't feel guilty about his death but she didn't feel blameless, either. A psychotherapist who was oblivious to a big chunk of a patient's life had to have doubts about her perceptions, her methods.

Maybe she would call Grace in a day or two, when her thoughts and the shock had time to settle. She might even take a drive down to Yale and they would go to their favorite coffee shop, assuming it was still there and that the Catholic history professor and renowned biblical archaeologist was in town. A face-to-face visit was overdue. For years after the breakup with Martin, the college friends had exchanged Christmas and birthday cards but they had not gotten together nor spoken. Not until Robert Lynch died. Grace picked up her phone messages and came back early from a dig in Turkey. She came to the Sticks and stayed for several days, comforting Martha and Darrell and helping to make sure the church service and funeral were organized. She and Sara never spoke of Martin Cayne. He was still at Yale and still unmarried. Sara knew that from the alumni mailings, which she read with a blend of burning trepidation and renewable hate as she braced for his name or photograph. But that was all that she knew. Sara suspected that the miserable creature was still allowing students to seduce him, still letting them believe in futures that would never be, still believing in the droit du seigneur, the God-approved right of a lord to sleep with a vassal bride on her wedding night.

Sara and Grace were back to normal after that. They usually spoke every few weeks, and Grace took a drive through the country every spring and autumn. They usually met halfway at an inn for lunch or dinner. Sara had not even considered going to New Haven. Now, though, the pain of returning might be a good distraction.

The late-afternoon winds had picked up and blew crisp, dead leaves around her feet. She buttoned her knee-length black leather coat. The fringes of her scarf blew gently behind her, tugging lightly on her neck. It was an especially lonely walk because she wanted to be with the other mourners when she reached the church. She wanted to counsel them and share her heartfelt thoughts about Fredric as an artist, as an independent thinker, as dark lightning on his bicycle.

As the church spire came into view above the trees, she also wanted to turn back. Her presence was going to upset the Marashes. She didn't want to witness that, let alone be the cause of it.

But Sara also did not believe she was responsible for what happened. Given the information she lacked, she could not have anticipated or prevented Fredric's death. To stay home would suggest guilt and shame, culpability and incompetence. It would be dishonest to herself and to her patients. If she didn't believe in her judgment, no one else would.

There was no entirely satisfactory solution. When she forced herself to answer the phone in her office that morning, she knew intuitively that hiding was not a smart or constructive response. As she did in the woods, Sara shut her brain from her body. She let her feet take her up the hill to Main Street and the church.

It was just shy of three forty-five when Sara arrived. Pockets of people were gathered along the streets. The Marashes were not yet there. Sara went up the stairs and walked inside the church. She ignored the cold stares of the ushers at the door. She knew these men by sight but not by name. They were retirees, old New England, judgmental New England.

Full of strong and unshakeable opinions, just like this place, she thought as she stepped to one side and stood in the darkness of the nave. She remained for several minutes looking at the stained-glass windows. They were so much brighter on the inside than they seemed from without. They made even the scourging of Christ seem wonderful and radiant. She envied those who found comfort here. For her, it was a place of intense loneliness.

Sara went back outside.

A few teenagers were gathered on the stone steps out front with Chrissie Blair. Most of them were dressed in black, with facial piercings and hair colored red, green, or raven-black. The three young women wore pasty makeup and purple or black lipstick. Chrissie excused herself when she saw Sara approaching the steps. The guidance counselor looked solemn, more mature. Or maybe the romanticized images from Fredric's room had been dancing around the back of her mind, supplanting reality.

Principal Harkness arrived as Chrissie was walking over. He came in a van with several teachers. The principal waited while the others got out. Trooper Brown pulled up behind him. She was on-duty and got out to direct traffic.

Chrissie stood close to Sara. "Did Mr. Marash call you?"

"He did."

"I'm sorry about that," Chrissie said. "He asked what your plans were and I told him."

"It's all right."

Chrissie seemed uncomfortable. "Actually, it probably isn't," she said as the wind stirred her blond hair. A black kerchief kept it from her face and forehead. She leaned closer. "They're talking about suing the school and the state. Negligence against Litchfield County High, malpractice against you."

"There's no merit to it."

"That's not what Principal Harkness says."

"I've never cared what John Harkness said," Sara replied. "I'm not about to start now."

Principal Harkness walked over. He walked proudly, with a little swagger, carrying the weight of the moment like an injury-riddled quarterback heading to the fifty-yard line to receive the applause of a grateful stadium. He stepped behind the guidance counselor. He did not look mournful. He looked flat-out hostile.

"Ms. Blair, I hope you're discussing the weather," Harkness said.

Chrissie said nothing. At least she didn't say, "Yes, sir."

Harkness regarded Sara. "Our attorney has advised us not to discuss Mr. Marash the younger with anyone, but especially with you."

"A mute educator," Sara said. "Only in Delwood."

"Save it for the depositions," Harkness said.

"Have you had information about that?" Sara asked. She was annoyed with herself the moment she said it. She knew she appeared vulnerable, afraid.

"Not yet," Harkness said. "But sure as winter you can count on it coming, Dr. Lynch." He put a large hand on Chrissie's shoulder. When he turned, she was supposed to. Chrissie hesitated. The principal stopped and looked back at her angrily. "We have duties here, Ms. Blair."

Chrissie managed an encouraging smile. "Take care of yourself, Sara."

"Thanks."

Trailing a scowl, Harkness followed Chrissie as they joined the other teachers, students, and townspeople filing into the church.

Sara stood where they had left her, on the uneven sidewalk beside a parked car. She felt increasingly lonely as the street emptied. Being alone was not the same as being excluded, and being excluded was not as bad as being ostracized.

There was no sanity or justice in any of this, just anger and ignorance fueled by misinformation and misdirected emotion. Sara didn't blame the Marashes necessarily, but the hateful, punitive withdrawal anchored by Harkness was disturbing. Like the edifice that loomed before her it was like something from the Dark Ages.

With the crowd gone, Sara noticed that Fredric's bicycle was chained to the rack beside the church. She gasped when she saw it, her first involuntary thought being that he had ridden it here. Bouquets of flowers had been tucked into the spokes. Franz Marash must have brought it back from the woods. It was a silent but powerful tribute to their loss.

"I'm flying!"

Sara started and turned behind her. It was the voice again, clearer than it had been in the kitchen.

She listened intently as she looked in the closed window of the car, walked between the cars and looked behind them, glanced along the street. No one was anywhere around her.

The church doors were closed as the bells tolled four. No one was walking by, or in, and she had been looking at the steps and the bike when she heard the voice. No one had walked out.

"Who is here with me?" she asked quietly. Her eyes drifted up to the spire and she suddenly wondered—

No. That thought is absurd.

There was no response. Sara remained where she was. She felt very silly to be listening for no one, and a little scared. But she was also intrigued. She tried to collect all of herself into that objective, professional place.

The wind grew stronger as the sun descended. It brushed roughly by, as though resenting the impediment. The leaves sighed in the trees and whispered underfoot. Her objective, professional self reminded her that the onset of auditory delusions usually occurred at similar times and in roughly similar places. They did not typically happen twice in one day or in very different locales.

"Is anyone here?" she pressed as a car rushed along Route 6. It whooshed by and disappeared behind her, leaving the street once more deserted and quiet.

"Yes," the voice said a moment later.

The answer startled Sara. She willed herself forward, like the wind.

"Who?" she asked.

She waited, her eyes moving here and there. The world was a moldy gray. The only bright colors came from the windows of shops across the two-lane road and a traffic light off in the distance. The lights in the storefronts were pumpkin orange and lemon-yellow behind plate-glass windows.

"Who's here?" she repeated softly. "Please answer."

There was a sudden tug on Sara's scarf. She felt it tighten toward the back. The wind was blowing in the other direction, against her back. Sara hooked an index finger into the loop around front. She pulled the scarf and it came free. It must have been blown against the tree, snagged on a branch. That had to be it.

The skies had turned darker, the winds were gustier. Leaves from the church lawn rode their stems into the street like little soldiers, describing oval after oval until they fell and drifted.

"Poor souls," the voice said.

"Who are?" Sara asked. "The people in the church?"

"The dead, the ignored, the forgotten," said the voice. "They march into limbo, brittle and flame-red."

"The leaves," she said suddenly. "You mean the dead leaves."

Sara knew now that the voice was not in her head. The male voice was so close to the back of her neck that it caused a tickle where the scarf had been. But it was definitely not on the inside.

She waited for an answer, but the speaker was gone. She sensed it, a sudden relaxing in the air, a loss of an almost imperceptible electricity.

Sara put her scarf back around her neck.

Though the voice was male, it had been a loud, breathy whisper. There was nothing familiar about it. Yet there was only one voice she could imagine it to be. Fredric. If that were so, either she was losing it or he was here as a spirit.

Invisible, as he always wished to be.

Had Fredric's research into the occult shown him a way to make his wish possible? Had the teenager found a way to become spirit and still move among the living?

Or was this just her own form of post-traumatic stress?

Sara decided to go. She had demonstrated her concern— and a little defiant innocence—by coming here. Anything more would be cruelty to the Marashes and to herself. She started to walk back toward River Road. Like her experience in the kitchen, the exchange now seemed more dreamlike than experienced, more imagined than remembered. But this much was true of self-delusions. If the speaker had been in Sara's head he would have given her answers, even if they were false. Imaginary voices do not posit questions or present riddles. Moreover, they tend to stay around for conversation. That is the reason they are generated by the subconscious. To illuminate thoughts, not throw more shadow.

Sara turned down her street. The familiar contours of the river loomed ahead. She was usually too busy or too preoccupied to notice. At the moment she felt comforted by that. Unlike the church, unlike the street filled with unwelcoming faces, Sara felt like she belonged here. The Sticks had always been a foundation from which she set out, whether it was to walk to the library as a child or to seek an education and a new life. It had also been a haven when she needed it. It was the place to which Darrell had brought her to recover.

She would take a little time to recover again. And then, after dinner, she would start on a new journey. One that she hoped would provide answers to a growing number of questions.

2

Like the rest of Delwood, like New England, the office of Dr. Sara Lynch, Ph.D., was dead—predictably but uncharacteristically.

On most days there were hourly calls from distraught patients, prospective patients, and patients who needed to change appointments. After a session there were always a collection of messages from guidance counselors or child welfare officers, teachers and officers of the law. Today there was just a message from Juan Patiz requesting an interview. She did not return the call.

Sara was neither surprised nor concerned to find her office so quiet. The town had its instant, uninformed thoughts about what she did or didn't do to help Fredric Marash. When they learned the truth, they would change their minds. The key was to find and deliver that truth.

Sara checked on her mother, who was napping, then went to the kitchen and picked on an early dinner from leftovers. Tonia was there baking a cherry pie. She offered to make something but Sara was happy with cold sesame chicken and broccoli salad from a few days before. She told Tonia she would be working and did not want to be disturbed.

"How was his art class?" Sara asked.

"Very nice, thank you, Tonia said. "He drew pictures—I think they were the fireworks we saw this summer. Very colorful."

"I'd love to see them later. I was wondering—does Alexander have any chalk?"

"He has white chalk for his little blackboard," Tonia told her. "Would you like some?"

"Please," Sara said.

Tonia went to the boy's room to get some. Sara did not want to use the chalk that had been in Fredric's box. Dr. Arul used to call what she was doing "a counterpush." During hypnosis, a guide could test the depth of a subject's trance by introducing something foreign to the moment. For example, if a subject was discussing medieval memories he or she should not recognize a battery or a pen. If they did, they were not committed and the results of the session would be unreliable. It was a valuable and important test. Conversely, one thing the hypnotist would never do was show them something of the period, such as an iron spike or a canvas sack. They were called "inducements." Even a drowsy conscious mind would know what those were and might use them as springboards for fantasies instead of memories. Inducements did not prove that the hypnotist had accessed the subconscious.

Sara was going to use Fredric's stencil. If it had any validity as a spiritual artifact, it should work regardless of the chalk. If she used Fredric's chalk, that might only serve to push a conscious mind that was apparently open to suggestion.

Tonia returned with a stick of thick white chalk. "I forgot to ask if you will need the chalkboard," Tonia said.

"No. I just need to mark out some measurements in my office."

"You are redecorating?" the housekeeper asked hopefully. "If so I would be very pleased to help."

"I'm just thinking of rearranging some things, that's all," Sara said with a smile.

Tonia made an "oh, well" face. Then she smiled. "Alexander was very cute. He asked if you were going to draw on the trees in the park."

Sara's neck went cold. "Why would he think that?"

"We see designs sometimes when we walk there," Tonia said.

"Oh? Where?"

"Off the hiking path at Yankee Dam," Tonia said. "We sometimes sit there to draw pictures of the birds in trees. He likes the crows and ravens. We see—what do you call them?" she asked and made a triangle with her fingers.

The shape caused Sara to start. "Figures?" she said. "Geometric figures."

"Yes. Geometric figures on some of the trees and on the rocks."

The chill spread through Sara's body. "How long have they been there?"

"Not long," Tonia said. "Just a few weeks."

She forced herself to smile. "Well, I'm not going to draw on the trees and rocks," Sara said. "They're so pretty the way they are."

"Oh, yes," Tonia said. "I am so grateful to be here."

Sara told Tonia to thank Alexander again, then went to her office. Markings in the woods. It could be nothing. Or it could be something significant, something she missed in the darkness the night before.

Sara kept a change of clothes in the closet. She put on jeans, rain boots, and a heavy sweater. Then she took the big, waterproof flashlight from the shelf. She kept it there for Delwood's not infrequent winter power failures.

It was odd. Dr. Arul once warned her to pack emotionally for the long journeys on which patients sometimes took them.

Sara always picked her way carefully with new patients, until her notebook was filled with data to help her take different routes, new chances. But no one, including Dr. Arul, had ever suggested there would be physical journeys. Perhaps they were missing an important area of treatment. Like forest conservationists, maybe they should also make clandestine observations of patients in their natural habitat.

Sara went out the back door of her office.

The river spun off several creeks through the length of the park. Yankee Dam was a small concrete barrier on the largest of these. It prevented flooding during heavy rains by creating a steady flow into the park. Built in 1966, it generated a twenty-five-foot waterfall onto tiered rocks along its face. The dam was one of the top tourist destinations in the region. It was the inspiration for the "I'll Be Dammed!" newspaper ads that ran briefly during the previous summer. Local conservatives found the theme objectionable and the campaign was quickly pulled.

The dam was almost directly west of the Sticks. Sara walked to the inlet and pulled Darrell's old rowboat into the water. It went in smoothly with a sloshing sound caused by the damp, rotted leaves that had collected around it. The river was still calm and the crossing itself would not be difficult. She would have to take her time returning. The early dark of autumn was descending, deepened by the cloud cover.

Sara stepped into the back of the boat. She lay the flashlight between her feet and picked up the paddle. She pushed off from the black mud of the shore and moved across with slow, alternating strokes.

She remembered playing on the river as a child. Her father sometimes took her out in this same rowboat, showed her, and later Darrell, how to "feel" the river. He taught them how to read the currents with the bottoms of her feet.

"You'll feel a little push as it rolls under," he told her. Sara was sitting in front of him that time, on the floor of the rowboat between his legs. He gave her shoulder a very gentle nudge. "If it's anything stronger than that then the river doesn't want you here. Pull over, tie your boat to shore, and walk home."

Sara had to be four or five years old and it was the first time she thought of water as a living thing. Since then, even when everything else was withering and dying from age or season, the river always seemed alive. It was sometimes cross, sometimes calm, sometimes bright, and sometimes gray. It was not always her friend but it was always her companion. And a damn—not to mention dammed—fine listener.

Sara felt a welcome hint of contentment as she crossed. The house was home but the river was Home. Unlike the rooms with their soft but ever-present echoes of unhappy times past, the good memories were still collected in the inlet while the bad ones were carried to sea.

The current bore her slightly southward. She came ashore on rocks at the foot of a deeply angled ledge. The slope was roughly in a line with the sycamore from which Fredric had hanged himself. The dam was to the north of that, to Sara's right. She climbed the thirty-odd-foot slope, wishing that she had brought gardening gloves. The ground was mushy and cool, but the exposed roots made climbing relatively easy. When she reached the top she was about one hundred yards north of the sycamore. She doubled back to look at the area in the fast-fading daylight.

It was difficult to look at the tree. Cadaver gray in the dim light, the sycamore was ugly, flat, and uninviting. Fredric had demonized it the night before. Now it was simply dead, with dying leaves that hung like curled and sleeping bats. She walked onto the rise where it stood, ducked under the crime-scene tape, and looked for markings. She kicked away fallen leaves and looked over the ground and the surrounding rocks. There was nothing written in chalk and nothing scratched in the wood.

Sara was about to continue into the park when she looked up at the branch from which Fredric had hanged himself. She needed to confront it, if just for a moment. As she did she saw, where the limb joined the trunk, a bare spot on the side of the tree. It was like a section shaved from the back of a dog, a patch with no covering. And cut into the pale buttercup of the naked tree were two letters: NJ.

Sara stood there looking up, certain Fredric had done that. The letters had a florid quality, they were not simply crude hackings. She imagined the young man having been on the limb one night, facing the tree, cutting by the glow of a flashlight. She also noticed now that the bare patch was in the shape of a triangle.

"But why?" she murmured. "What does it mean?"

"New Jerusalem," a voice said from behind her.

Sara jumped. A young girl was standing there. She was gaunt with hair the color of red pepper and a hoop through the left side of her lower lip. Sara recognized her as one of the girls who had been at the church.

"How do you know that?" Sara asked.

"I was here when Fredric did it," she replied, looking up.

"Which was when?"

"Like, a month ago?" the girl said. "I held the flashlight for him. It took forever. He was very careful." She shook her head sadly and sniffled back a cry. "I wish I'd been here last night. He must've been so upset to do this."

"What makes you say that?"

"Because he wasn't really ready to go there," the young woman told her. "None of us was."

Sara obviously needed to scroll this back, get in on the ground floor. She held out her hand. "I'm Dr. Sara Lynch. You are?"

"Marci Cello," the girl said, shaking the psychotherapist's hand. "I know you. Fredric talked about you."

"Did he? When?"

"When we were here. We met a couple of times a week to talk. He told us about your sessions. He wanted to tell you more about his stuff but he was afraid you'd give him shit."

Fuck, Sara thought. *Fuck, fuck, fuck.* "I never would have done that," Sara said. *Fuck.* "Do you know what he wanted to tell me?"

"About the New Kingdom," Marci said.

The teenager was as low-keyed and expressionless as Fredric. That was a cornerstone of the slacker personality but there was something comfortably, even smugly composed about these Goth youths. It was as though they had the key to a door that no one else could see, sort of negative-image Jehovah's Witnesses.

"What about the New Kingdom?" Sara asked.

The young woman did not answer.

Sara moved closer. "Marci, do you know why Fredric did this terrible thing?"

Marci was still looking up. She rolled a shoulder.

"You left the service to come here. Why?"

"Churches are creepy."

"More so than being out here at twilight?" Sara asked.

"Oh, yah. It's like here, now, I feel special. The animals are afraid of you or else they want you. It's extreme."

"May I ask a personal question?"

"Sure."

"How do you think Fredric felt about you?"

"I kissed him once. After he carved that," she said with a nod up. "I was all emotional and wanted to share the moment. He got squirmy."

"Why do you think?"

"It was New Kingdom stuff. He was all about that. It was, like, his mission."

"What's the difference between New Jerusalem and New Kingdom?"

Marci looked at her. "One's the gate, the other's the kingdom. We used to draw where we thought stuff would be, like the pools of lava and the towers of flame."

"The Dark Pope's domain?" Sara asked.

Marci seemed surprised "You know about him?"

"I know *of* him," Sara said.

"Lucky. Fredric only told a few of us, and the others got freaked after a while so it was just him and me."

"The others," Sara said. "You mean the young people who were with you at the service?"

Marci nodded. "I didn't want to be with them. I wanted to be with Fredric."

"But you felt he was here, not there."

Marci nodded again. "I can't believe he told you. He must've really trusted you."

Fuck, Sara thought once more. "Tell me about the markings," she said.

"His or mine?"

"There are two sets?"

She nodded. "Mine were decorative things. His were symbols and shapes that had a meaning. He didn't tell me too much about them. It was his job to know."

"I see. Will you show them to me?"

Marci started walking and Sara followed. They went to where the teenager had made the simple, triangular marks on stones and rock cuts, on trees and old fences.

It grew dark as they walked and Marci said she was glad she had found the psychotherapist. She had parked between the Marash and Jay homes after leaving the church but didn't know if she could find her way back in the dark. She said that Fredric was always prepared with things they might need, like flashlights and bottled water on hot nights.

Sara looked around then escorted her back to the road.

"Thanks for talking to me," Sara said as they reached the car.

"Sure. I feel bad."

"About Fredric?"

"That, but for you too," Marci said. "People are talking about you but I know, like, Fredric didn't plan to do this. He wasn't ready."

"You said that before," Sara said. "What do you mean?"

"He said he had to study more. He had books and shit but he never showed them to me."

"Are you going to try and 'study more'?" Sara asked with concern.

Marci rolled her shoulder again. "He knew a lot about

this, about how God lies and parents are not as understanding as demons."

"Demons," Sara said. She tried to make the word sound as ordinary as "bats" or "snakes." "Did you ever see one?"

Marci looked back at the park. "Sometimes, in the dark, you see stuff. You hear things like animal footsteps and birds flapping. And when we were lying down—Fredric said they were demons, and he had this voice that was really convincing, y'know?"

"I do," Sara said.

Leaving Marci with a hug, Sara walked back along the now-dark path. The Marashes were not yet home, and she hurried along. She did not want them to see her when they returned.

The woods seemed much different than the night before. When she ran along the path the previous night, it was just a park. Now it was a kingdom. The New Kingdom. She didn't visualize it; she didn't necessarily believe in it, but the idea was out there. Fredric's triangles were there, the points of the pentagram. It might not be a reality, but it was a fact. The difference, like the Devil, was in the details.

Sara felt the eyes that Marci had described. There was definitely a personality to the walk as night descended. More than just increasingly isolated as she moved north, it was apart from the mainstream of the world. There were no lights but what a hiker carried. There were no external voices, just the sounds of animals stirring: owls emerging, bats darting, raccoons scavenging. The sound of the walker's own footsteps was louder than at any other time, in any other place in Delwood. There was no comfort other than that which was brought.

Or created.

Now that Sara was looking for it, the silhouette of the sycamore was visible from quite a distance against the navy-blue sky. It was a formidable tree, tall and arched menacingly over the path. That powerful image, as well as its location and symbolism, made it ideal for Fredric's purpose. She wondered if he had selected the tree or whether it had chosen him in some sort of self-induced hypnotic state?

Night had descended by the time she reached the tree. As she crossed the path beside it she felt a sharp, sudden tightness on the nape of her neck. She was not wearing her scarf but it reminded her of what she had felt that afternoon. The feeling passed as she moved beyond the tree.

Or entered the New Kingdom or New Jerusalem, whichever applied.

Or neither. There was hypnotically induced aggression, when the subconscious was liberated and had its complete say, and there was unconscious-waking-aggression, when a powerful element of the subconscious managed to come forth on its own, like a volcano venting gas. Prodded by a sense of failure, Sara's subconscious was apparently expressing itself as a psychosomatic experience. She had to stop that. She had to remain objective.

The temperature dropped quickly as the sun did. That was not unusual in New England, but Sara was typically inside the house or her car when it happened. The river was going to be damn cold. Goose bumps rose on her arms just thinking about the crossing. She rubbed them in turn as she followed the bobbing flashlight beam into the darkness. Sara was walking slowly as she examined the markings Marci had pointed out. She didn't go to them. The psychotherapist moved among them, like a visitor to an historical excavation.

"What did you feel here?" she wondered aloud. "Marci said you were a leader. But from the books and your notes I know you were also a servant. You were a teacher and a student. Where was it all going, Fredric?"

Sara was hoping that the voice she had heard before belonged to Fredric and that it would give her an answer. But all she heard was her own voice and the rising cries of tenacious crickets that had not yet retired for the autumn. A breeze rolled from the river, causing the leaves to flutter. The sudden activity made her feel trapped, cut off from the civilized world.

The sky was virtually starless, obscured by a canopy of trees. Their leaves and limbs were as impenetrable as the ground below. The sounds around her were also a wall, close and amplified by the ridges on either side and by the darkness outside the cone of flashlight. Her father used to tell her that people hear better when they can't see. He didn't promise that they would like what they heard or that the enhancement would help them. Right now she wished she could see a little more and hear a little less. And not just in the woods. The words she had read were burned in her mind.

"Children intuitively sense His Satanic Majesty in the Dark. Adults lie and say there is nothing there. . . ."

There was something primal afoot, something more than the imagination of a woman alone in an exurban park at night.

Sara stopped by each of the markings in turn. Not the ones Marci had made, only those drawn by Fredric. Her heart thumped faster as she approached the last place she knew Fredric would have visited, a spot she suspected marked the northern boundary of New Jerusalem.

There was an old headstone on a ridge by a bend in the

trail. The path curved expressly to go around the resting place of Owen Kent, an early eighteenth-century settler. Very little was known about him, save that he was thirty-four when he died in 1778 "in a fight of honor" according to the carved inscription on the stone. That suggested he was killed in a duel. Sara had always wondered whether the fight was over independence or something else. Boundaries of a farm, perhaps. Or a woman. Maybe a doctor had misdiagnosed his son and he wanted revenge.

Sara had only looked up at the headstone when Marci was here. She wanted to take a closer look. The ridge was low here and she was able to pull herself up to the stone slab. It was cracked along the top, but the writing was still legible.

So were the chalk markings on the back. A passerby might not have noticed them from below. Up here they were clearly visible. Not just a triangle but an entire pentagram drawn within it, sketched vertically from Fredric's template. It was the end of New Jerusalem and the terminus of the New Kingdom.

This, she guessed, was the symbolic seat of Satan.

Sara noticed that the leaves lay extremely dead here. They were not dancing the way they had earlier in the street or along the path. Perhaps the stone and trees blocked the river wind. The branches of the surrounding oaks were drooped low over the plot, like divining rods looking for life. She turned the light around the area. There were no grasses here, nowhere for crickets to lunch and hide. She knelt beside the grave itself and picked up one of the leaves that covered it. The leaf was not quite dead. There was dampness and pale green life still left in it and in the others. They were supine, their ends curled toward the sky as though they were reaching up.

Maybe they were suckling on whatever was left of old Mr. Kent, seeping through the ground.

Sara stood. She could hear the dam to the north but had a sense she didn't need to go that far. She took a long breath. She had an idea and needed to know if it was true. Her legs literally trembled as she stepped behind the headstone. She looked down to prepare herself. The dead air here scared her more than the wind-stirred leaves below. She couldn't let that distract her as she looked out. She turned the flashlight back along the path to this tree, that rock, and finally the sycamore.

Her throat tightened, not from the imaginary scarf but from fear when she realized that she was right.

Fredric's markings defined the points of a much larger pentagram.

3

Sara's mind was now as restless as the leaves and crickets. But there were predators too, hiding in her brain, grim-faced Cerberi watching for her to take too large a step from reason.

Fredric must have believed that he had constructed or was in the process of constructing a realm that Satan himself could visit, or perhaps from which the Devil could reach out to others, perhaps even rule. Before one of the watchdogs could jump she reminded herself that this was not a question of reality. It was a matter of what Fredric believed.

Was the Devil supposed to help you last night? Sara asked the invisible Fredric. She thought back to Sunday school classes, to the New Testament passage from Luke in which the Devil bid Jesus to throw himself from the parapet of the temple in Jerusalem and said, *"If you are the Son of God He will bid His angels watch over you; with their hands they will support you.*" Did the young man imagine that Satan would catch him or hold him up? *Or perhaps he was simply furious with his mother, fed up with life, and wanting to be with a friend. A friend who, in his mind, may have offered him the kind of kingdom he had offered Jesus. Perhaps Satan had promised to make him the next Dark Pope if his faith was sufficiently strong.*

"Where is Heaven?"

The voice was in front of her and it was very clear. She raised the flashlight from the back of the tombstone and cast the beam through the dark. She thought she saw something by the twin footstones. They supported a chain that marked the beginning of Mr. Kent's grave.

The moon had risen beyond the hilltops. A shallow shaft of translucent light had punched through the cloud layer and was here then gone as it passed through the leaves. Sara thought she saw a shadow standing in the faint beam. She went around the plot and walked slowly toward it.

"Fredric, is that you?"

The shadow was still there, she could make it out in the darkness. The beam of her light passed through it. The shape, vaguely human, seemed to be bowed toward the headstone. It did not move. It reminded her of a supplicant in church.

"I wish you would talk to me, *with* me," Sara implored. "I'm trying hard to understand."

"Understand?"

"What happened here."

"What happened here?" the voice asked. It was definitely the same voice as before. The words sounded hollow, as when Darrell used to talk to her from the other end of a hollow log.

"Someone died," Sara said. "Was it you?"

Sara was near the foot of the grave. The shadow remained

stationary in the light, unaffected by the night breeze. Suddenly a portion of the shadow moved away from its side and extended toward the grave. It was pointing.

"Here is death," the presence said.

"Yes, but that is someone else," Sara said. She was enunciating very clearly, keeping her eyes on the shape. She wanted to try to connect with it. "The person I'm talking about was very important to me."

Sara suddenly realized that though she was coming closer to the footstone the figure beside it grew no larger, no nearer.

"What you need to know cannot be found here," the figure said.

"Where, then?"

Sara stumbled over a stone and her light moved. She quickly swung it up again and jerked back. The figure was right in front of her. It was no longer black but white, with dark but unformed features. It was eerie without being scary. To the contrary. There was a palpable sadness about the shape.

"Where can I find what I need to know?" she repeated, her voice cracking in the middle of the sentence.

"*His angels watch over you; with their hands they will support you,*" the speaker said.

All right, she thought. That scared her. Whatever the apparition was it knew what was inside her head. *That's because the manifestation and my thoughts inhabit the same place*, Sara concluded. *This vision is, has to be, part of your imagination*. She could prove it by touching it. She was close enough. She lifted her hand, then lowered it. Talking to an imaginary companion was one thing. Actually reaching out to touch it was an entirely different level of buying into a delusion. She was not there. Not yet.

"Why are you telling me about being supported?" Sara asked.

"Your hands. Where were they?"

"Fredric—if it *is* you—I would have been here for you if I had known. But you didn't tell me. I wish you had."

"Why do you call me that?"

"That's your name," Sara insisted. "Or—maybe wherever you are you have a new name? Do you?"

"I have no name."

"In your new place, you mean?" she asked.

"This is not new. I am not any place."

"I'm sorry," she said. "I don't understand." The last few times she had been with Fredric he had also talked in riddles. Either she was reliving those as a twisted psychodrama or this was his lost and confused soul. "Where are you and why don't you have a name?"

The apparition replied, "You never gave me one."

"I?"

"Who names?" it asked.

I? she thought. The realization hit her hard and Sara let go of the flashlight. The beam splayed across the barren earth. A moment later she dropped to her knees beside the footstones. There was not enough cruelty in all of Hell and its neighborhoods for anyone to do this to her. The woman shook her head slowly at first and then more violently. Her hands lay palms up and limp beneath her grounded knees. Her face was no longer immobile. It crashed and then exploded in tears. Her slender shoulders surged forward, pushing out the sobs that grew from the unreality of the moment. This couldn't be real but it couldn't be imagined. Sara did not think she hated herself so much—

"This isn't *happening*!" she screamed.

The woman grabbed the flashlight and shined it ahead and wiped her eyes. The glow struck the figure full. Still kneeling she screamed again, not in defiance but terror. There was a pale young man standing in a shroud. He was younger than Fredric, more gaunt and white with his eyes shut. He was hairless. Weeping openly again, Sara stretched out her left hand.

"It can't be," she said.

"It is," the thin lips said coldly.

Sara hesitated, her fingers resisting, wriggling, wanting to move ahead. "I'm so so sorry."

"Who am I?" the figure asked.

"I'm not entirely sure," Sara said. "May—may I name you now?" she asked. Then she pleaded, "*Please*. Let me name you now."

A small hand reached from the folds of the shroud. It was not the hand of a young man but the thick hand of a very small child. It did not seem to go with the owner. It touched her fingertips, as tangible as her tears, and then withdrew. A moment later the shadow was gone, like a thought that had slipped her mind. Only it hadn't.

Sara knelt there, shaking her head slowly.

"Is this what you want, for me to hang myself too?" she muttered into space. "Fuck you." She wasn't sure who "you" was, whether it was the Devil or Martin Cayne or her own miserable conscience or everyone who had a hand in corrupting the world for good and trusting souls. She blinked her eyes clear and looked out at the New Kingdom. She wanted to beg the apparition to come back but that was absurd.

Why? He was *here.*

No, she told herself. "*Something*" *was here.* It could not have been what she thought, the lost child of hers. That child had never been born. She had seen to that a decade before.

The flashlight only lit the ground a few feet in front of her but the woman did not have the energy to raise it. The moonlight was hidden by trees with just a few small, dusty beams reaching the ground. She continued to sit on her heels and look out at the darkness.

There was cruelty in this place. Sadistic evil bounded by a collection of chalk markings but defined by something else some*where* else. Sitting on the desk in her office, she suspected. It had caused Fredric to take his life and now it was seeking to hurt her as well.

That was not going to happen. Sara drew a long, long breath. She glanced at the headstone before her and quietly apologized to the occupant for disturbing his rest. He made no reply. At least some aspect of normalcy had returned.

The woman took a few more breaths and picked up the flashlight. She rose slowly, breathing through her mouth, her nose impassable and her head throbbing from the sobs. She turned from the headstone and hurried away.

4

Sara barely remembered picking her way back through the brittle, chirruping woods to the boat and then rowing across the river. Childhood reflexes returned and she made it across with some help from the gentle current. She didn't even feel the cold she had feared. Dragging the rowboat ashore she snapped to, somewhere closer to normal. Perhaps it was the exertion. She did not delude herself into imagining there was safety at the Sticks. The apparition had appeared to her here as well.

The apparition.

There *was* no child. What Sara heard and saw in the woods could not have been real. And the New Kingdom—it was just markings on the geography, chalk scratches put there by an obsessed young man. For whatever unconscious-waking-aggression reason, she was seeing things through the dead eyes of poor Fredric. She had been immersed in Fredric's life and this was an empathetic reaction.

Sara walked by the inlet. The sticks were at rest, weary from their long journey. She fancied she saw a little family down there, two large branches and two smaller ones. Perhaps if she looked at them long enough the moonlight would give them faces too. She might even give them a history too.

The Von Trapp family twigs fleeing oppression, she thought but only briefly. *Very* briefly.

This whole thing was in her head. It had to be. Sara passed the gazebo and crossed the backyard, which the moon had colored a pale ivory with the sharp delicacy of frosted glass. Even the grasses crunched underfoot, bent and dry until the morning dew gave them a last proud moment of autumnal old age.

She went to her office door and stopped. There was something behind her. She could feel it in the electrified small of her back.

"If you have something to say, say it," she said without turning. There was a touch of steel in her voice. She was glad to hear it. She didn't want to be harsh to a lost soul but there was her own soul to consider. If it were her own subconscious manifestation, then she forgave herself for yelling at it.

There was no answer but she still felt the presence. The tingling in her back climbed her spine until, after a few moments, she felt something pull lightly against the bottom of her sweater.

"Rake more leaves," it said in a strong, young boy's voice. "Wanna play."

"Who the hell *are* you?"

"Wanna play. With you."

Sara didn't look back. She was unnerved and ready to do something about this. The woman went inside and closed the door, still not looking back. The pulling on the sweater stopped. If it had been a "real" ghost, shouldn't it have come with her?

She crossed the waiting area and turned on the light and stood for a moment drawing strength from the familiar reality of her command center. The books, the diplomas, the computer and phone, even the box from Fredric's room; the answers. They were all here. Understanding this was a matter of doing what the psychotherapist did every day with every problem: staying rooted in reality.

Sara checked her messages. There were no cancellations, which meant she had two sessions in the morning. She already knew from today's messages that the children she saw in the afternoon would not be coming.

Sara lay on the couch. She heard Tonia talking to her son in the kitchen. They seemed very distant. She shut her eyes and savored the fact that she was away from the woods, from what she had seen there. She put her hands beside her. The leather felt good and strong. Nature tamed and used.

Animals raised and slain, blood—

"No!"

Her eyes shot open. For a flashing moment she had a vision of the throat of a cow being punctured with the tip of a dagger, its blood flowing in a strong, arcing stream. The sofa felt warm beneath her palms.

That's your own heat, she told herself. *You're inside the house now, warming, your blood circulating.*

She slid from the narrow couch, stood on the rug, and

looked around the office. Her eyes locked on the box she had taken from Fredric's room. She walked slowly to her desk and looked down at it, tucked between the computer and the stack of folders from her patients. She needed to know more.

"So don't look at it," she muttered. "Go through it."

When patients were stuck in an emotional state there was no way they could simply reverse direction and sail free. It was the job of the psychotherapist to try to walk them from it, one step after another. Sara knew she could not back from this uncharted quasireality in which she found herself. The only way out was ahead.

This was probably not the time to start something like this. Sara was tired but she was also afraid to go to sleep. Just lying on the couch, awake, had shaken loose strange shards of memory and imagination. The human mind had a strong logical component. Her own capacity for logic had obviously been suppressed tonight. She did not want to leave the interpretive and recollective aspects of her brain roaming free without a strong rational framework. She had to get herself back into reality.

Through it, she thought.

Her heart was drumming again but that was good. It would keep her awake and alert. With perspiration in her eyes now instead of tears, she went around the desk, sat down, and opened the box.

Nine

1

Through it.

The words were always easier than the deed. Words always were. As part of her studies, Sara had undergone psychotherapy to understand the process from a patient's perspective. Though the sessions were real there was still a laboratory feel to it. She was outside herself watching herself, a third party to her own analysis.

Not now. This was more like something that happened when she was four or five years old and her father took her out in the rowboat. She remembered asking him why they couldn't just walk across.

"Because you'll drown," Robert Lynch replied.

"No, Daddy," Sara said. "I mean on *top*."

"Only God can do that," he told her with a smile. "We need something to hold us up."

Sitting at her desk with the simple box before her, Sara felt like someone recklessly and impulsively wading across the Housatonic instead of taking a rowboat. She was already in and determined to get to the other side despite the unknowns. She knew the water was deep but she did not know how deep. Maybe just a few inches, maybe a few miles. She knew there was a current but she did not know how strong it was. She knew there were things living below the surface but she did not know all of them or how they would interact with her or each other. And the river was covered by a fine, cottony mist the way it was so many mornings. Sara was not even sure what she'd find on the other side. All she knew was that it was not possible to turn back.

She reached into the box and removed the paper. She took it, Alexander's chalk, and the *Devil's Bible* in her hands. Propelled by a quick, determined breath she rose and went to the rug. She put the items on the couch and knelt beside the rug. As an afterthought she got up and locked both the back and inside doors. Her mother rarely came to the office. If she happened to, however, Sara didn't want the woman walking in while she was performing an occult ritual.

You're really going to do this? Sara thought as she got back on her knees beside the rug. She began rolling the heavy carpet back from one corner. There was a foam rubber pad underneath and she simply flopped that over the rug. She placed the folded paper on the hardwood floor and opened it.

Through it, she repeated as she heard those watchdogs barking in her head, telling her that this was absurd, the kind of thing one does to humor a delusional patient. But then, there was a time she thought Dr. Arul's unorthodox methods were also without merit. She was wrong.

When the paper was laid out Sara took the chalk and used the side to sketch over the holes Fredric had poked. She did it lightly, so as not to tear the design. Crawling on the hardwood floor hurt her knees; she must have bruised them when she fell in the woods. She would probably be surprised to learn how many things happened to the body in a single day. Sara was so accustomed to uncovering repressed psychological scars in people she rarely thought about the physical slights, bumps, and journeys people experienced that were promptly forgotten. Except by the cells, the genes. Maybe one day humans would be built with knee pads.

Sara carefully transferred the design to the floor, reminding herself of how she used to draw in grade school: precisely. Sara enjoyed interpreting but did not like drawing abstract art. She liked trying to create a drawing that *looked* like the object. She hoped the physical act of drawing this symbol would either open her mind to the ceremony that must follow or else turn her against it. She also disliked abstract reality.

When the design was finished Sara made a small "X" where Fredric's feet had been. At least she hoped those were the young man's feet. It occurred to Sara that it could be a spot reserved for the Devil, or for the Dark Pope in absentia. If so, she hoped they'd be good enough to tell her in person. She had complaints for them as well.

She folded the paper and put it back in the box. Then she sat behind her desk, opened the tome, and stared at it without reading it.

"What the hell are you doing?" Sara asked herself.

It was a fail-safe question. Once she went ahead she was

no longer studying but acknowledging. She was allowing that some part of all of this was real. There was a psychological Pandora's box with a lot more inside than just a folded paper. As she had learned from Dr. Arul, opening the lid was not something one did without careful controls in place, without a guide.

She was on her own here.

Sara looked back at the book. *Thirteen steps*. That's all she had to take to discover whether the Satanic ritual had any validity, whether Fredric had unwittingly put himself into a mesmeric state, or whether the young man had actually found a key to the New Kingdom.

Sara began reading.

2

The ritual was simple, though the steps themselves were not. She glanced through the ritual to see if she would need anything she did not have. Except for candles, she had everything she wanted. The sycamore bark was not among those. She didn't want the Devil to be able to come and go as he pleased.

Instead of going to the pantry where she might be distracted by household matters, she went and got the two hanging citronella candles from the gazebo. They were there to repel mosquitoes. She did not think Satan would find them objectionable. If he did, she would let the church know.

The first instruction for the Summoning in the Book of Baal was to disrobe. Removing one's black clothes, it said, "allowed the flesh to enjoy the energy of the other celebrants and the heat of He who is to come."

Sara didn't know if that applied to the current circumstances. Though she felt a little foolish she decided to comply.

She took off her shoes, then stood and slipped off her sweater. She tossed it on the couch and unbuttoned her blouse. As she took it off she began to feel less foolish than flat-out vulnerable. Logically, that made no sense. Her clothing would not provide any kind of protection from a demon. It was probably the obeying of a male-skewed fantasy that bothered her. She removed her jeans and her undergarments feeling more and more like a prop instead of a participant.

Which is probably a good thing to feel, she decided. That would breed a healthy skepticism for what was to follow. It might help to counteract the vivid reality of her experiences in the park.

She sat naked in her chair and looked back at the book. She said the words aloud, then moved to step two.

She lit the candles and shut off all outside light sources. These were to be placed at the top and bottom points of the pentagram. Their pungent, unctuous smell filled the office. She put the aluminum containers on the pentagram, then went to the waiting room and opened the window to ventilate the smoke. The cool air was bracing on her bare skin. That was good. It was something else Sara could use to stay here and present in a dubious enterprise.

There were phrases to read silently. She read them.

The third step consisted of two parts. The first was to place blood from each of the participants in a receptacle and put it in the center of the pentagram. The instructions did not specify what the container had to be made of. Sara took the plastic lid from a soft drink cup Billy Roche had left in her trash can. Satan would have to live with a little Coke in his blood sacrifice. Then she punched a staple from the stapler and used it to prick her middle fingertip. No doubt this step helped to make some of the more giving souls a little woozy, a little more receptive to the process. She placed the lid inside the pentagram. While she was there, she was supposed to read a prayer aloud while she connected the dots to complete the outline.

With the book in one hand and the chalk in another, she read, "Gather ye children of the night, spirits of the wholesomely debauched, fly to this place so the pleasures of the flesh and life can be known. Abandon ye not hope but restrictions imposed by a possessive and selfish master."

Her cynicism was tempered as she completed step three. She was naked on a wood floor with simple chalk in her hand and an old book in the other, the wind curling through the anteroom and brushing against her back. Unlike the blind faith and drowsy predictability of a church service there was something very pagan about that, very tangible and real.

She stepped back from the candlelit design also feeling unclean. Perhaps it was her Catholic childhood reacting to the iconic image, or merely the secular fact that she was honoring a symbol and process that represented the basest aspects of humankind from bloodshed to carnality. Perhaps she was uneasy because these things belonged to Fredric, not her. They were his private trove and he had not given her permission to explore. Whatever it was, the plastic beverage lid no longer seemed to trivialize the moment.

Step four was to stand outside the pentagram, at any of the points, and hum in a low voice for three long breaths. This, she read, was designed to empty the body of impure vapors. She did this and it made her a little light-headed. Again, it was a good technique for corrupting the perceptions.

Afterward, she read silently from the book. It was more of the same, words that celebrated vice and maligned abstinence. Like politics, the theory seemed to be that if the officiant and his flock said something often enough it became real.

The fifth step was to strike a welcoming bell thirteen times. She had already decided to use a glass stein from Yale. She took it from the shelf and pinged it lightly with a letter opener. She happened to catch her reflection in the thick glass. It was distorted and flat, like one of Dali's clocks flopped across the couch beyond it. She didn't like the image of misshapen nudity and looked down as she finished the tolling process. She replaced the stein, recited another incantation, and performed step six, which was to stand at her place in the pentagram and close her eyes. She was to turn counterclockwise—just three times, happily—while contemplating the Master. There was one turn for each of the horns and one for his phallus.

Sara made the turns slowly. If this was part of the self-hypnosis technique Fredric had undertaken she needed to do it as well. When she opened her eyes she was startled by how bright the room had become. She knew her eyes were adjusting to the dark but the difference was noticeable.

The next three steps were to honor each of the dominant traits of Satan. For wisdom she was to stand at "her" point and read the rite of passage. She held the volume in her open hands and read, "Be receptive to us as we set our feet on the path to enrichment, learning, power, and sublime gratification. We seek your guidance, O Dark Lord, for the befouled White Lord has left the road in darkness." Step eight was to read the words of the same phrase backward, which she did. As she had read in the explanatory text, all passages ran two ways. It was just as easy to fall from Devilish grace as it was to achieve it.

The ninth step was to honor the sexual power of Satan. Sara had known going in that this was going to be the most difficult. It required her to prove that she was of-an-age to receive the carnal boons of His Satanic Majesty. The participants in the ceremony were required to achieve "sexual gratification in the proximity of the sacred star." This too was bound to weaken the resistance of the participants.

She assumed that self-stimulation was acceptable, and that it was okay to put the book on the desk. The text did not specify whether one was to sit, stand, or recline. So she sat on the edge of the desk with her legs extended before her. She closed her eyes. She hesitated.

Who was going to know whether she did this or not? There was no biorhythm monitor, no electrodes attached to her brain, no one watching.

You can't be entirely sure of the last, the psychotherapist reminded herself. It was what she was here to discover. Besides, she had gone this far. And if it was part of a weakening of the body to weaken the mind procedure, she needed to submit. She held the desk with her left hand and reached down with her right.

Sex had not been an important part of Sara's life. She had managed to duck all but heavy petting through high school and was not forced to make "the call" until her junior year of college. She had been dating her chemistry lab partner, Jefferson Dryfoos, for three months when the young marathoner asked if he could stay at her off-campus room. Sara agreed. Sometime during the small hours of the night, when she was feeling tired—like now—a little giddy, and just a little reckless, she asked him to make love to her. She didn't know whether to be flattered or annoyed that he had brought a condom. He assured her that it was part of every man's permanent "kit."

It was Jefferson's first time too, and while the prelude was exhilarating and it was wonderful to be held so close and tight, the drama itself was a little painful and somewhat disappointing. Even on subsequent nights, when they got more in touch with one another's rhythm, Sara felt less with Jefferson inside her than she did when he looked into her eyes with care and longing.

She and Jefferson drifted when the semester ended and they broke up after five months. Sara had another lover some months later, a clerk at the campus bookstore. He was a hard-working farm kid from Litchfield County. He had grown up with an outhouse instead of a bathroom; there was something earthy and very real about him. He proved to be very gentle and less combustible, but he had no imagination. Neither did Jefferson, and Sara realized that was something she needed in a lover. Someone who would look at her and talk to her before, after, and sometimes during, not just rest his weight on her chest and grunt.

She found that when she found Martin Cayne. Or rather, when Professor Cayne found her.

Sara remembered the man and his touch. She remembered how carefully he watched and circled her in the early days of that semester—

Her movements became more certain, more self-involved.

She remembered the first time she looked into his eyes and they were not those of Professor Cayne but Martin. Damn him, they were smart and dark and certain and inviting and just the slightest bit world weary. They were experienced eyes, the eyes of a wise fox, not the eager young bunny eyes of a student. Most of all they were curious. He wanted to know about you, your mind, and finally your body. When he took you he also gave of his entire self, for hours. The world outside your union remained outside your union. If there were music or garbage trucks or people outside the window they might just as well have been on the other side of the Long Island Sound. Sara felt respected, she felt cared for, she felt liberated from her old life and soaring.

She felt excited.

And loved?

She loved, and for the time that seemed enough. Love was something she had wanted to give for such a long time and Martin allowed her to do that. He accepted it graciously, if not gratefully, and though a piece of the relationship was missing she felt it could come in time.

Sara's teeth came together hard, locking in her moans as she shuddered harder. She thought of their first time together and their last time together, both of them equally ablaze—one with discovery, one with familiarity, the two with fire. Her right hand remained where it was, pressing hard, moving confidently, before stopping dead and finally relaxing. Then her entire body sagged.

Damn him.

Sara took a long breath and then another. Her eyes remained shut. She slowly became aware of the desk digging into her butt. After a minute or so she pushed herself onto a very wobbly pair of legs. She picked up the book, not just feeling bare and drained but also angry. This was nothing she hadn't done in private. It didn't even bother her that this was the first time she had masturbated "on command." It was clinical, a bit cheap, a little exciting. On the whole, neither a big plus nor minus. There was not even the usual sadness about being alone, questioning whether it was the right thing. What bothered her was where her mind had gone for stimulation.

Damn him. Damn it.

The tenth step was for the now-worthy supplicant to step back into whichever triangle of the pentagram she had selected. Sara shuffled her weakened self over to Fredric's spot with the book in hand. She said the words she was supposed to say. But her mind was on Martin, on how much he had disappointed her. On how much she detested him.

The eleventh step was to utter the seventy-nine "Maledictive Names" of the Devil. When she was finished, she tossed the book on the couch. She would not be needing it again.

Unclad and unguarded, she went to the twelfth step, which was to breathe deeply thirteen times and state her reasons for performing the ritual to summon a demon. Discounting the sexual climax, this was the one relatively improvisational aspect of the ceremony. She could imagine, with more people present, the low blending of sounds would have its own narcotic effect.

"I want to know the reason or reasons Fredric Marash hanged himself," she said. Sara phrased the question carefully and, instead of embellishing on it, simply restated it after every slow breath. She did not want to summon a demon only to get a trick answer. She had read stories like *The Monkey's Paw* where people used mystical methods to become wealthy, only to collect insurance money when a loved one died prematurely. There were also tales of genies who made someone wealthy but put the gold at the bottom of the sea.

The thirteenth and final step was for the priest or chief acolyte to name the demon the supplicant wished to have appear. Sara had selected the unspoken eightieth name: the Devil. The book advised even experienced dark practitioners not to summon the King of Hell. It did not provide the reasons, there was just the caution. Sara didn't care. She did not believe in working with intermediaries. Besides, as long as the penta-gram remained intact she could always send him back. According to the text, her command alone would be sufficient to that task.

Sara stood in the triangle, her arms at her sides. She looked at the smoke curling from the two scented candles, smelled the fragrance. The woman had no idea what would happen, of course. If the Devil did not appear it meant that Fredric had probably been delusional in his final minutes. That would support her belief that what he did could not have been predicted.

If the Devil did appear, if anything out of the ordinary occurred, then Sara was going to have to change the way she looked at the world. She did not believe that was something she would have to face.

As she stood there thinking about the Devil, Sara realized that she had at least one advantage Fredric did not have. She was a woman of reason, a scientist. She wanted answers, not boons. She did not want a place in the New Kingdom, she wanted understanding.

Just one word separated her from that knowledge. All she had to do was to speak it. A word, like a knife, to pierce the veil between reality and a new reality. Her lips barely moved as she looked down at the pentagram and said in a low, cautious voice, "The Devil Satan."

3

Sara didn't know what to expect. Over her thick, fast heart-beats she half expected howling winds from the river, groaning rafters, a rising or falling from the flames of the candles. She wondered if their smoke would form the shape of the Devil's face, like the great and powerful Oz.

None of those things happened. Nothing changed, save for the layer of perspiration that collected on her face and crawled down her neck. Sara continued to stand motionless in the triangle, unsure whether the ritual had been a success or a failure. And even that was relative, for failure to summon the Devil meant success in proving that the entire belief system was without material foundation. The book did not say how long she should stand there.

"Stand there until you are sufficiently sleep- or food-deprived to hallucinate," she muttered.

She assumed the results should have been instantaneous. She found herself drowsily wondering how long the trip from Hell was in miles. It shouldn't matter. She couldn't imagine the Devil needing a ferryman to cross the Styx.

Sara looked around and listened before stepping from the pentagram and going over to her chair. The room did not feel different than before. Neither did she, except for a half-formed sense of gullibility and maybe something more: a secret wish that this had worked. It would mean that spirits were real, that life wasn't the end, that her father and countless others were "out there" somewhere watching and waiting. It would mean that the Devil was real but also that God was real.

Which might not be such good news for you, now that she thought of it.

Sara put on her clothes, turned on the light, and blew out the candles. The world was rational after all. There was even an explanation for what happened in the woods. The spirit she "saw" had been a trick of light and mind and not something truly present. The voices she heard were audio hallucinations brought on by post-traumatic stress from Fredric's death, his unheard cries giving voice to her own latent, unspoken screams. The two coming together as the most profoundly powerful and disturbing vision her subconscious could push through.

Sara decided not to disturb the pentagram. She closed the window, then took her cell phone and a little-used key from her desk and locked the office door. She would wait until morning to replace the rug. Maybe she would try the ritual again tomorrow night, just to be sure she had done everything right. Or she could attempt to call forth a lesser demon. Perhaps a starter spell would have been a good place to start.

Sara moved slowly through the den and up the stairs. She thought about Fredric's motivation for having done this. He probably needed to know whether the authority figures and patriarchies he so despised were real and worthy of his hate. Perhaps he had prayed to God for explanations and received none. That would have fed his dislike of blind authority. Prompted by Goth postings, he may have web-searched the Devil, learned about the Dark Pope's book, and took another route of discovery.

Of course, the Devil said yes. Whether real or imagined, he told Fredric what the young man wanted to hear.

It was late—past midnight, Sara was surprised to note. She didn't think the ritual had taken that long. The house was very still. Even the TV was off in her mother's room. Sara stopped in the bathroom where she sat just long enough to collect the energy to get up again. Then she brushed her teeth, pulled on fall pajamas still smelling of cedar, and slipped into bed.

Unlike her spartan office, Sara's bedroom was full of "positive energy" as the more new agey psych publications put it. "A place of happy memories" was how Grace had described the room with somewhat less gravitas. There were stuffed plush birds ranging from an old Thanksgiving turkey dressed as a Puritan to a *Fruit Loops* toucan. She was not a bird collector per se; she just happened to have a dozen or so of them. The shelves were thick with childhood books. Beside the window was the old secretary that had belonged to her mother and her mother before her, where Sara used to do her homework. There were Duran Duran decorated boxes filled with 45s from the 1980s and a working portable record player beside neatly organized racks of CDs and a CD player. Most of those were collections containing the 45s. There were a few jazz CDs buried in the stacks. Dixieland Jazz and trumpeter Al Hirt in particular had been a favorite of Martin Cayne. Sara couldn't listen to them but she couldn't bring herself to throw them out, either.

The walls were decorated with framed drawings and finger paintings and photographs Sara had created from first grade to last. Her mother had hung them here, something to remind her of Sara when she was at school. As happy as the young woman had been to get away from here, her mother had been unhappy to see her go. That left only Robert and Darrell at home. Martha called her daughter two or three times a day as she fluctuated between caring for and about her men, and not.

"Don't you settle on a man who can't look you in the eye because he's drunk or lying," Martha would warn her.

Look at me, Mom, she thought when she came back here to live. *I didn't fall in love with an alcoholic*. What Martha forgot to tell her, or didn't know, was that there were sober men who could fix their eyes on yours and use it as a chute to pour lies into your head. Or truths that changed as the sun rose.

If there had been another generation of Lynch women

perhaps they would have gotten it right. *Maybe it wasn't too late*, she thought. With Darrell out there Johnny Appleseeding his way through the local population there might yet be one, if there weren't already.

Sara slipped into her queen-size bed and shut the lamp on her night table. It was a kitschy piece, an antique telephone that had been fitted with a high-intensity lightbulb in the mouthpiece. It suggested age and burning wisdom to Sara. Shutting the lamp always created a pleasant moment isolated from the rest of the day. She felt as though she were floating above the world, above her problems. It always made her smile. And a smile was a good way to end any day.

4

Sara fell asleep quickly and she was annoyed to be awakened by talking. She looked at the clock on the night table. It was two-thirty. Even before she lifted her head she knew where it had to be coming from. Now and then people came down the river at night, usually teenagers who had been drinking and had no business being on the water, let alone on Lynch property. She usually called Trooper Brown on her cell phone to come and chase the goons away.

The voice was that of a male, but it was different from the loud "yo dude" voices she usually heard. It was soft and smoky and slightly exotic. It reminded Sara of a priest in a Spanish church she had visited during her European studies. She couldn't make out the words and wondered if the interlopers were from the nearby Scatacook Reservation. The men sometimes traveled the river in the dark. She lay there half-awake, trying to hold on to sleep. She hoped that whoever it was were just passing through and were not parked at the inlet.

After a moment the voice said very clearly, and very nearby, "Come." And Sara realized the voice was not on the river.

Fully awake now, she raised herself on an elbow and looked around in the dark. She wanted to hear better, not see. She listened, heard nothing, and finally snapped on the light. There was no one in the bedroom. She must have dreamed it.

She waited. She could hear the faint hum of her electric clock. The crickets outside had retired and there were rarely owls after midnight. The river sounded distant behind the closed window. One reason voices from outside carried at night is because everything else was usually so very still and the kids were so very loud. She had a master's degree in what drunks sounded like.

Sara's breathing was extremely shallow as she listened. She remained propped on her elbow for several minutes. She was about to turn off the light when she felt something warm on her fingertip. She looked down.

There was blood where she had pricked herself.

The blood flowed freely, copiously. She pulled a tissue from a box on the night table. She wrapped it around the wound. The tissue went from white to red within moments. She pulled it away, dabbed the wound with another, looked closely. There was no gash, no cut, just the tiny prick from a staple. The blood flowed down her finger to her palm, pooled there for a moment, then trickled down her wrist.

"Why is this happening?" she asked no one in particular. And then she remembered what she had heard:

"Come."

Sara's breathing was no longer shallow. She threw off the covers, got out of bed, and lifted the window. She held her bleeding finger near the screen. She let the cool air move across her face.

She was definitely awake. She turned back to the room. "Tell me again," she said. "I want to hear it again!"

There was only the sound of the wind and river for a moment. And then, from somewhere beyond the light of the lamp, she heard the voice again.

"Come."

The psychotherapist wasn't dreaming now. She had not been experiencing a state of partial hypnosis caused by the ceremony. Her thought process was sharp and the bleeding was real.

So was the voice. Had the ritual worked? Was there a delayed reaction?

Or is the Devil playing with you? she wondered.

Sara took her comfortable white terry-cloth robe from the closet, careful not to stain it with blood as she slipped her hand through the sleeve. She noticed, then, that the bleeding had stopped. She cleaned off the residue with another tissue.

Sliding on her familiar old slippers she went into the hall. The woman moved swiftly but lightly on the balls of her feet. She didn't want to wake anyone. Even so, the old floorboards complained as she passed over them. They did that sometimes even when no one was here. As a child, Darrell had been convinced the house was haunted. His logical, rational sister told him that was silly.

"The grounds shift causing even old houses to settle," she told him with authority and sanctimony, before she even knew what that was. She was repeating something she had overheard her father once tell one of his rare clients. It made her feel guilty, now, to think that Darrell might have been more right than she.

Sara reviewed the Summoning ritual in her mind. Her thoughts were clear, her memory intact, nothing settling or shifting up there. She was certain she had done everything correctly. She wondered if perhaps the Devil *had* been in the pentagram when she left the office, but unseen. Maybe he let Sara leave just so he could summon her later, demonstrate his power over her.

Sara stopped at the top of the stairs. There were two large windows on either side of the door. She looked down into the moonlit darkness.

There were black silhouettes of leaping stags on the forest-green wool runner. The animals seemed to move as branches on the trees shifted the fall of the pale light. Maybe their hoofbeats—or limbs scratching the gutter of the house— were the mad nocturnal romps Darrell imagined hearing so long ago. Those sounds were probably as real to him as the voices in Sara's ear.

Sara wondered what would happen if she went back to her bedroom. If she waited until morning or the following night to visit her guest.

If there is a guest, she reminded herself. She had to know, though part of her—a very large part—did not want to ac-knowledge that he could be there. It would negate so much of what she had been taught, what she believed. On the other hand, if the room were empty she would be validated.

And if you ignore this moment he might choose not to partici-pate, Sara thought.

The text said the ceremony would cause the Devil to ap-pear. It said nothing about visibility or cooperation. Like prayer, the worshiper was guaranteed a place to be heard and someone to listen. The rest was beyond the control of the devotee. This was a "victory" she might have to give the De-vil, first contact at a time of his choosing.

And what do you have to lose by going down now? Sara asked herself. After all, she *wanted* to speak with him.

There were hollow whistling sounds as the wind picked up and blew under and around the old shakes. Sara watched the changing shape of the moonlight on the runner. The motion on the outside matched the unrest she felt on the inside. The corrosive power of disembodied voices, carnal gratification spurred by a brutally painful memory, performing a rite from which even a lapsed Catholic should run. Sara should be rejecting all of this, denouncing and denying it with intellectual resolve.

Yet she still wanted answers and there was only one way to get them.

Through it.

Sara went down the steps. The lighting and unfamiliar noises made the house a strange and hostile place. She was like a little girl unnerved as she walked through the den and unlocked the office door. She couldn't wait to get inside her "place" and was momentarily surprised to see the rug was rolled back and the pentagram exposed, the Devil's paraphernalia still on her desk and the air smelling of citronella. Her tired mind had defaulted to office-as-normal. There was no comfort here.

Through it.

She entered. The wind was gently rattling the windows in the waiting room and wrapping itself around the turret. She crossed the rug warily, as though it were a rickety rope bridge across a bottomless chasm. She did not feel the presence of the Devil, just her own fear. Maybe she had to set things back the way they were at the end of the ritual. Locking the door behind her, Sara went to her desk and set down the key. She relit the candles, opened the back windows, and turned off the light. She returned to the pentagram. She did not strip or step into her corner but stood to the side. She had come downstairs. The next move was up to the Devil.

She waited. The Devil did not appear.

God appeared to Moses, she thought bitterly. Sara might not be an Old Testament prophet but the Devil was not exactly Jehovah. Then she remembered what God had said to Moses as he approached the Burning Bush.

"Remove the sandals from your feet, for the place where you stand is holy ground."

Unhappily, Sara removed her robe and lay it on the couch. She slid off her slippers, unbuttoned her pajama top, then tugged off the bottoms. Naked, she decided there was nothing to lose by finishing her acquiescence. She stepped into the pentagram feeling far more exposed than she had before. Earlier, Sara felt that she had been alone in the office. Now she was not so sure.

The wind rolled through the waiting area, chilling the office. Tendrils of smoke wound upward from the aluminum holders. Sara noticed then that while the air moved toward her the smoke was oblivious to the gusts. The twin columns twined straight up, and as she watched they seemed to slow. After a moment the worming motion was so slight as to be imperceptible. The smoke began to darken. Sara noticed, then, that everything was getting darker as the flames slowly weakened and finally died. The room was in complete blackness.

That was stupid, she thought. Sara knew her way around in the dark but she didn't want to leave the triangle to get her flashlight. It wasn't just that standing here was part of the ritual: Fredric had told her that the triangle was a safe place. It seemed best, for the moment, not to move.

The smell of the candles, feel of the hardwood floor on her soles, and the lacy touch of the wind were the only external stimuli. As her eyes became accustomed to the dark Sara saw the faintest glow coming from her hibernating computer monitor. There were also multiple points of red and white light in the stein on her shelf, reflections and re-reflections of the tiny lights on the front of her computer.

Sara was getting impatient when the red lights in her Yale glass winked out. A moment later the exotic voice spoke again from behind.

"You came."

Sara jumped. She turned her torso partway around and reached back. She saw nothing, felt nothing. Breathing heavily, she looked toward the pentagram. The red lights were directly in front of her. They were larger now, two ruby ovals side by side and slanted slightly toward their center. They narrowed for a moment and then were once again full. Sara realized then that they were not reflections from the computer, they were eyes.

The eyes of the Devil.

Sara had never experienced anything like the dread that seized her mind and soul. Everything she knew—or thought she knew—was discountable. Death, after-death, evil as a thing and not a point-of-view—all of it had been jettisoned by a pair of piercing eyes. Her mouth was sand-dry and she could hear the blood rushing through her skull.

But if Sara's mind flattened under the weight of what it faced, her body did not. Something primal, survival-oriented, even defiant strengthened her legs, her arms, her backbone. Like a cave dweller cornered by a bear or great cat, she was not simply going to bow to his power. Besides, she had summoned *him*.

Sara found her voice. "Yes, I came," she rasped. At the moment she couldn't think of anything to add. Perhaps that was good. *Keep it simple, focused*, she thought.

The eyes narrowed again. "Why?" The voice was in front of her now. It was neither impatient nor intimidating.

Sara sucked a long breath through her teeth. Until she did that she hadn't realized how tightly her jaw was pressed together. "Before I say anything, is there a time limit to this conversation?"

"Of course," he replied.

"And what is that?"

"Death."

Sara's heart was in runaway mode. *You can't afford to get tangled in abstractions and "what-ifs,"* she told herself. If this were the Devil—and the evidence, however ephemeral, suggested it was—his frame of reference was going to be different from her own. She was talking to *the* Devil. The corrupter of Eden, the father of all sin. She had trouble just convincing herself to strip in private. She needed to keep this small and very narrowly focused.

"What will happen if I leave the pentagram?" she asked.

"Try," he replied.

"I'm asking you," she replied, surprised by her boldness.

A rolling laugh came from beneath the suddenly widened eyes. "Doctor, you confuse me with something else."

"What would that be?"

"A djinn released from his bottle."

The laugh faded. He was right in the sense that she did not get three wishes. But he was being disingenuous. She still had to watch what she said. The Devil was obliged to do nothing but appear. But he also wasn't obligated to answer any question or, when he did, to answer truthfully.

"This is what you did to Fredric, isn't it?" she asked.

"Chopin?"

Oh, Christ, she thought. The Devil had a sense of humor too. Or—was he being serious? How many geniuses had he known, had he patroned? Sara *had* to get control of this. She did what she did with her patients; she went with what he gave her. "Yes," she said.

"We never met. His lover, George Sand, was an acquaintance. Not a gracious woman."

"Are you trapped in the pentagram?" Sara asked.

"I am free within the pentagon."

That was the design on the inside, defined by the bases of the triangles. "Can you *leave* it?"

"Where did you first hear me?"

"If that was you in my room, it was just your voice."

"Are you certain?"

She wasn't.

"Who made you bleed?" he asked.

Sara looked into the crimson orbs suspended before her. The contents of the eyes were in motion, showing occasional swirls of darker red bordering on black. They revealed no information about their owner—except his location. Sara believed she could trust that. The Devil was inside the pentagram. Earlier, it was only his voice that came to her and that may have been inside her head. The Devil, or spirits, or her own reaching-out, acting-out, unconscious-waking-aggressive psyche, had shown she could hear things that weren't physically present.

"I made myself bleed," Sara replied. "Here, in this room."

Sara decided not to continue this conversation at present.

She had a great deal to learn about interviewing this beast, about getting the information *she* wanted. She believed that part of that was to demonstrate at the outset that she could ignore him, that she was in control—here, in her bedroom, in the woods or anywhere he decided to engage her.

The woman left the triangle. She walked toward the light switch behind her desk and flicked it on. The room looked exactly the same as before, except that the candles had been extinguished. She made her way slowly around the pentagram. Perhaps the triangle worked as a kind of "on/off" switch. That wouldn't explain how the Devil had communicated with her in her bedroom, but it was a starting point—

The candles flashed to life. They were not small flames like before but large ones, igniting the liquid wax, spilling onto the floor in tortured little puddles and churning black smoke into the room. As the burning pools moved toward one another, Sara rushed around the pentagram to the couch. She grabbed her robe and shook it out to throw on the flames. Before she could do so the vivid orange fires on the pools of wax flattened and died. The candlewicks themselves were extinguished and the residual smoke curled upward in thin, filmy wisps before dissipating. All that remained of the blaze were two ovals of dead, darkened wax.

"You lit the candles," the Devil said, his voice to her right. She looked there, saw nothing. "Did you make them grow?"

Sara pulled the robe around her shoulders. She stood looking at the pentagram once again. It seemed so innocent. The entire symbol was just chalk marks and two bug-repellant candles with a pinprick of blood in a plastic container. Could that combination really have summoned the Devil?

"Why did Fredric Marash take his life?" she demanded.

"Did you light the candle?" the Devil asked.

"We're talking about Fredric," she said.

"Indeed."

It took a moment for the remark to register. "You sadistic nightmare."

Sara got the key, went to the light, shut it, and left her office. She locked the door behind her. She began to regret this thing she had unleashed on herself.

But you are a scientist and this is a problem, she thought. The Devil was like a disease or any form of mental illness. He needed to be studied and understood.

Climbing the steps, Sara dropped into bed and stayed there until she was awakened by Tonia singing to Alexander in the kitchen.

Ten

1

Sara dressed and went to the kitchen. Tonia and Alexander were their usual upbeat selves.

"Good morning, Doctor Sara," Alexander said over jellied toast.

"Good morning," she said, mustering all the good cheer she could find. "Did you have a good night?"

"I did," he said. "I dreamed about sheep."

"I told him you were supposed to count them when you couldn't sleep," Tonia said as she poured cereal for her son. "It must have made a—what is it? A dent on his mind."

"Impression," Sara said.

"Yes, that's the word," Tonia said. "Can I get you something, Sara?"

"No thanks," the psychotherapist said as she poured black coffee. "I've got a lot to do this morning."

"It's Saturday!" Alexander said. "We are supposed to rest and play."

"That sounds nice," Sara said. It was difficult to keep up a facade of normalcy.

"Did you have a patient last night?" Tonia asked.

"Why do you ask?"

"I thought I heard talking."

"I was on the phone," Sara said.

"I thought I heard a man talking," Tonia replied.

"Speaker phone," Sara answered quickly.

"I heard talking too," Alexander informed her.

"Did you?" Sara asked.

He nodded. "My daddy."

Sara felt that disturbingly familiar sensation of her brain stopping dead, failing to make sense of what it had seen or heard. She hoped this had nothing to do with her own activities. It was one thing to risk her own well-being. But not another child, not *this* child.

"Piotr sometimes visits," Tonia explained in slow, careful English. She looked at Sara when Alexander wasn't looking and touched her head.

Sara took a short swallow of coffee. "This has happened before?"

Tonia nodded and stepped behind the boy. She kissed the top of his head. "God sends a sweet Russian angel to look after his son," she said, smiling. "I think, probably, Piotr needs attention too. Even angels must be lonely."

"Do you believe in angels?" Sara asked.

"Yes. I see their glass wings in the windows of the

Mrs. Lynch church and I think it would be nice if they were real—so they are real," she said with a little shrug and a smile. "I am just a person, not a holy priest, but I think that when souls go to heaven God must select special ones for some honor. For this kind of honor. It would make good sense, don't you think?"

"It would," Sara said. She was going to ask Tonia if she also believed in devils, but it did not seem an appropriate question to ask on a morning when the sun was out and the mother and son were in such glowing spirits.

Tonia went to the stovetop to prepare a spinach and mushroom omelette for Martha. Sara sipped more coffee, then topped off the mug.

"Was it all right last night?" Tonia asked.

"Was what all right?"

"With your patient?" Tonia asked.

"As well as could be expected, I suppose," Sara said. "He's got a long, long history of problems."

"That is too bad. Are you all right?" Tonia asked.

Sara smiled. "I'm fine," she lied. She wished the mother and son a good day and then headed to her office.

There is the flaw in theology, Sara thought as she unlocked the door. People can summon devils on their own. But to be reached by an angel they had to wait for God to send one or else beg Him. Most people called it prayer, but Sara called it a desperate plea. The idea of making herself contrite and even weaker so that *perhaps* a guardian spirit could rescue her seemed counterproductive. Even the rankings given some of the angels had always troubled her. *"Thrones, dominations, virtues, powers, principalities."* With the exception of the book-end names—the low-totem, cute-sounding seraphim and cherubim and the heroic-sounding, high-end archangels and angels—the bulk of the choirs were designed to humble people, not strengthen them. Instead of church, people should go to group therapy for the religion-dependent.

"Hi, I'm Sara and I'm a helpless, dependent, needy individual . . ."

Summoning the Devil might not have been the best idea in the world or the most fruitful. But at least it was proactive.

Except for the pentagram and spilled wax, the office was as determinedly neutral as always. She set her coffee on the desk, rolled back the carpet, and made sure there were no phone messages. She had a look at her e-mail and was surprised—and a little weirded-out—to see a message from Grace. It had been over a month since their last communication. She was glad to see it.

Grace Rollins was a thirty-seven-year-old nun with a strong religious core and a fiercely independent nature—New England to the bones. Though Grace observed her vows of poverty, chastity, and obedience, she did not live a cloistered life. After graduating from the Divinity School she joined the staff of the all-female Sister Mary Academy in New Haven, a school for troubled teenagers. It was through the school's community outreach program that Grace met Tonia Tsvardin.

Passionate about validating biblical events in the archaeological record, Grace used her connections at Yale to join digs throughout the Holy Land. Though Grace remained on the staff of the Sister Mary Academy, she spent most of her time at Yale.

Sara read the short note, which began with a salutation as though it were a real letter. Grace was a traditionalist in every way.

Dearest SJL: Been thinking about you. The weather reminds me of when we met, talking theology after class in the cool fall on campus among the dusty leaves. I want to see you soon. No reason in particular. Just "let's." Much love, G

It was a sweet and welcome sentiment. Sara wrote back that she'd been thinking a lot about religion lately—*"perhaps you felt the vibes?* ;-)"—and promised to drive down to Yale very soon. *All the way*, she wrote.

Those last words stared back at her. Unlike *"through it,"* they lacked motivation or conviction. It was going to be very difficult going back, even ten years later.

Sara sent the e-mail, then glanced at the rug. The lumpiness of the spilled wax was barely visible. Like events in life, she could cover it over and deal with it when and if she wished.

2

The morning seemed to drag.

Several patients could only come on weekends due to work schedules or having to watch children during the week. Sara was happy to accommodate them.

Her first patient was Claudia Cole, a twenty-nine-year-old closeted gay woman. This was Claudia's third session. She worked for a local Realtor and had always traveled to Hartford or New York to meet women. She was fearful that the conservative community would find out and ostracize her.

Now she had met someone and thought it might be serious. The other woman was a New York writer who had come to the office looking to buy a small house in the country. It was lust between the two from the moment the forty-three-year-old writer walked in the door, tucked into well-worn jeans and a leather jacket and as open and confident as Claudia was unsure. They made love in the basement of one of the homes Claudia took her to see. With the owner upstairs.

"Did she buy the place?" Sara had asked.

"Yes," Claudia told her. "And she wants me to move in."

Sara was an advocate of the don't-worry-about-what-others-think school, though she did hope Claudia was careful about getting too deeply involved with someone she didn't know very well. That didn't come just from Sara's schooling but from her own life. By the end of the session Claudia had resolved—with some persuasion—to wait. She needed to be comfortable with the decision or neither she nor her lover would be very happy.

The second patient of the morning was one of the local selectmen, Richie Wills. Richie was a fifty-year-old retired stockbroker who got rich during the heyday of the Internet. He got out before it crashed and went into politics. He had his eye on a state-level office. First, however, he had to get a handle on his anger. He had been an aggressive broker. Politics in Delwood did not encourage Type A bullying. Richie had been seeing Sara twice a week for three months. With a week to go before local elections, and a public debate still to come, Sara hoped they had made sufficient progress treating the childhood traumas that put him in that state, being physically and emotionally abused by his three older brothers.

Richie was politically savvy enough to say little more than an obligatory "I'm sorry" about the controversy surrounding the death of Fredric Marash. However, she noticed that he pulled deep into the driveway, where his car wouldn't be seen, instead of parking on the street as usual.

Sara went to the kitchen and had a late lunch after Richie left. On the counter was a registered letter from the school attorney, E. Edward Edwards, officially advising her that effective Monday morning she was not to treat any patients on behalf of the high school until the "situation involving your patient, Mr. Fredric Marash, has been thoroughly investigated and understood." The "your patient" reference was an obvious attempt to distance the school from potential liability in the event of a lawsuit. Since the appointments with other students had all been canceled there was no chance of her treating any of them. The letter really irked her. It was one thing when a relatively inexperienced public servant like Chrissie Blair covered her ass. It was another when a public institution did it. At least Chrissie made a few halting sounds of defiance while Harkness watched.

Sara did not hear any voices during today's lunch. She didn't know whether that meant she had made progress or had simply transferred her delusions from the kitchen to her office.

Martha came down the stairs as Sara was putting her plate in the dishwasher. The older woman seemed distracted. Though the sun was bright, Martha was not dressed to go outside.

"Is everything all right?" Sara asked.

Her mother shrugged. Sara let it drop. Her mother would get around to saying what was troubling her, though Sara had a good idea what it was.

"What are your plans for the afternoon?" Sara asked.

"I was going to have lunch, watch a show about gardens on Discovery, and then write a letter to the newspaper to straighten their tongues before they ask anyone else to comment about my daughter. I've been writing it in my head."

"Mother, please. Just let it lay."

Martha regarded her with surprise. "You've seen the newspaper this morning?"

"No," Sara admitted. "I sort of know what's been going on in town."

"Tonia put it in the cupboard until I came down," Martha told her. "Horrid little publication. We're going to cancel our subscription."

"This will pass—"

"A front page article quotes school officials insisting they had *nothing* to do with Mr. Marash beyond his education. They say that his mental health was entirely in your hands."

"Mine and the county—"

"Which claims, through an anonymous source, that nothing in their records suggests that Fredric Marash was suicidal or they would have taken appropriate action," the woman went on.

"He wasn't suicidal," Sara said. "There were apparently other reasons he did what he did."

"Then you should tell them. Call the paper."

"I can't. There are potential legal issues, insurance issues. I don't want to say anything that might hurt me if it comes to that."

"Do you think it will?"

"I honestly don't know," Sara said. "But I need to be prepared. I want to look into some of Fredric's activities that had nothing to do with our sessions."

"What do you mean?" Martha asked.

"I can't talk about it yet."

"But you *must*!" Martha said urgently. "You don't have to be specific, but at least tell the newspaper that they don't have the full story. You know how ideas get fixed in peoples' heads. You have to knock them out quickly, before they take root."

"A half-formed explanation will seem like I'm hiding

something," Sara said. "I need to do my homework before I talk to anyone."

Martha stood by the refrigerator, pouting and silent.

"Mother, please. You've *got* to let me handle this."

"A mother is supposed to fight for her children. Wouldn't you?"

"Only when she has ammunition. What will you tell them, that I'm a good girl? A brilliant doctor? That won't sell papers."

"You are—"

"This is not about local gossip or small town politics or a mother's heartfelt opinion—which, by the way, I do really and truly appreciate. What Fredric did could end my career—"

"Only if you let it."

"I won't let it," Sara said. "I promise."

Martha was thoughtful. "Are you sure?"

"Yes."

Martha thought a moment more. "What sort of activities are you looking into? Drugs?"

"No, Mother," Sara replied. "We'll talk about it when I know more, okay?"

"Do you promise?"

"I do."

"All right, dear," Martha said reluctantly.

Sara went back to her office. Before turning to her research, however, she did give some thought to the practical matter of how to explain the box when it came time to "go public." Sara could say that he gave it to her, or that she found it in the woods where Fredric hanged himself. His death, she would tell them truthfully, was part of some very private religious beliefs. Or antireligious beliefs, as the case might be. They were doctrines and practices he shared with only a few close fellow believers like Marci—not with his parents and not with his psychotherapist. Sara did not know if it would be necessary to tell the Marashes about Fredric's apparent asphyxiation fetish. It remained to be seen whether that had any part in what the young man had done in the woods.

Only one individual might know the answer to that and Sara needed to find out more before invoking him again.

She sat at her desk for the next four hours and read the *Devil's Bible* and Fredric's marginal notes thoroughly. The fact that the Devil did not appear or speak while she was alone made the events of the previous night seem distant; not exactly imagined but not quite lived either. Other than the spilled wax there was no evidence that anyone had been here, and she could have done that on her own.

Reading the text in its entirety reinforced what she had felt when she first skimmed the book. The *Devil's Bible* was less a volume of "how to" than of "why to." It was full of phrases such as, "Grant me indulgences, Lord of the Earth, for I have earned them," and "I rejoice in the life of pleasure which the Pit holds in abundance and for which the flesh was made." The Dark Pope did not ask worshipers to refrain but to indulge without limits. "Eve and Adam rejected the sterile Eden of God for good reason. They were woman and man and they desired the pleasures obtainable between woman and man."

There was nothing in the volume that would have helped Sara control the Devil any better than she did—if she had at all—though it did confirm several important points. First, no demon, not even the Devil, could leave the pentagon unless the original spell had been performed with sycamore bark in the pentagram, or if the lines of the symbol were broken. The latter, wholesomely and euphemistically named "An Invitation to the Celebration," could be intentional or accidental: a foot inadvertently dragged through the chalk mark, liquid spilled over it, or a strong wind blowing across it. Once released by either means, the demon would be free to possess the body of one or more of the acolytes or those close to them, depending upon the demon's power. The Dark Pope deemed this to be a good thing.

"It frees mortals from any remaining responsibility or inhibitions that may have been nurtured by a misguided belief in God. These deeds, from debauchery to thievery to the destruction of those faithful to the Plain Lord, will be executed with superhuman power and appetite, as befits the nature of the demonic spirit."

In other words, be careful where you step, Sara told herself.

She immediately got up, pulled back the rug, and made sure the pentagram and the interior pentagon were intact. They were. She left the symbol exposed to make sure it remained that way. To erase it when she was finished, the text said that she needed to first remove the "keys of flesh and blood": the candles—once made of tallow—and the sample of her blood. The order did not matter. The Devil could see or smell with equal acuity. Only a complete disconnection of these objects from the pentagram would break the bond.

The part of the text Sara found most fascinating had to do with what, if it were true, would be the oldest recorded example of "spin." According to the Satanists, the Devil was not subservient but equal. And his works were a way of keeping the peace between Heaven and Hell. The Dark Pope claimed that the key term of treaty between the leaders of the celestial and infernal hosts was that God the Fearful must permit Satan the Mighty to have subjects and a realm. In exchange, Satan had agreed not to attack the weaker kingdom of Heaven.

"The eternal struggle has never been a question of morality," the Dark Pope wrote. "It is a matter of numbers and of power. God fears Satan. To keep Our Imperial Lord happy, God permits him uncontested access to the souls of those who indulge their natural whims. The Plain Lord has the more difficult task of collecting the souls of those he has been able to turn from pleasure. But while our Great Lord Satan may interfere with the deeds of men, the Frail God Jehovah may not. That is the price of peace."

Sara didn't like this revelation. If true, the idea of Jehovah-as-politician, of detente between God and the Devil, was disturbingly mortal. At the very least, it was no different than the discredited religions of Greece and Rome with their petty warring gods.

But that didn't mean the interpretation was wrong.

Fredric concluded that unlike God worshipers, Devil worshipers had nothing to fear from eternal damnation. The Dark Pope agreed. According to the text, souls in Hell enjoyed eternal pleasures. The most worthy of these were sent forth whenever mortals called them, to help spread the word of Satan.

Had Fredric aspired to be one of those? In his last unhappy act on earth, did he give up on ever fitting among us as a mortal and choose to become a demon?

Had he succeeded?

Sara finished reading at dinnertime. She left to join the family. Darrell had come and she was glad to see him. He had not been drinking—yet—and was being gregarious rather than confrontational.

After a pleasant meal in which matters of substance and controversy were scrupulously avoided, Sara invited Darrell to have coffee in the gazebo. He seemed surprised but pleased to be asked. Martha was openly delighted that Sara had asked and that Darrell had accepted. There was a contented smile on the woman's face as her children went outside.

The night was mild and the sky was beginning to show stars. This was the time of day when Sara would ordinarily lay down the burdens of work. She could reflect instead of interrogate. Tonight, those labors were just ramping up. The woman felt energized, perhaps a little too much so. She needed to come down a bit. She did not want to make any mistakes when she went back to her office.

"How was your date?" Sara asked.

"When?"

"The other night."

"Oh," Darrell said. "It was okay." He laughed uneasily.

"What is it?" she asked. "Talk to me."

"It's nothin'."

They reached the gazebo. Sara sat. Darrell walked to the riverside and looked out. From behind, he looked like their father. He took a long drink of coffee. Sara wasn't going to push him the way she usually did. This was just about sitting outside and reconnecting, at least a little.

"I pulled a shoulder muscle working on a car today," Darrell said. "It's still sore, right up to my neck. I remember Dad complaining all the time about getting older, how this hurt or that ached and how he needed glasses to read and had to turn the TV way up to hear. Now I'm gettin' there."

"Are you scared?" Sara asked.

"Gettin' there," he admitted. "I'm thirty-three years old

and it's like I'm nowhere." He held the coffee cup toward the inlet. "Just another piece of wood floating along the river."

"Where do you want to be?"

"If I knew I'd go there. But you can't control things." He looked at his sister. "You have plans, a career. Then something unexpected happens and it messes everything up."

"Sometimes."

"Sis, I hate to break it to ya but Delwood is not a happy town right now."

"I know. I'm working on it." *Don't get into this, Darrell,* she thought. She didn't want to give a lecture *or* get one.

"Work hard," he said. "The shit is still young but it's rampin' up. Not everyone's against you. Some people blame the parents and some people blame the culture."

"I wish they'd just mind their own business."

"This town *is* our business. It's our only business, except for those who have sisters who are hip-deep in that business. It gets all tangled up. The last two days I've had to fight the urge to tell people they're fulla crap. I didn't because I don't have the facts and I wouldn't've changed any minds. But it makes me mad."

Sara was touched. "You know, I didn't want to come out here to talk about this. I just wanted to see how you were doing."

"Well, I'm doin' like I said. I'm achy and I'm miffed. I don't like what people are saying."

"Do you remember what they used to say about Dad?"

"Yeah," Darrell said. "I didn't like that either."

"And what we liked didn't change anything," Sara told him. "People thought what they wanted to think. And sometimes, they're right."

"Are they right now, about you killin' that kid?"

"No," she said evenly. It was not Darrell talking, it was the town. "Is that why you came here tonight? To check on me?"

He smiled boyishly. "Caught me."

"Thanks."

The grin deepened. "Also, I need to save money. Dating can be expensive. Especially the first-timers who need to be impressed."

They talked a little about the women Darrell had been seeing—mostly chat room connections and bar stool pickups—and he said he really had to change that too.

"I want someone I'm going to remember," he said.

"Be careful what you wish for," Sara told him.

Darrell faced his sister in the darkness. It took him a moment to understand her meaning. "Hey. You were young. We all make mistakes, some of 'em whoppers. Remember what Dad used to say, that it's only a mistake if we don't learn from it."

"I remember that."

"An' if we do something bad a second time, *then* it's stupid." He frowned as he swatted one of the macramé slings that hung from the east and west sides of the gazebo. "I was wonderin' why it's so dark here. What happened to the candles?"

"I brought them inside," Sara told him. "I needed a mosquito repellent in the office."

"This time of year?"

"Must be my sweet blood," Sara said with a big smile.

"That, or else the vermin are taking over," Darrell said.

"What do you mean?"

"There were rats down at the shop today," Darrell said. "Big ones. We haven't seen those fat boys for years."

"Any idea what that's about?"

"We figure some weekender brought 'em from New York without knowin' it," Darrell said. "They had that unafraid-of-people thing goin'. We set out traps, we'll see what we catch. I'm sure it's nothin', but if we get frogs and locusts next I'm outta here."

Darrell's glib comment about the plagues gave her a chill. Field mice were common in Delwood but rats were not. It was unlikely they would hide in cars when there were other warm, wet spots to hide in the city. She wondered if Fredric had summoned a lesser rat-demon to New Jerusalem as a trial run for the kingdom.

Darrell was silent for a long while. Sara could tell that he was looking down.

"What is it?" she asked.

"I was thinking of Dad. He was a good man, right?"

"I believe that," she said.

"I think he was a little messed-up from the war. Maybe a lot messed-up. Jimmy Bowen fought in 'Nam and boy is he a screwloose. Always pickin' fights at the bar and then never defending himself. Likes to get hit."

"Self-punishment. He probably did some things he isn't proud of," Sara said.

"Maybe. And this girl I went out with, Jennie York, she spent a year in Iraq and ain't in her right bean. She likes to be—well, have sex, but she doesn't like to be held. Says she doesn't like to feel trapped."

"The weeds of trauma sprout in funny places, as one of my first-year psych professors used to say," Sara said.

"This girl sure had the fertilizer," Darrell said. "But with Dad—he had his crazies but he loved us and was devoted to us. I wish I was like that. Devoted to something."

"It'll happen. You should start with a cat."

"I was actually wondering—you think it would be okay if I maybe spent spend more time with Alexander?"

The way he said that made Sara wonder for the first time if he might be a little sweet on Tonia. She didn't know why that hadn't occurred to her before. "I think Alexander would like that."

"You do?"

"Yes."

"Excellent."

They were quiet again for a long moment. "Would you think about something else too?" Sara asked tentatively.

"Oooh, I don't like the sound of that," Darrell said. " 'The category is Drinking for $1,000, Alex.' "

"Darrell, stop. I thought that since we were being open, talking about my own situation—"

"That's different. The thing with the Marash kid was a one-off. I been drinking for years. I *like* having a few with my friends," he said. "We work hard, and then we relax. There's nothing wrong with that."

"You just said you don't remember some of the women you date—"

"Not 'cause I've been drinking but because they're mostly unmemorable," Darrell said. "This is Delwood, remember? We've got to send to Russia or ship 'em to Yale to raise the standards."

"That may be true, but what I'm saying is you might choose more wisely if you looked beyond Sloppy Joe's," Sara said. "Maybe if you took some classes at the community college—"

"And met a nice professor to have an affair with?" he asked.

Sara scowled. She probably deserved that but it hurt anyway.

"Y'know, I think that Mom nagging Dad about his drinking is one of the things that made him drink," Darrell said. "She never asked him *why* he did it, she just chewed him out in her genteel little way. She didn't get that he was in a freakin' war when he was a kid. He saw stuff he could never talk about, stuff he probably couldn't get out of his head."

"And that was tragic," Sara agreed. "The thing about Southern Comfort is that it will make you forget what you don't want to remember, but it won't help you get what you want."

Darrell fell silent.

"I need more coffee and some cookies to go with," Sara said after a long sip. "You interested?"

"I think I'll probably head out," he said.

"Do you want company?" Sara asked.

"At the bar?" he asked.

"Sure. Why not?"

He snickered. "How could I drink if I gotta spend all my time defending your rep?"

"That's the point," Sara said.

Darrell frowned as he rose. "Touché big sister, but I think I'll go it alone." He kissed her on the forehead. "I appreciate the concern, though. I do."

"And I appreciate everything you've ever done for me."

"Anytime. I may be a fuckup, but I mean every good thing I manage to do."

Sara wanted to tell him he wasn't "a fuckup" but that would get into semantics. He was not the man he could be, and she wasn't sure how to make that point.

She drained the last of the coffee, then sat in the gazebo. It was William Blake who wrote that we become what we behold, and Darrell wanted to become their father. Robert was an uneducated man who worked with his hands so Darrell became an unschooled mechanic. There was nothing wrong with that, other than the fact that it left Darrell free to embrace every temptation that came through the door, from the call of a bright spring day and a fishing rod to women to going out "for a few" with his friends.

Whatever it was, in whatever combination, the habit bordering on addiction kept her auto-mechanic brother stuck in neutral.

She heard the screen door shut as Darrell went back inside. It sounded very far away. She stayed where she was for a minute more to give him time to leave. Darrell was a good faker. He would act as though everything were fine and their mother would go to bed happy.

In retrospect, Sara shouldn't have said anything about his drinking. But she feared for Darrell. It had killed their father, and though her brother did not have far to drive, she did not doubt that he did so under-the-influence. Maybe Darrell was right. Speaking their minds was a trait—or a flaw—of the Lynch women.

Even as she thought that, something else occurred to her. Something she had in common not just with her mother but with Fredric and many of her patients. Something the Devil would not hesitate to exploit.

Something she might be able to use to get the answers she wanted.

Snatching up the mug, Sara left the gazebo and walked to the back door.

Eleven

1

Darrell was gone by the time Sara entered the house. She heard his truck pull away. Sara brought her mug to the kitchen, sharpened herself up with more coffee—feeling the prick of hypocrisy after knocking Darrell for drinking—then popped up to her mother's room to tell her she was going to catch up on reading and filing. Martha was watching TV and knitting.

"Did you have a good visit with your brother?" Martha asked.

"We did, yes. Do you need anything?"

"I'm fine," Martha said, smiling and looking up.

There was a heartbreaking mixture of beauty and weariness in her mother's proud blue eyes, in the soft lines of her strong cheeks and forehead. Sara wished she could wash away the disappointment and leave just the beauty. The psychotherapist wondered if the Devil could scroll back time and events.

Don't even think about that, Sara warned. If there was any truth to the reality of the Devil, those were the kinds of thoughts and desires that could get a person into real trouble.

Sara patted her mother's shoulder and the woman blew her a kiss. She went to her office and returned the pentagram to its previous state. The blood had dried but there was nothing in the text that said it had to be fresh. She figured the Devil would let her know if he needed more.

Sara did not want to step into the triangle until everyone in the house had gone to bed. Instead, she sat at her desk and wrote questions to which she wanted answers. She rarely did that with patients. But free-form with the Devil obviously was not the most efficient way to get information.

After an hour she had filled several computer screens with questions. She went through these and cut many of them. She also added questions about some of the most horrific events in human history. Those were control questions, to find out if Satan was who he claimed to be. It seemed to her that an immortal being should know exactly what happened and why. Someone once said the devil was in the details. She would find out if the details were in the devil. If he was lying, if he hesitated, she would suggest to him that he was more puffery than substance. It was important, she felt, to keep the Devil on the defensive.

Sara heard her mother go upstairs around eight-thirty. Tonia put Alexander to bed, finished in the kitchen, and went up shortly after nine. Sara printed out the list and put it on a clipboard. She placed it on the couch where she could see it. She opened the back windows and locked the office door.

The candle wax had hardened and she relit the blackened wicks. She felt a little more confident and a little less anxious than before. In addition to the questions she had just composed, she had the one that she knew the Devil could not deny. The one that would help her to take control of this process.

Sara was about to disrobe when the phone beeped. She went to the desk and looked at the readout. The caller ID said **Franz Marash**. She hesitated. It could be bad news, a threat, anger—or his wife might need to talk. She picked it up.

"This is Dr. Lynch."

"This is Goldwyn Marash," said the surprisingly strong voice. "Our neighbor said you went in our house the night Fredric died. Were you in our house, Dr. Lynch?"

Mr. Jay on-the-job, Sara thought. "Yes," she replied.

"How dare you?"

Careful, Sara told herself. This was not the time for full disclosure. "I went inside to leave you a note," Sara said. "Something I thought might help you."

"What could possibly have helped us, you stupid woman?"

"What you're doing right now," Sara said. "I was going to invite you to vent at me, if you felt it would help."

"You've been a horrible, unthinkable curse on our lives. You want me to vent? You knew about the noose but you told my husband it didn't mean anything, it was just some kind of expression. *We* were worried but you said not to! If you had opened your *fucking* eyes and not been so smug, if you had a child of your own instead of borrowing everyone else's, our son would be alive today."

"Mrs. Marash—" she began, but the name stuck in her throat. She had to clear it, along with the inadvertent reference to her own child before continuing. "I do not believe your son was planning to kill himself."

"*Shut up!*" Goldwyn screamed. "Just shut up. You let my boy die and then you invaded our home. How could you think anything you had to say would help us?"

"That's why I didn't leave the note," Sara told her. "I was also in shock that night."

"You lying, ignorant, awful woman," Goldwyn sneered. "I hope you suffer like this someday. Don't come here again. Don't come to our shop. Don't look at me in the street or from your car. Is that clear, *Dr.* Lynch?"

Tears formed in Sara's eyes. She had to cover the receiver so Goldwyn wouldn't hear her sobs. She wanted to defend herself but said nothing.

"I'm glad you left the church yesterday," Goldwyn went on, weeping now. "I hope you die!" The woman slammed down the phone.

Sara held it for a moment longer before replacing the receiver. Her palms were damp and she was breathing hard as she sobbed. She was not surprised by the woman's hysteria. But the words hurt just the same.

Drained, she took off her clothes, got the flashlight from the closet, and lay it beside the design—just in case the candles went out. They had lost a good deal of wax but should burn for at least another two hours. Then she picked up her list and turned off the light.

The woman took a moment to collect herself. Sara was afraid but that was natural. It was also healthy. Fear would keep her alert, cautious.

She wondered if the Devil was afraid of anything?

Undoubtedly, she thought as she stepped into the triangle.

2

It was warmer than the previous night, and the wind was not as brisk. The silence was the same. She looked into the pentagon, at the spilled wax and the thin gray smoke curling from the candle.

"I want to talk to you," she said boldly.

There was no response. Why should there be? she reasoned. She had not said she wanted him to talk to her.

"Are you here?" she demanded.

"I am everywhere," the Devil replied. There were no eyes this time, just the voice. "I am angry with you," he went on.

It's off-topic but I'll bite, Sara thought. "Why?"

"When we parted last you called me 'a sadistic nightmare.' Why? Because I spoke the truth?"

"Are you telling me your *feelings* are hurt?"

"I am telling you it was a misstatement. You don't like hearing it about yourself and blamed me, the messenger."

"Thanks. When I want to be analyzed it will not be by you," she said.

"By who, then?"

"Not your concern," she replied. "My turn. What are you afraid of?"

"Afraid? Fear is an obstacle to clarity."

"I didn't ask for a definition—"

"A gift," he said.

"Look, you want me to trust you and I need a reason."

"I want nothing but your soul," the Devil replied, his voice deep and rumbling.

Hearing the words, and said so matter-of-factly, made her feel like a fish waiting to be filleted. In spite of the bravado it

scared her. It also made her mouth go dry. Next time she had
to remember the flashlight *and* a bottle of water.

"What do you fear?" Sara repeated. This time the confidence had to be forced out.

"Losing to God," he answered.

Sara couldn't believe that he'd answered. And answered
honestly, it seemed.

"In what way?"

"Any."

"The book says you have an arrangement—"

"We fight for souls, each in our own way."

"His way being to promote the Ten Commandments and
your way being to advocate sin—"

"No. *Living*," the Devil said. "You have been indoctri-
nated. Pleasure is not sin. Abstinence is sin. The world is that
simple."

"And the afterlife?"

"We dwell in the mansions we build," Satan replied. "Your
choice is the eternal pleasure of my realm or the boredom of
eternal self-righteousness."

"Death is that simple too?"

"It is," the Devil told her.

Sara was nowhere near where she wanted to be. But at
least the Devil was talking. "What about murderers? Rapists?
Child molesters? Where do they go?"

"God gets those who repent, I get those who do not.
They inhabit a very unhappy, servile place in purgatory flying here and there as needed."

"Flight attendants of the damned," Sara said.

The voice seemed to move closer. "Whistle past the
graveyard, Dr. Lynch, but *they* are corrupt, God and his fleas.
Indulgence is human nature. That is why God had to create

His neat little rules and enforce them with lies. To confuse your brethren, to deny them their birthright."

Her father was wrong. She could hear the words but without a face she couldn't tell if they had truth or meaning.

"You know, it's very difficult talking to someone I can't see," Sara said.

"You just did so with Mrs. Marash."

"That was different."

"Only in your mind," the Devil said.

This is a dead end. It was time to get back to the list. "I realized something before," she went on. "Your activities, your victories, depend entirely on our impatience. People who learn to pray are content to wait years, decades for their reward."

"Time helps God," the Devil agreed. "Older people become less active. They smell their mortality. They become fearful. Some turn to my demons for youth but most turn to God for salvation."

"Then you agree that people who ask for your help are impatient."

"I prefer 'hungry.'"

"What will happen to your kingdom when we lose our 'animal natures,' when we move farther from the apes?"

"There will always be a famine or power failure or someone to shatter your heart and drag you back," the Devil said. "My job is not in danger. Another million years of growth will not cause you to change."

"I don't believe that," Sara said.

"The father becomes the son," he said. "That is fact."

"The son can change," Sara replied. "I help people do that every day."

"So does God. And you still lose people every day, both

of you. You did better when the Church ruled Europe and there were fewer than a half-billion people on the globe. The dimensions and methods of human self-absorption have increased exponentially."

The room became aggressively quiet. Sara needed to stop this. Crunching numbers with the Devil was not why she had called on him.

"I want to know why Fredric hanged himself," Sara said.

"He chose to be with me."

"Is he with you?" Sara asked.

The Devil did not answer. Sara saw the swift, sideward movement of a large red hand. The palm was open, facing up, as it slashed the air before vanishing. Wind was pulled from the waiting room into the office, catching the smoke from the candles and moving it to the center of the pentagram. The twin columns drifted together into a single, upright mass. It quickly took shape and suddenly Fredric was standing before her. Though his body was hidden in thick black shadow—as it was in life—she could see the distinctive contour of his face. His features became sharper until she could see his familiar eyes and an unfamiliar smile beneath them.

"Fredric?"

"Hello, Dr. Lynch," he said.

Sara's shoulders felt weak. Her fingers shook. She held her list tightly and could hear the paper rattle.

"How are you?" Sara asked. The question, shallow enough in a session, seemed entirely ludicrous now.

"I'm fine," the young man replied. He sounded relaxed, the way he had when he first told her about the triangle.

She continued to shake, partly from the cold but mostly from the apparition. Sara suddenly realized that she was naked but chose to ignore it. Fredric was not interested in her. Besides, she was not convinced any of this was real. "Why did you do this?" she asked.

He was silent as he stood suspended in the filmy mist.

"Do you remember what happened? Why you took your life?" Sara asked.

"Who wouldn't remember his own death?" Fredric asked with bemusement. "I wanted to be free."

"From what?"

"You know the answer to that. Disappointment. Judgments. Lies."

"We were working on those—"

"For ten years! And you were losing your way."

"*I* was?"

"Why did you lie to my mom about going in the house?"

"To protect myself," she answered truthfully. "Why did *you* keep things from her?"

"To protect *her*," Fredric said. "You see how different you and I are?"

"We are *very* different but I cared about you," Sara said. "You could have come to me. The magnitude of this—it shouldn't have been decided in a moment of anger."

"It wasn't. I've known for a while there is only one place for the unloved and discarded."

"You weren't unloved. I met someone today who cared deeply for you, Marci Cello."

"I will talk to Marci about joining me."

"No!" Sara said.

"She misses me, I know that. I will show her the contentment she can share."

"Fredric, she does miss you, which is why you *mustn't* confuse her."

Sara wanted to run into the pentagon and grab him, shake him. Reacting threatened, the smoke thickened protectively, instinctively, like a living thing. It swallowed Fredric, then it thinned. The candles returned to normal and Fredric was gone.

"You prefer Marci to be in pain," the disembodied voice of the Devil said. "Or does your misery want company? Is that what you truly take from your patients?"

"Whatever she's feeling will pass," Sara said, ignoring the charge. "She has time to make choices, to experience things that will help her choose."

"Marci Cello will end up no different than the women your brother uses and discards. Do you think you can change that?"

"I have to believe that."

"*If* you are allowed to see her," the Devil said. "The pious of Delwood have gone into your room and taken your scarf and left you nothing to play with."

"I will change their minds—"

"You will fail," the Devil assured her. "The future is written in the past acts of your kind."

"Not always! Christ *Jesus*!" Sara snapped, losing it for a moment.

The Devil laughed humorlessly. "I tried with Him. I did try."

The remark startled Sara as she realized with cold-water shock that this voice was, in fact, the same one that had tempted Jesus in the wilderness. This creature *knew* the Son of God. Whether or not she was a practicing Catholic, it caused her other thoughts, her "control" questions about history to fade to insignificance.

It also gave her a flash of courage. If the Devil *was* real, then so were Christ and God. If she needed them, if reason failed, then faith could be her lantern and repentance her re-demption.

Still trembling, Sara glanced at her notes. This wasn't about her. There were other souls to save from the Devil, Marci's among them.

"What is New Jerusalem?" she asked.

"What do you think it is?"

"Your kingdom on earth. But then what is the New King-dom?"

The Devil was silent. Sara suspected that the New Kingdom was the name for what would spring from New Jerusalem. But she hadn't summoned the Devil so she could make educated guesses. She wanted information and she fought her own admonition about impatience. She fought the desire to lash out at the God of Goats by sending him back to Hell.

"Do you think you can?" he asked suddenly.

"Can what?"

"Return me to Hell?"

"I do," Sara said. The way he asked made her uncertain, as it was surely intended to do.

The Devil's liquid red eyes suddenly appeared again, duller than the candles and barely discernible against the darkness. They rose until they were some seven feet off the ground, then moved toward the edge of the pentagon and looked down. They seemed as large as they did when they were eye level.

"What makes you think I cannot leave?" the Devil asked. "Was there a pentagram in the cave when I communed with the Nazarene? Did I not just appear?"

"There may have been a symbol," Sara replied bravely. She tried to keep her voice steady, her posture confident.

"Yes. Perhaps my devotees carved one in the rock," the Devil said, chuckling. His eyes narrowed. "Or maybe Fredric summoned me in the woods and released me."

"Those designs were unbroken," she said.

"Perceptive," the Devil replied.

"You can't leave the symbol," Sara said. "I believe that."

"That may be true," the Devil replied. "Or it may be false. My kingdom runs right below your feet, from one end of civilization to another, from the beginning of time to its final moments. That is not a frail, tiny chalk mark on the floor. What do you think would happen if I burned the wood and the chalk vanished?"

The candles began to bubble. Boiling wax crawled from the containers, not on the floor but along the chalk line. The fire went with it, creeping along the sides of the pentagon in the middle.

"Are borders real or are they merely suggestions for the weak and unimaginative, like the Commandments?" the Devil asked. "What kind of a leader has to demand fealty?"

The subject had changed. She tried to keep up. "You tell me," she said.

"Ah, the psychotherapist ascendant," the Devil said. "A leader instills loyalty. He earns it by deeds, not commands. My followers come to me by choice, not by fear."

"They *are* afraid. They're afraid of life."

"And who has made them that way? Who but the one who began our war by flinging them from Eden for daring to feel. There was no need for any of this. He and I are brothers, unparented and eternal. We are the genesis of all deities in all times and all cultures. He was the destroyer of Eden and peace, not I."

"The gods of all cultures," Sara said. There were analogues, the warring deities in Greece and Rome, in Norse mythology. She thought of the phrase she had heard earlier. "*Proserpine ad portas*," she said.

"Proserpine is at the door," the Devil said plaintively. "You heard that before?"

"Yes. How?"

"It is everywhere, if you listen," the Devil told her. "Lost love, suffering. The legacy of a jealous God, He who must be loved above all. This world is the veil of tears. There is no suffering for the souls who come to me willingly."

"No," Sara said. "I don't believe any of this. It's what you tried to do to Jesus, confuse him—"

"Having delusions of extreme grandeur, aren't you?"

"Not I. The empty promises *you* gave to Jesus are no different than those you told Fredric."

"I told no lies!" the Devil bellowed.

Sara was surprised by his sudden rage. And sobered. These were the kinds of tantrums that had destroyed ancient cities.

"The New Testamentarians cleaned it up. What I told my nephew was that he was going to die cruelly and soon. I urged him to have a word with his father about that. Jesus declined. He trusted his father, but I knew better. I knew my brother would have him executed to secure his hold on masses of souls. It was a brilliant move. One death, millions of converts. God took that from me, don't you see? One snake, millions of so-called sinners. What I didn't know was how cruel Jehovah would actually make that death and the death of those who followed. Crucifixions, disembowelings, food for lions and bears. And they call *me* a monster. But then our siblings surprise us, don't they?"

Sara didn't answer. She was too busy trying to process what she was being told.

The red eyes moved again. For the briefest moment she thought she saw them fixed in a face, something that resembled the grotesque masks she had once seen hanging in New York's Chinatown, faces with big, fixed grins and high sinister foreheads. But Sara could not be sure. She had been so rapt in the Devil's narrative she even forgot the flames on the chalk. They had completely surrounded the interior pentagon and now the smoke began to rise. It filled the center of the symbol, a churning column, until the ruddy eyes were barely visible.

"You asked a question before," the Devil said in a deep voice. "Am I your prisoner?"

"Are you?"

"Can you see my arms?"

"You know I can't."

"They are stretching upward," the Devil told her. "They are reaching through the ceiling into the floor. I feel a young boy, in bed."

Sara tasted dinner in the back of her mouth. She struggled to keep it down. "What are you doing?"

"Tucking him in."

"Leave him alone," she said.

"Then you *do* believe I can touch him."

"I don't know." She glanced down at the pentagram.

"I am still within it. I must be lying."

"Yes—"

"Let me show you I am not," he said with cool meance. "I'm moving on. Another room. There's a body in a chair. Your mother. I feel the scars and wrinkles and the aches underneath her robe. I feel the soreness and the unhealed places where she can still feel the back of your father's hand or the toe of his shoe."

"Stop," she muttered without thinking.

"The television is on, but her eyes are shut. She is dreaming. Dreaming of a grandchild."

Why was he doing this?

"I did not say yours," the Devil said. "That pain comes from you, not me. Your mother thinks of her unmet grandchildren often. Right now she dreams of your brother. He has had many lovers, and they have slain many children."

The flames were rising, not as a wall of fire but as a reverse rain, blazing droplets that rose and evaporated in angry little puffs. There were more and more of them as the Devil spoke.

"Here are the souls of the unborn," the Devil declared. "They are not mine, nor do they belong to God. They are fire, they are wind and water and earth. They are the dumb, unwritten stuff of the world and have nowhere else to go."

"No more," Sara cried.

The fire died in an instant. There were only the candles again and the eyes, still high and dim.

Sara felt as though she had been pummeled. She was hot from the fire and exertion. Perspiration trickled down her bare thighs, along her sides. It dripped onto the floor, onto the pentagram. She couldn't take any more of this. Not now.

"You asked about Fredric Marash," the Devil said.

"I did but I can't do this anymore."

"What do you think you know about the young man's final moments?" the Devil asked.

"I was there, I saw—"

"Not externally," the Devil said.

Sara stood there, limp and spent. She wanted to go but this wasn't just about her. "He was lonely and confused. He ran from his home in rage and panic."

"Fear breeds desperation breeds unreasoning behavior," the Devil said. "Your mind is linear and unexciting."

"Delineate me," she said, finding some anger.

The Devil laughed. "You still don't see. That is what Fredric *did*. A delineation is frozen motion, arrested life, the essence of a being locked in a single descriptive form or act. Fredric delineated himself. He knew what he was and what he wanted and expressed them both in a single deed."

"Fredric was a confused teenager," Sara said.

"In fact, his clarity was astonishing. He saw the limitations of his world and he chose mine."

"I saw him hanging from a tree. He did not seem very happy."

"That was the shell his mother had left him." The Devil moved closer invisibly. "It was not his *soul*. We spoke before his flight from the house. He had been sitting on his bicycle in New Jerusalem, surveying his work. I told him that a parent would soon cause him pain. It was nothing less than I told Jesus."

"His mother cleaned his scarf. It was innocent. You stirred him up for your own gain."

"His mother was looking for evidence of freakish sexual activity."

Sara was openly surprised.

"Goldwyn Marash had eavesdropped on his intense enjoyment, had knocked on his locked door while he was within," the Devil said. "She was ignored. When he was gone she entered his room. She sought evidence to support her own linear fear, that her son had inherited her own unorthodox sexual nature." The Devil laughed. The candles rose slightly, throwing their own laughter along the bookcase and rug. "Goldwyn found none of the diversions she had sought, barely noticed the images of Chrissie Blair. She took the scarf to clean because she needed an excuse to cover her fruitless search. Without realizing it, the stupid woman had seized the one object that had any libidinous function." The Devil was silent as his eyes retreated toward the center of the pentagon. "Fredric chose to escape that kind of scrutiny and looming suppression, the unwarranted judgment of an ignorant convert to God. He made that choice bravely and emphatically."

"He was too young to have done that," Sara said. "There were other ways to deal with the problem."

"Do you speak from experience?"

It took a moment for the words to go where the Devil had aimed them. "You keep returning to the abortion. Is that my only sin?"

"I returned to nothing. I asked a general question."

"You hit me with innuendo about my mother, my decisions, the vision in the woods beside the grave—"

"Why do you assume the apparition was sent by me?" the Devil asked.

The question was a surprise.

"The boy appeared on a cemetery plot consecrated by a priest, outside my realm," the Devil replied. "My brother is a master of confusion and deceit. That image was from him."

"I don't believe you."

"I am never wrong."

"*I don't believe you!* I'm not even sure I believe *in* you!"

"That would make you somewhat—insane?"

"I don't think so. You could be corporealized guilt over Fredric."

"Only Fredric?" the Devil asked. "In any case there is no need for me to lie," the Devil said. "Look around you. You hear the confessions of the happily licentious, you see Darrell drawn to women and decadence and you know it is natural and true. Yet you hold to your chaste superiority. You are not like them, you tell yourself, and that is true. *They* are honest. You say I lie yet you speak falsehoods to Goldwyn and Tonia, to your mother and brother. Who is the abomination?"

Sara had heard enough. She stepped from the triangle. The eyes vanished. The candles burned low again, leaving the room a bleak orange. The air outside was motionless, the house quiet.

"What have I done?" Sara asked. She walked on wobbly legs to the couch and plucked her blouse from the arm. She hugged it to her chest and stood there sweating, tortured, racing inside yet barely able to stand. "What have I brought on myself?" She put on her clothes, her hands were shaking.

You did what was necessary to save Marci, perhaps others, not to mention your reputation and career, she reminded herself. Even if the Devil was real, even if her soul was the prize, the battleground was her mind. Dr. Arul had told her that she was firmly in command there. She needed to assert that command. She needed to fight the Devil with other ideas.

Unfortunately, right now Sara didn't have any. Not one. She had nothing in her mind or soul except disorientation and a dull, aching sadness and there was nothing on that list she had so proudly crafted that could help her. Finding out who killed JFK was not what she needed.

Fortunately, there was nothing to do now except go to bed. Tomorrow would be a different matter.

And tomorrow she would seek help from the other side.

Twelve

1

Sara woke up shortly before seven the next morning. She felt worse than when she had gone to bed. Her limbs were like sacks of sand and her head was cloudy. The latter lasted but a moment. Thoughts started trickling, then rushing back, so many that she couldn't focus on any one.

What should you do?

It was Sunday, so she couldn't do much. On Monday she could talk to Chrissie Blair—*And tell her what?*

Explain what was happening? Tell her that other students might be in danger? Go to Marci and warn her? Check the Goth chat rooms for other local names and get in touch with their parents, alert them to the danger?

That what? A dead teenager is coming after them? That would be pointless without more information. Without armor. Without utterly believing it herself. The Devil would wish her to be impatient, to run in without credibility or solutions.

The Devil. *The Devil.* In the gray, cave-mouth light of a new autumn day she didn't believe it herself.

Sara got out of bed. She had no evidence that the visitations were real. Even if she had recorded the session who would be convinced? They'd say it was fake, she was channeling voices from her subconscious. For all Sara knew that was exactly what had happened. A post-traumatic response to the death of a patient.

Sara went to her office and called Grace Rollins. The professor had just finished with her morning devotions and was about to join the girls of the Sister Mary Academy for breakfast. She was very happy to hear from Sara.

"How are things?" Grace asked.

"Wonky," Sara replied.

"Oh, you and your psychobabble," she teased.

"Do you have time to see me today?" Sara asked.

"I'll make time. What's up?"

"I'd rather tell you in person," Sara said.

"Is everyone all right?"

"We're fine and it's serious in a theological sense," Sara said.

"My favorite kind of serious," Grace replied. "I'm going to mass and have a Sunday school class to teach until two-fifteen. Does that time frame work?"

"I'll be there," Sara said.

"Bless you. Courage. Why don't we meet at the coffee shop at two-thirty," Grace suggested.

"Glad to hear it's still there."

"It's a bulldog, one of the last holdouts against the chains."

"That's the kind of hind legs and teeth I need."

"Sara, are you sure there's nothing I can do now?"

Sara took the plunge. "Not unless you can tell me about the Devil, hell, and how you get in and out and rid of him."

There was the briefest pause. "I'll see you later. Drive safely," Grace said.

Tonia was in the kitchen making waffles. Pouring a half cup of coffee and biting into dry toast—her stomach was feeling a little unsettled this morning—Sara told the housekeeper she would be gone all day. They had her cell phone number if they needed anything.

Tonia was facing the waffle iron. She nodded silently.

"Is everything all right?" Sara looked around. "Where's Alexander?"

"He's eating in his room."

"Why?" Sara asked.

"I did not want him to spoil your morning," Tonia said. "He is very angry and upset."

"About what?"

"He woke during the night from a nightmare," Tonia said, turning slightly.

The psychotherapist felt a tingle along her backbone. "What kind of nightmare?"

"He said his father was reaching through the floor trying to pull him down," Tonia replied.

The tingle became lightning. It snapped Sara's tired neck and head upright. "What happened then?"

"I held him until he went to sleep. When he woke this morning he was very upset. He yelled at me for keeping him here. He said he wanted to be with his daddy."

Sara went to the woman and turned her around. Tonia's eyes were red, her pretty face drawn. "I want you to stay with him today," the psychotherapist said. "Play games, go for walks, hold his hand."

"Why do you say this?"

"Strong dreams often have a powerful influence on young, imaginative minds," Sara said. "Things they see in their heads sometimes seem real in the day, what we call waking nightmare. Alexander might *think* he sees his father in the street or in the duck pond. He might try to go to him."

"Father in Heaven, no," Tonia replied.

All of what Sara had said was true, though she omitted the part about the Devil having reached through the ceiling the night before. She did not want to frighten the woman by telling her that Satan may have infected her son with visions. Fredric would have called that a lie. Sara called it protective care.

"Will Alexander be safe?" Tonia asked.

"I believe he is very safe if you do as I've said," Sara told her. "I'll try and get home before you put him to bed, make sure everything is okay."

"All right, Dr. Sara. Thank you very much."

Tonia always called her Dr. Sara when she was giving advice. It was endearing, a little sparkle of diamond in the mine.

"Did you check on Mother?" Sara asked.

"Yes. She is up," Tonia said.

"You saw her?"

Tonia nodded. "She called to me when I walked by, asked me what the weather was like. I told her raining and she asked for her bathrobe. Then she made a moan and pulled the robe to her chin."

Sara smiled. Her mother was fine.

Tonia went back to the waffle iron. Sara took a big bite of toast, another swallow of coffee, then grabbed an umbrella and went to her car. She was surprised to find Darrell's truck parked behind her Jeep in the driveway. He was sitting in the driver's seat, staring ahead. The window was up, misted by drizzle. Sara rapped on the glass. Darrell rolled it down.

"Hi," he said.

"Good morning." Sara could not only smell the alcohol she could practically taste it. There was an open bottle of Jack Daniel's on the seat beside Darrell. It was nearly empty.

"I came here to shit," he said. He turned away and stared out the windshield.

"Do you need help getting out?"

"Nope. Doin' fine."

It occurred to Sara that what he had meant to say was "sit." She opened the door and gently took his hand. "Come with me anyway."

"Where to?"

"Inside."

"Gotta stay here, inna car."

"Why?" Sara asked.

"Dad tol' me ta wait," Darrell insisted.

Sara felt the same electric chill she'd felt just a few minutes before. "Darrell, Dad is *dead*."

Darrell fluttered his lips. "Tell *him*! If Dad was dead he wouldn't have told me to sit here."

"No one's here."

Darrell wrenched his hand away. "Course no one's there. He went inside."

"What? Why?" Sara asked.

"Said—said he had to get you an' Mom."

Sara looked back at the house, at the north tower. She needed to go to her mother now. She started back when suddenly the front door opened. Martha was standing there in her bathrobe.

"Is everything all right, dear?" Martha asked.

Sara nodded. She went back to the truck.

"See?" Darrell said. "There she is! Wonder where Pop is?"

"He's gone," Sara said. She looked at her brother. "When did you see him?"

"A moon ago. It was still dark." He chuckled. "'Moon' ago. Pretty funny, huh?"

"Were you here?"

"Yep. Came back to talk to you but Mom said you were in your office. I didn't wanna bother you so I watched TV with her till she pooped out. Then I left." He looked at Sara. "Then I came back. Dad came out and I talked to him. He said he would go and get you guys and we would all have breakfast at the Cheyenne Diner like we useta."

"Darrell, I need you to sit here, okay?"

"You just said to come—"

"In a minute," she said.

"Okay. Not movin'."

Sara hurried to Martha.

"What's going on?" the woman asked. "Is Darrell all right?"

"He's a little out of it," Sara said. "Look, I'm going to bring him in and then I'm going out."

"Oh? Where?" Martha asked.

Sara didn't feel like answering questions. "For a drive. To clear my head."

"That's a splendid idea." Martha smiled. She looked out at the rain. "Just be careful. The roads will be slick with wet leaves."

"I'll watch myself."

Martha continued to stare at the drizzle. "I was going to get the papa—"

"Sorry?"

"The newspaper," Martha said. "I was going to get it, but the rain—"

"I'll go," Sara said. That wasn't what she heard, but then everything was a little off this morning. Sara got the newspaper from the foot of the driveway, shook the water from the wrapper, then tucked it in the pocket of her trenchcoat. Then she went back to Darrell's truck. "Come on," she said, taking his arm.

"But you said—"

"It's okay. We're going inside."

"But Dad said—"

"*Mom* wants you inside," Sara said. "Who's the boss?"

"Mom is," Darrell said.

Sara made sure the keys were still in the ignition. Then she half-helped, half-pulled her brother from the truck and walked him to the door. He moved like the Frankenstein Monster in lurches and shoulder-heavy stumbles, his arms swinging as though they were asleep. He called for his father as he went along, telling him he wanted to wait but the boss told him no.

"The two bosses," Darrell said with a laugh, giving his sister a sloppy peck on the ear.

Sara led him to the first-floor guest room. Martha followed behind. Drawn by the commotion, Alexander met Sara in the hallway and helped her.

"What's wrong with Darrell?" the boy asked.

"He doesn't feel well," Sara said.

"It's *women*!" the man shouted. "Women make me *crazy*!"

"Alexander, go help your mother in the kitchen," Sara said.

"I want to help Darrell."

"Go to serve woman!" Darrell yelled. "It's not just a cookbook anymore. It's a friggin' life manual!"

The boy's big eyes shifted from Darrell to Sara.

"Please take Alexander," Sara urged her mother.

Martha took the boy's small hand in hers. "Let's go get some of your mother's waffles," she said.

The boy left with her. He was obviously over his nightmare but affected by what he had just witnessed. Darrell had never been this bad during the day when the boy was around.

"See, he's whipped jus' like me an' Dad," Darrell said. "Hey, 'member Ellen Caroline Meade, sis?"

"I can't say that I do."

"E. C. Meade. They called her 'Easy.' I was crazy about her in high school but she was crazy about the editor of the school paper and his reporters. She liked 'em smart and she liked 'em aggressive, all of which I wasn't any of. See? Is that grammar right? I don't even know." He laughed. "Maybe if I did she'd've liked me. I couldn't spell. All I could do was *fix* things."

"There's nothing wrong with that," Sara said.

"There is if you want a smart chick," he said.

Sara got him to the bed and let him drop.

"But nooooo. I couldn't spell. Or punk. Chew. Ate. So Easy went off with that fuckin' journalist fuck Steve to Panama and take fuckin' pictures to go with his fuckin' stories. She probably fucked the fuckin' Panama-people journalists too. 'Hold me, you smart motherfuckers. Let me dig your diggable brain.'"

Sara lifted his legs onto the bed. They were dead weight. "I want you to stay here and sleep," she said.

"Yessir, ma'am," Darrell said with a sloppy salute at the ceiling. "Women *are* the man. Dad didn't build Mom her plantation on the river so he was a bigtime floperoo. Maybe if she'da told him it was okay, she only wanted him and not *things*, maybe he woulda been okay. Who knows?" He started to sob. "At least Easy told me I was a loser. She said she wanted someone who was '*stim*ulating.' She said the 'stim' like it was a good hard fuck. I was just a grease monkey." He feigned disgust. "Ewww. Who is *that*?" He laughed suddenly. "Who? Who's on first? I dunno! *Third base!*" He laughed. "'Member the videotape that had that routine, sis? How Dad and I useta watch it and it would make us laugh each time?"

"I remember," Sara said. She took off his work boots, then stood and watched as her brother wound down. The sentences became fragments, then just words, and finally he was silent. She shut the door and went to the kitchen. Tonia was setting their breakfast on plates. Martha was in the dining room with Alexander. They had gone to the boy's room and gotten him an action figure. Normally he wasn't allowed to have toys at the table. Martha had obviously made an exception. Sara was proud of her. She was not a woman who typically broke with tradition.

Sara put the newspaper on the counter, then leaned into the dining room. "I'm sorry to leave you like this."

"Don't think about it," Martha said. "I am not a stranger here."

"I will help," Alexander assured Sara, holding up his little action figure.

Sara didn't know whether the boy was talking to the soldier or *for* him.

"I'm counting on your help, Alexander," Sara said.

The psychotherapist felt a little uneasy about going but

there was no choice. Leaving their eclectic little family with a smile, Sara went out the side door. She moved her brother's truck to the street, got in the Jeep, and drove up the hill.

It felt good to be ascending, even if it was just up a cloud-darkened River Road.

2

A fine rain continued to fall as she drove along the winding Route 6. Sara flipped the wipers on low and slid *The Magic Flute* into the CD player. That opera was her favorite classical work, about a lowly bird seller who triumphs over the evil Queen of the Night. She related to the queen's daughter, Pamina, who was the center of everyone's attentions—including a bold but clueless prince.

Mozart was light and spirited and she liked having him in the car. The only drawback was that the wiper did not keep time with the music. She wondered what ordinary people would have heard in the time of Mozart, other than music, that had a regular beat. Horse hooves and wagon wheels. Water mills. Snoring. Their own heartbeats. But they wouldn't have heard those things in a concert hall. What a world this had become, a symphony unto itself.

Was anyone conducting? she wondered. Or was the Devil right? We were essentially on our own while he and God vied for our souls. It was a dismal thought. Even a nonpracticing Catholic had, somewhere in her muscle memory, a fundamental hope—if not belief—in the existence of a paternal God.

Sara left the two-lane route after twenty miles, taking small country roads toward Waterbury and Route 8. That was the major artery that would take her to Interstate 95 and New Haven.

The farther south she traveled the more there were leaves still on trees. It wasn't life but it wasn't quite death either. The leaves that had fallen were damp and slick and she drove the tight, blind curves cautiously. She would hate to perish without a clear idea of where her soul should go.

Do you really doubt that? she asked herself.

Even as a girl, Sara had never quite believed in Heaven. The idea that Jesus would have time to greet everyone personally and put them at ease about being dead, that her father would be sober and her relatives would all get along, that she could learn the Celtic spoken by her remote ancestors, that she could enjoy life without coffee—none of that made sense. Now that she was exploring the idea of Hell, Sara was not so ready to disbelieve. But what the Devil had said made sense. She was more frightened by that than she was by the possibility that there was no afterlife. The idea of souls as toys in a petulant, fraternal spat between God and the Devil was terrifying. It did reduce her to the self-image of an animal.

Quite by chance, the Queen of the Night was just now singing that if her daughter failed to obey her wishes she would be her daughter no more. She wondered whether Mozart's talents had come from God or the Devil, or neither. Perhaps, like Fredric, the young composer had come by his talent through the gene pool. Perhaps he experienced all he wished to in this world and was ready for another. Maybe the Devil helped him along. She wondered if some souls were prized above others, like veal. The younger the better, the holier the better, the more brilliant the better. Satan had expressed particular pique at failing to persuade Jesus. Some of that was his desire to strike back at God. But his brother's son, his nephew, would have been a plum soul for his farm or spa or whatever was down there.

There was too much to contemplate and too little information even to try, especially since she had only heard from one side. The Queen of the Night had her reasons for holding her daughter back. In the end, though, they weren't good ones.

The trip to New Haven took nearly two hours. When Sara arrived she parked in a public garage and sat there for nearly a half hour. It was time to shift her thoughts from one hell to another, her private purgatory. Driving back was easy. Returning was not. Sara had expected some insulation from the past: new storefronts over the old ones, chain stores instead of the mom-and-pops. Even this parking garage was new. But Sara knew that the ambiance would be very much the same and there would be difficult memories on so many corners.

Through it.

It was definitely time to face some of the lesser demons, the ones without form or voice or liquid red eyes. The ones that were in her head and haunting these streets but no less real for it.

Sara was early but she left the car anyway, walking from the drab concrete structure toward State Street. The old hangout was on Elm Street, not far from City Hall.

The pavement was gray and the rain was cool and the bottoms of her pants quickly turned from tan to wet-brown. The wind from the Long Island Sound hit the funnel of the New Haven Harbor and moved briskly along the streets. Sara kept her umbrella angled ahead, watching for the feet of oncoming pedestrians so she didn't poke them. Shielding herself not just from the rain but a chance encounter. She didn't know where he might turn up. Cars and buses sped by with an increasingly hollow slosh that reminded her to stay away from traffic or get splattered.

A little like life itself, Sara reflected.

Sara zigzagged through the town green and emerged on Chapel Street. She walked down College Street past the famed Shubert Theater, legendary home of pre-Broadway tryouts.

We need a tryout venue for life itself, she thought. Perhaps that's what college was supposed to be. But failure there hurt for real and could last forever, and kids had miserably few defenses to deal with it.

Sara stopped in front of the old theater marquee. She had come here many times during her studies, usually with Grace or another girlfriend. Martin Cayne wasn't one for musicals or rock concerts—or so he said. He preferred poetry and literary readings, and dramas, preferably by angry young voices. He liked to know what people were thinking and feeling in a raw, emotional state.

He liked to cause that too.

It started raining harder so Sara headed for the coffee shop. Ted was no longer behind the cash register of Teddy's, with his yellow fingernails and the lumpy ashtray his grandson had made in ceramics class. The curled wallpaper was gone, replaced by paint, but the pictures of old New Haven were still there, along with photos of Ted with various stars who had appeared at the Shubert.

It was after lunch. The church crowd had gone and there were plenty of tables. Sara selected a booth toward the back, facing the door. The bathrooms had new doors, she noticed. These probably closed all the way, and locked. She used one. The smell of disinfectant was much less pronounced than it used to be. The soap no one dared touch had been replaced by a soap dispenser with fresh-smelling pink liquid inside.

Sara ordered coffee—there was a choice now, and she

selected hazelnut—and waited. It felt good to be here, very comfortable and safe. Martin had never come here. It was too low-rent. This was her spot with Grace. And when Grace arrived the comfort level grew.

Grace folded her black umbrella outside and shook it off before turning. She looked into the coffee shop and smiled when she saw Sara. She hung her black poncho by the door, unshouldered her big book bag, and walked along the carpet that had been laid over the wet linoleum.

Grace was a tall woman, nearly six feet, with gray eyes and high cheekbones. She wore a traditional habit, eschewing the license of Vatican II to wear civilian clothes. To Grace, the habit was a statement of her devotion to Christ and her belief that God's work was to be done twenty-four/six. As she told people with a wry smile, even God took a day of rest. Of course, Grace rarely took one. When she wasn't lecturing, researching, or writing, she studied languages: Greek, Latin, Hebrew, Arabic, and Aramaic. As she once told Sara—when she was learning modern Hebrew—she didn't want to stumble on a great find in the Negev Desert and have no idea whether it was a prayer or a menu.

Sara slid from the booth. Grace dropped the bag and umbrella beside the table. The women hugged very long and very hard.

"Good for you," Grace said.

"Thanks." Still smiling, Sara broke the embrace and regarded her friend. "I finally made it back to New Heaven."

"That name," Grace said, chuckling. "I'd forgotten."

Sara had nicknamed the city when Grace decided to remain. There hadn't been an occasion to use it since.

Grace sat down, ordered coffee, and spoke a small, quiet

blessing for the gift of shelter and food. Then she looked at Sara with her wise young eyes. "How was your drive?"

"Long and slippery, but I remembered the way," Sara said.

"You were always so good at those things," Grace said.

"How's your back been?"

"When I'm in the field, doing hard labor, it's fine," Grace said. "When I do nothing but talk and think, it's less fine. I actually wished you were with me this past summer."

Sara sat down. "Where were you?"

"In Jerusalem. I got lost on the very small roads in the southern sector. The streets, you see, conform to the original layouts. They're small and crooked with very few modifications for modern traffic. I could never tell which way I was going."

"I know how that feels."

Grace scowled. "No psychological metaphors allowed," she said.

"Yes, sister."

"How is your family?" Grace asked as the waitress returned with coffee and menus.

"Mother is fine, Darrell is Darrell, and your two Russian angels were the best gifts you could have given us," Sara told her. "But I need you to stay in lecture mode for a little bit."

"Business first?"

"I really need it, Grace."

"Shoot."

Sara lowered her voice and leaned in slightly. "Talk to me about the Devil. Anything you can think of."

Grace had been spooning sugar into her coffee. She finished, took a sip. "I've been thinking about that since you called," Grace said. She pointed to the spoon. "He is sugar."

"How do you mean?"

"He is the prime sweetener, the one who makes everything taste good."

"And that's a bad thing because—?" Sara asked.

"Where there is no trial, there is no reward. When Adam sinned, it was the will of God that his children be denied the beatific vision of happiness. It is our job, all of us, to return to a state of sanctifying grace through deed and worship."

"A bootstrap operation," Sara said.

"Not entirely," Grace replied. "Jesus took the big step for us. All we need do is heed His words and follow His teachings and we'll do fine." She took a sip. She looked at Sara across the top of her cup. "What's this about? A patient, I hope?"

"Partly. The patient—a teenager—is dead. He was an occultist who took his life. I wanted to know why."

Grace put her cup down and pushed it aside. She folded her hands on the table. "Honeybun, what did you do?"

"I asked the Devil to pay me a visit."

"And did he?"

Sara nodded as the waitress arrived to take their order. Sara ordered pea soup and a Caesar salad. Grace ordered grilled cheese.

"Well grilled, burn it," she said. Her eyes were still on Sara.

"My patient had a book, something by the Dark Pope," Sara continued when the waitress had gone.

"Bruce Perry of Denver," the nun said.

"What?"

"He's the current Dark Pope and that's where he lives," Grace told her. "His work is supposedly based on writings that somehow survived the burning of the Library at Alexandria during the time of Cleopatra. You used a spell from that volume?"

Sara nodded.

"Do you have any idea what you are tempting?"

"I'm starting to, which is why I'm here," Sara said. She took a sip of her own coffee. "Grace, I have seen the Devil. I have conversed with him in my office—at least I think I have. We spoke for hours and he told me things."

"Lies. Every word."

"I have no proof of that," Sara said. It was just like their old debates on campus, though with more at stake.

"Sara, the Devil is not just a bad guy. He's Evil-with-a-capital-E. The word 'boundary' has no meaning for him. He will do whatever it takes to win souls."

"Okay, back up," Sara said.

"Let's," Grace agreed. "You were distressed because of your young patient. You raised the Devil who said things, some of which made wonderful, soothing sense. He convinced you that your patient was in a better place, that God and the church had misrepresented Hell, and that you should get to know him better. Is that what happened?"

"More or less," Sara said.

"The Devil stinks of conviction. There is rarely the wise guy in him. He is courtly but accessible, godlike but human, impervious yet quick to wound. But these are just *parts* he plays. His true nature, his reason for being, is to tear down what God wants us to become."

"How do you know that?"

"It's in the Bible, in accounts of possessions and exorcisms, in other texts in many tongues," Grace said.

"You've never had a personal encounter."

"Why would I want one? It's like watching an execution. I have no desire to lay eyes on what is worst in us. And before you say it, no. It is not like me giving someone a lecture about sex."

"I wasn't going to say that."

"You were thinking it."

Sara grinned. So did Grace, a little.

"It's more like reading Shakespeare instead of performing it," Grace said. "I get the meat without the ham."

"All right," Sara said. "Let's put aside what I did and stick to theology for the moment. What do you say to Satan's claim that he and God are brothers?"

"God created all things. He is the one infinitely perfect spirit, exalted over all things. God has no brothers, only a Son."

"See, that's where I start having problems," Sara said cautiously. "What you just said is the party line. How do we know it's true?"

"You mean, why should we believe God over the Devil? The Devil reveals his doctrine in his methods," Grace said. "I say this to my students all the time. When Satan turned against God and fell from Grace, the once trusted and beloved angel could no longer see all. He had to crawl among us, search for weak spots in Eve, Judas, others. I'm sure he did that with you. Did the Devil talk to you about Martin?"

"A little."

"Paul warned the Corinthians that Satan seeks strained or tortured relationships," Grace said. "Finding them, he attacks the weakened heart and tempts the flesh. Look how his pestilence spread from just one soul to two in Paradise, then outward turning brother against brother. Even after God cleansed the earth with His Flood, Satan was there. He is an eloquent seducer and a master survivor. He seized your patient and now he preys on you. If he succeeds, he will go after those you know, your mother, your brother, Tonia and Alexander, your other patients."

"A chain letter from Hell."

Grace nodded. She took a slug of caffeine, not a sip.

"Why does God allow him to exist?" Sara asked.

"We cannot know good without bearing witness to evil. It has been so since Original Sin. But our great strength, our defense, our salvation, is our power to choose. It's what distinguishes us from the other animals, makes us children of God."

The waitress arrived and set the plates down. Sara was glad for the interruption. Grace had made her feel reckless and a little stupid. She picked up her fork and stared at the table.

"You'll have more luck with a spoon."

Sara looked up. "What?"

"The soup," Grace said.

Sara set the fork down and picked up the spoon.

"We're exposed to all kinds of challenges and temptations every day," Grace said softly. "Since we're in full disclosure mode, let me tell you—whenever I see a hot guy I wonder if I made the right choice with my life."

"You?"

Grace nodded enthusiastically. "Not so much in Preppytown here, but on some of the digs where these swarthy heroes are working bare-chested under the hot sun? Oh, yeah. The key is to make the right choice, even if they're not optimal."

"You make sense. So did he. How do I know who's right?" Sara asked.

"You can't have certainty. That's why this is called 'faith.' But I haven't described anything you haven't experienced. All I've provided is context, which is something the Devil will never give you."

"He did, but it was different."

"The brother story, designed to appeal to your sense of family." Grace picked up her sandwich. "I've been doing a lot of talking. How about I put something in my mouth to keep it busy. You talk."

"I've been talking so much over the last few days," she said. "I don't mind listening." She suddenly felt very tired.

"Tell me about the Devil. What does he look like?"

"Red eyes and smoke," Sara said. "That's all I've seen. It's strange. You don't doubt that I've seen him, spoken with him."

"Why should I?" Grace said, crunching on hard, blackened bread. "I speak with God all the time."

"Has *he* ever answered?"

"No. I've never heard from the Devil either, but I don't doubt that he's always nearby, curled under a wormy rock or hiding in a pint of ice cream. God is very present when I pray. That's all the answer I require."

Sara gazed at her upside-down reflection in the spoon. "I saw Fredric's spirit and my dead child," she said. "They came too."

Grace sat motionless for a moment then reached across the table and took her friend's hand. "My poor honeybunch. How can you doubt his capacity for affliction after that?"

"He said that the manifestation of my boy, the baby, was God's doing. I don't believe that God would be so cruel." Sara looked at Grace. "Yet God allowed his own son to die on the Cross. Isn't that cruelty?"

"God became flesh to suffer and die for our well-being," Grace said. "That is not cruelty. It's love."

"But God allows us to suffer. I was stupid for getting pregnant, you told me so yourself. Remember the night I called from the train station?"

"I do. But—you were waiting for Darrell. I offered to come and sit with you. You didn't want me there. I said *that* was stupid, not you."

"Oh," Sara said. She felt the Devil laughing at her. "All these years I thought—shit."

"It's all right," Grace assured her. "You were upset."

"Jesus," Sara said.

"Move on," Grace said.

"Right." Sara looked for her mental footing. She found it in the pain of that night. "I—I screwed up by getting pregnant. But I don't feel like I sinned. I feel that God did by not helping me."

"He sent you your brother—"

"*He* did not do that," Sara said.

"Darrell could have been any number of places when you called," Grace said.

"Then maybe the Devil sent him, because if I couldn't reach him I may have seen you and you would have talked me out . . ." Sara's voice drifted.

Grace squeezed her hand.

Sara took a steadying breath. "Whoever sent him, Darrell drove me home and took me to the abortion clinic the next morning. But I'll tell you this. God never helped me. Not then or when my father was drunk or when my mother was crying or when Fredric was jumping from a branch with a chain around his neck. He was missing in action, unwilling to get his hands dirty."

"The way the Devil does?"

"Why not?"

"Sara, God asks us to make a personal effort toward spiritual recovery. But we need to take that first step. The step of faith. I want to ask you two questions that won't be easy to answer."

"You can't be any rougher than the Devil." Sara snickered.

"I don't know about that," Grace said sternly. "He sugarcoats. I won't."

Sara's cocky smile wavered. "Go ahead."

"Are you entirely certain you *shouldn't* have had the child?"

"Yes," Sara said. "I would have hated him for whose son he was."

"All right. Now give me a reason you should have had the baby."

Sara had half-expected the question. Grace had taken psychology, knew that devil's advocacy—ironically—was a way of testing a positive statement. Back then they called it 'purging' because it was like being forced to vomit.

"Purging" as in "purgatory," Sara thought.

"My mother would have been happy," Sara said, thinking back to what the Devil had said the night before. "She would have had trouble explaining single momhood to the ladies at the nail salon, but she'd have been very excited."

"Any other reason?"

"*Any*? Instead of feeling guilt I would have felt hate," Sara said. She thought of Barri Neville and what she said about her own children. Instead of shame, Sara felt emboldened by the confession. "I would have been enraged whenever I saw Martin in the child's eyes or mouth or manner."

Grace released Sara's hands. She went back to her sand-wich.

"So?" Sara asked. "What did that tell you?"

"Nothing," she admitted. "I was showing you how the Devil works. You came up with two arguments in opposition to the most wrenching decision you've ever made. If I kept pushing, cajoling, consoling, you might have come to regret what you did. The Devil finds your weak spot and pushes. You're tormented about Fredric. The Devil tells you the boy is happy and, by the way, you could be happy too. He works it. In time you start to believe. He tells you to sign on the bottom line and bring your family. You do." Grace shook her head slowly. "Terminate the debate. Send the Devil home."

"You're telling me I made this trip to hear 'Just say no'?"

"Pretty much," Grace said.

Sara ate some soup. *That isn't enough.* She needed more. She needed reasons. Instead of clarity she had gathered more confusion. Faith alone was not going to get her out of this.

"Would you care for some other advice?" Grace asked.

"It's a seller's market."

"You should go to the Becton Center."

Sara picked up her fork and speared a leaf of romaine. "Why?"

"Martin Cayne is lecturing today."

"Fuck him." Sara's voice was firm, but her insides went liquid.

"You need to confront him, maybe even forgive him."

Sara held up the fork. "What I need to do is put this in his throat and bleed him out."

"It's not healthy to hold on to so much anger," Grace said.

"I *said* 'fuck him.' Anyway, I hear God's still pissed about that apple."

"Not really. He laid down the law to Adam and Eve. That's what *you* need to do, get in the man's face and finish old business. Lift the pall from New Heaven and from your soul."

"Thanks, but I can only deal with one devil at a time," Sara said sharply.

Grace disengaged with a conciliatory bow of her head. It wasn't high-handed or disapproving, but Sara felt chastened just the same. The women ate quietly for several minutes.

"Look, I'm sorry," Sara said. "I didn't mean to snap at you."

"I'm fine."

"It's just this whole thing has me a little spooked."

"There's a Beatitude that might be appropriate."

"I don't doubt it." Advice from Grace was personal and welcome. A lecture from God and His Son was propaganda she didn't want.

"You mustn't give up on faith," Grace said.

"I can't 'give up.' I never had it."

"Faith isn't just about embracing God. It also speaks to accepting the help and love of another. I'm not Satan. I'm your devoted friend. We have shared a great deal on nothing more than our mutual trust. I wish you'd give my ideas the weight you're giving his."

"Convince me that a kind and loving and forgiving God is real," Sara said. "I *know* the Devil exists."

"Last year I met an old missionary in Botswana," Grace told her. "He said to me, 'Sister, I know God is real.' I asked him how he knew. And this gentle, generous, open, bony face turned to me with his brown eyes full of confidence and said, 'Because if he did not, I would change nothing in the way I live.' He was right. By nature, we wish to be what God has asked us to be."

"A serial killer would probably say the same thing about the Devil."

Grace frowned. "You're being provocative."

"I'm being *realistic*," Sara said. "Both factions say, 'It's true because I say so' but only the Devil has 'said so' to my face. That's not the ego projection of some pious African priest. That's real." Sara asked for the check.

"You're angry at God the way you're angry at Martin Cayne, and you've lost sight of what you must do," Grace went on. "This isn't a duel where the better shot gets to go home, or a school debate in which the best argument wins. You've opened the door to Hell. The Devil has come through. He will work you over and he won't leave empty-handed unless you command him to."

"I can't do that until I find out what happened to Fredric."

"You won't find out from the Devil."

"He makes me think."

"He makes you weak."

Sara paid for lunch. They left the restaurant in silence. Sara had heard from the other side. She had to think about what Grace had said and make decisions. One thing Sara was sure of: she was not using this investigation to beat herself up. Just the opposite. The Devil, damned or not, gave her comfort.

The rain had let up, leaving behind a sharp gray pall and damp trees and grass that smelled like wet cardboard.

"Thanks for lunch," Grace said. She nodded toward the campus. "Want to walk a bit?"

"I'm not going there."

"Just to the campus, then," Grace said.

Sara nodded. They crossed the street.

Entering the grounds was far more difficult than walking the streets. Except for the cell phones and laptops, very little had changed. The stone buildings, the storied ivy, all were just as they had been.

One thing was very different, however. The last time Sara was here she was emotionally hemorrhaging inside. She had transferred from Martin Cayne's classes, she had avoided old routes and patterns, she spent more time with new classmates. Sensing Grace's disapproval about the abortion, she had seen less and less of her old friend. She felt isolated and alone.

Now, she simply hated.

"Are you all right?" Grace asked as they moved along the leaf-covered walks.

"It's strange," Sara admitted. "Painful."

"In Deuteronomy—this isn't a lecture," Grace added, "the Israelites are commanded, 'Remember what the Amalekites did to you,' referring to the enemies of God who came from Egypt and attacked them from behind. They killed the infirm, the children, and other stragglers instead of facing the warriors. Not just evil but all wrongdoing comes at us in our weakest places. And because they are weakest those voices cry loudest. I understand why being here still hurts."

"Being *everywhere* hurts," Sara said. She was surprised to hear herself admit that, but it was true.

Grace regarded her old friend with a mixture of sadness and compassion. "The Beatitude you didn't want to hear before was, 'Alas for you who are rich; you are having your consolation now.' Sara, I have few possessions. 'Bupkis,' as my friend Rabbi Chelmow calls it. But I am building toward something, I know it. I can *feel* it. That's why I asked you to have faith *in me*. Kick these troubles in the butt. Look for something else. It has to be better than this."

Sara's mouth twisted. "I am. I guess I picked badly—again."

Grace embraced her friend. "I have to pick up some papers in my office. Why don't you come with me?"

"I have to get back," Sara told her. "Everyone was a little cranky on the home front and I want to see how they are."

"Go, then," Grace said as she released her friend. "And get rid of the extra tenant."

Sara smiled noncommittally as Grace gave her a long, last look. The nun touched her arm reassuringly.

"Whether you want it or not, may God look after you," Grace said before walking off.

The psychotherapist stood on the path and watched Grace hurry along. She collected students as she moved through them, distinctive in her habit and obviously respected for her work. Sara continued to stand there for several minutes. These young people flocked to Grace to be challenged and uplifted. Teenagers came to Sara because they were troubled and depressed.

"No wonder you're always so damn cheerful," Sara said, not with rancor but with envy.

One thing the nun told her did have resonance, though: butt-kicking. Sara was here and she felt motivated. Maybe it *was* time.

Taking a long, deep breath, she headed off quickly in the direction of Becton Center.

Thirteen

1

Sara was all speeding heart and wildly firing nerves as she approached the tall white building on Prospect Street. It had always reminded her of a large waffle iron, ready to impress ideas on the best, the brightest, or the most privileged.

And sometimes scandalous sons of bitches are even there to pour syrup on a select few.

The lights were on in the corner lecture hall that Sara knew so well. Martin was still giving the extracurricular weekend lectures, holding court in the oddly shaped wedge that fanned out from a small stage. A stage where Martin Cayne came to full, flowering, self-impressed life, where he got to play Socrates on the stoa.

Sara walked up to the double glass doors. There was a guard in a small booth outside, a cabinet really. She was dressed in crisply pressed blue and had arms like Samson. Sara was almost relieved she was going to be turned back.

"Can I help you?" the woman said as Sara approached. Her voice was a bored monotone.

"I'm here for Professor Cayne," she said. The words tasted dirty, like grounds on the bottom of a coffee cup.

"What's your name?" the guard asked.

"Sara Lynch."

"May I see a photo ID?" the guard asked as she checked her computer.

Sara reached into her shoulder bag and flipped out her driver's license. The guard printed out a pass and slipped it through a slot.

"Third floor, room 333," the guard said.

Shit, Sara thought. "Thank you," Sara said. She glanced at the pass. Grace had put her name on the guest list. Sara was not only predictable, now she was busted. She went inside. The years evaporated. So did a little of the anguish. She was outside herself watching herself as an eager student, her life ahead and her heart open, her conscience clean and healthy.

Sara decided to take the dark stairwell, try to burn off some of the unrest that was roiling in her gut. She took the climb quickly, blowing past the two male students who were smoking on the second-level landing and shouldn't have been. They didn't even try to hide their cigarettes. One of them was absently flicking his lighter, tossing his thin shadow against the green wall. The young men did say hello, however. From their designer clothes and haircuts—and the Rolex one of them was wearing—Sara could tell they were accustomed to special privileges like smoking indoors. Confident, gilt-edged, cheeky discourtesy. Now that she thought about it, Sara preferred Fredric Marash. He had been a striver, not one of the entitled.

She reached the third floor and waited for her heart to slow from the climb. She listened. There was no one in the halls. Class was still in session. When her heart was racing merely from anxiety, Sara opened the door.

The corridor was the bottom of a squared-off "C" that ran through the building. Room 333 was on the other end of the "C." Sara entered, moving slowly, cautiously. She was aware of the possibility that classes could end and he could emerge before she was ready to see him. He rarely stayed after class to talk to his students. He preferred that they make an appointment and come to his office. As she did along with who knew how many others.

Sara wondered if Martin would recognize her. She had longer hair then and fewer lines. She wore less pounds and shorter skirts. She walked behind not toward him. But she didn't doubt that she would recognize him by sight, sound, and smell, by the very presence of him. She would recognize Martin's modest build, but more than that, the charismatic radiance of his intellect, draped on the outside with swagger and confidence, presented to the world to force it to bend toward him as though he were a superpowerful magnet.

Not bend, she thought. *Bow*. As she had willingly, because he focused that attention on her. It filled her, uplifted her, grew her, and then crushed her—not in the application but in the withdrawal. Like a sword. It ruined her for others, spoiled her for anything but *that*.

She walked faster down the long corridor, eager now to get to the other end. At first she thought she was being drawn to it, wanting to feel that life again. But as she reached the top of the corridor where room 333 lay around the corner, she slowed. She heard his familiar voice through a closed door.

"Linear models of psychosomatic crises in adults do *not*

give us the full picture of the cause or treatment," Martin was saying. "Open systems models are required before we can have a full picture. Esther, will you come forward and walk the class through the conceptual framework you worked up?"

"Yes, Professor Cayne."

Sara was very good at inferring intention from inflection. The woman's words were formal but her voice was unstressed, familiar.

Another lover.

Or a wannabe. Or a will-be. Martin had referred to her by her first name, something he had done with Sara when they were very close to becoming lovers. It was a way of inviting her farther in. Afterward, he referred to her in public as "Ms. Lynch," a way of maintaining a seemly distance.

Sara edged toward the door. An oblong glass panel looked in on the classroom. She stopped just short of the window, frozen in midstride. Everything came back to her. She knew just where Martin would be while Esther made her presentation. Off to the student's right, beside the first row, looking at the class and toward the door. Mildly claustrophobic, Martin did not like it when he could not see a way out. There were windows in the room but the shades were pulled nearly to the bottom. He did not like distractions when he was working. In his mind, only the sun was competition for Martin Cayne.

Barely able to breathe, Sara inched toward the window at an angle. She could see the back of the stage and the woman as she stepped behind the podium. She was a tall brunette, slender, and wearing a skirt that came to the tops of the knees. Sara felt sorry for her. She edged ahead. She saw the stage end, the crossed legs of students in the front row, and then the row itself.

She stopped and looked down at the linoleum. Why did she want to see him? *To let him know what he did to you.* But could she? Would he even listen? If not, then what? Grace had told her to forgive him but Sara couldn't do that. Partly because of anger and partly she feared that his raw appeal to her would command the space and the moment. Even if she said the words, he was an even better people reader than she was. He would know she was lying. She *didn't* forgive him. She wanted things back the way they were, before she met him. She needed to move back before she could move on.

She moved back against the wall, hitting it hard.

". . . predisposition to this condition, and the manifestation of symptoms, if not predictable within a conceptual framework, are unquestionably definable therein," Esther was saying.

Sara's legs were shaking. She fought the desire to slide down the wall to the floor in a used and useless heap. The only thing that kept her standing was an opposite desire to go to the door, fling it open, and hurl her fists at Martin Cayne. She balled her hands and squeezed. She wished her breathing would slow and her mind would clear and the past would *leave her head.*

"We should begin with a fundamental awareness of the parameters of the model," the student continued. "Illness that cannot be defined as organic is what we call 'functional.'"

Let me tell you about functional illness, Sara thought angrily.

And then she heard him. She heard that still-so-familiar voice as he interrupted Esther.

"Since there are only five minutes left, I want to stop Esther and ask her to finish the presentation at our next meeting. In the meantime, I invite you all to join us immediately after class and video-observe our ongoing study of psychosomatic asthma at the clinic. Esther and I believe that only seven of every ten cases are the result of real respiratory illness . . ."

Everything was the same. The surefooted intellect, the folding of a female student into his work and then into his confidence. The experiment they had worked on together was about past-life regression. That was how she first became familiar with the work of Dr. Arul.

Sara could not walk up to this monster and forgive him. She did not want to give him another cheek to slap. But even if she told him about the abortion, confronted him with her pain, there was no guarantee that he would give a damn.

What will you do then?

Sara didn't know if she could bear another rejection. She turned from the classroom, her legs no longer weak as they carried her down the stairs, away from the greater pain she feared to the one she knew.

2

The heavy early darkness was dramatically accented by the piercing white of the oncoming headlights. It was rush hour and the highway was crowded. Sara was grateful. It kept her mind out of her head and on the road.

That changed when she left the main thoroughfare for the back roads.

Forgiveness.

In a moment of candor she admitted that she couldn't forgive her father for hurting her mother; how was she going to forgive *this* contemptuous bastard.

Sara noticed every stark reality of the journey, a trip of loneliness and despair. The endless black asphalt of the country roads, the helplessly fallen leaves, the jagged road cuts in heart-red sandstone, and now and then the hungry bright-eyed fox or raccoon or the more frequent squirrels and chipmunks whose eyes no longer gleamed and whose blood and torn pelts stained the damp street. Sara felt it all because most of the time she was part of the stark pageant—stony, dead, or hidden. The only time she felt open and empowered was when she was angry.

You don't want to leave that terrain, do you?

She moved through the countryside, the ribbon of dark road . . . her life . . . furtive moments of living and scattered pieces of death, starting and ending at the same place in a small town with wickedness afoot in her home.

It was just past dinnertime when Sara reached the house. There was shouting inside. Sara parked and hurried to the front door. Darrell was just inside. He was yelling at their mother and she was yelling at him. Sara couldn't make out the words, only the volume. She looked toward Alexander's window. The light was on. She hoped that he and his mother were together, away from this. Sara did not want the boy to have her memories.

Sara walked in. Darrell and Martha were in the foyer, by the steps. Darrell was holding a can of beer. They went silent as she entered.

"Good evening," Sara said.

"Hello, dear," Martha replied thickly.

Sara looked at her brother. "How were the pork chops?"

His brow dipped in confusion. Sara pointed to the side of her own mouth. Darrell had mustard on his. He only ate mustard with hot dogs and pork chops, and Sara didn't smell grilled franks.

"Fine," Darrell said as he rubbed it away with the ridge of his hand, transferring it to the side of his jeans.

"Well, I'm going upstairs," Martha said.

"You're running upstairs," Darrell snarled.

"No. I'm walking," Martha said as she turned to go.

"You're running like you did from Dad, to sit in your stupid chair and knit another fucking sweater—"

"Language!" Martha barked over her shoulder.

"—another *fucking* sweater and watch something about gardens or the South on TV and forget that there is a man in the house who could really use some encouragement and attention."

Martha continued up the stairs.

"You made him what he became!" Darrell yelled. "He was a lonely failure because you never had anything good to say!"

Martha stopped halfway up the stairs. She turned back with eyes of fire. "I supported this family while your father played on the river and drank. I didn't mind the playing so much because it was with you or your sister. But it was not easy to carry him. He expected or needed or just wanted a lifelong vacation because of what he went through." She came back down the stairs with sharp, aggressive steps. Sara had never seen her so openly hostile. "But I had needs too, and ideas, and a past, and hope for a future that went beyond delivering his children. I wanted to be with him. That meant he had to come back from the war he was fighting in here." She tapped her temple. "He just wasn't ready to do that. Ever."

Sara eased between them. "Mother, why don't we all go to the den and talk this out."

"Because there's nothing to talk *about*!" Martha said. "Your brother believes what your father believed, that the small, safe world in a bottle or glass is better than this one. I'm afraid for him, for the way we found him this morning, and I had the audacity to suggest otherwise."

"No one tells me how to think or what to wear or the right way to behave. And by the way—it's a can," Darrell said. He drained it, crushed it. "Now it's an empty can, like my fucking *life*."

"I think we need to stop this," Sara said.

Darrell shook his head. "I think *we* need to remind our mother that we weren't deaf and dumb. I listened at my door and I bet you did too, sis. I heard Dad beg. I heard him cry. Maybe if you had learned to play cards like he asked or held him the way he wanted he wouldn't have had to *go* out drinkin'. Maybe I wouldn't have been so goddamn stuck on the guy. I loved it when he smiled and laughed. That's why I hung with him. Someone had to."

Martha was standing on the bottom step, her eyes level with Darrell's. She was looking past Sara, her gaze hard and unyielding.

"Your father didn't just want to play cards," Martha said. "He wanted to play poker because that's what he played with his shipmates. When we went out he wanted dinner at a greasy spoon, not anywhere nice. He liked to smell the smoke from the grill, the oil in the fryers. He didn't want to be held out of love. He wanted to be held like his whores held him. He got angry because I didn't like him to talk as his shipmates had or when I had to stop whatever we were doing—not because we were under attack but because one of you woke from a nightmare or had a cough. I tried *very hard* to please him but there were babies and there were bills and there were times when he was so drunk he didn't even know I was there. And yes, one day I stopped trying. Because when I asked him to get help or come to church with me he refused. Maybe you didn't hear that part because I spoke very softly to try to get him to trust me."

Darrell snickered. "Well. The angel Martha has made her case. Unfortunately, we can't ask Dad for his side. We'll never know how disappointed he was when you talked him out of hiring an artist or photographer to render his ideas so he could print brochures and expand his carpentry business—"

"We would have needed to take a second mortgage when we could barely pay the first."

"—or why he turned his son into a drinkin' buddy because he wanted to be with someone who cared about him, who loved him."

"I loved your father."

"On your terms, not his!" Darrell shouted. "That isn't love. It's control."

"Let's give this a rest," Sara said. She had waited till she heard the steam leave their voices, when it was safe to reinsert herself.

"Okay, sure," Darrell snarled. "You can help Mom back onto her cross, then get on the one beside it." He flung the can toward the kitchen, missing the garbage. He left it where it lay and went out the door, slamming it. The women stood facing one another in the terrible silence that followed.

"I tried," Martha said, her voice cracking.

"Don't talk about this now," Sara insisted. She had always known that her parents tried the best they could to build a life. They had been able to overcome some of their little differences but not their big disappointments. They hid their anger as best they could as they moved along paths that— somewhat by need but more by design, Sara suspected— rarely intersected. "Come on, Mother. I want you to lie down."

"I ran the house, the shop, and I looked after the two of you. I tried to give your father what he wanted." She turned tearful eyes toward her daughter. "He didn't want a wife and family. He wanted someone to write to from a battleship. He wanted to be out in the world, doing whatever he thought a man was supposed to do. That was why we came to Delwood. I thought it was to build a home. He was only looking for another adventure."

Sara took her mother's hand, walked her from the step, and held her tight as she cried out years of frustration. Her mother's tears wet her neck, pain and sadness in a tangible form. She rubbed Martha's back as she held her, kissed her ear, then heard from her own ears the sound of cries from upstairs.

"Give that to me."

"No, Mommy! *No!*"

"*Now!*"

Sara sat her mother on the steps.

"Wait here, all right?" Sara asked.

Martha nodded and Sara hurried up the stairs to the south tower. The door to Tonia's room was open. Alexander's door was closed. They were in there. Sara approached cautiously.

"Alexander, I want that toy."

"It's mine!"

Sara rapped on the door. "Alexander? Tonia? It's Sara. I'm back. I wanted to say good night."

Tonia opened the door. She looked absolutely haggard. "Sara, I am happy to see you. Would you please come in?"

"Sure," Sara said as she entered. "What's up?"

Tonia pointed. The psychotherapist looked at Alexander. He was sitting on the foot of his small bed, facing the door. He was holding the same action figure he had that morning.

"How was your day?" Sara asked the boy.

"All right," he replied. "You shouldn't be here, Sara. My father says it's dangerous."

"Your father?"

The boy glared and nodded.

"Why is it dangerous?" Sara asked.

"We're in a combat zone," he said.

"I see. Who is fighting?" Sara asked. She crouched in front of the boy.

"My dad," Alexander told. "He says there is fire all around him."

"What kind of fire?"

"Enemy," Alexander said.

"I should have realized that, shouldn't I?" Sara said with a mock edge of self-reproach.

Alexander nodded gravely.

"Who is the enemy?" Sara asked. "Did he tell you that?"

Alexander nodded with pouting gravity. "*ангелы*," he said.

"I'm sorry?"

"He said 'angels,'" Tonia told her, a sliver of panic in her voice. "He said his daddy is fighting with angels."

"Really? That's a strange enemy," Sara remarked. She didn't like where this was going.

"They're trying to kill us," Alexander said. "Daddy will protect us. He says the first one is coming for you. It's a big and mean one."

"Are you sure you don't mean devils?" Sara asked. "Angels are good."

"Not this one," Alexander replied.

Sara didn't like this at all.

The psychotherapist motioned for Tonia to come into

the hall with her. Reluctantly, the woman left her son with the doll. Sara kept the door open a crack.

"How long has he been like this?" Sara asked.

"Since dinner."

"Did he hear Darrell and my mother fighting?"

Tonia nodded. "I am so sorry. I like them both very much—"

"They'll get over it," Sara assured her. "Tonia, I've heard your son talking to his action figures before—talking to them *and* for them. It's perfectly natural. Children do that."

"Yes, but the angels—"

"He may have seen them on the stained-glass windows of the church. They're big, powerful-looking images with flaming swords. In Alexander's mind they probably make good supervillains." She smiled. "And his father probably makes a pretty good superhero."

"That isn't what I mean," Tonia said. "I never taught him that word."

"He may have heard it somewhere—"

"I don't know where. We only have spoken English since we came to this country, even in my cousin's house."

"Maybe it was in a storybook, or something he remembered from his very early childhood."

"We read Russian fairy tales, not church stories," Tonia told her. "There were never any angels."

"Well, he obviously heard it somewhere. From a friend in Russia, or on the radio or television—"

"He *says* he heard it from his father."

"You know that's not possible," Sara said, without quite believing it herself. Not now, not in this house. "Tonia, I think you should let this go for tonight."

"I'm scared," she said. "Your boy, Fredric—was he behaving like this before he went to the woods?"

"Fredric had problems that went back for years," Sara said. "The situations are entirely different. Let Alexander play. Stay with him until he falls asleep and we'll look at this again in the morning. I have a feeling things will be better then."

"All right, Sara. Thank you. But I'm going to keep the doors open when we go to sleep," Tonia said.

"That's a good idea," Sara agreed. "I'm going to bring my mom upstairs. If you need anything, I'll be in the office. Call me."

Tonia thanked her and went back into Alexander's room. Sara was not willing to ascribe this to supernatural causes. Pre-adolescent language retention was a fact, and calling on an imaginary protector in a suddenly hostile environment was not unusual in children. And he may very well have seen the stained-glass windows in town or on his way to school.

But Sara was not as sure of all that as she wanted to be. Her own anger and despair, Darrell and their mother clashing more bitterly than ever; there was madness at large here. It was walking furtively but insistently and it could well have another place of origin.

Sara brought her mother to her room. Martha still seemed distant as she lay on the bed.

"Do you need anything?" Sara asked. "Decaf, a snack, water?"

"Not just now, dear," Martha said.

"What about a book, your knitting?"

"I think I'll just lie here," Martha replied.

Sara kissed her on the forehead, then backed from the room. She hated seeing her mother this way. Whatever her flaws, the woman *had* worked hard to keep things together for so many years. She deserved adoration, not an attack.

She left the door open and marched downstairs. Things *would* be better in the morning, as she had promised Tonia.

Sara would see to that.

3

Shut the office door. Lock it. Pull back the rug. Take the candles from the shelf and put them in the pentagram. Remove clothing. It was already becoming a familiar drill, which was dangerous. Sara knew she couldn't afford to become complacent around the Devil.

Sara had done the first three and checked her voice mail—there were confirmations of the changed appointments, nothing more—when the stillness of the room was broken by a sound like rippling silk.

"I'm here," the Devil informed her.

Sara was startled but continued what she was doing. She didn't want to show the Devil uncertainty.

"Do I need these?" she asked, holding the candles toward the pentagram. "Or has our relationship moved beyond that?"

"Relationships are very much in your thoughts."

"A palm reader's perception," Sara said. She was in no mood for sayings or riddles. "Answer my question."

"I have. We're speaking."

She replaced the candles and sat in her chair, facing the pentagram.

"You've been to see Grace Rollins."

"Did you follow me or did you have business at Yale?" Sara asked. She was growing tired of the Devil's smug omniscience.

"I'm a Harvard booster myself," the Devil replied. "The cleric John Harvard and I have a history of discord.

"You came away empty-handed," the Devil went on.

"Grace didn't give me any reason to trust God over you," Sara agreed. "But that doesn't mean you 'win.' I have no reason to waste time on either of you."

"Too bad."

"Yeah."

"Keep in mind, Sara, that this involves more than just you. It affects your family and your town."

"That's one of the things I don't get," Sara said. "Fredric summoned you. I summoned you. Why should anyone *else* suffer?"

"His Pushy Greatness is displeased. God does not like the hateful interaction of his children."

"Then he should *help* us, not punish us. I know better than most people that we are a work in progress. The mistakes we make are part of our search, they're built into the system. But what you and God do—that's an abomination."

"I?"

"Alexander's condition—is that your doing?"

"Yes."

"How has that boy sinned? Why is *he* being haunted?"

"Visits from a father he barely knew is not a haunting," the Devil said. "I sent the boy visions to give him strength."

"Against what?"

"I told you."

"Right. God. What's he going to do, send plagues and destruction?"

"Step outside."

Sara hesitated. "Why?"

"Go to the backyard. Tell me what you see."

Reluctantly, Sara went to the waiting room and peeked through the drawn shades. She saw nothing but the sparkling river and the dark base of the hills beyond.

"Outside," the Devil said.

Sara went to the door. She opened it slowly and stepped outside. Her eyes were immediately drawn to a light beyond the hills. In that light was a shape. An angel was coming toward her. It was standing well above the river, magnesium-white save for a glowing red-orange sword. She wanted to feel comforted by the appearance of an emissary of the lord. But there was intimidation in its majesty, omen in its fire, coldness in its still, marble features. It was especially disturbing to feel closer to the demon behind her than to the heavenly messenger in front.

"You're frightened," hissed the demon.

Sara said nothing.

Satan leaned closer. "This is not poor Jesus, the lamb of God," he whispered in her ear. "This is the agent of the Lord who Smiteth."

"What is it?"

"The Angel of Death."

Sara watched as the angel drifted lower and closer, its robes writhing slowly, hypnotically, like liquid porcelain.

"How do I know it's from him? *You* may have created this vision."

"Be sensible," the Devil said. "I could have summoned demons last night, frightful things that would have driven you into my protective arms and straight to Hell. It is not by my hand this judgment comes." He whispered softly, "I do not send angels."

Sara heard movement behind her. Though the candles had not been lit she saw red smoke filling the pentagram. Something unseen was clawing at the floor within.

"What is that?" she asked.

"Your guest and protector," he said.

The voice was about to get a body. Sara looked back at the angel. It was over the riverbank behind her home, near the gazebo. The face was lost in light. Locks of golden hair were visible, framing the face like the sun.

"He is not here for me," Sara said. "He is coming to oppose you."

"That would be an uncommon waste of his time," the Devil said. "The pentagram is like a foreign embassy. He cannot enter. No"—the Devil sneered even closer—"he is here for you. He will slaughter you as he did the firstborn of the Egyptians, without mercy or feeling. And your soul? That will go into limbo, not to the mansion of God but also not to me. God will occasionally settle for a draw."

Sara watched for a moment longer, then went inside. She shut the door hard and looked out the window. She had no trouble seeing the angel now. It was low and approaching rapidly.

"Am I the only one who sees him?" Sara asked.

"You are the only one who is about to die."

Sara thought of her father's banshee tales. "This is not real."

"How do you know?" the Devil asked.

Sara ignored him. The Devil was doing it to her again. She had come to her office determined to take charge, to force him to answer questions before dismissing him. He had taken the discussion elsewhere. She went into her office and stepped to the edge of the pentagram. The tower of red smoke was thick and oily, like paint floating in a tank of pure water. It reached halfway to the ceiling and curled outward, like a beaker of dry ice. As she watched, a muscular forearm pushed upward through the smoke, uncoiling like a rising cobra. Sara jumped when she saw it. The flesh was red and glistening, the fingers long and serpentine. The arm stretched higher, above the churning cloud.

"It is real, Sara Lynch, but I will not let him have you."

A second arm shot skyward and the two limbs moved sinuously, one after the other as though they were climbing an invisible rope. Sara could see the elbows and then the rest of the arms, each thickly knotted with sinew. As the arms reached up the smoke rose with them. In a few moments the powerful limbs were covered.

Sara watched with fear and expectation. She fought the urge to return to the window. If there was danger and the Devil was her salvation, this was where she belonged. The psychotherapist didn't know how long she stood at the foot of the pentagram; probably no more than a few minutes, though it felt much longer. Suddenly the column swirled inward, swallowing itself. The arms vanished with it. Sara watched it go, then took a moment to catch her breath.

"What just happened?"

The Devil did not answer. Sara was about to go back to the waiting room to see about the angel when she heard shuffling in the hallway. She kicked back the carpet, went to the hall door, and opened it.

Alexander was standing there with his doll. He held it in front of his face as though sighting down the tiny plastic gun. Tonia was behind him, gripping his shoulders and urging him back.

"Bang! Bang!" the boy said.

"I'm sorry, Sara," Tonia said. "He ran down—he said it was important."

"The man told me to," Alexander told her.

Sara looked down at the boy. He was still holding the figure high, one eye tightly shut.

"What man?" Sara asked. "Your dad?"

"A red man," Alexander replied. "He told me you were in trouble. My daddy and I came to help."

Sara smiled bravely. "Thank you. That was very sweet."

"Вырадушны," the boy said in a deep voice.

"It means you're welcome," Tonia said uneasily.

"I thought it might," Sara said.

"I don't know where he's hearing these things," Tonia said as she led the boy away. "I am sorry again."

"It's all right," Sara said as she shut the door. She walked unsteadily to the waiting room and peered out the window.

The angel was gone.

She leaned on an aluminum-frame chair and shook her head. "You did this to scare me," she said, "to make me trust you."

The Devil laughed. "Men do not believe that there are dire events in which I do not have a hand. Senator Daniel Webster actually accused me of encouraging the slave trade to turn God from America."

"That encounter was fiction," Sara said.

"If you say so, Dr. Lynch."

"*Everything* you say and do is a twisted lie."

"The remark is in the Congressional Record, along with more blasphemous lies than have been spoken by all the demons of every era since the expulsion from Paradise." The Devil's voice grew harsh. "As for your other charge, do watch what you say. There may come a time when I decide not to intervene on your behalf."

The Devil left. It was nothing Sara could see or hear; she just knew. More rattled than she had been since she uttered the incantation, Sara was tempted to undo the spell by dis-mantling the pentagram. She resisted for one reason.

What if the Devil is right? About everything.

Sara was about to make her way to the couch when she noticed that her voice mail indicator was beeping. A call must have come while she was outside.

"This is Dr. Sara Lynch. I can't come to the phone right now; I'm being chased by the Angel of Death . . ."

She listened to the message. It was from the attorney for the school district. He said he realized it was late but asked if "it would be convenient" for her to attend a meeting at the school the next day at seven-thirty A.M. Mr. E. Edward Ed-wards said he wanted to discuss "the Marash situation" and invited Sara to bring her personal attorney if she wished. He asked her to call back and let him know one way or the other.

Maybe Satan or God or whoever has him will lend me Daniel Webster, she thought. That would tell her which divinity wanted the Lynch vote.

Sara had one patient in the morning and two in the after-noon. She called the attorney and left a message that she would be there without counsel. This despite the fact that she had demonstrated a remarkable ineptitude of late at repre-senting her points of view.

Sara chuckled dejectedly at the word "demonstrated." She wondered if Satan were influencing her vocabulary now. Or perhaps the word came from her subconscious, along with every damn thing else that had happened over the past two days.

Her eyes shifted from the telephone to the *Devil's Bible*. There was no point going through the book again. She had traveled its pages, sucked up its indignation and outrage, and come away with little else. She had a feeling that even additional sessions with the Devil would only deepen this paralyzing muddle.

"*Trust me,*" Grace had said.

Maybe Sara *had* had enough. Her tired and stinging eyes drifted up to the bookcase. Upon her confirmation, the Church had given Sara a Catholic encyclopedia. She took it from the shelf, sat on the couch, and began paging through it. The title page was inscribed, "*To Sara Jacqueline: God loves you—Bishop Reilly.*" Below it she had written in very light pencil, "*How does he know this?*"

The book was full of tenets, articles, and symbols she had forgotten along with a few she had actually annotated.

"Younger than Fredric and just as dubious," she said as she read her criticism about the rules against the ordination of women and what a funny word she thought "Homoousios" was.

But the entry that stopped her short was about Limbo. According to the text there were two realms with that name. One was *limbus patrum*, the home of the Old Testament saints; the other was *limbus infantium*, the abode of unbaptized infants. However, there was more to *limbus infantium* than children—the "flamelets," as Satan had portrayed them.

"You lied to me," Sara said. "You tell me you and God agreed to rules and then you lie about them!"

If the Devil was still within earshot he didn't answer. Sara wasn't surprised. A deceiver was also surely a coward. But he wasn't deaf. She replaced the encyclopedia and walked toward the pentagram, which was still covered by the rug.

"You told me the Angel of Death would take me to limbo," Sara went on. "According to canon, the only baptized souls allowed in limbo are those who died without repenting original sin but who are themselves blameless. I have committed sin for which I have not confessed. There is no way God would take me there!"

Sara looked down at the rug that was flat and innocuous.

"Maybe you can't hear me," she said. "Let's see if I can fix that."

Sara reached for the edge of the rug. As she went to pull it away, the corner suddenly exploded.

Fourteen

1

The edge of the rug whipped high in the air, knocking Sara over before falling back on itself. The edge was folded over with part of the pentagram exposed. The area inside the pentagon was matte-black, without light or substance.

Flat on her backside, Sara scuttled back several feet and watched as the red arm emerged again, rigid and strong. The palm was extended toward her as though it should be holding a tray. The thumb and pinkie splayed, the three middle fingers pressed tightly together.

The horns of the ram, Sara thought. She didn't know how far to let this self-generating process go. The void ended at the chalk mark that defined the interior pentagon. Sara assumed, *hoped*, the external lines of the larger pentagram would contain this new visitation.

A gleaming black orb parted the flat darkness; the top of a head. It rose from the center, followed by a bowed neck. The red flesh looked the same as the smooth, oily arm that rose as the head did. The head was bent forward and covered with fine, slick hair. The strands were pressed together so tightly that they resembled a skullcap. The neck straightened, raising the head and bringing two long, straight horns from the darkness. Each horn was the length of the forearm and were pointed directly at Sara. Rising from just behind the ears, they radiated outward matching the angle of the thumb and pinkie. They rose from shallow craters in the skull and tapered to fine pinpoints that didn't so much end as vanish. The untextured horns were a brilliant golden white, like a halo, only they did not suggest peace. They were delicate yet threatening, like the stinger of a wasp. The horns rested between large pointed ears; these were bent back and wrapped slightly *around* them. It was said the Devil could hear equally well in all directions. A sharp widow's peak drew attention to the swirling reddish-black eyes below.

As the rest of the face emerged Sara saw a straight nose, high and clearly defined cheekbones, and thin lips stretched across a wide mouth. The goat's beard was represented in the form of a black goatee. It was as pointed at the bottom in the same way as the horns on top, coming to what seemed like an infinite point.

The eyes locked on to Sara as the Devil continued to rise from the unrippled black surface. His muscled chest emerged, bare save for a very thick covering of hair. The hair followed a narrowing line toward the Devil's waist that formed an inverted triangle. The tip of the triangle disappeared into a belt and loincloth made entirely of dull golden rings. They were large and layered, hanging straight and reaching almost to the tops of the Devil's knees.

The Devil's right arm rested along his side. It held a scepter made of fire. The flames licked one over the other, like the feathers of a bird, burning without flaring. At the top of the scepter was a large, perfectly round blood-red opal that bobbed and floated on the fire. The flames cast no light on the surrounding bookcase.

The Devil's powerful legs were also thickly haired, ending in feet and not the hooves Sara had been expecting. They seemed to float rather than stand on the black void. There was no tail. Save for the horns—*of light?* Sara wondered, thinking of Michelangelo's *Moses*—this was a being made more or less in our own image.

Except that he has no navel, Sara noticed. The Devil eternal.

Satan's silent arrival had taken just a few moments. Nothing but the rug had been disturbed. When the nearly seven-foot-tall being had emerged, the fingers of his outstretched hand closed slowly to form a fist.

"You dare quote *books* to me?" the Devil hissed. "I am older than the first thoughts of man. I was stung by the first deceptions of God!"

Sara decided that she did not want to speak to the Devil on her knees. She pushed herself up and stood on the rug facing the Dark King. She didn't feel any taller. The Devil remained an imposing presence.

"You lied," Sara said. She felt emboldened by terror, which was the only thing filling her now. She shoveled it out as bravado. "You lied about the angel taking me to limbo."

"I told no lie," the Devil growled. "The failure is that of man and woman, their willingness to believe what they think or feel and not what *is*."

Sara finally agreed with the Devil. She knew that failing well.

"The ancient Egyptians spoke of *b't* as the savior of the child Moses," the Devil said. "It was the word for the House of Pharaoh, misinterpreted by Hebrew scribes as *bet*, the daughter of Pharaoh. Slave scholars were also unaware that *mases* meant 'son' and so failed to realize that their Deliverer was not a Hebrew castaway pulled from the Nile but an Egyptian prince born to the House of Pharaoh. And so a lie becomes the foundation of the Greater Lie."

"But you spoke of Adam and Eve, of being the serpent in Eden—"

"Convenient metaphor for the birth of strife," the Devil replied. "Cain and Abel were not men but places, the warring city-states of Sumer and Akkad. You miss the joke of it all."

"What is that?" Sara asked.

"The authors of the Bible were composing a *testāmentum*, from the root *testārī*. They were writing their will."

Sara shook her head. It was too much to contemplate.

The Devil's fingers uncurled. "Come to me if you wish to know the truth."

"No."

"God has abandoned you, Sara Lynch. Unless you truly and absolutely repent your sins, your soul is mine whether you believe or not. You may as well accept that and join those who have joined me."

"My soul," Sara said. "I don't even know what that means."

"It is you without the body," he replied. "A soul comes to you at conception—I'm afraid, Sara, your people got that part right."

His glibness was like a razor across her belly. Of all the things the Devil had said, that was the worst. She tried not to let the hurt show.

"The soul is a pure thing, then. It is shaped and imprinted by the choices we make. At some point the soul decides on a direction, whether to seek or to simply accept. You, for example, have not yet decided. You want to explore yet you stay rutted in hurt. Then there are some souls that mature quicker than others—Fredric's, for example. When that happens there is no choice but to change clothes as it were, shed flesh for light."

"Is that what you told Fredric?"

"Do you believe I needed to persuade him of anything?" the Devil asked. "He had pushed his flesh to its limits. Bravely, against custom. He had nowhere else to go."

"He had all of life ahead of him."

"What kind of life?" the Devil asked. "Fredric was already hiding behind walls, taking pictures of Chrissie Blair as she left the school. How long before he went to her home and raped her when he could no longer control the desire for her flesh?"

"You don't know that."

"I do. He believed in taking aggressive bites from life."

Sara felt helpless and sickened.

"I don't like to see you this way," the Devil said. He stretched his hand toward her. His fingers ended in opaque white nails that tapered to a point. They reflected the light of his scepter in a milky, hypnotic glow. "Let me show you my kingdom. It is not pain, Sara. It is indulgence without torment."

"A fat-free afterlife," Sara said.

The Devil grinned. "There you go," he said. "God does not appreciate sarcasm but I treasure anything a little—off. The eternal skin he offers is the security of his own controlling, unchanging radiance. In my realm, you seek your own comforts and rewards." The Devil's eyes shifted to the scepter. "The sun or the flame—his blinding domination or my guiding torch. It is your choice."

"You do your job very well," Sara said.

"My *job*?" he said, some temper in his voice. The open hand closed and shook slowly. "You do not yet understand. I am passion incarnate, the curiosity of mind and soul given flesh. I am the god of eternal *living*, not eternal death. You doubt me. Yet you believe what you read of limbo in a book penned by uneducated men who barely understood the lingua franca. You believe a theological construct written by those with no proof. The Dark Pope has spoken with me directly. He has been to my realm. He has communed with those who have come to me, many of whom you have studied, whose teachings *you* follow." He extended his fingers again. "Come and see."

"Fire and dirt," she muttered.

The Devil arched an eyebrow. Even in Satan there were the remains of a curious boy. Sara felt the stubble of confidence return.

"God doesn't have to beg for fealty," Sara said. "He isn't unsure of himself."

"Ah. You want to do *your* job," the Devil said. "Suppose I agree to cooperate. I will hear you out, answer your questions, if you grant me a favor."

"I won't come in there with you," she said.

"I will not ask that."

"I won't involve anyone else, either."

"I'll not ask *that*."

Sara couldn't afford to let him cow her. Not when she finally had the chance to get her hands around this. "All right," she said.

The Devil lowered the hand he had extended. He looked down at her, his horns brilliant, his eyes charitable. They seemed almost benign in the reflected gleam of his scepter.

"You confuse interaction with entreaty," the Devil said. "Unlike God, I am not afraid to present my case directly."

"Your way takes a great deal of work," she said.

"Idle hands, you know," he said, smiling.

"Is this something you chose or was it forced upon you?"

"Both. My brother has convinced the world that piety and chastity are rewarded in Heaven. He has sent forth His own range of acolytes, from the soft-spoken to the near-mad to spin lies of eternal pain for disobedience. I must operate in my own way to neutralize their effect."

"Fredric was not ready to go with you," Sara said. "He was running on emotion, not thought. God would have given him time."

"God *has* time. Men do not. The great tragedy of humankind is you know nothing of the crushing emptiness to which so many eventually turn."

"You talk about great souls who have come to you. What exactly do you offer? What does one experience in your fire?"

"Come to me. Find out."

"I told you I won't," Sara reminded him. "You agreed not to ask."

The Devil smiled broadly. She suddenly felt very uneasy.

"What happens to a soul in your care?" she repeated.

"Thank you."

"For what?"

" 'Care,' " the Devil said, "for that is exactly what my souls receive. They enjoy eternal gluttony of every kind which, despite the claims of the misguided, is not a deadly sin. It is a great reward. Imagine being able to join with the souls of others, sharing their collective experiences. There"—he gestured upward—"they suffer only what my brother allows them of his own being."

"I don't want to learn from sadists and killers."

"Fredric was on the edge of becoming one of those," the Devil said.

"I'm not sure I agree, but even so—"

"The horrors of Purgatory are separate," the Devil said. "*That* is the Hell of lore, the pit of Tartarus, the fabled realm of unrelenting chastisement. It is where God sends his failures."

"You're simply the manager."

"Hardly that. The door to Perdition is locked from the inside," the Devil said. "We scourge evil from the wicked. That is what fuels the flame. After a cycle of seven years in the seven levels the souls are sent to me for judgment. If they are purged I release them into the company of the others. If not they are returned." He smiled. "Most are returned. Do you know that Albert, Duke of Clarence, still does not understand—not in his soul—that what he did was wrong?"

"I'm sorry?"

"Grandson of Queen Victoria," the Devil replied. "Jack the Ripper."

If this was a delusion of some kind, at least it was world class. And it might be. That was one of the questions on her list.

"Am I a killer?" she asked pointedly. "Would the soul of every woman who has done what I did be sent to Purgatory?"

"No," the Devil assured her.

"But you said humans possess souls from the moment of conception."

"Unformed souls are still just spiritual clay," the Devil told her, writhing his fingers as though sifting through sand. "It is death but not murder." He moved closer and whispered, "Another misconception—if you'll pardon the expression. Those people outside, the masses. They speak solemnly of God's commandment that we shall not kill. What God said to that raving puppet Moses was that we should not 'murder.' Protecting the life of others by ending the life of a madman, of one in pain, of one who is only potentially formed, of one who is an unwilling or unwitting burden— that is not murder. It is charity."

The Devil straightened. As he did, the rings of his loincloth jangled like church bells. The tones of the circlets were rich and soothing.

"Do you know what these are?" the Devil asked.

Sara shook her head.

"Halos," he said.

Once again the Devil had surprised her. Sara looked at the rings anew. It was as if they had suddenly blossomed with light, each possessing a humble luster that matched their music.

"They were turned over to me by those who tired of Heaven and the dull grace of God," the Devil told her. He fingered them without taking his eyes from Sara. "Philosophers, scholars, even a saint."

"This is preposterous," Sara said. A willing suspension of dogma was one thing. What the Devil had just described was absurd, like a sports team where unhappy players were traded.

The Devil's face was suddenly much closer to her own. His mouth was hard and his eyes were livid. "Do not doubt my devotees or converts," he warned. "God has turned his face from yours. I may yet do so."

"And how will that play out?" Sara asked. "Do you have your own Angel of Death?"

She had experienced aloneness in her life. She had felt miserable isolation and despair. But until this moment she had never known the kind of terror that made her want to pray.

"I have the Reapers of Purgatory, as you may yet discover," the Devil said. "They collect the souls of the damned and forgotten. Like the Angel of Death they carry your soul to Vocīvus, a limbo unrecorded in books and chronicles. It is a void between God and myself where emptiness is reflected and magnified by the unseen souls around you. It is not punishment, it is not reward. It is nothing."

"But I avoid this fate by joining you," Sara said. "An overdose of Ambien or a noose around my neck."

"Perhaps you would prefer to risk the forgiveness of God," the Devil said. "Pray for weeks or months or years or longer, hope that he will hear and grant you artless immortality."

"You talk about the arts, about the mind, about fiery passion. But there is no body. What do we experience?"

"Roll back the rug," the Devil said.

"Why?"

The Devil shook his great head. "You are an insufferable contradiction of inquisitiveness and doubt. You agreed I could ask something of you and this is it. Turn the rug over."

Sara continued to hesitate. But as long as the Devil was inside the pentagram she had nothing to fear. The psychotherapist bent and carefully pulled back the overturned end of the rug. The world came into terribly sharp focus as she looked down. The triangle in which she had been standing during their other sessions had been scuffed by the carpet blowback.

The pentagram was broken.

Sara looked up at the Devil as he stepped forward. He was staring down at her, his expression harsh.

"I could have left the symbol at any time tonight," the towering creature told her. "I chose not to."

Sara backed from the demon. She wished she had a crucifix right now. If that was faith, she had found it.

"You have nothing to fear," the Devil assured her.

Sara didn't believe him. Not that it mattered. She felt helpless and vulnerable, but most of all stupid.

The Devil tilted his scepter toward her as he approached. "You asked about exhilaration. The orb can show you anything you wish. Your father, his father, anyone you can name, anything you can imagine."

"They wouldn't be real," Sara said. "They'd just be shades, idealized constructs from my subconscious."

"The teachings of the estimable Dr. Arul," the Devil said.

"Are you going to tell me that he's with you?"

"Would you believe me if I showed him to you?"

She shook her head.

"Then we won't inconvenience him," Satan replied. "But I will make a bargain."

A deal with the Devil. She should have seen that coming days ago.

"I will return to the pentagram and you may fix the outline," the Devil said. He stopped directly before her. "All I ask is an embrace."

"You need a hug?"

"Step next to me. Place your cheek against my chest."

"Then you'll return to the pentagram?"

"I have said I would," the Devil told her. "Despite what you've been told and experienced, not every male is a self-interested pedant, hedonist, or bully."

"And if I decline?"

"My Reapers will embrace you," the Devil said. "Get you out of the way, off the list so that God and I can move on."

"A few minutes ago you said I would have the time, years if I wanted, to pray to God for forgiveness—"

"I said 'perhaps,'" the Devil told her. "For a psychotherapist you do not always listen carefully."

Sara was in no position to negotiate. She took a step forward until she was standing beside the Devil. This was the closest they had been. He had a musky scent, very masculine and not unpleasant. She thought of Fredric's scarf.

"Do you ever appear as a woman?" she asked.

"Would that appeal to you?" the Devil inquired, a trace of surprise in his eyes.

Before she could answer "no," the Devil changed. He stood before her a woman slightly taller than Sara with pale, flawless skin. He—she—had raven hair and eyes and brilliant red lips. No longer a heavy loincloth but a cloak of golden halos hung about the Devil's shoulders. Satan still held the scepter, the flames casting a dull yellow glow on a body that seemed to have been sculpted from alabaster.

"All beings have a male and female nature," the Devil said. He reached out and touched Sara's shoulder. "Do I seduce men? I do. Were you going to ask if I seduced Fredric?"

"Yes," she said. She felt the touch from cheek to feet, a warming of the blood as it moved through her body.

"It wasn't necessary," the Devil replied. "Fredric was an astonishing young man who made his own discoveries. I was not needed—there. You have neglected the needs of your body."

Sara flushed. This was none of the Devil's business.

"But it is," said the Devil, reading her thoughts. "When

you come to me you will be soul where the distinction between male and female has no value." Her black eyes were close, wide, bottomless. "You do not need form to experience bliss. Put your arms under my cloak."

Sara had no room to maneuver, nor the will or strength to resist. She stretched her arms around the Devil's waist. Her actions were hesitant, awkward. She did not want this.

"Close your eyes," the Devil commanded. "Move closer."

Sara shut them, tightly. Her tense fingers stretched along the demon's body as she took a half step forward. Sara felt smooth, warm, unfamiliar skin against hers and fought the desire to pull away.

"Put your cheek against my chest," the Devil said.

"You only said embrace," she reminded him, her voice weak and broken, though less so than her spirit.

"Forget the flesh. Embrace the energy."

Sara turned her face to the side. Shaking, she moved closer and rested her head against his chest. It was male again, hot and damp. His hair felt soft against her jaw. She thought it would be more wiry.

Like a goat.

The curls seemed to expand and draw her in face first, as though she were sinking into bath bubbles. His flesh thinned and dissolved beneath her palms, like the smoke from the pentagram, leaving only intense heat that reached through her skin without burning it. Her fingers stopped trembling and the tension left her body. The warmth rolled through her leaving only an ethereal contentment, a sense of drifting that contrasted with the delightful, weight-free sinking sensation. Her arms and head seemed to be in very different places. The warmth stuck in her loins with bullish strength, entering her muscles and bones and cells. It shifted in all directions at once and she experienced a moment of explosive ecstasy that drove fever to her heels and mouth, causing her to cry out before vanishing. Her body and that of the Devil had been joined and then erased. Sara had neither eyes to open nor fingers to move. There was only the narcotic afterglow that subdued her senses yet enhanced her awareness.

She heard a voice ask, "Again?"

"No," she replied. "I'm still—happy."

After a moment of disorientation Sara began to feel the faint proximity of others. Their presence grew more insistent as moments or hours or centuries passed. She felt joy, peace, security, curiosity. She felt buoyant and wanted and eager to experience what those others had to offer.

The sensations came quickly: a sense of welcome, belonging, unheard music and unseen art but no less real somehow. They registered *somewhere*.

In your soul?

Sara felt safe and wanted. She was relaxed in a way that she had never been. There was no past, only the present. Hate was already a half-forgotten feeling. Without a face to hang it on, or memories to keep it alive, she was free.

And then a reasoning part of her said, "You did this with Fredric. Held him, took him with you. I can feel him here."

"We embraced in the woods," the Devil responded in his female voice.

"You said you didn't seduce him."

"Nor did I," the Devil insisted, her voice a rippling river somewhere inside of Sara. "It was the night before he fled. He could no longer endure being apart from Chrissie Blair. He summoned me, asked for my help. I showed him there was another way to contentment."

"Fredric was not ready to die."

"His body died. His soul lives."

"His soul was unfinished," Sara said. "He needed time." Memories of her own life returned. "I was unfinished, once. I was not prepared for the life I faced. Time," she said suddenly. "That is why God gives us time. To finish our souls."

Sara suddenly felt a heavy falling sensation.

"Then finish," the Devil said. "Quickly."

"I don't understand."

"A moment is as useful as a millennium," the Devil said. "You could toil from now to the end of time and never be finished to God's satisfaction. You would be wise not to try. My Reapers await."

"No!" Sara cried. "You asked me to embrace you and I did. You asked me to trust you and somehow that happened. This was not part of our agreement."

"There was no agreement about life or death," the Devil replied. "I told you the Reapers were out there and I said you might meet them soon."

"That is not a choice!" Sara screamed. "You said repeatedly we all have one."

"Choose."

"When *I* am ready!" she said. "You have no power over me. You are a tempter, that is all."

Sara was suddenly afraid of her own body. She was fearful of the brain that forced reason on her, fearful of the perishable flesh she would inhabit when she stopped falling, aware and ashamed of her limitations to feel.

But she wanted it back.

The speed of her fall was marked by change. The comforting nimbi that had engulfed her were replaced by darkness. The sweet, pre-dawn silence was driven away by a building drumbeat, the sound of her heart.

Contentment was replaced by overwhelming sadness, followed closely by hate and despair. It was worse than Sara remembered.

"Remember what it is to inhabit your own skin," the Devil said as a man. "To feel the pain lurking in every moment, the cumulative hurt of every trial you have endured. Consider what Fredric was spared, not what he lost."

Growth risks pain, she thought.

"Only in this crude animal realm," the Devil said. "I give you choice. Use it wisely. Embrace what I have shown you."

The woman felt her arms again. They were where they should be, with her head above them. Her skull was throbbing, pushing swirling red masses against her eyelids. She heard wind and creaking, smelled the last failing remnants of her deodorant, felt her fingers tingling and her palms perspiring.

A moment later Sara felt the floor as she struck it.

2

There was weather outside. That was her first cohesive thought.

The wind was knocking the trees against the house and scratching the edges of branches against the gutters.

Sara opened her eyes. She was lying on the office floor, her back to the desk. Her cheek was on the hardwood with the hem of the rug against her jaw. Her right arm was beneath her, the other thrown across the rug. The turned-back edge of the rug was by her feet. She looked past it. The pentagram was empty.

Sara lay there, drained and hurting. Her head was pounding and her right arm was sore. She must have struck them both when she fell.

From where? she wondered. *The side of the desk or a journey with His Satanic Majesty?*

The Devil did not answer. It felt good to have private thoughts again.

Sara squeezed her fingers together to get the blood circulating, then wearily pushed herself from the floor. She got as far as her hands and knees before stopping. Her head did not agree to go farther. She held that position for a long moment, looking down at the hardwood floor.

"What just happened?" she asked herself.

"You went to Hell," the Devil replied.

No! Sara's eyes snapped toward the room. The Devil was standing beside her, on the rug. She scrambled to a sitting position, wincing as she discovered bruises on her legs and side she hadn't noticed till then.

The Devil walked toward her slowly. "Why are you afraid? There are no Reapers here. Just two new-old friends."

Sara grabbed the edge of the desk and pulled herself up. "We are not friends. I want you to leave."

"The symbol is broken," he said. "You have no authority."

"Then please. I'm *asking* you to leave."

He crossed his chest with his scepter. "I'm hurt. I'm also unpersuaded. If I am not your friend, then I am your adversary. If I am your adversary, why would I grant any request?"

"Because I'm very tired," Sara said.

"The sad price of mortality," the Devil said. He crouched beside her, his flaming scepter lying casually across one knee, his eyes penetrating. He seemed to be studying her. "Do you remember the Ten Penny bar in Bridgeport? You waited tables there during your senior year of college."

"I remember," Sara said.

"You picked up a man one night. A handsome man, a man with money and a yacht and a promise to sail you to Bermuda. What happened?"

"We went to his hotel room."

"And?"

"I fucked him," she said.

"Good for you. And when you were finished?"

"I wanted to get as far from him as possible as quickly as possible," Sara said.

"Why?"

"I don't know. You tell me."

"Did you feel used?"

"No," Sara said. "I liked what happened. Where is this going?"

"To Rome," the Devil replied. "Did you think he would actually take you on his boat?"

Sara shook her head once. Her thoughts were windswept, too scattered for her to resist.

"So it was a little play, a fragment of one night when you indulged a prince and peasant girl fantasy."

"Something like that."

"And when reality returned you were angry," the Devil said. "He was no rajah and you would never be his rani. You felt stupid for letting yourself believe, even for a moment, that you could be more than what you were."

"If you say so," Sara said.

The Devil thrust a big hand behind her head. He clutched her hair tightly in his fingers and yanked her face toward his.

"I am not that sorry, pampered yachtsman," the Devil snarled. "You don't dismiss me."

Sara was panting with shock and fear. His breath was hot against her face, his teeth sharp and threatening. Knowing that he could not take her life did not diminish his ominous power.

"You thought, smug and sure, to whistle me forth, to command answers to your questions," the Devil said. "In Rome, where I was known as Pluto, they had a saying. '*Si vi pacem para bellum*.' 'If you want peace, prepare for war.' You were prepared for *nothing*." The Devil relaxed his grip but did not release the psychotherapist. "You have *learned* nothing since Martin Cayne drew you into his bottomless abyss. Your life has been a glaciated *thing*, motionless save for the events that drag you from one shallow, vacant point to the next."

The Devil's hand moved to her ear, to her earlobe, to the sensitive back of her neck. He closed his lips on her temple. The terrible disorder in her mind vanished, washed away by remembered rapture. Against all reason she felt cared for. She savored that almost as much as the Devil's touch.

"Heaven is as I have just described," Satan went on. "An endless melody from an uninspired, inhibited muse, dressed up by a formidable choir. Their voices sing loud and high to cover the emptiness of the experience. Be warned, Sara. Choose wisely. Join me and dwell in perpetual joy."

Sara's pulse and breathing betrayed her, both of them quickening as she responded to his touch.

"I give you until tomorrow to decide," the Devil said.

"What happens then?" she asked, not really paying attention to the answer. The Devil's smooth, enveloping lips had moved to her jaw, along with all the nerve endings in her body. She shut her eyes.

"Then?" he said. "I return, and not alone."

A moment later the kiss ended and the Devil's hand was gone. Sara opened her eyes.

She was alone again, though hardly herself. The psychotherapist felt as though she were waking slowly from a dreamlike state. It wasn't as dramatic as before but she was grateful for that. Sara didn't savor the feeling but forced the descent along. She couldn't remain on the floor. There was something she had to do.

Marshaling her energies, Sara raised herself up with the help of the desk. Her arms were vibrating like cello strings. Her legs weren't any better. She recalled from the ritual that one of the infernal names of the Devil was Amorist Magnus, the King of Lovers. She now understood why.

Steadying herself on the side of the desk, Sara reached her chair and opened the *Devil's Bible*. She turned to the Summoning and went to the footnotes. In particular, the one about the sanctity of the pentagram.

"'If in the course of the ceremony an acolyte causes a break in the symbol, it is a danger only if it remains unrepaired. The blessed Devil and his demons are an independent and at times willful race. They can, left to their own natures, create considerable mischief and mayhem.'"

It was one of the few examples of understatement by the otherwise hyperbolic Dark Pope.

She read on. "'At the converse of the Devil's hour, when a demon is weakest, the pentagram may be repaired and control restored.'"

Sara looked up the Devil's hour in the appendix, just to make sure it referred to midnight. It did. If she redrew the outline at noon then, in theory, she should be able to return the Devil to Hell. When he was gone she could solemnize the closing of the door by erasing the pentagram as dictated by ritual. That wasn't a guarantee but it was a hope. A hope she was careful not to think about long or cohesively in case he was lurking nearby.

Sara shut the book and grabbed a tissue from the box. The scent of the Devil was in her nose. She didn't want it there.

"Sorry, Fredric," she said wistfully. "I'm glad I got the scented ones."

When she was done, Sara kicked over the carpet and staggered from her office. She went to her room and fell on her bed.

Before going to sleep she remembered to set the alarm. Her soul was not the only thing she needed to save.

Fifteen

1

Sara awoke to the sound of wailing.

It drifted mournfully through the house, as though it were coming from the walls themselves. It took a moment for her to be sufficiently awake to swing from bed. She glanced at the clock. It was nearly six and she shut the alarm. Half awake, she went to the door and listened.

There was only silence. She noticed then that her cheeks were damp and warm and her eyes were swollen, that she was filled with a sense of profound oppression and heartache. She remembered her dream.

The sound had been her.

She recoiled. For a moment the wood of the door had felt like the lid of a coffin. In the dream it had been and she stepped back from it, remembering who had come through.

It was Robert Lynch and his grandson, both of them alive and smiling. The boy was nine and her father was older but fuller, healthier. He smelled of "grandpa" instead of scotch, like pipe tobacco and flannel.

"*Bless you,*" Martha said in Sara's ear, only her mother wasn't there. "*Robert Junior changed your father's life. My husband became whole again, and clean, and Darrell as well—*"

"It isn't my fault!"

"*Of course it was,*" Martha said with a laugh. "*You didn't even tell me or your father. You told your brother but he adored you and thought everything you did was right.* Whose *fault, then, dear?*"

"Let me guess," a voice said from behind. "The Devil made you do it."

Sara turned slowly. The Devil was standing there in his female form. She was white-faced, red-lipped, and ebon-eyed. She was dressed in a red robe that moved even though she was still.

"What are you doing here?" Sara demanded.

"Quite a spectrum of experiences last night," Satan said. "But you know, they say many people are actually happier in the workplace than they are at home. Something to do with personal fulfillment. You understand that, don't you?"

"I asked you a question."

"I'm not obligated to reply," the Devil pointed out. "But I will. You aren't the only one who wants something."

"I'm sure."

"Your son wants his mother."

Sara had expected that. "Leave me alone."

"I can make him a part of you again," the Devil said, coming closer.

"I said leave."

The Devil put her hand on Sara's belly. "I can put him here."

"Is there nothing you won't do?" Sara said through her teeth.

"For a friend? No." The robe suddenly flared with endless layers of flame, like a field of matches that had all been lit at the same time. There was no heat, only light. "I brought the flamelets with me," the Devil said. One emerged from deep within the blazing sea. The Devil's red mouth smiled. "There. Robert Junior. Ask for him and he is yours. Again."

"I don't believe you."

"Go ahead. Make the same decision again. I want to hear how it sounds, see what it looks like."

"Weren't you there the first time?" Sara asked.

"People don't need my help to sin."

"I did *not* sin."

"You broke—how many Commandments? Four? There was murder, and you surely took His name in vain affixed to a 'damn' or two or more. Your actions dishonored your parents and you coveted a man who belonged to another."

"I have a meeting," Sara said, moving from the Devil.

"About a boy who wasn't yours. This is a meeting about a boy who was."

Sara spun. The Devil was gone. Her son was standing in his place. He was whole and smiling, not the cadaverous thing she had seen in the woods.

"Hi, Mom," said the fresh-faced lad. "Grandpa and Darrell wanna go fishing. Can I go?"

Sara almost said, "*It's too cold for that, honey.*" Instead, she turned away. She wanted to hit something. "The boy is not here," she told herself. She was surprised to find that she wasn't upset. She was angry, and not about the abortion. It was the psychological hammering.

"Mommy?"

She ignored the child's voice.

"Let me guess," Sara said to the Devil she knew was near. "I can be reunited with my son but not here. I would have to come with you."

"It would work better," the Devil admitted from behind her. He was male again. "In this plane Robert Junior exists only as a flamelet, the manifestation of his being in *limbus infantium*. In you, grown to maturity and birthed as he might have been, he would be a son."

"This is what you did to Fredric," Sara said angrily. "You coaxed and cajoled until the moment of weakness when he bought in."

"What ego to imagine that everyone thinks as you do," the Devil sneered.

"We all want to live!" She faced him.

"The sentiments of Robert Junior, concisely stated."

"You monster. Grace was right. You spread confusion and discord," Sara said. "I gave you a fair hearing and I don't believe this honors the intent of your one important precept, that we must come to you *by choice*."

The Devil chuckled and walked toward the woman, stopping just a few inches from her. The demon's red eyes were iridescent. "Don't blame me for that. People *always* have a choice. The trick is to make the right one."

The Devil touched Sara's cheek. The psychotherapist pulled away. The demon pouted playfully. "After everything we shared last night?"

"New day," she said defiantly. In six hours it would be, anyway.

The Devil's brow crinkled. "That sounded—confident."

Sara said nothing.

"The clock," the Devil said. "This is about time."

"What about it?" Sara's stomach was burning.

"You want to run it back," the Devil told her. "You want to pick again, differently."

"I don't," she said. The burning subsided.

"What do analysts call it when an individual refuses to accept the obvious?"

The answer was "clinical denial" but Sara did not intend to discuss it with this creature.

"You suffer from it," the Devil told her. "You've become a cold and barren shell, hungry to be filled. I saw that, I touched it, and for a time I took that away. Your choice is whether to remain so and spend eternity in Vocīvus, or to do what you advise your patients—be 'proactive.'"

The psychotherapist said, "I choose to go to my meeting."

She turned and went to her dresser. She didn't have to look back to know that the Devil was gone. Soon, she would make that arrangement permanent.

2

Hurrying to make up for her little delay, Sara reached the school exactly at seven-twenty. She went directly to the principal's office. The other three were already there. It was strange to see Chrissie Blair again in the flesh, head and body together, this woman who had drifted unaware through so many thoughts and moments. Harkness was present, surly and big behind a desk that seemed too small to contain him. The third attendee was a slender, balding man in a loose-fitting brown suit. He looked to be about forty and had recently lost a lot of weight. That was Sara's guess, anyway, to explain the clothes and the slightly hungry look in his eyes. A well-worn leather portfolio sat on his lap. It had his initials, E.E.E. It had probably been a gift from his parents when he passed the bar. He rose when Sara entered. He was the only one who did.

"E. Edward Edwards," the man said in a clipped voice. There was nothing in his serious eyes or the dead-straight line of his mouth that suggested he possessed a sense of humor.

When the bone-spare welcome was finished, Harkness suggested they begin the meeting.

"You've elected not to be represented by personal counsel?" E. Edward said as he took a chair.

"I have so elected, at present," Sara replied.

"You understand that I represent the school district and that we may find our interests at cross-purpose."

"I understand," she replied.

This kind of formality did not suit her. However, tired as she was, Sara was pleased to note that her experiences with the Devil had made her an even more careful listener than before.

"I want to point out," said Harkness, "that we have not been served with legal papers. I want to make sure we're all on the same page in case we are."

"When does that usually happen?" Chrissie asked.

"Anywhere from two days to weeks," E. Edward said. "It's a wide window."

E. Edward had pulled a white legal pad and pen from inside his portfolio. "Dr. Lynch, as you may know, the aspects of your professional relationship with Fredric Marash that do not pertain directly to his death remain privileged. That said, is there anything you can tell us that might indemnify the school and yourself from legal liability in the apparent suicide of the young man?"

"It wasn't apparent," Sara said. "He jumped from the branch with a bicycle chain around his neck. His father and I both saw him hanging there."

Chrissie seemed to shrink at that and looked away.

"Question," Harkness said. "Isn't *this* meeting confidential? Shouldn't she be able to tell us everything?"

"This meeting is privileged, but the courts have ruled that patient-doctor confidentiality does not terminate upon death," E. Edward replied. "What we learn here may not be admissible, so I would rather not have that information exposed. If it were to leak into the body of our defense, we would have to reveal the source. That could jeopardize Dr. Lynch."

"Thank you, Mr. Edwards," Sara said.

Harkness made a face. "It seems to me we should be using every tool in our kit."

"That's true," the attorney said. "But there's also no point bringing a sander to fix a leaky sink."

Sara liked that. Harkness did not.

"Dr. Lynch, on the day of Fredric's death you reportedly told the young man's father that he did not seem suicidal," E. Edward said. "Is that accurate?"

"It is. He wasn't."

"You sound confident."

"Fredric exhibited none of the signs of an individual on the verge of ending his life," Sara told him. "The young man was not behaving recklessly. He was not uncharacteristically depressed or withdrawn. In fact, there was a new openness about some aspects of our sessions. He had not suffered a major loss or death in his life, showed no indication of putting his affairs in order, and did not appear to be abusing substances of any kind."

"Do we have a toxicology report?" Harkness asked the attorney.

"Not yet," E. Edward replied.

"I grew up in an alcoholic household," Sara said. "I know the signs."

"The police report said you and Mr. Marash arrived together," E. Edward went on. "Did you discuss the situation when you were in the woods?"

"Not really. We were shouting for Fredric."

"Did he answer?"

Sara shook her head.

"But you were working in a cooperative way," E. Edward said. "Mr. Marash was not blaming you for Fredric's actions."

"He was not," Sara said.

"Does that help us?" Harkness asked.

"It reinforces that there was an ongoing, trusting relationship between the father and Dr. Lynch, even in the midst of this crisis," E. Edward informed him. "Doctor, do you know if Fredric Marash went to the woods on other nights?"

"He did."

"Why isn't that privileged?" Chrissie asked.

"His father told me," Sara replied.

"That's important," E. Edward said as he made notes. "Mrs. Marash was concerned enough to call Dr. Lynch, whom she obviously trusted, and Mr. Marash was sufficiently worried to go after his son this night. Clearly something unusual, apparently catastrophic happened at the home *after* Dr. Lynch had visited the shop."

"That's good," Harkness said.

"It appears to help," E. Edward said, "though a suit from

the Marashes would not be keyed solely to the events at the home that night. It would address the core issue of potential ongoing negligence that caused this crisis."

"That's buck-passing," Chrissie said. "We worked hard to help Fredric."

"I said he looked like the 'walking dead' that day, but nobody listened to me," Harkness said.

"You meant it as a dig, not as a perception," Chrissie said angrily.

Harkness leaned back in his chair and glowered at her. The guidance counselor was not cowed.

"Did Fredric seem to mind?" E. Edward asked.

"No," Harkness said. "He didn't give a damn what anyone said."

"Is that in his psychological dossier?" E. Edward asked.

"It isn't, and it's also not true," Chrissie replied. "He just didn't care what *some* people said."

Way to go, Chrissie, Sara thought.

"Getting back to the night of the boy's death, there is hearsay, Dr. Lynch, that you entered the Marash domicile following the incident in the park," E. Edward said. He looked up from his notepad. "Is there any validity to this talk?"

"You mean, did I do it?" Sara asked. She was stalling, thinking.

"That's the question on the table," Harkness said.

Through it, Sara decided. It was true and she would say so.

"Yes," Sara said. "I went into the house because I wanted to spare Fredric's parents additional trauma."

"Pure genius," Harkness said. "What the hell could be worse than their son dying?"

"Knowing the reason why," Sara replied.

"Principal Harkness, Mr. Edwards," Chrissie interjected. "As a certified grief counselor I should point out that on the night of the suicide Dr. Lynch was probably very distraught—"

"I knew what I was doing, but thanks," Sara said with a smile.

"Is there anything you can tell us about that?" the attorney asked.

"My reasons for going into the house had nothing to do with Fredric," Sara said.

"What the hell does *that* mean?" Harkness asked.

"I needed information. I needed names. I had reason to believe that our town is home to a cult of teenage devil worshipers of which Fredric was a member."

There was a long, long moment of no one breathing.

Harkness slapped his desk. "It's those damn Goths."

"That's just an expression of the problem, a form of acting-out," Sara said.

"Wait," E. Edward said. "You said you had 'reason to believe' there's a devil cult here. Can you elaborate?"

Sara was going to have to fudge a little. "I live across the river from the area where Fredric died. I row over on occasion. The other day I noticed strange markings on the rocks and on fences. I looked them up. They resembled symbols used in Satanic rituals."

"There's a reference to fresh petroglyphs in the state trooper's follow-up report," E. Edward said.

"I thought that might have had something to do with Fredric's actions but I wanted to be sure before I piled additional trauma on the Marashes. What I told Mr. Marash that afternoon was true. There *was* no clinical reason for Fredric to commit suicide. But when I saw where he died, I thought there might be religious reasons. I was concerned there might even be plans for a Jonestown-style mass suicide."

"Which is why you trespassed, to protect other young people," the attorney clarified.

"I couldn't afford to wait for a search warrant," Sara said.

"You might not have gotten one, based on the evidence of a few marks in the woods," E. Edward said. "And you're saying that you found occult materials in the house?"

Sara nodded again.

"Do you think the parents were involved?" the attorney asked.

"No. This seems to have been just a small group of teens. I met one of them in the woods the next day." She looked at Chrissie. "Marci Cello."

"I know her from grief counseling," Chrissie said. "Thanks, Dr. Lynch. I'll have a talk with her."

Everyone in the office fell silent again. The din of arriving students seemed very distant. Sara watched the attorney as he wrote on his pad. She noticed that he wasn't wearing a wedding band. She felt a pinch of loneliness though she wasn't sure who it was for.

"It may seem insensitive to say this, but what you've just told us is very good news," E. Edward said. "Not about the cult, of course, but about our own exposure. The emerging scenario speaks to the concern Dr. Lynch has for the community and of her willingness to risk her career for it. It also addresses an unrevealed outside influence on the boy's actions."

The mood of the office shifted from confrontational to something that—bizarrely, Sara thought—resembled bonhomie. She did not want to be buddies with Harkness. Yet with the big issues seemingly marginalized, the little slaps and jabs that brought them to this point were forgotten.

Legal tribulations obviously had a way of making strange bedfellows.

The meeting lasted forty-five minutes. When it was over, Chrissie hustled off to her first student appointment and to schedule one with Marci. The guidance counselor would not let on that Sara had told her anything. Harkness warmly told the attorney he appreciated his coming and coolly thanked Sara without expressing his appreciation. She would survive the affront. She left the office with E. Edward.

"I want to thank you for your frankness and cooperation, Dr. Lynch," he said as they walked toward their cars. "I can't imagine how this has been for you."

"Fredric was very dear to me," she told him. "He was an artist and not an easy young man to know, but the effort was worth it. He had a rich soul."

"I'm surprised to hear you say that," the attorney said.

"Why?"

"The analysts I've worked with always talk about the mind."

"Souls have been a lot on my mind," she said. "I was lucky to see that side of him."

The attorney stopped. He seemed distracted. "Dr. Lynch, I didn't want to ask in there but I sensed you and the Marash boy were close. Forgive me for asking, but if there is a suit this may come up. Was there anything—"

"Inappropriate in our relationship?" Sara asked.

The attorney nodded.

Sara was glad he had brought that up. She was wondering how to get into the other significant aspect of Fredric's behavior, one that was covered by privilege.

"No," she assured him. "Fredric was not interested in me. But there was someone else, someone unreachable, someone he adored. Someone he was happy to see every day. She was another reason I didn't believe he was at risk."

"You're talking about a student? A cheerleader?"

"A teacher," she said.

And then it hit him. His eyes widened with understanding. "The guidance counselor."

"There is a classic, frenetic behavior pattern that follows unrequited adoration," Sara explained nonspecifically. "It very aggressively involves living, not dying. It involves pursuit, potential stalking. If *that* fails, there is a risk of self-destruction. But that takes months."

"And we weren't there yet."

Sara didn't have to shake her head. E. Edward got it.

"I'm guessing Ms. Blair doesn't know," the attorney asked, cocking his head toward the school.

"I don't believe she has a clue," Sara said. "But anyone who might go into such a devotee's room, clean it out, could not miss the evidence. You might want to pursue that."

"I will," E. Edward said enthusiastically. "Thank you. I appreciate the compass reading."

"And I appreciate your discretion," Sara said. "Now there's something I wanted to ask you. Also something personal."

"It's Edward," he said.

"Sorry?"

"The 'E,' my first name initial. It stands for Edward. My parents couldn't resist."

"I kind of assumed that," Sara replied. "Not what I was going to ask. I was wondering why you practice here, in this county. Are you a native or just drawn to the place?"

"I went to school nearby and stayed because my kid sister is an invalid," he told her. "Jumped into a shallow pond as a kid, broke her neck. She can't walk and has no fine motor control in her hands. She has to use them like flippers. Our parents are gone and our childhood house is Edie friendly, so here I am."

"Edie." Sara smiled.

The attorney shrugged. "Like I said, my parents couldn't resist."

Sara felt tears, not just for Edward Edward Edwards but for herself.

"Did something keep you here?" he asked.

"Something," she replied. "Several somethings."

The attorney had a smile in him and he gave it to her then along with a hug.

"Whatever it is I hope you're doing okay," he told her. "As for this other thing, I'll try to keep it as far away as possible."

"Thanks," she said sincerely.

As they parted, Sara noticed Principal Harkness standing behind his desk, watching from his office window. She could not imagine what he was thinking.

Happily, she didn't care.

3

Tonia was out shopping when Sara returned home. Alexander was at school and Martha was in the kitchen eating toast, drinking coffee, and reading the newspaper. She said that Alexander had seemed better than the day before, though he was still talking to his toy soldier.

"In English or Russian?" Sara asked.

"Why, English, dear," Martha said. "You know he doesn't speak very much Russian."

Sara poured coffee and sat down.

"Toast?" her mother asked, pushing over the plate and jelly.

Sara took a slice and ate it plain.

"Where did you go so early?" Martha asked.

"A meeting at the school," Sara said.

"About the situation?"

Sara didn't have to ask what "the situation" was. She nodded.

"How did it go?" Martha asked.

"Very well," Sara told her. "I think we removed some major concerns from the table."

"I'm so glad to hear that, dear," Martha said.

"What about you? Have you heard from Darrell?"

"I left a message on his machine while you were out. He hasn't phoned."

"He will," Sara assured her. She took a last bite of toast. "I saw Grace Rollins yesterday."

"Did you?" Martha exclaimed.

Sara nodded. "I ended up near Yale and gave her a call."

"How is she?"

"She seems very happy. She's been traveling a lot, teaching—"

"Spreading lies."

The words fell like boulders. Sara stopped chewing. A terrible silence filled the small room.

"Why did you say that?" Sara asked.

"I suppose God was traveling with Grace Rollins when I needed Him," Martha said harshly. "That's why he didn't answer my prayers."

"What do you mean? Yesterday or—"

"Ever!" Martha snapped. She returned to the newspaper. "I prayed to Him when your father was failing and then for

Darrell. I might just as well have been talking to a doll, like Alexander."

The sentiments sounded sincere but the tone was ugly and distorted. Sara went to her mother and gently removed the newspaper from her hands.

"What brought this on?" Sara asked, kneeling beside her. "You've never spoken like this before."

"I never felt like this before."

"What's different?" Sara asked.

"I had an epiphany this morning," Martha said. "I was dreaming that I was free to say what I wanted to anyone I wanted, and I did."

"Did you talk to someone in this dream?" Sara asked.

Martha fixed her eyes on her daughter. "You, dear."

"What did you tell me?"

"That I was angry at how you killed my grandson."

Sara had to swallow before words would clear her throat. "Who said I did that?"

"No one, dear. It was just there, in the dream," Martha said. "But you were young and afraid and I forgive you. You may not be the warmest daughter in the world but you keep a roof over my head."

"You're the reason I'm *here*," Sara said, fighting nausea.

"Thank you. I wouldn't want to depend on the kindness of strangers." Martha frowned. "Someone said *that*, or something like it. Who?"

Sara turned away. *Don't listen to this*, she told herself. *It isn't real*. The Devil had put these thoughts in her head. *Or did he simply bring them out?* No. Darrell wouldn't have said anything about the abortion. Even when her brother was drunk, some subjects were firewall-protected.

Her mother didn't even seem as if she were entirely

there. Maybe part of her was still asleep. Dr. Arul used to have patients who didn't fully shake the effects of hypnosis. Now and then he would be called to help someone who had a relapse in the middle of the night or on the street or in the underground.

Sara did not go directly to the office. She stopped in the hall powder room, shut the door, and knelt beside the toilet. The toast and coffee came back. She pulled a scrap of toilet paper from the spool and wiped her mouth. Then she went to the sink, tugged a paper cup from the holder, and rinsed her mouth. She drank several cupfuls slowly, then washed her face.

If the Devil was doing this, she couldn't understand why. Tormenting people was hardly the way to get them to commit their souls.

Unless the goal is to turn up the heat until surrender is the only option.

Hopefully, after noon, it wouldn't matter.

She left the powder room and went to her office. She fell heavily into the chair behind her desk. There was just one message and it was from Grace. She was calling to find out how Sara was doing.

"Lousy," Sara replied.

Her office seemed stuffy, which was hardly a surprise given who had been there and what had transpired. She grabbed a shawl, opened the window, and went to the gazebo. She sat in the clear morning air and looked out at the slate-gray water. The small whitecaps were spiking fitfully as the river rushed by.

What have I done? she asked, feeling the kind of empty despair she had not known for years. *What have I brought into this house?*

It wasn't just the Devil. He was right about this much: she felt like a shell with nothing but red, roiling bile inside. Whatever joy had been present in the last decade, from being with her mother or watching Alexander and Tonia learn their new lives or helping patients, was being sucked away. That too was not just the Devil. It was her own sense of loss and surrender. That wasn't exactly a revelation, but like her mother's bitterness, it was closer than ever to the surface.

"You're giving up," the wind whispered in her ear. It came as a familiar, unwelcome sound.

"Were you there?" Sara wondered aloud. "Were you watching when Martin Cayne pushed a knife in my chest? Did someone set you free long before I did?"

"Sara Lynch again pays tribute to Sara Lynch," the Devil said, laughing. "I have been liberated since before Eden fell. All you did was ask to talk."

"Fine."

The wind brushed her cheeks, tangible as satin. "I am everywhere. I see everything. I hear everything."

"Talk about paying tribute," Sara said.

"I've claimed millions of souls. You've taken one. I win."

Sara shook her head sadly. "You said God was the one who enjoyed handing out punishment. You do a pretty good job of it."

"The truth is not punishment," the wind replied. "It is information."

"Did God make my son appear to me this morning? Or was that 'information'?"

"You did that."

"You had nothing to do with the vision?"

"You know how the subconscious works. That I was in it doesn't mean I created it."

"And my mother?"

"That was mine," the Devil admitted.

"To give her information?"

"For her and also for you," the Devil whispered. "You can't move ahead if secrets force you to watch your step."

"That wasn't your decision to make."

"But it was, and you knew it," the Devilish wind replied. "You spoke the name that speaks the truth. Peripipteinus. The maker of change."

One of the infernal names. Sara had no idea what it meant; perhaps she should have.

"So honest, so good," Sara said. "So selective. If you don't want to hurt us, why don't you show us *good* things?"

"These are the ghosts that haunt you." The wind seemed to smile. "You enjoyed being with the attorney today. Good comes of misfortune."

"I enjoyed talking to him," Sara admitted. "It was the first positive experience I've had in a while."

"I recall a 'positive' moment you had the other night."

"A loveless orgasm?" Sara said.

"Self-love," the Devil corrected her.

"Even that wasn't genuine," Sara lamented. "It was imposed by your book. And it was nothing compared to that embrace in the parking lot of the high school."

"Do key experiences always occur to you in parking lots?" the Devil asked.

"Fuck you," Sara said. It was all that came to mind.

The wind continued to blow. "Was Martin Cayne a loveless orgasm or a close embrace?"

"Neither," she said truthfully.

"What was he?"

Sara didn't answer and the feeling of satin faded and the

winds calmed. She rose. She wished there had been something stronger than "fuck you" but she couldn't think of what it was.

She also didn't have an answer to the Devil's question, and that was more disturbing still.

4

Sara called Grace and got her voice mail. She asked her friend to call back as soon as possible, then rolled back the carpet and looked at the damaged pentagram. It was a heartbreaking sight, such a tiny distortion with such a dreadful impact. The smallness of it was irritating, like the pea under the mattress, worse than if the entire thing had been smeared.

The phone beeped as she was folding back the rug. Sara grabbed it across the desk. It was Chrissie calling to make sure Sara was all right.

"I'm fine," the psychotherapist told her. "You okay?"

"Sure. Principal Harkness got pretty p.o.'ed awhile after you left, though," Chrissie said.

"Why?" She had a good idea, though. In his Neanderthal mind she was using her charms to seduce the attorney.

"He doesn't like the idea that there's some kind of devil cult based in his school," Chrissie said. "He thinks you made that up to cover your butt."

"He's worse than wrong, he's stupid," Sara said. "Maybe he'll send the football squad out to eradicate the problem. A SWAT team to hunt down Goths." He would do it if he thought he could get away with it.

"I suggested his players join up," Chrissie replied with a conspiratorial snicker. "I thought it might help their game."

If one good thing had come of this, it was that Chrissie Blair had begun to assert herself.

"Principal Harkness said he saw Attorney Edwards hug you in the parking lot. I didn't realize you knew him. It seemed like you didn't."

"Never met him before," Sara told her.

"I guess you got along then."

"We had a nice chat afterward," Sara said. "It had nothing to do with this situation—"

Sara stopped talking as she looked across the office. The locked inner door was opening slowly. She half expected to see her mother with an old skeleton key and a new complaint. But there was no one on the other side. Maybe she hadn't locked it or it hadn't been properly closed. The open window in the waiting room could have caused a reverse draft.

"Well, it doesn't matter I suppose," Chrissie said. "I've made an appointment to see Marci during sixth period study. I'll keep an eye on things from this end."

"Thank you, Chrissie."

"We'll fix this," the guidance counselor replied. "I believe that."

Hold on to your faith, Sara thought. *You may need it.*

When she hung up she walked over and closed the door. The lock had been undone. Or maybe it was never done. She turned the flange on the knob and made sure the door was securely shut before going back to her desk.

Sara's first appointment came at eleven, dental hygienist Meg Jackson. The fifty-three-year-old Delwood native was thinking of leaving her husband, a sanitation worker, for the dentist. While the fifty-year-old Dr. Holmes had not shown any interest in Meg she did not want to court him without being free to do so. The sessions—this was the woman's fifth—had pointed up the inherent instability in her thirty-five-year marriage. That was what Sara had been exploring at the close of the last session.

The psychotherapist had to work hard to dig her mind into the subject and keep it there.

"You said last week that the first three years of your marriage were the happiest," Sara reminded the woman. "Your husband dropped out of college—"

"Community college," Meg said. "Norwalk Community."

"All right. And he took a job as a loading dock foreman at a printing house in Brookfield. What had he been studying in school?"

"Business," Meg said. "But with a new wife and a child on the way we needed to earn more money."

"You continued your own studies."

"Yes," Meg told her. "I was going to Fairfield U. I took my two-year Associate of Science degree. I didn't get to use it, though, until after our second child started going to school."

"Do you think your husband resented the fact that you stayed in school and he did not?"

"No," Meg assured her. "He always said that one of us should have an education. He didn't mind that it was me. He was very supportive back then."

"When did that begin to change?"

Meg was about to answer when Sara heard a noise in the waiting room. Her next patient was not due for another two hours.

"Hold the thought," Sara said as she went to check.

She opened the door, stepped in, and saw Fredric sitting there. He was dressed in black, seated in one of the straight-backed chairs and staring at the wall in front of him. His neck was healed and he looked peaceful, the way he did that last session; almost jocular.

"Their relationship began to change when Mrs. Jackson became so busy with the children and part-time hygienistry that she stopped giving her poor husband any attention." Fredric looked over with his soulful eyes. "Go ahead. Ask her. She knows that he started shacking up with a secretary at the printing house."

Sara returned to the office. She had to get through this session; just this, then she could send the Devil and his visions back to Hell.

"Sorry," the psychotherapist said. She smiled tensely and sat down.

"That's all right. It gave me a chance to think," the woman said. "Things began to change when Little Joe went to kindergarten and I took a part-time job. My husband felt I should stay at home and have another baby but I had my eye on private school for our son and that wasn't going to be cheap."

"Did Little Joe end up going to the school?" Sara asked. She avoided shifting her eyes toward the waiting room. She had to be here for Meg Jackson.

"He did not," Meg said. "My husband and I tried to talk about it one night over dinner—the conversation wasn't very pleasant," she said. "Big Joe got upset." The woman hesitated, looked down. "He got really, really upset."

"Did he hurt you?"

"He raped her," Fredric said, shambling into the office.

"He did get rough," Meg replied.

Obviously, she neither saw nor heard the young man.

"Come on, Meg. He got a lot rough," Fredric said. "He got up from the dinner table, pulled you from the chair, and fucked you on the linoleum. You didn't scream because the kids were in the next room."

"What did he do?" Sara asked. She leaned forward, trying to stay with Meg while Fredric walked over. He stood between them, off to the side, as the hygienist began to sob.

"We had sex."

"Was it consensual?"

"Did I let him?" the woman asked. She hesitated, then nodded.

Fredric crouched beside her. "Your fat husband threw you down, dropped on top of you, and kissed with his big dog tongue while he tried to pull up your housedress—the green one with white raindrops that he gave you for your first anniversary. It hurt when he took you and you can't forgive him. But you can't hate him, either. Tell the doctor why."

"Meg—when was your daughter born?" Sara asked.

It took a few seconds before the woman answered. "Nine months later," she said and began to sob.

Sara pushed over the tissues.

"It would have been weeks before she confessed that," Fredric told Sara. "I just saved the two of you a lot of time."

Sara waited until Meg quieted somewhat. "Mrs. Jackson, did you ever talk to your husband about what he did?"

She shook her head.

"Do you ever feel anger toward your daughter because of it?"

"I don't know," Meg wept.

"That means yes," Fredric said. "You hate your daughter because of how she was conceived. Was there ever a day you looked at her and didn't see your husband's twisted face when he attacked you? Is that image branded into your eyes?"

Fredric turned suddenly and looked at Sara. "Any of this sounding familiar, Dr. Lynch?"

"It may be true," Meg said suddenly.

Fredric clapped his hands triumphantly. "There. We have no control over how we're conceived, or when, or where, or *why*, yet we catch the backlash. My grandmother tried to sleep her way to stardom. It didn't work. So she became Saint Goldwyn and my mother and I were supposed to be the same. I hated that."

After a long cry Mrs. Jackson suddenly turned to her right, to where Fredric was standing. "Who is he?" she asked.

Sara straightened from neck to toe. "You see him?"

"I'm sorry?"

"Do you see—someone?" Sara asked.

"No. I mean my husband. I don't know who he is. All these years together and I still don't understand why he got so mad, why he wanted to hurt me. I haven't been able to open up to him, to trust him since that night. I don't know who he is or what he's become."

"Do you think he's different now?" Sara asked.

The woman shrugged a shoulder. "He tries, sometimes. With flowers or little notes, or a look. He'll take my hand in the mall."

"Has anything like that night happened again?"

"No. I'm always watching, even when we make love. So is he, I think."

"How often do you make love?"

"Once a week, maybe once every other week," Meg said. "It was months later before we did—and it's never been the same. I don't like the weight of him, the smell of him, his touch."

"I don't blame you," Fredric said. He leaned close. "Maybe

I'll come to you in a dream tonight, let you see how gentle that big slob of a husband is with the secretary at work."

"No!" Sara said.

Both of them looked at her.

"You have to move on," Sara insisted.

"Which one?" Fredric snickered.

"Both."

"Excuse me?" Meg said.

Sara bowed her head, took a moment, then looked back at her patient. "You and your husband need to address what happened that night. Otherwise this hate will stay with you."

"Not if he's gone," Meg said.

"Getting rid of someone doesn't get rid of the pain," Sara said.

"You would know," Fredric said.

Sara looked at Meg and smiled sweetly. "Mrs. Jackson, I'm—I'm not feeling very well at the moment."

"Can I get you something?" Meg asked.

"No thanks. It's been a difficult week."

"I know and I'm sorry," Meg said. "I don't believe any of the things people are saying."

"Such as?" Fredric asked.

"They come into the office and talk and talk, even when I'm cleaning their teeth," Meg continued. "They say the boy was on drugs, that he may have been in love with you, all sorts of things. I can only imagine what they say about me when they're at the beauty parlor or nail salon."

"If you want I'll tell you," Fredric said.

"Mrs. Jackson, I was wondering if we might continue this whenever it's convenient for you," Sara said. "We can start again from the top of the session and there won't be any charge."

"All right," Meg said, blowing her nose. "I should probably do some thinking about this anyway." She gathered her handbag and took her jacket from the coatrack. "I think I can come back Friday, if that would be okay."

"The same time," Sara said after checking her Palm Pilot. She noted the time. It was twenty minutes to noon.

"Thanks. I'll be here." Meg smiled. "I think I needed that little cry."

Sara smiled at her.

"I'm sorry about all the rest," Meg said, "but I know things will work out." She clasped Sara's hand. "You're a good woman."

Sara was still smiling as Meg left.

Fredric watched her go. "She'll forgive him but it'll never work out."

Sara ignored him. She went to the rug and drew it back.

"What are you doing?" Fredric asked.

Sara didn't answer. She got the chalk from her desk and carefully repaired the pentagram.

"Someone got a little careless," Fredric said.

Sara used a letter opener to scrape away some of the wax that had spilled onto parts of the pentagram. She drew over that as well. She wanted to make sure everything was perfect. When the psychotherapist was done, she retrieved the *Devil's Bible* and recited the Spell of Disestablishment. As she spoke, she used tissues to rub away the pentagon. She removed the candles and erased the symbol as dictated by the text, from the center outward in a counterclockwise direction.

She did not look up as she worked. Sara used the old hardwood floor the way Dr. Arul had occasionally used crystal trinkets: as a sure, clear focal point. She saw shapes in the grain, a profile here and an animal there. She even saw what looked like an angel. Unlike the ethereal glass bars and spheres, the floor represented hard reality; Sara's past, the seat of her practice, a place of reason. It would be her anchor as she flushed away the strange, surreal disorder of the past few days.

When she was finished, Sara stood. She kept her eyes on the clean floor. When she looked to her right, where Fredric had been, he would be no more.

The teenager was still there. Her body went cold.

"You look like you've seen a ghost," Fredric said.

"You shouldn't be here," Sara said.

"There's an impediment," Fredric said. "Remember when you helped pull me off the tree? Messy business, not just in the head but on the sweater."

Sara had no idea what he was talking about.

"Leaves dislodged—bark, too. Flakes of it landing all over, including on you. You carried some of those back here. Pieces of sycamore."

"They kept the portal open," Sara said, her throat tight and her voice infirm. "The Devil can come or go."

"All of us can," Fredric said. He went to the chair Meg had vacated and plopped down. "Since I'm here and you can't just shoo me away, why don't we have that session we missed? Maybe it would help if we talked about what it was like before you and my father showed up the other night."

"All right," Sara said. "What was it like? Why did you feel that was your best option?"

"I was hounded and alone," he said. "Judas without the crime."

"You weren't alone. I wanted to help you."

"You wanted to rewire me, defuse me, make sure I didn't blow up when people walked all over me."

"It wasn't like that at all," Sara said. "The system wasn't built for people like you, Fredric. I wanted to understand you, find ways you could channel your imagination, satisfy your curiosity—"

"Let's see."

"What?"

Fredric rose. "You say you wanted to help me."

"More than anything."

"Then do it," he said, his voice a dare. "Here's the past. Change it."

5

The darkness behind Sara's eyelids filled with stars and dark sky, the woods at night, the wind moving through them. The breeze had substance, the honeysuckle on the ridge had a smell, and the rocky earth was lumpy beneath her shoes. Sara opened her eyes. She was in the woods, holding a flashlight. She moved her hand from side to side. The beam was under her control.

Could this be real? Had she gone back, made it in time? Or had everything been a horrible projection of things that had not yet occurred?

Sara saw Fredric climbing the tree with the chain slung across his shoulder.

"Don't," she muttered. Then she yelled. "Fredric, *don't!*"

"Go away!" the young man shouted as he continued to climb. "I can't take this anymore!"

Sara ran forward. She felt herself getting winded, inhaling the dirt kicked up by her desperate dash. Perhaps there *was* a chance to save him.

"Fredric, stop and talk to me!"

"You can't help me. *He* can."

"The Devil?"

Fredric stopped. He looked back, shielding his eyes from her flashlight. "What do you know about him?"

"I know he can't fix things except by ending them," Sara replied. She slowed to a jog.

"How do you know that?"

"I've spoken with him," Sara said. She lowered the beam slightly. "I've spoken with him *and* her," she added, remembering that the Devil might have appeared to Fredric as a female.

"You raised the Devil? Yourself?"

"Yes."

"Why?"

"To see if I could help you, if I could understand what you were experiencing," she said.

" 'Were'?" he said.

"*Are* experiencing," she answered. *Thank you, God,* she thought. *If this is real, give me the wisdom to get him through it.*

"Did he show you the children of *Avernus*?"

The lake in southern Italy, she remembered. "No."

"If we don't trust him we will be like them," Fredric said.

"I don't understand."

"Flocking, dumb servants instead of masters," he replied.

"Is that what you want to be? A master?"

"Yes."

"What would you do then?"

"I would make her come to me," Fredric said. "Imagine wanting someone so bad it makes you crazy."

"I did, once," she told him.

"What happened?"

She was walking now but still continuing toward him. "ASD," she said with what she hoped was a companionable laugh.

"What's that?"

"It's my brother's expression for when he's dropped hard and fast by a woman he's dating. He calls it 'ASD'—Ass So Dumped."

"That happened to you?" Fredric obviously wasn't amused. He was living the emotion, not hearing the words.

"Yes," Sara said.

"What did you do?"

"I hurt for years," she told him. "I still do."

"Is that what you want me to do? Hurt for years?"

"No," Sara said.

Fredric held up the chain and rattled it. "Good. 'Cause I can fix this and go right to him, get what I want."

"You can't have Chrissie Blair if you're dead."

He seemed surprised. "How do you know about her?"

"I'm—perceptive."

"Can I have her if I'm alive?"

"You don't want her," Sara said. "You're smarter than she is, more talented and creative—"

"She's beautiful," Fredric said. "When she looks at me it's like looking at the deer that sometimes come to the backyard—she's so delicate."

"Let's talk about that," Sara suggested. "Come down so we can do it face-to-face."

"You come here," he said.

"Fredric, that's a skinny branch—"

"Big enough for me," he said and began to tie the chain around the limb. "I want to see my savior. I need his help."

"No, I'll come up!" Sara shouted.

Fredric stopped.

The psychotherapist went to the steep ledge of the road cut and clawed to the top. She reached the trunk of the sycamore. There were no low branches or good footholds, so she tucked the flashlight in her deep pants pocket and struggled on the knobs and twigs while Fredric lay down. He continued with his plan, tying the end of the chain into a figure eight around the tree.

"Fredric, don't. I'm trying to get there," she said.

When he finished securing the loop, he tossed the other end to Sara. She exhaled with relief and used it to help pull herself up. She made it to the limb. Fredric had been crouching in the crook where the branch met the bole. He moved outward to allow Sara access. He held an overhead branch to steady himself. Sara leaned against the trunk. There was a slight slope to it that made her feel somewhat balanced. She put her hands behind her butt to steady herself.

"Talk," Fredric said.

He looked like the Fredric she knew. Black clothes and pasty face with smart and curious eyes, a sullen expression but with underlying sweetness.

"Promise you'll hear me out," she said.

She was still holding the loose end of the chain. Fredric held out his hand. She hesitated.

"I can probably break my neck just by jumping," he pointed out.

Sara gave it to him. He stood with his arms at his side. That wasn't exactly a promise, but in the Visual Dictionary of Fredric it was, at least, a pause.

"Before we talk about Chrissie, I want to tell you something," Sara said. "I'm pretty angry with your mom. She had no right to go into your room."

"Hypocritical witch."

"Why didn't you tell me what was going on between you two?" Sara asked.

"You couldn't have helped."

"You don't know that," Sara said.

"Oh, like you could convince them to accept my life?" The young man rattled the chain. "Well, I'm in control, not them. I'll be free *and* I'll get my Chrissie."

"Fredric, you'll be *dead!*" she cried.

Sara raised her hands to try and slow things down. "Listen to me, *please!* I admire you. You've got the courage of your beliefs, more than I had at your age. I'm still exploring, thinking about religion and the things I've done or didn't do. It can be a great adventure but not if you end it."

"I'm not ending the adventure. Only the pain."

"They're inseparable," she said. "But you needn't shoulder it alone. There's no reason we can't do this together."

"Actually, there *is* a reason," the young man said.

"What's that?"

"You said it yourself," Fredric grinned. "I'm dead. So unless you want to join me—"

"No, *don't!*"

Fredric lifted his arm, looped the chain around his neck, then stepped off the branch. It happened so quickly that Sara actually screamed. She reached for him reflexively, nearly lost her own balance; she grasped the tree behind her to hold on. Sara wailed miserably at the ugly crunching of bark as Fredric's weight caused the chain to snap taut.

The woman closed her eyes and shouted into the faintly rustling canopy above. When she stopped for breath and opened her eyes, she was no longer standing in the tree. She was sitting in her chair in her office, quite alone.

Sixteen

1

It was several minutes before Sara felt like moving. She was shocked and she was spent. Her limbs were weak from what seemed like a very real climb up that tree. Her soul ached from what felt like a second chance to save Fredric.

Sara didn't know whether this had been a haunting, a reverie, or if the Devil was still afoot and playing games. Perhaps Sara could have handled Fredric differently in life if she had possessed all the information, in time. She was aware of the importance of everything she said or did. Sara had learned that lesson when they used to visit her mother's Uncle Bob, a commercial pilot who flew gliders for fun.

"When you fly a sailplane you only have one chance to land, one approach at whatever place you pick to set down," the big,

white-haired man used to say. "*Mess that up and you become part of a wrecked aircraft.*"

That was how Sara looked at her sessions with patients. If she missed a mumbled comment or said the wrong thing someone's life could be destroyed.

The beep of the phone pulled Sara back. It was Grace. Sara had never been so glad to hear from someone.

"What's happening up there?" Grace asked.

"I honestly don't know," Sara replied.

"Are you still playing with Bruce Perry's book?"

It took Sara a moment to remember that Perry was the Dark Pope. "Not really," she replied. "I followed the instructions to get rid of the Devil but I don't think it worked."

"Of course not," Grace said.

"What do you mean?"

"The ritual of the pentagram is purely symbolic," Grace said. "I've encountered dozens of symbols of darkness on archaeological digs—pentagrams, evil eyes, totem poles, even clay jars that supposedly contain djinn and the souls of great wizards. These objects and pictographs serve the same purpose the world over. They are graven images that, as God himself told us, have no place in faith—either good *or* evil. These are not where any demon figure resides. He is everywhere at every time, a single being with countless facets."

"Great. You agree with him."

"Other way around, please," Grace said. "The point is, when we worship a fetish or golden calf, what we're really doing is opening *ourselves* up. We're inviting Mammon to enter a different vessel, one that is much closer to us."

"The soul?"

"No. That is yours. He gets into the head, the heart. He

manipulates those. That is where you must confront and purge him."

"How?" Sara asked.

"You harness an equal and opposite reaction," Grace told her. "You pray."

"But I don't believe!" Sara said. "What am I supposed to do, just fake it?"

"If you want to be rid of this fiend you have to reject him, as Jesus did," Grace said. "Did you believe in the Devil before you summoned him?"

"No," Sara replied.

"Do you believe in him now?"

"He's walked around my office and dialed up the dead to talk to me."

"So he's real. I said it before: Doesn't it reason that if there is a force for evil there must also be a force for good?"

"All I've seen of God is a wafer," Sara said. "I've seen this evil up close. And it's spreading, affecting my mother, the Tsvardins."

"You need to do something about that, and quickly," Grace urged her.

"I know."

"If you can hold him back until tonight I'll come and pray with you—"

"No," Sara said. "If you're right I need to do this myself. Otherwise, it'll come back when it wants, like Mr. Hyde."

"Fair enough. But I witnessed an exorcism in Peru. The Devil does not leave a place without a struggle."

"Alexander beat back the Angel of Death with a plastic action figure."

"Pardon?"

"Long story, but he did it."

"If so it's because he *believed* in what he was doing," Grace said. "You must earnestly atone for calling the Fallen Angel and accept the rightness of divine faith. St. Mark tells us that Jesus expelled the Devil by the will of his command. It can be done."

"Sure. By the Son of God."

"He will work *through* you, if you let Him," Grace said.

Sara was silent. That wasn't going to happen. She simply didn't believe, not strongly enough for that. If the Devil were still here she needed something else to boot him out. She just didn't know what that was.

"I guess I've got some soul-searching to do," Sara said.

"When you do, remember two things," Grace said. "The Devil required a ritual to come into your life. Evil is not your natural state."

"Good point," Sara said. "What's the other thing?"

" '*Through it*,' " Grace said.

2

Sara had an afternoon session with Chun Park, a twenty-nine-year-old computer repairman. The son of South Korean immigrants, Chun lived with them in Farmington, halfway across the state. The young man's very private parents would not have approved of him seeking help so he did it discreetly. Chun was here because he had fallen in love with an American-born receptionist at the firm where he worked. His parents wanted him to find and marry a Korean.

It was easy enough for Sara to get through the session. It helped, of course, that neither Fredric nor the Devil appeared. But she also felt a connection with Chun, who had a logical, scientific mind. He wanted to marry the woman he loved. He and Sara both saw it as her job to help him make it on the path he had chosen. It helped, of course, that Sara herself was not a traditionalist, someone who believed that a son should not be forced to live the life of his father.

Chun sat expressionless throughout this, their tenth session. But when he left there was gratitude in his handshake. It made Sara feel good about her work. It wasn't enough to battle the Devil, but it was something.

It was midafternoon and the sun was struggling against early nightfall and gathering clouds. The result was an unusually rich orange cast to the backyard, from the stoop to the river to the mountains beyond. Sara knew she had to go and see how her mother was doing. She needed to brace herself for that, just in case nothing had changed. She took her cell phone and went outside and drew long, invigorating breaths. She looked out at the fallen leaves that covered the lawn. They had not yet been raked into neat pyramids.

She thought about the boy she had seen in her room this morning. She didn't fight it but went with the vision.

Her son. Despite the autumnal beauty there was a hole in the landscape. It was small but significant, and it moved here and there with a ball or a balsa wood glider or a Frisbee and a dog.

He would have been nine and playing in the leaves. Yes, she thought sadly. Maybe even with his grandfather.

If it was possible, would you undo it? Would you be like Meg Jackson, disturbed by the sight of your own daughter, or would you have gotten over the fact that it was Martin's child playing out there? Might the Great Professor even have come around one day when he learned the boy was his? Perhaps out of curiosity or vanity. Or love. Might he even have married you, or at least devoted some of his life and a portion of his libido to you—those parts of each that weren't earmarked for his students?

She would never know the answer, any more than she would know what would have happened if she'd gone to school closer to home and helped with her father, encouraged and finally badgered him to get into rehab. She remembered being disturbed by his weakness, even though she understood it. Her dad, her daddy, was supposed to be stronger than that.

Sara punched a number on her phone. She put the receiver to her ear. She did not know whether she wanted Grace to answer. She almost hung up when her friend picked up.

"Sara, are you all right?" Grace asked.

It was a struggle to keep her voice steady. "You busy?"

"Answering e-mails," she said. "What's wrong?"

"I—I was just thinking that maybe I made a mistake," Sara said.

"I know. You're going to fix that—"

"I mean back then," she said. "I don't know if I should have had the abortion. But—I couldn't let his child grow inside of me. I wanted it out."

"Child, I can't begin to understand what that's like," Grace said. "You made a difficult decision under terrible stress. You can't punish yourself for it."

"How do I *not*?"

"By allowing yourself to repent and letting go," Grace said. "God gave us rules for how we conduct our lives, but He knew we wouldn't always follow them. That was why He gave us other rules about how to obtain absolution. God will forgive you when you forgive yourself. The one thing you need to remember, Sara, is that the door to Hell is locked from the inside."

She laughed.

"What's so funny?" Grace asked. "Did the Devil tell you that too?"

"Kinda."

"The best liars use as much truth as possible," Grace said.

Sara nodded as she looked out at a yard that was not only dying but empty by her own hand.

"I want to get out of this hurt," Sara said.

"You can."

"I don't know what to put in its place."

"Before you can figure that out you have to empty it," Grace reminded her.

Sara was still looking out at the backyard. Her mind had retreated further into a more comfortable past, stopped at a time when she and Darrell used to play out here in the fall. Responsible Sara would rake, doing what she had been told, while Darrell ran around with a rubber-band gun their father had carved from balsa wood. He would shoot at birds and squirrels and occasionally at his sister. It all happened right here, so immediate yet so remote.

What was *time, anyway?* she asked herself. Dr. Arul used to say that if we had never gone to sleep between our childhood and now, those distant things would have occurred "that day."

"*Of course, we would also be grievously sleep-deprived and hopelessly irrational,*" Arul had added, "*but those distorted perceptions would be no less real to us than well-rested 'reality.' And who knows but that past events might be that much sharper to us. Infirmly anchored to the present, we might even be able to spirit-walk back to those days and re-inhabit them.*"

That would be nice, Sara thought. Darrell would still be a happy kid and she would be too, able to change the course of her life—

"Are you going to be all right?" Grace asked.

"Gonna try. Thanks for everything, Grace."

"That sounded a little too final."

"Only if you mean 'determined,'" Sara replied.

"I'll keep the phone on and with me day and night," Grace said. "Call if you need *anything*."

"I absolutely will," Sara said, still thinking of a time when there were more options in more colors than just black and white.

Sara folded away the phone and walked toward the center of the yard where she used to make the piles of leaves. The ones Darrell belly-flopped on, flattening them until they were a wide carpet instead of a hill. Then he would bring out his G.I. Joe figures and pretend they were attacking a Russian fort.

The days of innocence, before mothers had to worry about mold and deer ticks and whether army toys were bad for young boys.

Sara went to the garage. She got out a rake, an old one with floppy and indecisive wooden prongs. She went to her stoop and began pulling leaves toward the center of the yard. It felt familiar and comforting and she did not end her half-attempted "spirit walk" until the sun slid behind the tops of the mountains and the surroundings went from red-orange to blue-black and a high, muffled scream rattled against the closed windows of the tower where Tonia and Alexander lived.

3

"Please, baby no! *Don't!*"

Sara heard Tonia cry out as she rushed into the house. She tore through the kitchen toward the staircase, meeting her mother at the bottom of the steps.

"I was napping in the den and I heard them," Martha said.

The woman appeared to be normal again. Maybe the counterspell worked in a kind of delayed reaction. She ran up the stairs as Tonia shrieked again.

"Alexander, *no!* Please don't move!"

And maybe it did not.

"Mom, please wait here," Sara said sharply. If the Devil or one of his minions was upstairs she didn't want to have her mother flip out on her.

Sara took the stairs two at a time, something she also hadn't done since she was much younger. She ran down the carpeted hall toward the second tower. The doors to both bedrooms were open. Sara couldn't imagine what was going on in there. Alexander was not saying anything back.

Sara swung into the child's room.

Alexander was kneeling on the floor facing the far wall. His back was to them. Tonia was several steps behind her son. She was leaning toward him, her arms extended, but she was not moving.

"What's going on?" Sara said softly as she walked up behind Tonia.

"His father is telling him how to dismantle a bomb," Tonia replied. "That's what he says."

Sara moved along until she could see past the boy. The metal cover and screws of the electrical outlet were lying on the hardwood floor. She slipped her cell phone from her pocket and entered a number. The house phone rang. Her mother answered and Sara spoke quickly, quietly, then put the phone away.

"What is he using?" Sara asked softly as she eased around the terrified woman.

"The Swiss Army knife Darrell gave him for Christmas."

Sara put her hands on Tonia's shoulders to reassure her and keep her where she was.

"Alexander, I never thanked you for saving me the other day," Sara said.

"My daddy did that," the boy answered. His normal cheerful voice was a dull monotone. Not like her mother's voice had been before, more like someone who was concentrating very, very hard.

"I never thanked him either," Sara said. "Will you do that for me?"

"When I'm finished," the boy said gravely. His right hand was cupped in his left, guiding the knife blade into one of the top slots. But it wasn't Alexander or his father who was doing this. Piotr Tsvardin had been a second lieutenant. They would have corrected her.

"May I assist you?" Sara asked.

"This is dangerous work."

"I'm trained for it," she replied.

"*Нет!*" he shouted. The *nyet* was more of a bite than a word.

Sara continued to move toward the side, into Alexander's peripheral vision. She was not worried about distracting him and having his hand slip. If she was correct, the objective *was* the boy's electrocution and death. All she wanted to do was slow him down for a few more moments.

"You like saving lives?" Sara asked.

"It is what I do."

"I've seen you work. You are very good."

"*Quiet!*"

Even as the boy barked the order there was a distant *thunk* and a heartbeat later the lights went out. Sara reached out, seized the boy by the upper arms, immobilizing the arm with the knife, and pulled him back. He squirmed and slashed at her with a snaking wrist, cutting the back of her left hand. She dropped him on his side as his mother groped toward them in the near-darkness.

Alexander managed to wriggle free. "*Stay away!*" he shouted.

"Mom, reset the breaker!" Sara yelled.

There was another loud pop from downstairs and the lights came back on. Alexander looked like he had cast off the burden of civilization: he was crouching, scowling, holding the knife at his side, his eyes shifting here and there as though searching for something to poke. Sara glanced at her hand. He had given her a nasty cut and she did not intend to underestimate his ferocity or resolve.

Snarling, the boy glared at Sara and then sprang at her. He never reached his target.

A pillow came roaring in from the left. Tonia had plucked it from the bed and swung it outward like an Olympic hammer. She caught her son in the face on the upswing as he jumped, knocking him to the floor. He lost the knife and Sara scrambled for it before he could recover. She stuffed it into her pocket.

"My baby, I'm so sorry," Tonia said. She dropped the pillow and fell beside her dazed son.

He struggled a little as she hugged him toward her. "Mommy! Mommy!"

"It's all right," Tonia cooed. "You're safe now."

Sara picked up the pillow and removed the case. She wrapped it around her hand. The cut was superficial but wide. She held it in place as she stepped behind the mother and child. Alexander was crying.

"He is back. My boy is back," Tonia said. "Thank you."

The psychotherapist crouched behind Tonia and ran her hand through Alexander's hair. He looked up at her briefly, his eyes crinkled with tears. He was definitely back and Sara gave him an encouraging smile.

Martha entered wearing strength as well as concern.

"I'm glad you didn't let the answering machine pick up," Sara said.

"I thought it might be your father," Martha said.

Sara shot her a look. "You mean Darrell."

"I mean your *father*, dear."

"When was the last time you spoke with him?" Sara asked, her belly tightening.

"About an hour ago, when he went out for groceries." Martha's expression soured. "But I'm sure he stopped at the bar."

Sara didn't bother to tell her that it wasn't Robert Lynch she had heard any more than it was Piotr Tsvardin who was instructing his son on how to dismantle a bomb. The Spell of Disestablishment had not worked. Instead of beating Sara up through her unborn child he was obviously taking a different tack.

"We've got things in hand here, Mother," Sara said, rising. "Why don't you go back downstairs?"

"You're hurt, dear," Martha said, taking her daughter's hand. "Let me take care of that."

"All right," Sara said. She turned to Tonia. "I'm going to close the door. Stay with Alexander and don't leave the room."

"What is wrong?" Tonia asked.

"Something I'm going to try to fix, but I need you to stay here."

"Will you be all right?"

"I'll be better if I know you two are safe," Sara said.

Tonia smiled and nodded and Sara left with her mother. They went to the bathroom where Martha cleaned and bandaged the cut.

"What was happening in there?" Martha asked.

"Alexander was missing his father," Sara said.

"He did this to you?"

"By accident."

"Children can be so unpredictable," Martha said as she worked. "Not my Sara, of course. Maybe girls are different."

"Why don't you go back to your room and rest," Sara said. "I'll wake you before dinner."

"All right, dear," Martha said when she had checked her handiwork. "This *has* been rather exhausting. All those boxes in the basement, in front of the fuse box. If only your father had been here."

Sara didn't try to reach Martha by entering her delusion the way she had done with Alexander. She just couldn't pretend that her father was alive. Instead, Sara walked her mother to the bedroom, made sure she was comfortable, then gave her water and an Ambien. She wanted to make sure the woman slept for a while.

Sara headed downstairs. The house was unusually quiet. The steps creaked as they always did and the wind hissed through the eaves and rattled the drainpipes. But the interior life was gone. There was no one about, the TV and radio were silent, and she neither smelled nor heard anything from the kitchen. But Sara suspected that the silence was just an interlude.

She went to her office. If the Devil returned she wanted it to be here, away from her loved ones. Not that she had any control over that. If he decided to rattle around in the attic or knock over the boxes in the basement she would have to go there. In the office, at least, she felt a little bit of reason return undistracted by the past or lost hopes. She had some measure of control—over herself.

As she sat behind her desk it bothered her, deeply, that God had sent visions to a French peasant girl who was minding her business, and in no particular jeopardy, in Lourdes. Yet He couldn't spare a moment of the Virgin Mary's time for an American woman being stalked by the Devil. He couldn't show her something that might give her a *reason* to believe.

Why? she demanded. *Because I summoned the Devil? I'm desperately sorry. I sincerely repent.*

Sara decided to call her brother's cell phone. She needed someone to keep an eye on their mother while she worked this out. Darrell did not pick up and she left a message for him to call her in the office.

With nothing else to do, no other plan, she set the Bible and the *Devil's Bible* before her. Between them, she hoped to find the answer. She decided to start with the Bible, with Revelation. It couldn't hurt to give the "other side" equal time. She read through the saga of the Apocalypse, through the extravagant symbolism looking for clues about the Devil's ultimate plans and nature. She read about sacred scrolls and mystical seals, about the lamb and the trumpet and the beast with ten horns and seven heads and ten diadems on those heads—

"*Boo!*"

"Jesus!" Sara cried. She was on her feet and facing the waiting room door even before her brother began to laugh.

"Hah! Just like the old days!" Darrell cheered. "Sara full of Sara, reading or cleaning up toys—"

"*Not* funny, Darrell!" Her heart was skipping rope.

Her brother stepped into the office. "Sorry. I had to."

"Why?"

"Because we had words last time, and I wanted to show you there were no hard feelings."

"By acting like a six-year-old?" Sara shook her head. "I might have been with a patient."

"There were no cars in the driveway, the inner door was open, nobody was talking. Columbo Darrell doesn't miss clues like that." Her brother came around the desk smelling of oil but nothing more. "Anyway, we had some of our best fights when I was five or six."

"Fine," Sara said. On the plus side he seemed to be the normal Darrell, not someone with visions. Maybe those were restricted to the house.

"I saw your caller ID," he said. "I was down the street and decided to come and see what you wanted and what was for dinner."

"There's nothing for dinner," Sara told him. "Do you have a date?"

"Nothing official. I was going to meet a gal at Sammy's. Why?"

"I need you," she said.

"Sure. What's up?"

Sara closed the Bible with its not-very-helpful mysticism, collected her thoughts, then started over. "I was wondering if you might be able to stay with Mom and Tonia for a while."

"Not a prob." He smiled. "Do *you* have a date?"

"No," she said. "Why would I need you to stay here?"

"Maybe Mom's still on a tear, or who-knows-what," he said.

"It's not a date," Sara told him. "It's—a very long story."

"What's the short version?"

"Nothing," she said.

"That means something." Darrell leaned on the desk and looked at her. There was no longer anything flip about his manner. "Come on, sis. You've always told me the score. Is Mom sick?"

"It's nothing like that," she said. "Not as such, I mean."

"You lost me."

Sara took a breath. "I did something stupid," she told him. *God, was this conversation a chill-inducing déjà vu.* "I was researching Fredric Marash's last hours and I found out that he was a devil worshiper."

"A customer said that at the shop," Darrell told her. "She said there's a cult in town or something."

"She?"

"A secretary at the school. She overheard."

"Jesus," Sara said. Damn this town. *God* damn this town. "Is it true?"

"Yes," Sara said.

"Wow. Father Colgan is *not* going to be happy."

"That's the least of our worries," Sara said.

"I knew you'd say that—"

Sara's hand shot up and she half turned toward the office door. Darrell fell silent. They both listened.

"Do you hear a noise?" Sara asked.

"No."

"A kind of scratching—like mice in the wall," Sara said. She walked around the desk.

"I hear it now," Darrell said. "In Mom's tower."

Sara nodded.

"What could she be doing?" he asked.

"Nothing. I gave her a sleeping pill."

The psychotherapist left the office followed by her brother. They walked quickly down the corridor.

"Why'd you conk Mom out?" Darrell asked.

"That's one of the things I wanted to talk about," Sara told him. "She said she saw dad. She said she interacted with him, thought he was still living here."

"So I'm not the only one who's been a little loopy."

"Darrell, I don't think anyone's loopy." She wished they were. Delusions were treatable.

"Then what's going on?" Darrell pressed. "We got devil-kids running around casting spells? Wait. You said *you* did something stupid—"

"We'll talk about it in a minute," Sara said. She was suddenly too embarrassed to tell her brother more.

Sara hadn't heard the sound after leaving the office but that didn't mean anything. The old walls directly under the tower were very communicative. Side by side, they crossed the short, carpeted hallway that ended in their mother's bedroom. The heavy six-panel door was closed. The scratching was on the other side. It was more like a slow sawing, moving in a line from the top right corner to the left center.

"What the hell?" Darrell said. "Mother?"

"I'm here," she answered. She was standing directly behind the door.

"You sure she took that pill?" Darrell asked Sara.

Sara nodded. Darrell reached for the knob. Sara grabbed his wrist.

"Darrell, strange things have been happening in this house. You have to be prepared for anything."

"Like what? Mom naked or something?"

"Or something," she said. "Just follow my lead."

"I'll step away so you can come in, children," Martha said.

The sound stopped. Sara looked at her brother. He nodded. She reached for the knob and cracked the door. Her mother was standing in the center of the room, facing the door.

"Mom?" Sara said.

"Hello, dear," Martha said.

Sara opened the door a little farther. "Why aren't you in bed?"

"Your father woke me."

Sara opened the door farther. Someone, some thing in the likeness of Robert Lynch was standing beside Martha, her hand in his. He was just as Sara remembered him the last time they were together. He was wearing Robert's clothes, his posture, and his expression—smiling benignly, as he so often did in life, unconcerned with anything beyond the moment.

Sara stepped in. Darrell leaned in behind her, his hand on her shoulder. Sara felt his fingers tense as he looked in.

"No fucking way," Darrell muttered.

"This isn't Dad," Sara said to him. "You've got to believe that."

"Sis, are you sure?"

"Of course it's your father, dear," Martha said with a smile.

"How can I see Dad if he's not there?" Darrell asked Sara.

The white-haired man leaned toward his right. "Son?" he said. "Is that you hiding behind your sister again?"

"Dad?"

"It isn't him," Sara said. "It's one of those trance-things. We have to get Mom out of there."

Darrell shook his head. "Man, it sure sounds like Dad."

"But you know it *can't* be," Sara told him. "Our father is dead."

"Dead?" The man laughed. "I'm right here."

"*Something* is here," Sara said. "It isn't Robert Lynch."

"How silly you're being, Sara Jacqueline," Martha said.

The older man's smile broadened. "It really is okay, son. You can come in. I'm not going to spank you." He extended his free hand. "Those days are over. Everything's going to be all right."

"When you go back to where you belong," Sara said. She walked forward very slowly. She wanted to look behind the door.

"Damn, I want to believe you, Dad," Darrell said.

"You need to get a grip, Darrell," Sara told him.

"And *you* need to stop telling your brother what to do," the man said sternly. He shook his head slowly. "Always so sure of yourself. But even you make mistakes."

"Sis, maybe you only think you did what you did. Remember from Sunday school?" Darrell asked. "The universal judgment, the final resurrection of the dead. Maybe it's that time and Dad *is* back."

Sara faced her brother, hard. "That is *not* what's happening."

"How do you know? Dad's right, you don't know *everything*."

"I know because I'm responsible for this. I wanted to find out what happened to Fredric so I took his books and his notes. I read them, made the design, spoke the chants. I'm the one who summoned the Devil."

Darrell stared at his sister. He reminded her of a comic strip character, all eyes and mouth.

"Son, your sister is a little undone. Why don't we go outside and have a sit by the river?"

Sara grabbed her brother's arms and held them tightly. "Darrell—I need you to trust me."

"I want to." He looked past her, shook his head. "Man, this is really messed up. And I haven't even been drinking."

"You haven't," Sara said. "You're sober, and you know Dad's dead."

The young man's eyes narrowed with sadness. "Dad, she's right." His mouth twisted with longing. "This is one time I wish I didn't believe her."

"Then don't, son."

"I miss you," Darrell said. He tried to step around his sister.

Sara continued to hold his wrists. "I need you to concentrate. We *buried* Dad."

"Obviously we didn't. He's here."

"That *isn't* our father!" Sara insisted. "Think. You see the green polo shirt he's wearing? The old leather belt? The brown loafers? We gave them to Goodwill, remember? You helped me pack his things in boxes when he died."

"Right. We did do that," Darrell said.

"I don't like all this talk of *death*!" Martha exclaimed. "You're beginning to upset me, dear. Very much!"

"Calm yourself," the man said. He put a comforting arm around Martha and gave a squeeze. He glowered at Sara. "I think it's time the two of you left. Your mother and I wish to be alone."

"I don't think so," Sara said over her shoulder. She continued to look at Darrell. "Are you here? Are you with me?"

The younger man nodded vigorously as though trying to convince himself. That would have to do.

Sara turned and stepped deeper into the room. "I know that Dad is dead and that a demon—possibly the Devil—is pretending to be him."

Martha laughed. "Of all the silly things."

"That terrible business with the Marash boy must have confused you," the man said. His relaxed expression was unchanged except for the eyes. They were darker, threatening. "Darrell, why don't you take your sister to her room? Give her one of those sedatives."

"I'm not going anywhere," Sara said as she edged to her right. There was a bureau just beyond it, with a letter opener on top. There were small, curled wood filings on the tip of the metal. Sara took another step in and looked behind the door. Her mother had used the letter opener to cut a large pentagram into the door.

"Darrell, get Mother out—" she said.

"Leave her!" the older man barked.

Darrell walked forward slowly. The man raised a hand across his shoulder. Darrell stopped.

"Get out," the older man yelled.

"You can't hurt us," Sara said. "That's why you need the pentagram. You need help."

"The story of Sara J. Lynch. She reads a few books and thinks she know everything," the older man said.

"I know that and I won't let you finish it," Sara said evenly.

"Won't you?" The man chuckled.

"Even if Mother has said the words there are no candles and no blood."

The man moved so quickly that Sara didn't have time to react. He snatched the letter opener from beside Sara, slashed behind him cutting her mother's arm through her sweater, and with a slicing return of his arm sprayed droplets of blood across the back of the door.

"Darrell, help Mother!" Sara shouted.

The young man rushed in and cradled his mother, who was slow to realize that she'd been cut. The woman looked at her wound and then gasped. She slumped and Darrell laid her on the bed.

"You aren't real," Sara said. "You're the Devil wearing a disguise, something pulled from our subconscious."

"I'm very real," the older man said. "*This* is real. Reality once came from nothing. I was there. I saw it all." The man laughed and took cigarettes from his pants pocket. They were her father's brand. He shook one out. "There are improvements this time around, though. I don't have to worry that these will kill me."

"Did you ever?" Sara asked. It was difficult to remain focused. The Devil had just tempted her with the secrets of Creation.

He lit the cigarette. "I lived life the way I wanted. But I loved you all. I still do. It would be wonderful if you all came with me."

Sara looked over at the bed. Darrell was kneeling beside their mother. He had tugged a handkerchief from his pocket and was pressing it on her arm to stop the bleeding.

Sara looked over at the bureau. She would use the letter opener to destroy the pentagram before Martha or the Devil could complete the ritual. "I don't think any of us will be joining you," she said.

The man drew on the cigarette and blew smoke. "I do," he said and flicked the still-lit match at the back of the door.

The blood on the pentagram sparked and ignited, spitting flames outward from across the pentagram. Sara was momentarily paralyzed as the wood in the pentagon vanished, replaced by a familiar matte-black void.

"There are advantages to being the Lord of the Pit," the older man said, chuckling.

Sara heard sounds from within the void; scraping, clucking, hissing, echoes from somewhere beyond the room. She moved toward it, listening.

"They are coming," the man said.

The Reapers of Purgatory, Sara thought. Unlike the Devil, they could hurt her and her family.

Sulphurous heat rolled from the pentagon. The sounds were growing louder. There was an undercurrent of howls and clanging, like small chains being pulled. Bicycle chains. Over it was a louder wailing. It was more war cry than pain and it was coming toward them.

The New Kingdom, New Jerusalem, she thought. Euphemisms for places of disorder and moral confusion, the Devil's beachheads in this realm. She was not convinced the Devil's eternal indulgence was worse than the idea of God's endless neutered bliss. But she liked the idea of having a choice.

"Come with me and I'll spare them," the older man said.

Sara couldn't speak. She stepped back as the din increased. She wished she *had* read more, but she knew that the Devil's ultimate purpose was to collect souls. He had tried to talk Sara into joining him. He had sent "Piotr" for Alexander, domestic discord to weaken her and her brother, and "Robert" to woo Martha. He had failed. Now he was simply going to rip their souls out and take them. Because Sara and her brother were unconfessed sinners, God wasn't going to do anything to help. When they were gone, the distraught Martha would turn to "Robert" for consolation. She would agree to go wherever he might lead.

Sara continued to back away. The sounds were just beyond the edges of the pentagram. She took a quick look back at the bed, saw Darrell folded protectively around their mother.

"I did this," Sara said. "You can take me but leave them alone."

"You're giving me *permission*?" a familiar voice said.

Sara looked over. The Devil was standing where her father had been. He was an inflated presence now, his shoulders higher, his chest inflated, the sinew of his arms knotted with the strength of looming conquest.

"I'm sorry." He grinned, speaking in Robert's voice. "I love you, Sara Jacqueline, but I want my family reunited."

And suddenly, in that taunt, Sara heard what she had been missing. The answer she had been looking for. She went to the bed and stood in front of her huddled brother and mother. That was how the Devil had taken Fredric. Satan had turned his mother against him, broken the bonds and set the young man adrift. That wasn't going to happen. Sara and Darrell may have sinned but they were not sinners. They may have strayed but they were still brother and sister.

The sounds were no longer distant. They were sharp and near and just beyond the horizon.

Sara turned toward Darrell and leaned close. "I don't know what's coming through that opening, whether it will fly or walk or crawl," she said. "But we can send them back."

"How?" Darrell asked.

"Have faith," she replied.

"In what?"

The Devil stepped to her side. The glow of his flaming scepter cast a bloodred light in every corner, on the air itself. "There isn't enough faith in this room to stop what's about to arrive."

A quote from Matthew popped into Sara's head. It was something she remembered because her father had been sitting beside her in church when Father Colgan said it, and he had said a quiet "amen":

"If you had faith the size of a mustard seed, you would be able to say to this mountain, 'Move from here to there,' and it would move."

Sara looked past the Devil as a charcoal-dark shadow fell across the floor. It washed toward the bed like an oil spill. An unfinished breath later, dozens upon dozens of what appeared to be very large ravens screamed through the opening. The birds had brass talons and beaks, with glowing red eyes. They fanned out, filling the room and rushing through the partly open door. They were cackling and wailing as though maniacal with the sudden freedom that had been given to them.

The Devil smiled. *"Your* handiwork, Sara Lynch. Within minutes they will be everywhere in Delwood, appearing to people as what they miss the most. A loved one, a pet, the chance to undo a choice regretted. An idea or inspiration. A shop owner will think of a gimmick to increase sales and, tomorrow, an amateur painter in her atelier will see a vase or a fruit in a different way. Pleasure, riches, fulfillment. That is what we are sending into the town. Why do you fight that?"

"Because we're human," Sara said. "Whatever good or bad we do, the choices must come from within."

"The rewards of life in the cloister known as Delwood," the Devil said. He touched her chin. "A head filled with Yankee platitudes."

Sara jerked from his touch.

"Why work so hard?" the Devil asked. "You didn't, once, in the time of Eden."

"That was the problem," Sara said. "We were easily distracted. My dad knew this much, that a thing meant more if you built it yourself."

"He did indeed," the Devil said. "He spent years crafting his own coffin."

Several of the winged creatures began circling Sara's head. Their wild flapping and loud, echoing cries were in contrast to the sharp, unnerving click of their metal claws. They sounded like clacking bones, the patter of plastic wind-up teeth. They came nearer and nearer until they brushed Sara with their wings. She dropped to her knees and leaned against Darrell's back to protect her face. She threw her arms around him and, together, they hugged their mother closer.

If there was ever a time to pray—

But Sara would not pump out prayers that were more desperate than heartfelt. That would only satisfy the Devil, and if God was listening, it would piss him off even more. It would also waste time. She needed something that she believed in, something that might work.

"What's happening?" Martha asked.

With "Robert" gone the woman was herself again.

"Don't worry," Darrell said. "Just keep your head down. Sis is workin' this thing out. Right, sis?"

The question was sweet, trusting, and naive.

The birds began to swarm over the Lynches, pecking and scratching.

"Sis?!" Darrell cried. "Am I right?"

"You are!" she shouted. Her right arm was pinned beneath her. She slipped it out. "Hold my hand!"

"What?"

"*Take* it!"

Darrell freed a hand and snaked it back. Sara pulled it

toward her. It had been a long time since she had held anyone's hand, even a member of her family. She remembered a
time when that simple act had saved her sanity, when they
were sitting in a doctor's office and he reached over—

"Do you need me to do anything?" Darrell asked.

"Just what you're doing," she said as talons raked her
neck and ears. "Believe in us, in our family."

"I always have," he said. "It's all I got."

The statement was poignant and powerful and exactly
what Sara needed to hear. She held his fingers tightly, reminded herself that the pain in her head was *in* her head. She
thought about the one thing in which she did have unshakeable faith, the devotion and selflessness of her brother. Darrell possessed a good and generous spirit, interred to keep it
safe from the disappointments life had hurled at him. That
included an imperious sister and mother who disapproved of
the way he lived his life.

"Is that the best you've got?" asked the Devil. He
stretched out his hand and touched her neck. The pain ceased
where the Reapers had scratched her. "God doesn't care about
your suffering."

"*I don't need him to!*" Sara cried inside.

"No?" the Devil replied as though he had heard. "What
do you need?"

Sara held tighter to her brother's hand.

"Approval? Acceptance? You may get that from family,
from friends, even from a lover. But unless you repent on
God's terms he does not want your soul."

"I can't answer for God," Sara said. "But you will *not* take
me or my family."

"No. You will not," said another voice.

Sara felt a tickling on the back of her hand. It was her

mother, moving her own hand onto those of her children. Her soft flesh showed surprising strength as it clasped the joined hands.

Sara felt strong and humbled. *We won't go*, she thought. *If you can read my thoughts, read that.*

There was hot breath against her ear. Her neck stung where perspiration filled the scratches and lacerations. The cries of the birds were a continuous squall.

"Life is heartache and disappointment," the Devil said. "Surrender and enjoy peace."

"I'll find it on my own," Sara said. It was a promise to herself.

"You only know how to *lose* it," the Devil sneered. "To give it up."

"Go to Hell," Sara murmured. "Leave us alone."

Sara felt the two hands on hers. Their fingers flexed, moved, insinuated themselves deeper in her own. It was a small gesture with extraordinary scope. She felt grander on the outside and greater on the inside. Her burdens seemed lessened. She felt, in that moment, like a god with many heads.

The Devil came closer. He kissed her ear. "You can bundle yourself in the flesh of your flesh but I will be waiting," he said, deeper in her ear . . . inside her head. "You cannot change who you are or what you've done."

Sara braced her body and soul for an attack that never came. The sounds faded quickly, the hot breath of His Satanic Majesty yielded to cool sweat. The ruddy darkness faded like a nightmare in the dawn. Martha and Darrell relaxed their grip without releasing their hold.

Sara knew without raising her face from the pile of Lynches that the Devil and his thralls were gone.

Seventeen

1

Sara finally raised her face and looked behind her. All that remained of the terrible encounter were the marks on Sara's
neck and the pentagram carved on the back of the door.

And the bruises on the inside. But those would heal and the
tissue would be stronger for it. *Because you did it yourself*.

Sara released her brother's hand and rose unsteadily. The
room seesawed for a moment. She turned back to the bed
and lifted the handkerchief from her mother's wound. It
wasn't serious. She would get something to dress it. She noticed then that the wound Alexander had given her was
bleeding again. She'd need a new bandage.

With Sara off his back, Darrell was able to get up.

"How'd you get away without a scratch?" Sara asked him.

"Maybe I was prayin' harder than you," he said. He

looked up at Sara. "We did it, right? We kicked the god-damned ass of the Devil."

"Language," Martha said into the bedcover.

"'Goddamned' is pretty much on-the-nose," Sara pointed out.

"I meant 'ass,'" Martha told her. The woman sat slowly and looked out at the empty room. "Your father used to say 'butt.' If that locker-room reference must be used, I prefer 'butt.'"

"Sure thing," Darrell said. He frowned. "When were you ever in a locker room, Ma?"

"I've seen sports on ESPN," she answered. "I like the Braves."

Darrell smiled. "The things we don't know about our folks," he said. "I'll get first-aid stuff."

Darrell left and Sara sat beside her mother. She put an arm around the older woman.

"Thanks," Sara said.

"For loving my children?"

"For trusting your daughter," Sara said.

"It was you or the Devil, dear," Martha dead-panned. "Did that all really happen?"

"It happened," Sara said as she gently touched her mother's upper arm below the wound. "What do you re-member?"

"I remember seeing your father," Martha said. She smiled sadly. "That wasn't really him, was it?"

"No," Sara said confidently. "Dad had more texture."

"That's a good word," Martha said. "When your father was alive and he smoked you could smell the tobacco *and* scotch on his breath." She was silent for a moment, then said, "But when his eyes were clear you could see the love in them. There were lines in his face that told you a little of what he had seen in his life." She traced them along the side of her own eyes and down her cheek, like a tear. "He didn't talk about it much. I wish he had." She lowered her hand and nodded confidently. "No, it wasn't him. I don't believe he would be with the Devil. I don't believe that at all." Martha looked at Sara. "I don't know exactly how this happened, but I need to know. Do you think it will be happening again?"

"I don't believe so," Sara replied.

"Good," her mother replied. "I believe my ears will be ringing with bird calls for quite a while."

"We'll have to find a better sound to replace them."

"Church bells. I'll bet that would work," Martha said. She looked sharply at her daughter. "I would like very much if you would come with me on Sunday and help me listen."

"I will do that," Sara said. She resisted adding, "*For you*." This was not the time or place for that discussion.

Darrell returned and ministered to the women. He said he had also gone to check on Tonia and Alexander. They were asleep and probably hadn't heard a thing. Martha expressed some surprise at that, but Sara explained that there was apparently a kind of damper within the area of demonic visitations. It made the immaterial and soundless seem real and loud only to the participants.

"Like a conscience," Martha suggested quietly as she watched her son work.

It was exactly like that, Sara agreed as he reapplied her bandage.

2

Sara slept well for the first time in days.

Before going to sleep she had used wood putty to dismantle the pentagram on the door, according to ritual. She would have the door replaced and destroyed as soon as possible. For now, this would do.

Ironically, the putty smell brought back her father more powerfully than the Devil ever could.

Sara believed the Devil was gone. She was not convinced of it, and probably never would be. Yet she was too tired to stay awake and worry.

She dreamed about being lost at Litchfield County High. The doors were locked, the corridors were unfamiliar and empty, and the only people she saw were Chrissie Blair and a janitor.

Lost in your own head without practical knowledge and very little help to sweep up negative thoughts, she reflected upon waking. Interpreting dreams didn't get much simpler than that. But a dream was not life and she was determined to make changes.

It was nearly eight. Sara had a session at nine. She dressed and hurried to the kitchen. Darrell had slept over and she was glad to see him. He was drinking coffee and making a pan full of scrambled eggs. Alexander was seated at the table drinking orange juice and eating Raisin Bran straight from the carton. His little fist didn't fit in the box as readily as it used to. He was dressed for school. He had his backpack beside him. There was no toy soldier as far as Sara could tell.

"How are you today?" Sara cheerfully asked the boy.

"I'm very well, Sara," he told her. "I had very funny

dreams but my mommy says things in our head can't hurt us."

Sara smiled. "Where is your mother?"

"In the shower." He smiled devilishly. "I got there first so she lost the Soap Derby."

"You have a contest each day?" That was sweet news.

"Yup," he said as he crunched on a fistful of flakes. "It's the Tsvardin Morning Olympics. We see who gets up first, who showers first, who gets dressed first, and who is the first one down here."

"What's the prize?" Darrell asked.

"A gold hug for the winner," Alexander replied.

"I had no idea." Sara grinned.

"Amazing what ya don't know about people you think you know," Darrell said over his shoulder.

Sara walked over to her brother. She gave him a short hug.

"That felt like silver," he said with a frown.

She hugged him again.

"Better," he replied.

"How are you?" Sara asked. "Any 'funny dreams'?"

"Nuttin,' honey. My imagination must feel completely dissed 'cause it has left the building." He leaned close. "It couldn't have come up with anything like what we saw. What about you?"

"Nothing major."

"How're the hand and neck?" he asked.

"The hand hurts, the neck stings. But I'll be fine."

"We got worse than that when we used to play in leaves," he said.

"You played. I raked."

"Yeah, but I shot you with rubber bands from under the piles. Remember?"

"Like it was yesterday."

Darrell used the spatula to sever a section of eggs. He slipped it on a plate and handed it to her with a fork. She stood beside him as she ate. "Y'know, sis, I *did* have a sort of waking nightmare before I crashed."

"Oh?"

He nodded. "I took a look at that wood putty job you did on the door," he said. "It sucks."

"Language!" Alexander said.

"Sorry, sir," Darrell said.

"I guess I didn't get the carpentry gene," Sara said.

"Don't worry. I'm gonna destroy and replace that baby today."

"Thanks," Sara said. "Just make sure you keep it filled until then, okay?"

"Not to worry. Treating it like nitroglycerin *and* wearing a cross," Darrell assured her. He portioned the remaining eggs onto a plate and checked the sausages he was cooking on the back burner. While he was still standing close he whispered, "Can I ask a personal question?"

"Sure."

"This is gonna seem weird."

"I doubt that," Sara said.

"Yeah?" He leaned close. "I was wondering what you'd think about me asking Tonia out. On a date, I mean."

Sara grinned. "I think she'd like that very much."

"It's not like dating a cousin, is it?"

"No," Sara assured him.

He nodded. "Okay. Thanks. One more question."

"She likes tulips," Sara said.

"Not about that," Darrell said, "but thanks. Is there any chance o' that shit comin' back?"

"I'm going to make sure Trooper Brown has the Park Service clean up the marks in the woods. We'll talk to the other kids who belonged to the group. But this is a constant vigilance kind of thing. It's been here since the dawn of civilization and it isn't going away."

"Got to remain alert—and sober," Darrell said.

"Yeah," Sara said, beaming. "That would be good."

Martha came down, followed by Tonia. If there were scars from the night before they were all inside. Martha seemed unusually chipper. She looked at her children and smiled more than usual, happy to have them nearby—and close to each other. Tonia was watchful but relaxed. Her son might not have remembered anything but she did, which was probably just as well. Years from now Alexander might suffer nightmares or half-shaped visions of a time he remembered but couldn't place. Tonia would be able to help him, or whoever he turned to for healing.

Martha dug Sara's World's Best Daughter mug from the back of the cupboard and handed it to her. It was something her father had given her years before.

"Thanks," Sara said.

"My pleasure, dear," her mother replied. She kissed Sara on the forehead. "Have a good day."

"I will."

Sara filled it with coffee and went to her office. She had a call to make before her morning appointment.

E. Edward Edwards was in his office and took the call.

"How are you?" he asked.

"Very well," she replied. "Mr. Edwards, we need to talk about this cult."

"I agree," he said. "But before we get into that I want to tell you about a conversation I had with the Marashes last night."

"Oh?"

"You were right about his fascination with Ms. Blair," E. Edward told her. "They admit he had her pictures on his wall. They also went into his computer."

"Let me guess," Sara said. "Some variation of her name was the password."

"It was a simple 'Chrissie.'"

Fredric was an artist, not a wordsmith.

"They found links to asphyxiation sites, including auto-erotic stimulation," E. Edward told her. "There were also e-mail exchanges with individuals who practiced the technique."

"They just offered this information?"

"Mr. Marash did," the attorney replied. "He wants closure. He said he needed to talk to you to try and understand what happened. They've agreed not to pursue legal action against you or the school. They don't want this information made public and our agreement will remain sealed."

"Couldn't they have had court files sealed since Fredric was a minor?"

"He was above the age of sexual consent," E. Edward said. "The information would have been allowable in court as it spoke to a possible cause for the method of suicide. And jury members might have talked. The family did not want that."

"Understandably," Sara said.

"Of course. I spoke with their attorney and we've agreed on the gag points. I'll be receiving the formal draft agreement this morning. I'll need your signature. I can fax it; or I can bring it to you."

There was the slightest hesitation between "fax it" and "or I." Sara decided to put a toe in the gap. "I can drive by and pick it up later."

"It's a bit of a hike," he said. "Why don't we meet halfway? The Millerton Inn is right off Route 6—"

"I know the place," she said. "Sounds good."

"Excellent. Tonight at eight?"

"I can do that."

"Great. See you there," the attorney said. "I'm very sorry about Fredric but I'm pleased that you've been vindicated."

Sara hung up feeling not bad. "Good" would take time.

She placed another call, this one to Grace Rollins. Sara left a message saying that she would be coming to the Yale campus early in the afternoon and would like to see her for a few minutes.

"You helped me get a very bad situation under control," she said. "I want to thank you. I'll also need a pep talk and a pass when I face another demon."

3

Sara had her session with Charlie Dana, a forty-four-year-old former New York advertising executive who ran a small agency out of his garage office. He had done that for the last eighteen months and had been seeing her for the last seventeen months. The father of two was paying the bills but felt that he had chickened out by leaving the high-pressure major leagues for the relative ease—and commensurately low rewards—of Delwood.

Sara had been trying to nudge him from his fixation that picking berries made him less of a man than hunting mammoths. Removed from the big game he had to be reminded that the highs had been intoxicating but the lows were dismal. At one point he asked her a question that she had been expecting for a while. It was fitting that it should come now.

"Does it ever bother you that you're a Yale graduate practicing in a small town instead of in a real city, pulling in big fees?" he asked.

"It bothers me that it never bothered me, which makes me wonder if I'm just looking for trouble," she replied.

"I don't understand."

"If you're content, why shake things up? Some people do, compulsively. They are unhappy with peace, unaccustomed to stability. They manufacture pain and disharmony because they know that territory."

"That's what you think I'm doing?" he asked.

"I think you're drawn to the negatives instead of the positives, yes," she told him. Sara didn't say that she understood the problem both clinically and personally. The important thing was to get better.

Charlie promised to think about it.

She told him that was his problem. "Don't think. Just go through it. Things will look a lot clearer on the other side."

4

The drive to New Haven was different than it had been two days before.

The sun was out, the air was cold but dry, and Sara's head was clear of all but two things. One was the objective, the kind of resolution she had just suggested to Charlie. The other was the impediment she faced. Her hatred of Martin Cayne.

Sara made it in under two hours. She even had time to stop for a burger at a roadside shack past New Milford. She sat outside on one of the weather-beaten picnic tables. Someone had carved something in the side of the wood nearly thirty years before. She wondered if JD still loved VE. She wanted to believe they did.

The smell of the cooking meat, the cloud of beefy smoke, the crackle of the fries in the oil, were sounds she had grown up with. The air was sharp but it smelled of natural pine. There were migrating birds and squirrels of all shades and only a few cars on the country road.

No, Charlie. She didn't regret living in a small town at all.

Sara parked in the same garage as before and walked to the campus. She needed to get her blood circulating before going to Becton Center. She needed to get her mind off the drive, off the events of the past few days, so she could focus—ironically—on her anger. It came quickly and easily, as rich as the day it been born. It was the only thing of his that Sara had allowed to live within her.

More people were out than there had been the other day. Sara was glad for the life, the activity, the distraction. There was too much motion, too many people talking—in person, on cell phones, and to no one at all as drama students ran through monologues—to allow the woman to grab other pieces of the past. She did not want to fortify the impediment by reliving the good experiences, the warmth she had felt, the growth she had experienced when she was with Martin Cayne. Coming back to the campus was about one thing.

Sara walked to the hall, her heartbeat rapid, nerves complaining. She did not know which was worse: the idea of confronting Martin or of living without his hold over her, filling that dark place with light. Sadness had been a way of life for so long.

Sara hoped she would know soon enough.

She reached the building, went over to the guard. Grace had called ahead. Sara was admitted after showing her driver's license. She waited in the small lobby until five minutes before the bell, then hiked to the third floor. She stood on the landing to catch her breath. She didn't want to be winded when she confronted Martin.

Sara was all energy, hyper-alert but breathing normally when she finally opened the fire door and entered the corridor. She stood at the far end of the floor like a fighter in her corner before a bout. Her arms folded as she waited for the dismissal bell. She noticed her reflection in a bronze plaque with room numbers on the opposite wall. She walked to it and pushed hair from her forehead, relaxed her mouth. She wanted to see a secure woman and not the dependent, doting kid she was in her head.

Sara looked into her own eyes for a moment. She had a sudden, fierce desire to get out of here. It was probably too late to fix this and confronting the bastard might only make it worse.

Is that what you came here for? To run from him again?

Through it.

The bell rang. It was a sound Sara knew well. It was in her muscle memory. She started walking, straight and sure. For tactical reasons she switched her bag to her left shoulder. If she needed to gesture with her right arm she didn't want the bag falling to her elbow and pulling it down.

The sound of doors opening and students talking took her back. Despite her efforts she felt herself sinking through every layer of what she had been—the eager young student, the love-struck girl, the wounded child. Her legs carried her forward even as her will drifted again. She had no armor for this. Psychiatric training typically worked in the third person—

Through. It.

Sara rounded the corner and headed toward the classroom. The door was open. Bright sunlight caused the inside to shine white. Her body had momentum. It would complete the journey with or without her.

Students were leaving, intense little birds migrating to new grounds, thinking they were smart, sure, on a rocket ride to wisdom. All they got here was the propellant, not the arc or the destination. That came from inside, not out.

The door was a few steps away. Martin would be the last one out with some adoring co-ed or another. Maybe Esther.

Sara stood aside while the biggest crowd of students moved through. Then those determined legs carried her inside, fueled by a deep breath that the woman exhaled quickly.

Professor Martin Cayne was standing with his back to the windows. His features were in shadow. He was wearing the navy blue blazer he always wore but there were no students clustered around, no teaching assistant. He was gathering lecture notes and sliding them into the slots of his old leather briefcase. Sara remembered when it was new. She crossed along the foot of the front row. Martin did not look up.

Martin Cayne seemed shorter than Sara remembered, his shoulders a little rounder, his hands a little smaller. She did not see a wedding band. She remembered how strong those hands had seemed the first time he drew her toward him and pressed his fingertips against her shoulder blades. It didn't take long for him to know her body as well as he knew her mind.

"Too bad you only cared about one of them," she said, stopping when she was a few steps away.

Martin looked up. He studied the woman for a moment, his face in darkness. "Sara Lynch," he said. "Or is it something else now?"

"It's Lynch," she replied.

"Still living at home?"

"Still," she said.

Martin regarded her a moment longer, then finished closing his briefcase. "What can I do for you?"

She wanted to say, "Die." She said nothing, which was almost the same.

"No comment?" he asked.

The man's voice a little raspier, perhaps from years of lecturing, and his manner was curt and defensive. He had never been patient, sentimental, or uncertain. Those were qualities she had once regarded as weak.

That's all beside the point, Sara told herself. *This is not a reunion.*

"Did you come here to blame me?" Martin asked. His voice was cold.

"Are you to blame?"

He snickered. "Don't even try to use interrogative impeachment on me, Lynch."

She had expected the vanity, the arrogance. Now she would use it.

"I have a professional question," Sara said.

"Is it short or will you need an appointment?" he asked.

"Short," she assured him. "What would you tell a young woman who feels guilty for having aborted her child to show hate for a deceitful lover?"

His eyes came up. They held hers for a moment. There was nothing in them. Nothing at all. "I'd say next time she should use birth control." He snapped his briefcase shut. "If it helps, he would have seconded the decision."

"It doesn't. Should the father have been there for the procedure?"

"I'm sure the woman managed without him," he replied.

"Barely."

He shrugged. "I would also point out that this was a possibility she should have considered before getting herself in the danger zone."

"Getting *herself*?"

"Returning to someone's home and removing her turtleneck sweater so 'she could breathe.'"

"She was impaired by the champagne she'd had at dinner, impressed that Dom Perignon had been ordered to celebrate what her companion told her was a special occasion."

"It was," Martin replied. "Two people had connected. It was strong that night, and for a little while thereafter, and then it wasn't. She failed to see the signs and now she blames him for her shortcomings."

"She was in love."

"She was infatuated."

"She was *in love*, taken somewhere special by a smarter and more worldly partner."

"What was it, the fucking *Isola di Amore*?" he snapped.

"Yeah. It was."

He shook his head. "She was a willing participant, free to give or take or *leave* whenever she wished."

"She trusted him."

"To do what? Marry her? Raise kiddies together?"

"To be truthful."

"His body language was truthful. She should have done a better job reading it." Martin picked up his briefcase, rolled his shoulders back, and glared at her. "In any case, I would remind the lady of the Erasmus we discussed, that the human mind is far more susceptible to falsehood than to truth. Deceit is not the fault of the observed but of the observer."

"This man definitely lied about what he was doing another night."

"The man had every right to be where he wished."

"The man was a coward."

"The man was free. The man still is. And the man is leaving."

Martin Cayne went to move around her. Sara turned with him. She slapped him so hard with her free right hand that he stumbled forward a step. Her palm burned from the force of it.

"Read *that* body language," she said.

The professor stopped and rubbed his cheek. "That was extremely childish."

She hit him again. "No, that was. You deserved the first one. You were a mistake," she said, finally answering the Devil's question. "And you're over."

Sara looked at him with steel in her eyes. He looked back with surprise. That was good enough. She turned and left.

There were no students in the hall, no young ladies waiting. Maybe she had come on an off day or maybe some of the Martin Cayne magic was gone. Perhaps his heart had been seized and squeezed and dropped by someone and he had sworn off relationships. She didn't know. She would never know.

The beauty was, for the first time in years what he thought or did or *had* done simply didn't matter.

5

Sara walked to the Ingalls Rink. The arena itself was closed and she sat on one of the benches outside. The air was cold but the sun was warm. The balance was just right. She opened the top of her jacket. She was sweating after her encounter, shaking with a not unpleasant touch of post-traumatic stress.

She couldn't believe she had done it. After all these years, after all the tortured thoughts that kept her from sleeping, after all the waiting and vengeful planning and plotting it was over. Martin Cayne had been undemonized. He was just a man and a slapped-silly one at that. It felt good. She couldn't undo what had happened years before and that would always weigh on her soul. But it helped knowing that even if she had gone to Martin at the time nothing would have been different. Sara would have made the same decision, hating him even more for his dispassion.

Grace phoned when her class was done. The women didn't speak long, then. The nun told Sara to stay put as she made her way to the arena. There were several students bobbing in Grace's wake as she arrived, each of whom she introduced before sending them on their way.

"They're heathens mostly," Grace said jokingly as she sat beside her friend. "But it's the indentured duty of the young to question. Jesus questioned." Grace regarded her friend. "You saw Martin Cayne."

"I did."

"It went well, I can see it in your eyes," Grace cheered. "They're alive."

"I feel good," Sara acknowledged.

"Do you want to talk about it?" Grace asked.

"Not really," Sara said. "Unless you want to hear about how I made him turn the other cheek."

"Ow. I can imagine," Grace replied.

Sara grinned. "And I'm meeting a man for drinks or dinner later—I'm not sure which."

"Does it matter?"

"No," Sara admitted.

"Who is he?"

"The school attorney," Sara said. "He has papers to give me. I don't know if anything's there personally—"

"Except a fresh start," Grace said.

"Exactly," Sara said.

Sister Grace lost a little of her gleam. "What about the other situation. The one at home?"

"That was messy but we got through it. Mom, Darrell, and me."

" 'My mother protected me from the world and my father threatened me with it,' " Grace said.

"Which prophet said that?"

"Quentin Crisp. *The Naked Civil Servant*," Grace said. "I fly a lot. I've a great deal of time to read. I'm glad it worked out that way. Love is a leap of faith too."

The women sat side by side in quiet contentment.

"Was it really the Devil?" Grace asked at length.

"If you're asking whether it was Pareidolia, it wasn't," Sara said. She showed Grace the back of her neck. "A mass hallucination didn't do this."

"What did?"

"Birds," Sara said. "Big black ones with very sharp claws and beaks."

"The Strigoi," Grace said.

"They have a name?"

Grace nodded. "The Eastern Orthodox Church in Romania holds that demon birds rise from graves at night to feast on human flesh and blood. They are the favored soul-gatherers of Satan and are said to have brass claws and beaks."

"You can put the talons and beaks in the 'definite' column," Sara said. "What about an Angel of Death? Could that have come from Satan too?"

"You saw one?" Grace said.

"One?" Sara sounded surprised.

"Satan rules his own host of fallen angels who are known as Destroyers," Grace said. "Adriel, Yetzerhara, Yehudiam, Abaddon—their numbers are legion. If you saw one, it was probably Rahab, cursed for having refused to part the Red Sea for the Children of Israel."

"How do you know?"

"He alone retains his true form, a daily reminder of the glory he lost."

"You think that's what I saw?" Sara asked. "What my whole family saw?"

"People have visions all the time, many of them valid," Grace said. "There's no reason to believe you didn't."

"I might have been crazy."

"You, yes," Grace said. "Not the Tsvardins or your family."

Sara marked an imaginary one point on the outside scoreboard of the rink.

"You got the big win, Sara," Grace said. "God does not give us all the answers but the Devil gives us none. You've seen how love enriches us. The Devil is a satisfied under-achiever, content with lust. There is always more than we know, more than we can imagine. Don't forget that."

"Not likely," Sara said.

"Speaking of enrichment, I could do with some coffee before my next class," Grace said. "The History of the Second Vatican Council. The kids always get feisty when it comes to Divine Revelation. They want to know how we can be sure the natural intermediaries aren't making things up."

"How are we sure?" Sara asked.

"We're not," Grace admitted. "That's the part called 'faith.' It's why I keep digging 'out there,'" she said, nodding toward distant, unseen fields.

Maybe the differences between them were not as vast as Sara imagined. "Let's get caffeinated," Sara said, smiling as she rose.

They walked together in the slanting sunlight, enjoying the moment while Sara looked ahead toward her own unseen fields.

Eighteen

1

The surroundings were red and empty. There was no noise and no movement. Even so, the place was not as vacant as his soul.

He did not begrudge Sara her victory. It was fairly won. But it was bitter nonetheless.

He watched the women go, his skin flushed and warm and red, his eyes as richly aflame as the sun beyond. With a wicked smile, he dropped the corner of the shade and walked from the lecture hall.

TOR

Award-winning authors
Compelling stories

Please join us at the website
below for more information
about this author and other great
Tor selections, and to sign up for
our monthly newsletter!